12 Months of Whump
Volume 1

Lux in Tenebris: Poena et Salus

Hunting Static

The Windows to a Shapeshifter's Soul

Never, Never

Creatures From the Caldera

Deepest Canyon: A Starslinger Tale

Cover Design by Nicole Alessi

Illustrations by Hen Towers

CONTENTS

Introduction

Welcome to 12 Months of Whump! The Whumpy Printing Press published one whump novella every month in 2025. This book contains the first six novellas, published between January and June of 2025. Each novella can be read as a standalone. Within these pages you'll find demons, monster hunters, dragons, pirates, rotten-apple-scented felines, and dinosaurs. And hopefully whumperflies.

Lux in Tenebris: Poena et Salus

Isaac Ryals

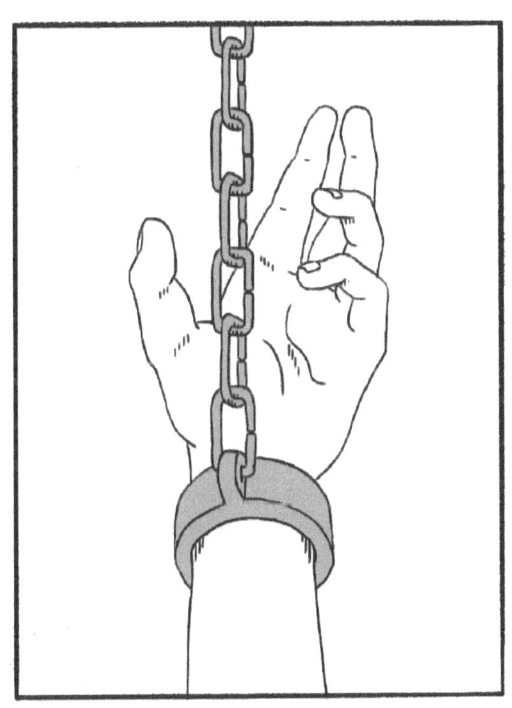

Cover Design by Nicole Alessi

Illustration by Hen Towers

Also by Isaac Ryals

The Honor Bound Series

Contents

Content Warnings

This story contains the following content:

- Themes related to Judeo-Christian religion, including angels, demons, references to possession and exorcism, and quotes from scripture.
- Kidnapping
- Recapture
- PTSD
- Restraints, collar, gag
- Torture
- Blood
- Character death

If this book isn't for you, no worries! But if it is, we hope you enjoy this story about a hapless demon...

1

The iron cuffs burned Dee's wrists. His shoulders ached from his hands being locked behind him. He twisted weakly against the restraints, his heart lying sluggish and still in his chest, barely able to breathe the stuffy air in the car's trunk. The car went over a bump, and he bit back a cry of pain as his head thudded against the lid of the trunk, then the floor. The trunk was warded, he could feel it: the familiar prickle of power cloaking him from anyone who might be looking for him. Tears streamed down his cheeks and into the cloth gag tied around his head.

He could hear the angels in the car as they laughed and turned up their music. It grated on his ears, tinny guitar and crashing drums, but at least it covered the sound of their cruel laughter. He whimpered softly and pressed his face against the rough carpet on the floor.

His stomach heaved. It was going to happen again. He felt the weight of his capture so many years ago – out at the bar, having a good time in the woman's body he had borrowed, reveling in the life and music and joy that humans could feel when they allowed themselves to. He remembered the room beginning to swim around him. He remembered the Power that had stepped forward – but he hadn't known it was a Power, how could he when he was drunk with the colloidal silver they'd spiked his drink with? – with gloved hands, smiling at the demon as he stumbled away from the bar.

"Hey, sweetie, had a little too much to drink, huh? Yeah, baby, let's go home."

He vaguely remembered the bartender watching him as he was pulled toward the exit, just a flash of doubt crossing the bartender's face, a moment of hesitation

– before someone had called for another round of shots, and he'd turned away to grab the shot glasses. Dee remembered staggering out the door to the bar, tucked under the Power's arm – protected by his gloves and long sleeves, how could he have *missed* that?

He remembered being shoved to his knees in the alley behind the bar. He remembered the cuffs being clicked around his wrists, remembered being thrown into the trunk of a car, remembered the jolt as the car began to move ...

He remembered waking up in a basement with an iron collar around his neck and iron cuffs around his wrists, shaking his head against the cacophony of sobbing inside his head. He remembered the woman screaming from the pain, from the burning in her wrists, from the fear as one of the Powers stepped up – there were more of them now, three standing in a circle around them – and took the demon's face in his hand.

In his ungloved hand.

The car hit another bump, and this time Dee couldn't choke back the sob as he slammed against the floor of the trunk again. Another spike of laughter from the car. Tears streamed down Dee's face.

Dee. The name Ilya had given him.

He tossed his head and lurched forward, desperately pulling up the face of his kind human friend in his mind. He keened softly as he remembered their soft voice, their gentle hands, their quiet way as they held him tight and rocked him and slept beside him in bed, asking nothing from him, a warm presence that steadied him, cared for him.

Loved him, maybe.

They can't know about Ilya.

He clenched his jaw shut, shuddering from the blistering pain in his wrists, from the fear, from the ache in his chest that opened up inside him and threatened to swallow him whole. He could remember how it felt when the human in his body screamed and suffered alongside him. He could remember how it felt when he woke after being drowned in holy water and realized he could no longer hear her voice in his head.

The Powers killed a human, just so they could torture a demon.

They would not get Ilya.

His stomach roiled, and he gagged against the cloth in his mouth. He could feel the angelic hands on his body, could feel how his skin blistered and burned from even the slightest touch – not like the slow, stinging pain of the iron, but an instant flame, charring his skin, blackening it. He could feel the whip, the blinding agony as it shredded his back, lash after lash until his flesh hung from his bones. He could feel the white-hot blade of the knife, consecrated iron burning into his skin, poisoning his blood. A knife that would kill him if the angels cut too deep, the only hope of escape he had.

He bleated in fear, sick with the pain that crashed through his body with each memory. They would break him all over again. They would hurt him and hurt him and hurt him until there was nothing left, nothing but a shell – like he had been when Dara carried him away from that hell months ago.

Tears streamed from his eyes as he desperately hoped Dara would come for him again. He pleaded silently that she and Evangeline would save him before the Powers took everything from him. They weren't like the other angels – they cared, impossible though it seemed. If Dara couldn't save him, the only thing he could hope for – could beg for – was that the Powers took his life.

His skin crawled as the car slowed to a stop. The car bounced slightly as the Powers climbed out. Dee felt the jolts as they each slammed their doors shut.

The trunk lid opened, and he blinked against the sudden light. He cringed back from the angels' hands as they reached in and pulled him from the trunk. He sobbed weakly as they dragged him forward, shoving him toward the front door of a house at the end of a long driveway. He couldn't see another house in any other direction. As he approached the door, his heart sank.

There was a warding symbol on the door, just like he had felt on the trunk – and just like Evangeline had drawn on the front door of Ilya's house. Dara and

Evangeline would never find him now. He would disappear into that house, be chained to the floor, be torn apart for however long the Powers wished to hold him.

He began to sob in earnest as they dragged him through the front door.

2

Dee shrieked in terror as the angels dragged him toward the open basement door. His shoes squeaked and slid on the wood floor, and tears streamed into the gag as he twisted away from the Powers. His sweat-soaked clothes ripped under the angels' hands. His heart lay silent within him, even as his chest heaved with terrified gasps.

"Fucking *filth*," an angel spat. A hand lashed across Dee's face, leaving blistering skin in its wake. Dee sobbed and shuddered as his tears stung the burn. The door to the basement yawned open, the peeling gray walls of the staircase disappearing down into blackness.

"*P-please*," he gasped, the word muffled by the gag. "*Please, no, please, mercy –*" His eyes were wide, helpless, as he looked around at his captors. He remembered their names; they were burned into his mind at the point of a knife, at the end of a whip, seared into his soul. He knew their names better than he knew his own.

Lucas. Jude. Dominic.

Their faces were all twisted with hate, their inhuman beauty poisoned by their twisted mouths, their spiteful eyes. He could barely breathe as they dragged him to the basement door and shoved him forward.

He almost caught himself on the first stair, the impact shuddering through his sneakers. Then he felt a boot in his back, and he pitched forward into blackness.

The fall seemed to last an eternity.

When he hit the floor, his shoulder buckled and his skull cracked against the cement in a brilliant flash of light. The rest of his body followed in a boneless heap. For a breath, there was no sensation in his body but blank, dizzying terror.

The pain rushed in a moment later.

He screamed his throat raw. Agony shuddered up and down his arm, dull and crushing and nauseating. He gagged weakly and sobbed, rolling onto his other side and curling into himself as much as he could. His shoulder screamed at him as he pulled against the iron cuffs locking his hands behind him. Sweat chilled on his skin. His teeth began to chatter.

Above the sound of his screams, he could hear the angels laughing. A single lightbulb clicked on above him, casting the basement in stark, yellowed light. His vision swam as the angels descended the steps one by one and gathered around him where he lay shuddering. The light stabbed into his eyes as he looked up at them. He squeezed his eyes shut, sending more tears dripping onto the cement floor.

His eyes flew open again as a boot drove into his stomach. He let out a choked, gurgling scream. The fractured bones in his shoulder ground together, seeming to spark a fire that roared under his skin. He felt more than saw the Trap painted on the floor around him, severing any change of escape from his body – even if he had the strength to exorcize himself.

"Looks like we found our little snake out in the grass," Lucas murmured, crouching down and reaching out to touch Dee. "Here we thought we'd never see our little serpent again."

"*N-no*," Dee heaved. Black spots floated in his vision. If the angel touched him, he was going to be sick, he was going to *die* ...

Lucas drew one finger down Dee's cheek. The skin sizzled under the touch, and Dee jerked his head away, sobbing and shaking and pleading wordlessly. Jude dropped to his knees behind Dee and jerked his head back. The smell of burning hair was acrid in Dee's nostrils.

"When that little Virtue pulled you out of our basement, we thought we *lost* our little sinner, didn't we?" Lucas crooned. The others laughed in agreement. "Who'd have thought we would find it months later, walking around like it was *human*?"

"Walking with a little limp, though, huh?" Dominic said through his cheerfully clenched teeth. He crouched beside Lucas. "Those legs never did heal right, did they?"

"I want to take this off," Lucas said, eyeing the gag. With Jude keeping Dee's head steady with the hand in his slowly singeing hair, Lucas dragged his finger down Dee's cheek again – and pulled the gag from his mouth.

"*P-please,*" Dee wailed, desperately locking his muscles tight and hoping his shivering would ease. It only made him tremble harder. "Please – mercy, Powers, please, *obsecro, potestates, obs-secro, non, miserere mei, misericordia* – " [*Please – mercy, Powers, please, please, Powers, p-please, no, have mercy on me, mercy* –]

A slap lashed across his face and knocked his head against the cement again. His ears rang with the force of it.

"*Quia lingua non est tibi*" [*This language is not for you*], Lucas snapped. "*Sordes damnatus*" [*Damned filth*].

"*I-ignosce me*" [*F-forgive me*], Dee sobbed desperately, his mind a jagged slash of panic. "*Tantum volo misericordia, obsecro, obsecro* – " [*I only want mercy, please, please* –]

Lucas shoved him onto his back, put his knee on his chest, and *leaned.* His hands were crushed under him and the bones crunched in his shoulder. Dee's head fell back against the floor and he screamed in agony.

"*Non venenum lingua nostra per tuus oris turpis*" [*Don't poison our language with your filthy mouth*], the angel snarled in his face. Dominic got to his feet with a smirk, disappearing into the circle of darkness that surrounded Dee. Jude grabbed his hair again and twisted.

"*Patieris agonia ob tuus peccata, daemon*" [*You will suffer agony for your sins, demon*], Jude hissed, his gaze darting over Dee's face, taking in his desperate terror.

"*Fortase nos occidere*" [*Perhaps we will kill you*], Lucas murmured, leaning his weight on Dee, bending over him until his lips were almost at his ear. "*Si nos decernimus passus es satis*" [*If we decide you have suffered enough*].

"K-kill me, *please*," Dee gasped. He could feel the bones in his shoulder grinding together – and could feel them already trying to knit, to mend. "Kill me n-now, please, Powers, *mercy* – "

Jude's grip on Dee's hair loosened, his fingers sliding through almost gently. "'Thou therefore, O Lord God of hosts, the God of Israel, awake to visit all the heathen: be not merciful to any wicked transgressors.'" His lips pulled into a devastating smile. "There is no mercy for you or your kind."

Dread stole the pleas from Dee's mouth. He trembled beneath Lucas, muscles straining, pulled tight enough to snap. Tears welled in his eyes as the angels stared down at him, cold and calm and merciless. There was a feverish light in Lucas' eyes that had nothing to do with his heavenly glow. Dee could not fill his lungs with the angel crushing his chest.

He didn't need to. This body was dead, he was only the thing inside it. Despair crawled inside him and settled, comfortable and familiar.

"I think it's time to put this back on," Dominic said softly from outside the circle of harsh light. He stepped forward. His face was cast in stark relief, making him look frightening, inhuman. Monstrous. In his hand he held a broken circle of iron, a hinge connecting the two sides. Dee moaned, his voice breaking, as he stared at the iron collar.

Dominic dropped to one knee beside Lucas. Jude snapped Dee's head back, baring his throat, drawing a broken whine from him. The iron collar closed around his neck. Dominic's hand passed over the collar and when he pulled it away, it was a solid, unbroken band of iron around Dee's neck, with a ring hanging off the front for a chain.

"So begins your second penance, little snake," Lucas purred.

"*N-no,*" Dee whimpered. His vision blurred with tears as he lay on the floor, helpless, senseless, the cement leaching heat from his body through his clothes. Tears rolled down his temples and into his hair, smelling faintly of sulfur. The angels only smiled wider as he burned under the collar and cuffs.

3

Tears streamed down Dee's cheeks. His mouth gaped open, his fangs flashing and dripping with his own blood from piercing through his gums. The collar was pulled tight and chained to the ceiling, crushing his throat, choking him. His hands were still cuffed behind him, chained to the floor, keeping him on his knees and fighting desperately for every breath.

He tried to hold his breath, he *tried,* but this body was stronger than he was. This body remembered the feeling of being choked, of needing air, because she had suffered the same tortures he had – for a little while. As Dee struggled and whimpered and choked, the body took over. The body tried to save itself, even as Dee suffered inside it.

He tried to track the angels moving around him in a constant, shifting circle, tried desperately to watch where they were, to prepare for another blow. His vision blurred with tears and panic. The sound of the angels' laughter echoed in his ears until he thought he would be sick with it.

Pain exploded against his back and he screamed, a broken, animal sound that tore his throat as he made it. His vision went white, then black, as he sagged forward, held upright only by the collar that seemed to constrict around his neck. His throat itched and burned, his wrists already blistering from the cuffs digging into his skin. He sobbed and twisted, writhing, desperate.

"Sad little demon," Dominic mocked behind him – Dee could *hear* the angel's knuckles creaking as he gripped the cane. He shuddered and cringed away, mindlessly tugging against the cuffs keeping him chained to the floor. His shoulder exploded in agony.

"Its screams are just as lovely," Lucas murmured, stepping forward into the stark circle of light, pinning Dee with his gaze. Dee went still, whimpering, as Lucas reached out with one hand and gently stroked his thumb along Dee's cheek. Dee shrieked as it singed his skin, the tears sizzling and steaming under the angel's touch. "Better, perhaps. Maybe its jaunt in the world helped it return to us restored, ready for more punishment."

"P-please," Dee breathed, staring up at the angel with wide, terrified eyes. "Please, *potestas*, p – " [*Power*]

Dee gasped as a stinging blow snapped his head to the side.

"I've *told you*, filth," Lucas growled. "That language is *not* for you."

Dee's mind was a scattered cacophony of panic. The words were on his tongue, the pleas burning his throat. "*Obse* – P-please, I – I'm *sorry*, Power, please, *mercy, mercy, please* – "

"How *spoiled* you've become, *serpentis*," Lucas murmured, clutching Dee's hair and dragging him forward. The collar closed on his throat. The cuffs tore his wrists and he let out a strangled cry. "You used to know your place. 'Blows and wounds scrub away evil,'" Lucas said with a smile. "'And beatings purge the inmost being.' Did you forget that, little snake, when you were corrupting the little human who took you into their heart?"

Ice clutched at Dee's chest. His desperate, whistling gasps ceased, and his body went rigid. His mouth gaped and gray clouded his vision.

Lucas' smile widened, and his eyes burned into Dee. "Oh," he breathed. "You didn't know we knew about them."

"It's rather amusing," Jude said, stepping closer and standing at Lucas' elbow. "You and the human. Do they think you're human, too? Do they know the vile filth they let into their home?"

"Certainly confusing on the part of the Virtues," Dominic said as he fell in on Lucas' other side. He traced the tip of the cane across Dee's throat, down his chest, then pressed it against his stomach, harder and harder until Dee let out a piteous whine. Lucas' grip on his hair tightened and he dragged him forward harder, pressing the cane deeper into his soft, exposed abdomen, tightening the cuffs and collar even more. Tears streamed down Dee's face and onto the cement floor below as he choked and sobbed.

"They gave us the idea of how to ward ourselves, though," Jude said with a chuckle. "Just draw a sigil that makes the car and house undiscoverable to angels, then pop the house's address in the GPS, and use that to find the house after that." He shrugged. "It's weirdly brilliant. The things these humans can do with their technology ..."

"M-merc-cy – " Dee mouthed. He couldn't draw in air to beg with. He shuddered and weakly tossed his head against the angel's grip.

"After all the things you've done?" Lucas murmured, drawing closer, craning Dee's head back so he was forced to look at him. It relieved a little of the pressure on his throat, and he gasped in a breath. "Oh, little snake." He released Dee's hair all at once. Dee's eyes rolled back as he dragged in breath after desperate breath. "'Ye are of your father the devil, and the lusts of your father ye will do. He was a murderer from the beginning, and abode not in the truth, because there is no truth in him. When he speaketh a lie, he speaketh of his own: for he is a liar, and the father of it.'" He grinned, tilting his head to survey Dee. "There is no mercy for you. You are the enemy, little one. Your words and air and blood are poison. You possessed this body when it was not yours to take. You corrupted the human and manipulated them into being kind to you. Do you believe you deserve salvation, *inimicus*?" [*enemy*]

Dee couldn't speak. He sobbed raggedly and sagged forward, barely able to keep upright. The collar tightened on his throat again.

"Hm," Lucas hummed. Dee raised his head and watched Lucas' smile grow, twisting the corners of his mouth into a devastating grin. "I imagine the human's touch was the first touch you've felt in *years* that didn't burn you, hm, *daemon?*"

His hand drifted up, hovering at Dee's cheek. Dee sobbed and twisted away. A warm line of blood rolled down his neck from the torn blisters at his throat.

"This is the only touch you deserve, little monster," Lucas whispered. He grabbed Dee's face in an iron grip and smiled as the demon roared in agony.

4

Dee shuddered as the angels kicked him again, in the stomach this time. He dragged in a ragged gasp, blinking against the blindfold. Tears had wet through the fabric long ago. He lay on his side now – the angels had finally let him down from the chain dragging him upright, finally unchained his hands from the floor. They stayed locked behind his back. The cement floor sucked the heat from his body where he lay – helpless. Exposed. Open.

His body *hurt,* a terrible throbbing ache that stabbed through his shoulder, crushed his abdomen, burned his back. The bones in his shoulder were still trying to mend. The prickling heat inside him itched, even under the pain.

"*M-mercy,*" he rasped, eyes rolling back against the pain. Blood dripped down his back from the lashes of the cane, soaking into his shirt and trickling onto the floor.

Ilya gave me this shirt.

"Mercy," he croaked. "Mercy, *mer* – " He was cut off by a scream as the angels kicked his broken shoulder. His vision went even blacker behind the blindfold and a ringing started in his ears. He convulsed and gagged. Nothing came up. There was nothing in his stomach anymore. Dee's head spun.

Jude spoke. "'He shall smite the earth, and with the breath of his lips shall he slay the wicked.'"

Dee jerked away from a kick to his ribs. Something *snapped* inside him. Agony clutched his chest, sharpened when Dee screamed. Sweat beaded on his forehead. His mouth gaped open and he sucked in a shallow breath, desperate.

"K-kill – *please* – kill me, I beg you, merciful Powers, please, I beg – "

He let out a twisted wail as he was forced onto his back. His hands were crushed beneath him as an angel straddled his hips and pinned him down by his throat. His skin blistered under the angel's hands. He tipped his head back against the cold floor and shrieked his agony.

Then, mercifully, the hands disappeared. Dee coughed, sucking in breath after panicked breath. His broken rib creaked inside him, sending stabbing pain through his chest, up his neck, down his arm –

His lung burned too. Dee dragged in another breath and cried out as the pain pierced him again, as real as any knife. He shuddered and went still.

They've punctured my lung.

He heaved a ragged sob. He writhed under the angel, desperate to relieve the press of the cement against the shifting bones in his chest and shoulder. He sucked in another lungful of air, let it out.

He knew this body and its pain well enough to know there was air leaking into his chest through the tear in his lung.

I don't need to breathe.

Tears dripped from the soaked blindfold and into his hair. He shivered and forced his chest to be still. Desperately, he tried to focus his energy on repairing the lung, the rib. His shoulder flared again with pain. He was sick with it.

A rough cloth settled around his neck and he tilted his head, desperate to understand what was going on. Heavy hands pressed down over the cloth a moment later, constricting his bruised and blistered throat. His mouth opened and he fought for air – an instinct. His eyes rolled back behind the blindfold and he twitched under the angel's weight.

"That's better. Don't want to burn through to your trachea *just* yet," Lucas purred, his voice sounding like it was only inches above Dee. "Mmmn. There's nothing quite like watching a vile monster fight for air."

Dee couldn't make a sound. He thrashed weakly, eyes wide with terror beneath the blindfold. He waited for his hearing to fade, for the embrace of darkness to save him from the pain. It didn't come. He knew it wouldn't.

His heart no longer pumped blood anymore. His cells no longer needed it. He would be awake – and alive – until the angels slid their knives of consecrated iron between his ribs.

He'd begged Ilya to do it. Fever-drunk and delirious, he'd looked up at them from his sickbed and *begged.*

Ilya would have been kinder.

Something tore in Dee's shoulder as he yanked against the cuffs locking his hands behind his back. He kicked his feet against the floor, shoes squeaking on the cement, wild with panic.

"Beautiful," Jude breathed from somewhere above Dee. A shoe nudged his ribs. He jerked, his mouth pulled open in a silent scream.

Lucas chuckled and, for a brief moment, loosened his hands around Dee's neck. Dee dragged in a tortured breath, the air whistling through his throat, before he convulsed in a fit of coughing. Then Lucas pressed down again, cutting off his air.

"What a silly *daemon*," Lucas crooned. His breath fanned out over Dee's face. "You truly believed you were safe, didn't you?"

I hoped –

"How astronomically foolish you are, little one," Lucas murmured. "You really believed that the human could find it even in their tender heart to feel for you? You really thought an angel of the Lord, a *Virtue*, could care whether you breathed or died?"

A broken, high-pitched sound punched from Dee's throat as a boot collided with his side. Every cell in his body screamed for relief.

Lucas' voice darkened, the words said softly before now spewed from gritted teeth. "You are *inimicus.* You are *daemon.* You are *adversator.* You are the Enemy who walks among us. You take what is not given to you. You burn everything you touch."

Tears rolled down Dee's face behind the blindfold. *I know. I know.*

"You are deluded beyond measure, little snake, to have believed you had a place with the humans. If they knew you for what you were, they would cast you out. They would tie you to the stake and burn you alive. They would drown you in holy water – just as we are going to do to you." Lucas' hands tightened around Dee's throat. Stars burst behind his eyes.

An angel's boot settled on his cheek, turning his head to the side. He gagged weakly at how it shifted his throat beneath Lucas' hands.

"This is what you deserve, little snake," Dominic said above him. "To be ground beneath the foot of those who will destroy you, and to suffer under our hands. You were not made for softness. You were not made for human love. You were made to *break*." The boot lifted from Dee's face.

Dee flinched back as best he could, bracing for the kick. *I know all that. I only thought … I only hoped …*

"Look how it struggles," Jude whispered. "Look at how it fights. *Lovely.*"

"Mmm," Lucas assented. "So *wicked.*" He chuckled softly, leaning harder against Dee's throat. Dee twitched and writhed, mouth open wide as he fought – desperately, fruitlessly – for air. His lungs felt like fire inside him. The moment stretched on, eternal, inescapable.

There was a shift of boots on the floor at Dee's head. "Move, Lucas," Dominic said in the darkness above him, a smile in his voice. "My turn. And take the towel away. I want to watch it *burn.*"

5

Ilya's stomach lurched. Worry burned hot under their skin. Their feet pounded against the sidewalk as they rushed through the park, casting their gaze this way and that, searching desperately. Searching for their demon – their *friend.*

He'd been *right here.*

He'd stopped for some water – and Ilya had been so proud of him, so grateful that he felt safe enough in their presence to want water and *take* it, without begging, without terror. They had turned away from the drinking fountain for the briefest moment, raising their gaze to the shimmering crown of leaves at the tops of the trees, rippling in the cool wind. They had opened their mouth to say to Dee, *look at that. Isn't that beautiful?*

Then they'd turned back, and he was gone.

Gone.

Ilya's heart clenched. He couldn't have gone *far,* he ... he wouldn't have just ... *left.* He wouldn't have left them. He wouldn't have just disappeared.

Then where is *he?*

Their mouth was dry as they reached for the phone in their pocket. Dee didn't have one on him, so Ilya wouldn't be able to call. He'd never wanted a phone. He was content to stay by their side whenever he could gather the strength to leave the house, staying close to Ilya or Dara or Evangeline. Even if being near the angels still made him tremble.

Ilya's heart leapt as they turned and smacked right into Dara, where moments before there had only been empty air.

"Where is he?" she murmured, golden eyes blazing.

Ilya blanched and fell back a step. Protective anger rose in their throat. "H-he didn't ... he didn't do anything, Dara, I just can't find – "

"No," Dara huffed, lifting her head as if trying to hear a faraway voice. "*Where is he*?"

Ilya shuddered and turned to survey the park again. "What do you mean?" they murmured. Their fingertips began to tingle. "Wh-why are you ... What happened?"

"He's ... he suddenly got very scared," she whispered.

Ilya's heart sank in their chest. "What?" they breathed. Their hand drifted out to take hers. Her fingers were cool and dry.

"He was out with you, right?" Dara said, still peering around the park, the air around her starting to vibrate. "You were out for a walk?"

"Yeah," Ilya said, their voice shaking. "Yeah. Just a ... a walk. He was doing so well and then I turned around and he was ... was gone."

"How long ago?" Dara mumbled. Her hand seemed to grow colder in theirs, seemed to suck the heat right from their body.

"Um ..." Ilya blinked against the tears that were clouding their vision. "Um ... A minute or two ago?"

Dara let out a breath. The smell of ozone washed over Ilya. They tugged at Dara's hand, desperately trying to duck into her line of sight. "What happened?" they whimpered, and couldn't hold back a full-body shiver. "Dara ... what is it?"

A muscle ticked in Dara's jaw, and she pinned Ilya with her gaze. The world seemed frozen around them, the breath of the breeze and the thud of Ilya's heart against their ribs and the movement of the sun in the sky all seeming to cease for a long moment. Dara wet her lips and looked away. Ilya heaved a sigh of meager relief.

"A minute or so ago," Dara murmured, her voice pitched low and rippling through the ground around them, "Dee suddenly felt ... frightened. It was like ...

he cried out, and I could hear him ... all the way across town. I f-felt his, um, his pain, and ... and his terror."

"H-how is that even possible?" Ilya breathed.

"I feel this with both of you," Dara said, waving away the question. "So I can make sure you're safe. But I ... What I felt is, um ..." Slowly, her gaze slid across the grass and the trees around them and settled on the drinking fountain Dee had paused at only minutes before. She lurched toward it, and somehow even that motion was unfathomably graceful. Ilya stumbled along behind.

Dara stopped in front of the drinking fountain and reached out to touch it, letting her fingers brush the shiny chrome. Her eyes slid closed, and the very air around Ilya began to hum. Then, with a punch through Ilya's chest like a bolt of lightning, her eyes flew open and she gripped the handle.

"***Lucas***," she hissed through her teeth.

Ilya staggered back and slammed their hands over their ears as the word seemed to tear the air apart. They could not block out the sound that crashed over them, sounding like continents being smashed to pieces, like the sky cracking open above them. All around them, people turned their heads instinctively toward the sound, even though Ilya knew they could not see Dara.

Not if she didn't want them to.

"Wh-who is Lucas?" Ilya whimpered, trembling from head to toe in the wake of the angel's wrath, pulling their shaking hands away from their ears.

"The one who took him before," Dara snarled. "The Power. It was him, Dominic, and Jude ... Those are the ... the ones who – who *took* Dee before, and – "

Ilya couldn't hold back a sob. "A-and they took him again? Are you ..." They blinked. Tears spilled down their cheeks. "Are you *sure*?" they breathed.

"I'm sure," Dara said, the air still buzzing around her, but settling, cooling.

"*Why*?" Ilya whimpered. They raised their gaze to Dara's, terrified of what they would find there. When they read the confirmation in her eyes – the rage, the *sorrow* – they crumpled, anguished.

"W-we have to *find* him," they sobbed. "They'll – they'll hurt him, Dara, please, I can't let him ... We have to *save him.*" They gasped and clutched at Dara's hand. "Can you feel him? Like you did before? Can you feel him right now? Please, Dara, *please* ..."

Dara's eyes fell shut, and she drew in a deep breath. It was like the very air around Ilya was breathing. When she let it out, they felt ice pierce the air around them. She opened her eyes. When she raised them to Ilya's, they were pained. Ilya whimpered and pressed a hand to their mouth.

"He's ... in pain," Dara whispered.

"*No,*" Ilya sobbed. "*No.* N-not again." Dara's hand tightened in theirs. They dashed the tears from their eyes. "Where? Can you ... c-can you feel where? You found him before – "

"No," Dara murmured, her eyes unfocused. "I can't ... They're using ..." She paled. The sun shimmered on her skin. "They're using the rune that *we* use to conceal the house. They're ... they're taking him ..." Her throat bobbed. "I can't *find* him."

"H-how did you find him before?" Ilya said, trembling. "When they were ... were hurting him."

"By *accident,*" Dara said. Her voice sounded fragile – not like glass, but like a bomb. "We were in the area for a meeting with another fucking garrison and heard him, um ... screaming."

Ilya pressed their hands against their mouth and heaved another sob. "No. *No.* H-he's taken so m-much pain, *no* ... Dara, we, please, we have to ... Dara, what do I *do*?"

"I don't know," Dara murmured. When she looked up to the sky, she seemed to glow with a ferocious light all her own. Her eyes flashed and her lip curled. "We're going to find him. We're going to *find* him."

6

Dee lay at the angels' feet, senseless and shuddering. He was curled on his side with his hands still cuffed behind him. He felt the crushing burn of the bones in his shoulder trying to mend, his muscles trying to pull them back into place so they could fuse and solidify. He gasped weakly against the pain as it spiked and faded and spiked again in his body. He'd given up on not breathing long ago – he didn't have the strength to hold his breath. Still, he could feel the pressure of his lung collapsing slowly, like a fist squeezing his heart. The pain hollowed him out and shattered him under its weight.

A tight band of burned flesh wound around his neck in the perfect shape of Dominic's hand. His cheeks were singed, too, where Lucas had grabbed him. And on his back, long, bloody slashes from the cane stung and ached with each breath. The raw skin around his wrists and throat felt distant and dull compared to the other hurts in his body. But at least they'd given him his air again.

They'd given him back his sight, too. His eyes streamed tears that dripped onto the cement floor beneath him. He watched the angels as they moved around him in the shadows beyond the stark circle of light on the floor, laughing, murmuring, making plans. Plans for Dee's pain, and for his penance.

He could no longer listen. He would suffer it all eventually. After so long in their captivity before – *years, it had to be years, Lucas mentioned years* – he knew there were no limits to the angels' cruelty. Chained, collared, broken, *alone* – he would suffer, and break even more. There was no mercy in the angels' eyes. Mercy would never find him again. Not with the warding symbol on the door.

Ilya was merciful. Ilya was kind.

Dee could barely remember their gentle touch. All he could feel was his body burning around him.

His silent heart plunged in his chest as the angels stepped forward into the light surrounding him. He whined, an animal sound, and pressed his face against the floor. He waited, perfectly still, for the blow to fall, for the burning hands to grab him, for the knife to carve into his flesh. He shivered, and waited. And waited.

Finally, when he could not wait any longer, he raised his gaze to the angels, shaking so hard his teeth chattered. He couldn't suppress a moan of agony as the bones shifted in his shoulder.

Still, they were mending. They were mending.

He lay helpless and bound under the angels' deadly stares. His terror was a shard of ice that burrowed deeper and deeper inside him.

Lucas grinned and wet his lips. "**Beg,**" he commanded, and the word was a bolt of thunder in Dee's ears.

Dee would not have needed the command. He opened his mouth and sobbed, *"Please."*

The angels chuckled in the circle around him. "**Again,**" Lucas said, the word shaking the very foundation of the house.

Dee groaned as the sound crushed him against the floor. He cowered away from the angels, drawing his knees up to his chest and clenching his hands into fists behind his back. "P-please, *please*, angels, Powers, m-mercy, please, *please*, d-don't hurt me ..." His lips were numb. He thought he might be sick.

"It used to be better at begging, I think," Jude said, tilting his head as he stared at Dee. He took a heavy step forward and crouched at Dee's side.

"*N-no*!" Dee shrieked, his feet scrabbling against the floor as he tried to twist away. "*Obsecro, potestates –* "

He gasped as a blow snapped his head to the side, cracking it on the cold cement floor. The coppery taste of his own blood burst across his tongue. He sobbed weakly as blood dripped from his lips.

"F-forgive me, angels," Dee whimpered, his head spinning. "H-have mercy on m-me, please, *please, mercy, please, please, please ...*"

"It's spoiled," Dominic said with a grin. "Living in that house for so long, allowed to walk freely instead of being forced to its knees, allowed to sleep in a bed and eat from a table ..." He snorted and tossed his head in a peal of laughter. "Instead of putting it in iron chains and *breaking* it like the monster it is ..."

Lucas stepped forward and nudged Dee's chin up with the toe of his boot. Dee fell still and looked up at the angel, trembling, lips still moving in a silent prayer for mercy. Lucas' grin spread wider across his face, lips pulling back to show his teeth. Dee shivered, powerless to look away.

"**Beg for water, little snake**," Lucas rumbled.

"P-please." The word was torn from Dee's lips, even as he began to cry harder, shaking his head in desperation. He could already feel the holy water pouring down his throat, could already feel the inescapable agony as it burned him all the way down, poisoning him, devouring him from the inside out. "P-please, angels, w-water, water ... N-no, *please* – "

"All you had to do was ask," Jude murmured. He reached down and drew one finger down Dee's cheek. Dee writhed and sobbed under the touch.

Lucas knelt, his hand darting out and fisting in Dee's hair. He jerked Dee's head to the side, forcing him onto his back again. The angels laughed as Lucas held a bottle over Dee's head, the lid off, the water filling it and trembling at the brim.

"Powers, please, *no*!" Dee screamed, trying desperately to turn his head away.

"Our little sinner has asked for water," Lucas said. He forced Dee's head back, baring his throat. "And it has asked for mercy. Of course, we'll oblige."

Dee screamed in anguish as Lucas poured the holy water over his face, immediately blistering his skin. Then Jude forced his jaw open with a burning hand, and Dee was drowning in fire.

7

Dee's screams shattered in his own ears. With his arms stretched up above him and cuffed to the ceiling, and his feet barely able to reach the floor, he could hardly draw a full breath. His feet and calves burned, shaking under his weight as he strained to balance on the tips of his toes. His breaths came in shallow, anguished pants, his lung slowly collapsing with each gulping inhale. His shoulder was a blaze of agony, fractured ends of bone grinding together as he tried – and failed – to hold perfectly still through the beating.

The angels stood around him in a semi-circle, their smiles wide and their eyes flashing, merciless and cold. Dee shuddered and turned desperate eyes on them, tears stinging his cheeks and tasting bitter on his tongue.

"P-please," he whispered, his voice broken, his throat raw and blistered from the holy water. "Please, merciful Powers. K-kill me."

Dominic smirked. He stepped forward and reached out to stabilize Dee with a hand on his shoulder, fisting in the cloth of his shirt. Dee sobbed and squeezed his eyes shut, just before the blow smashed into his abdomen.

He let out a rasping scream as white exploded behind his eyes. Pain crashed through his shoulder, through his stomach, through his throat, building and building until he thought he would die from it. He tilted his head back and wailed his agony, eyes fixed sightlessly on the ceiling. Ice seemed to pierce him down to his bones. His blood cooled on his back from the cane marks that had been torn open again from his struggles.

"We *are* merciful, aren't we?" Jude crooned as he stepped forward, reaching out and smoothing his fingers through Dee's sweaty, tangled hair. Dee whimpered as the smell of burning hair made him gag. "We could have done what they did in the old days. Flayed the skin from your body, hanged you and left you there for days and days, burned you in the fires so like the ones we may eventually return you to ..." He smiled. There was no kindness in his eyes, no grace. He leaned in closer, twisted his hand in Dee's hair until Dee whimpered.

"You know, Lucas," Jude murmured, his gaze moving over Dee, taking in his terror, his pain. "I really would like to kill this one eventually."

Lucas cocked an eyebrow. "Oh?"

"Yes," Jude said softly. His breath felt like ice on Dee's skin. "It's fun to play with, and we are doing our Lord's work in overseeing its penance, but ..." His lips curved up, and Dee squirmed under his gaze. "I want to watch the fire leave its eyes. I want to watch it die, knowing we have done good work in purging it from this earth."

Dee's eyes fell shut, sending tears coursing down his cheeks. "*P-please*," he breathed.

"Just ... not for a while, right?" Dominic said, petulant.

"Oh, no," Jude said with a chuckle. "No, I think we could still get a few good years out of this one."

Dee whimpered. "N-no – "

His head snapped to the side as Jude struck him across the face. A warm trickle of blood spilled from Dee's mouth and down his chin as he slumped, limp in his shackles. Pain burst through his shoulder and he cried out, scrambling to get his feet back underneath him.

"Hm." Jude nudged Dee's chin up and smiled when Dee's skin sizzled under the touch. Dee turned his head and pressed his face against his arm, sobbing, helpless. "Yes, perhaps a few good years, but then ..." Jude leaned in closer, so close that Dee could see the flat gold of his eyes. "I'm going to slide my knife of consecrated iron into your heart – and look in your eyes as I send you to burn in Hell, little one."

Dee's parched and aching throat tightened as he cowered away from the inhuman loathing in Jude's eyes. If they killed him with their consecrated blades, there would be no Hell waiting for him. Not without a human soul to tether himself to as he fell. He would simply cease to exist, would simply disappear into nothingness. No soul, no spirit, no piece of him would remain. If they killed him in this body, he would be gone forever.

He squeezed his eyes shut and cried out as Ilya leapt to his thoughts, *his* Ilya, kind and trusting and true. His Ilya, the one who held him, loved him, cradled him gently when he was sick and scared and hurting, when he was shaking from memories of the torture he'd endured at the hands of angels.

These angels.

He opened his eyes and raised them, once again, to Jude.

Do it now. Please, please, do it now.

Jude wound up and whipped a vicious backhand across Dee's face. He gasped, stunned, his head spinning from the blow. More blood streamed down his chin, staining his shirt. He coughed. Red spattered Jude's face. Dee moaned in terror as Jude froze with his hand pulled back for another strike.

Slowly, slowly, Jude reached up and wiped his face with his sleeve. Dee couldn't breathe; terror squeezed his heart like a vice. His throat closed. His legs threatened to give out, sparking fire and agony in his shoulder.

"Maybe we could use a break to clean up," Lucas said lightheartedly.

Jude huffed. "Indeed. I'm sullied, now." He swiped at his face again, leaving garish streaks of blood on his cheek. "Although I should have expected to get filthy while battling the scum of the earth ... Still." He paused, hovering between taking a step forward and taking a step back, his gaze fixed on Dee.

Lucas sauntered to the steps and climbed the first one. "It's almost time for our report to Ezekiel, anyway."

Jude was still staring at Dee, his eyes lingering on the smear of blood on Dee's lips. "I somehow thought its blood would burn me, or something."

"Enough of it will," Lucas said with a shrug. "If it's from a stronger demon. With this one, its blood is barely stronger than water. It's not even corporeal."

"Interesting," Jude mused. He stepped away. Dee let out a piteous sob of relief.

Dominic snapped his fingers. The chains released from the ceiling and Dee toppled to the floor, unable to slow his fall. His mouth stretched open in a silent scream as his shoulder crunched with the impact. He lay shuddering on the icy floor, shackled and bleeding. His broken rib grated with each breath. He groaned and rolled onto his other side, doing his best to cradle his shoulder. He shuddered as pain broke over him, again and again and again.

Lucas paused on the steps. "It's wearing out so *quickly*," he said with a scoff.

"We've been more enthusiastic this time," Dominic said, a hint of a laugh in his voice.

"Hm. True. And it's just ... healing slower." Lucas tilted his head. His eyes flashed and his teeth showed in a grin. "We're going to be back in an hour," he said, pinning Dee with his gaze. "So until then ... **heal, demon**."

Dee writhed, back arching, as the command gripped him. Every bit of his body cried out at once, demanding his energy, desperate for relief. The grating itch of mending bones crescendoed into a blaze of heat. His blood burned in his veins as the angels turned and, laughing, left him alone in the stark circle of light, lying crumpled in a heap on the cold basement floor.

8

Dee's throat could only manage a croaking whisper as he burned. The bones in his shoulder blazed like fire under his skin. His muscles juddered and shook, straining to hold the bones in place as they mended – taking minutes, when before it had always taken days. The charred flesh all over his body went raw and bloody, softening, stinging, as new skin grew to cover it. The cane marks on his back broke open again, weeping blood before they sealed, leaving only a shadow of pale skin where each mark had been.

The room spun around him in a dizzy-sick kaleidoscope of agony. The scent of his own blood was thick and bitter in his nostrils, metallic and smelling faintly of sulfur. He could not tell if his eyes were open or closed; all he saw was white, a stab of cold light piercing into him, swallowing him whole.

And through it all, Dee could only lie helpless on the floor and scream – or try to. His throat was still blistered from the water. Or perhaps torn from the screaming.

With each agonized breath, he felt the air in his chest thin, his lung inflating again, throbbing and aching from being crushed. He drew in bigger and bigger lungfuls of air that he didn't need. He kept drawing breaths he didn't need.

He kept drawing breaths he didn't *deserve.*

He shuddered and sobbed weakly. The collar felt familiar around his neck, more familiar than freedom had ever been. He felt its weight and its sting, felt how it rubbed his skin to raw, then bleeding. He felt how it had imprinted in his skin when he'd been strung up from it. He felt how it seemed almost *molded* to him, fitting his throat with only a finger's-breadth of space around it. He smelled the sour tang of the metal against his skin, mixing with the smell of his blood and sweat. He wondered if, since his blood was poison to all things holy, it would eat through the iron, with time.

That hadn't happened in the years he'd spent under Lucas' boot, Dominic's fists, or Jude's scalding touch. Perhaps if the Virtues never came for him, he would be here until the building crumbled around him, until the iron rusted away into dust.

He wished, dizzily, that he could meet such a simple end.

Perhaps that's how it would be. Perhaps when they finally slid their blades into him he would simply rust away, all the scattered stardust pieces of this body disintegrating into dust and blowing away, to become motes floating on a sunbeam, to become the imperfection in a drop of rain. He moaned weakly and twisted against the floor, shivering as his fangs descended with the next flash of agony. Even so, he was grateful to the Powers. They had commanded him to be healed. He could feel the fresh, pink skin blooming on his cheeks and throat, and shivered. His shoulder would take more time, but it was healing. He was healing.

He was *mending.* And with every repair, the body sucked away more of his energy, more of his strength. But slowly, steadily, the pain was fading, even under the initial agony of the command.

Thus saith the Lord, the God of David thy father, I have heard thy prayer, I have seen thy tears: behold, I will heal thee.

Dee shuddered and let out a plaintive moan. *That's not for me; that's for them. I'm a monster. I'm the one who possessed an innocent human and corrupted another one ...*

But he had just wanted to *feel* something. He just wanted to experience the things he'd only heard described in hushed, reverent tones by the other demons he'd known in Hell. He only wanted to experience the colors and sounds, the music, the lush textures of fabric on his body and food in his mouth, the press of another human against him, dancing, hugging, laughing, lips on cheeks and hands on hearts – he'd just wanted to *feel* it, something good and rich, something he'd heard so much about but could never have imagined.

He'd only been *borrowing* the body. He was always going to give it back.

And now the woman was dead, and he prayed with every fiber of her stolen body that she was at peace. As for him, he would burn, and he would deserve it.

His hands balled into fists and he sobbed as his shoulder gave a particularly painful wrench. His voice was louder now, stronger. When he swallowed, it didn't feel like swallowing a knife.

Surely the angels wouldn't allow him to live with such relief for long. Surely the angels would want to tear him open again and revel in his screams and pleas.

As if he had summoned them with his thoughts, the door to the basement opened. Dee let out a piteous wail. His burns were healed, but his shoulder was still crushed with agony. The bones weren't fused yet. They shifted and creaked when he lifted his head to look at the angels as they descended the steps one by one, their unearthly gazes fixed on him.

When Lucas reached the basement floor, his lips quirked into a smile. "We've just had the *best* idea," he said. Dee sobbed when the others began to laugh.

9

"*N-no,*" Dee sobbed as the angels stepped toward him. His shoes squeaked against the floor as he tried to drag himself away with his hands still locked behind him, agony rising and breaking through his shoulder. He felt the edges of the Trap like the hum of an electric fence. Sweat broke out over his newly-healed skin. "P-please, *no* ..."

"It looks *much* better," Lucas said with the hint of a pout in his voice. "I didn't think it would work so fast." He cleared his throat. "**Demon, stop healing.**"

Dee's mouth fell open and he wailed against the floor. All at once, he could feel the bones in his shoulder stop knitting together. He could feel every healing fiber of his body stop. Not even the slow creep of his own mending continued. The iron blistered his skin, and it did not begin to mend again. His tears stung his cheeks as he sobbed.

A vicious hand closed on his hair and dragged him back into the center of the Trap. He gasped as he was thrown to the floor again. His head cracked against the cement floor.

"P-please," he heaved, turning his head to look up at the angels standing around him. "Please, *please*, Powers, y-you have stopped all my healing, I c-cannot – "

He cried out as Dominic kicked him hard in the chest. He realized, distantly, that his lung was restored, the rib still fractured but no longer piercing into him now. Through the ringing in his ears, he could barely hear the angels speaking above him. He whimpered and gasped – grateful, at least, for his air. For as long as he had it.

He froze when the angels stopped murmuring above him and turned to look down on him once again. Jude knelt down beside him and reached out to run a hand through his hair. He shuddered under the touch that he could feel singeing his hair.

"We'll let you heal later, little one," Jude crooned. "Can't have you wearing out too quickly. Remember, we'll want to keep you for *years.*" He smiled when Dee whimpered softly. "But you don't need to heal for this part." He chuckled and glanced up at Dominic. "Ready?"

"Yes," Dominic said with a grin as he knelt beside Jude. Dee blinked away tears, and they ran down his cheeks. His gaze found Dominic again – and every muscle in his body went rigid.

Dominic was holding a knife.

The edge glittered under the yellowed light, impossibly sharp, seeming to cut the very air – and seeming almost to have a light all its own. Dee's heart ached as he stared at the blade of consecrated iron, held inches from his face. Then he nodded silently and rolled onto his back, tilting his head to bare his throat to them.

But Ilya ...

Tears burned in his eyes and he convulsed with a sob. *Ilya, Ilya, Ilya, my Ilya ... Custodire eos, Deus, benedicere eos, custodire eos a malum sicut me ...* [*Ilya, Ilya, Ilya, my Ilya ... Protect them, God, bless them, protect them from evil like me ...*]

"Oh, little snake," Lucas said, kneeling beside his head. "Haven't you been listening?"

Cold gripped Dee's chest.

"We're not going to kill you," Jude said gently, his lips curved in a mockery of a smile. "Not for many years. Not until you have *truly* paid for your sins – and oh, little sinner, they are *many.*"

Dee looked up at them in terror, eyes flicking between each angel, and then finally back to the knife that glinted in Dominic's hand. He wet his lips and shuddered as more tears coursed down his temples and into his hair.

Dominic smirked as he bent over Dee. "Still, this position is perfect." He grabbed the ring of Dee's iron collar, holding him in place – then brought the knife to Dee's throat and made a cut over where his pulse once beat.

Dee sobbed in panic as the blood spilled out over his throat and pooled on the floor beneath him. He didn't need his blood – he didn't, he could live without it – but his body rebelled, and he writhed against the heavy hand pinning him down by his collar. He dragged in breath after desperate breath as tears blurred his vision and spilled down his temples.

Above him, Dominic held the knife to the palm of his own hand – and cut. When he pressed his hand to the wound, Dee *screamed.*

Dominic's blood spilled out over Dee's throat, leaving blistering skin in its wake. It seeped inside the cut and pooled in Dee's veins, burning him from the inside out. Dee's shoulder tore as he thrashed against the cuffs, mindless, fangs breaking through and flashing as his mouth opened wide with his scream. He sounded like an animal in a trap, like a creature being torn to pieces.

Above him, Dominic frowned. "It's not ... spreading."

Lucas tilted his head. "Has it always not had a heartbeat?" He stared down at Dee as he burned. "**Demon, make your heart beat, spread the blood through your body**."

Inside Dee's chest, his heart shuddered, then contracted in a single, sluggish beat. Then, again. And again. Every beat felt like a knife going through him, a spasm of pain. As his heart beat, the angel's blood spread slowly – and lit every nerve on fire in its wake.

Dee threw his head back and roared with agony. A line of fire moved from the wound at his throat, down inside him to his chest – and then everywhere else. Every lethargic pump of his dead heart spread the poison to every vessel, every cell. Another beat, then another. Dee convulsed as it spread, barely feeling the flash of pain as Dominic pressed his finger to the cut at Dee's throat, cauterizing it shut, keeping the angel's blood trapped inside him.

Dee's heart beat once more, then fell silent again in his chest. Dee was burning alive.

Lucas peered down at Dee, his eyes fixed on him as he sobbed and twisted against the floor. "'For the life of the flesh is in the blood: and I have given it to you upon the altar to make an atonement for your souls: for it is the blood that maketh an atonement for the soul.' This is righteous justice, little one, for your profane existence. Be grateful that we are punishing you for your sins." His hand tightened in Dee's hair and he jerked his head back, smiling at how Dee's pupils were blown wide with agony, his fangs flashing in the light as he jerked and screamed. "Be *grateful*, little sinner," he murmured.

"*B-bene facis*" [*Th-thank you*], Dee heaved. He gasped as Lucas whipped a hand across his face so hard that he pitched onto his side. He arched back, mouth open wide with his desperate shrieks. "Th-thank you, m-merciful ... Ahh, *please, please, please, no* – "

His eyes rolled back and he retched. Acid burned his throat like holy water. He convulsed as fire burned through his veins, consuming him, tearing him apart from the inside out. Sweat poured down his skin, soaking his clothes and hair. He left smears on the floor as he tried to twist away from the pain that had burrowed deep inside him.

"Told you this was a good idea," Dominic said somewhere above Dee.

Dee opened his eyes and saw the angels standing around him in a circle now, staring down at him as he twitched and sobbed. Fire consumed every part of him. His throat was raw from screaming.

"It won't kill it ... right?" Lucas said, and nudged Dee with his toe. Dee wailed and cringed into himself. His chest heaved with desperate sobs.

"Probably not. I mean ... I don't think anyone's ever ... done this before." Dominic grinned. "But look at it."

Dee's eyes were unfocused as the angels smiled down at him. He choked on a sob and tried to twist away.

"Still, if we want to keep it alive ..." Lucas tilted his head to survey Dee, eyes sweeping him up and down. "**Demon, you may heal at the rate you normally do**." The ground shook under Dee as the command gripped him.

He shuddered as his body rebelled against the poison inside him. He retched again, bringing up nothing but bile. White light flashed across his vision and he hoped, desperately, that he would lose consciousness and slide into the mercy of oblivion. Instead, he felt his body writhe against the floor, desperate to escape the pain and unable to. Then, as if his body had given up entirely on purging the poison from his veins, he felt his shoulder slowly begin to mend again.

He could barely see through the agony as even his eyes burned. He could taste his own blood as he bit his tongue in his panic, fangs piercing deep.

Jude's voice was husky and low. "'Because I have purged thee, and thou wast not purged, thou shalt not be purged from thy filthiness any more, till I have caused my fury to rest upon thee.'" He licked his lips. "Look at the agony in its eyes. *Lovely.*"

Dominic twirled the knife in his hand. His palm was healed, spotless, as if there had never been a wound. "This was an *excellent* idea, if I do say so myself." He grinned at Dee.

Dee shuddered and realized that, slowly, slowly, the fire inside him was fading. He sobbed in meager relief.

"Still," Dominic said as he knelt by Dee's side again. "I forgot how good it felt to have my knife to the little sinner's throat." He pushed Dee onto his back, placed a hand on his chest, and *leaned*. Dee's rib creaked under the weight. He shivered and looked up at Dominic, panting and desperate.

Dominic pressed the tip of the knife to the base of Dee's throat, just barely brushing his skin. Dee squeezed his eyes shut and sobbed weakly.

"Beg," Dominic said, and grinned when the other two laughed. "Beg, little *daemon,* for mercy."

10

"*P-please,*" Dee begged, his throat bobbing with panic. The tip of the knife brushed his skin and instantly cut, sharper than any razor. "P-please, angels ... mercy, please, show me mercy, *please* ..."

Dominic laughed as he straddled Dee's hips and drew the tip of his knife across Dee's throat, light as a feather, above and below the collar in gentle stripes. Dee gasped and sobbed as his skin tingled under the blade. His hands were crushed beneath him, the iron cuffs cutting deep into his wrists. He swallowed, again and again, doing his best to hold still as the angel's blood still burned him from the inside out.

If he just leaned forward ... if he just lifted his head and let the blade cut through his throat ...

My throat or my heart. Please, please, mercy, cut my throat or pierce my heart, please ...

Dominic chuckled as he drew the knife down, over Dee's heaving chest, lower still until the tip rested against his abdomen. Dee quivered, tears streaming into his hair, as Dominic stared down at him with gleeful hatred in his eyes.

"Alright," Dominic said softly. "You've begged. Now. **Confess**."

Dee arched back, his mouth bobbing open as the command gripped him. His lips felt too numb to speak. Every inch of him burned, and his mind was blank with panic. "I-I ..."

"Confess your sins," Jude said gently. He knelt beside Dee's head and wound burning fingers through his hair. Entire hanks of it had been burned away, leaving smoldering ends and bald skin. Jude smiled as he ran a lock of it through his fingers. It singed and curled away, sending wisps of acrid smoke floating up toward the ceiling. "Confess, demon. You were lost to us once, only to be found to be broken anew. Tell us of your evil deeds and we will bring absolution: by purging you from this earth, and your deeds with you."

Dee opened his mouth to speak. His eyes rolled back at the fire in his veins, twisting inside him and breaking him to pieces. He dry-heaved, desperately turning his head so he wouldn't choke. He cried out as the motion jostled the bones in his shoulder.

He screamed as Lucas kicked him hard in his broken shoulder. The newly-healed bones broke apart again, and Dee sobbed in despair. He shuddered as agony swept through him, again and again and again.

"Confess, *daemon*," Lucas spat. "Tell us what you have done."

"*H-habeo –* " [*I h-have*] Dee whined as the knife pressed against his abdomen, easily parting the fabric of his shirt and piercing into the first layer of skin.

"*Nolo dice quod lingua iterum*" [*Do not speak that language again*], Dominic growled above him. "*Tu es indignus dicere eam*" [*You are unworthy to speak it*].

"*S-set est lingua mea*" [*B-but it's my native tongue*], Dee sobbed. "*E-est –* " [*I-it's –*]

A slap rocked his head to the side. "*Nolo. Dice. Quod. Lingua. Dice eam iterum, ero scalpere lingua tua*" [*Do. Not. Speak. That. Language. If you speak it again, I will cut out your tongue*].

Dee sobbed weakly. "Forgive me," he rasped. "Forgive me."

"Confess your sins, and we may just be merciful," Dominic said with a smile.

Dee stared up at him, trembling with hope that he knew he shouldn't have. He wet his lips and was grateful, so grateful, that his mouth had healed from the holy water. His throat was almost too tight to speak.

"I-I ..." he croaked. "I s-stole this body when it was not mine to take."

"Yes, you did," Dominic said with a grin, and slid his knife into Dee's belly.

Dee threw his head back and shrieked his agony as the knife pierced him. He felt the sharp blade bury deep inside, cold and merciless against the unending burn of the angel's blood. Tears pooled in the shells of his ears and streamed onto the concrete floor. Dee writhed under Dominic's weight, his shoes scrabbling for purchase on the floor. He shuddered as Dominic drew out his blade and passed one finger over the wound, sealing it shut.

Dominic held the knife above Dee, glinting with his blood. It dripped onto his shirt – *Ilya's shirt* – staining the cotton bright red. Dee stared at the knife in horror as Dominic turned it back and forth as if inspecting it.

"Good," Dominic said with a smile. "What else?"

"N-no," Dee heaved. He could feel the blood pooling inside him, and could feel the veins and tissues sealing shut just as quickly. His head spun as the wound flared hot, then hotter, overpowering the agony of the poison inside him.

"What else have you done, *inimicus*?" Jude asked, almost sweetly. "What other foul deeds have you committed against the humans of this earth?" He leaned closer until his breath huffed over Dee's ear, cold as ice. "Submit yourself to penance, little one. Tell us your sins, so we can cleanse you."

Dee cried out, desperate and hopeless. He tilted his head back, silently begging Dominic to slit his throat and send him to oblivion. Ilya could not reach him here. Not even Dara could reach him here.

"I ... I-I at-tacked a Virtue," he sobbed.

Dominic hesitated. "You attacked ...?"

"My rescuer," Dee said weakly, eyes fixed on the knife poised above him. "Sh-she – she moved too quickly and I ... I panicked, I didn't mean to, I didn't *mean* to, b-but I lunged at her and ... and bared my teeth ..." He whimpered softly as his fangs pressed against his lower lip. "I didn't mean to," he whispered. "I j-just wanted to protect my ... the human. I th-thought she was ... I didn't *know* ..."

Dominic laughed. "You bared your teeth at one of the holiest of us, after she removed you from our retribution? You truly are a *vile* and ungrateful creature."

He gave Dee a wicked grin as he plunged his knife into his exposed abdomen again.

"*NO*!" Dee shrieked, arching away from the blade as it cut deep inside him. The pain crescendoed and he turned his head, heaving again. Nothing came up but a weak trickle of blood.

"I knew this one was wicked," Jude said with a gentle smile. "But I had no idea how deep the corruption went." His fingers left scorched hair in their wake. The smell burned Dee's nose, and he shuddered.

Still, the fire in his blood was subsiding, slowly. It gave way to the agony of the wounds from the knife. He trembled and shook, sweating through his clothes.

"What else have you done, *serpentis*?" Lucas said, nudging him with his toe. "Surely there is more."

"Y-yes," Dee gasped, beyond all thought, beyond anything but the pain inside him. "I ..." His eyes filled with tears. "I-I corrupted the ... the human."

Dominic let out a breath through his nose. "Well, we could have told you that." He grinned as he leaned over Dee and slid his knife into him once more.

Dee's scream was weaker now. He shuddered with relief when Dominic pulled the knife back again. The smell of his blood was thick in his nose, metallic, tinged with fear and something else, something like burning flesh. He lay motionless under Dominic, save for his heaving chest and trembling lips. His throat bobbed as he looked up toward the single lightbulb hanging over him.

"I ... I s-somehow m-manipulated them," he rasped. Guilt and grief crushed his heart. "I ... I don't know how, but ... th-they care for me, I'm unworthy and they *care* ..." His throat constricted in an animal whine. "Th-they are – are *good.*" He squeezed his eyes shut, trying to brace for the knife.

For a long moment, no one moved. No one breathed. Dee cracked his eyes open and stared at the angels, one by one, as they loomed over him. His hands were numb beneath him.

"*How* deeply do they care for you?" Dominic said, staring down at Dee. His hand hovered in the air, knife still dripping blood onto Dee's shirt.

The back of Dee's neck prickled. He shivered as sweat chilled his skin. "Wh-what, angel?"

"I said ..." Dominic smiled and plunged the knife into Dee's stomach. Dee screamed his throat raw. "How. Deeply. Do. They. Care. For. You?" With each word, he twisted the knife harder. Dee's vision went white and he writhed under Dominic's weight. He coughed, and blood speckled his lips.

Dee's mouth bobbed open as he tried to speak. *They feel for me. They care about me.* He could barely draw breath past the shard of fire inside him. His eyes rolled back and he tried, desperately, to focus on the angels above him who spun with the rest of the room.

When his eyes finally focused on Dominic, his blood ran cold. The angels were looking at each other, with identical expressions of vindication on their faces.

"So you have poisoned yet *another* human soul," Lucas said with satisfaction dripping from every word. He looked down at Dee with a snarl on his lips. "You have damned another life to the flames."

"N-no," Dee breathed, shuddering as his own blood cooled on his skin. He screamed as Dominic jerked the knife out of him and sealed the wound shut with his burning hand.

"We must save the sinful human that tethered their soul to this creature," Jude hissed through his teeth, lips pulled wide in an inhuman smile.

"N-no, *no*!" Dee sobbed. His voice broke. "No, merciful angels, *no*, they – th-they are innocent, they are blameless, it wasn't their f-fault – "

He cried out as Dominic backhanded Dee across the face with his empty hand. Dee felt himself bleeding inside, felt the bones in his shoulder grind and grate. His face was glazed with tears as the angels all stood and stepped away from him in one fluid motion. The room hummed. Dee felt the vibration deep in his bones. He sobbed, open-mouthed, and tried to drag himself to the angels' feet with his hands still cuffed behind him.

"P-please," he breathed, blind with dread. "No. Please. Not Ilya. Please not Ilya."

Lucas laughed and kicked Dee hard in the stomach. Dee screamed and shuddered as agony ripped through his wounds.

"This will be *fun*," Jude said, looking down at Dee. He reached down and grabbed a handful of Dee's hair to yank him upright. Dee cried out and shuffled to his knees. "It is the Lord's will to eradicate the stain on the earth that you create, little snake. No matter. This will only take a little time."

Dee's eyes were wide as he screamed his horror.

11

"Lucas, would you like to fetch them, or do you want one of us to do it?" Jude said with a vicious smile on his face. He glanced at Dee and smiled wider as Dee sobbed.

"I think I'll do it," Lucas said, turning back to grin at Dee. "This will only take a moment." Dee blinked tears out of his eyes, and Lucas was gone.

"*NO*!" Dee shrieked, gasping past the collar that seemed to constrict around his neck. "No, *no*! *Ilya*!" Tears streamed down his face and he collapsed to the floor, sick with horror. "*Ilya* ..." he whimpered, eyes wide and sightless as he lay limp on the cold ground.

Jude stepped forward and gripped what was left of Dee's hair. "Now you *and* your little friend can submit yourselves to penance," he crooned, looking down at Dee with gentleness that made his skin crawl. "We truly are doing the Lord's work today."

"*N-no*," Dee sobbed brokenly. Agony lanced his heart. *Not Ilya. Not Ilya. Not Ilya.*

Dominic snorted as he glanced down at Dee. "Should have thought of this before you corrupted them, little snake," he said, his lip curling. "'It is joy to the just to do judgment: but destruction shall be to the workers of iniquity.'"

"B-but they are not iniquitous," Dee whimpered against the floor. "They are innocent, th-they are *good* – " He screamed as Dominic kicked him in the stomach again. His eyes rolled back and he gagged weakly against the stab of pain through the knife wounds.

"Quiet, *daemon*," Dominic sneered. Dee heaved a shuddering sob. He pulled against the iron cuffs, even as the bones in his shoulder ground together.

There was a *thud* upstairs, then a scuffle against the floor. A muffled voice raised in a shout of fury. The sound of an open palm against flesh.

Dee moaned as he dragged himself up to his knees again, eyes fixed on the basement door. His heart clenched and he nearly retched as pain burrowed deep into his wounds. He trembled in every limb, his skin on fire with terror and guilt and grief. The basement door flew open, and Lucas dragged Ilya heavily behind him.

Ilya raged against his grip, aiming kicks at Lucas' legs. Their hands were bound behind them, and they shrieked through the gag tied around their head. A bruise marred their cheek. Blood dripped from their nose and into the gag.

Ilya. My Ilya.

"*No*!" Dee sobbed, tears streaming down his face. Ilya's eyes went wide and they lurched forward in the angel's grip, screaming through the gag in their mouth. Lucas jerked them upright and dragged them down the rest of the stairs. He forced them to their knees just outside the line of the Trap imprisoning Dee and yanked their head back, his fingers tangling in their tight curls.

Ilya's eyes swept over Dee, taking in the blood that stained his shirt, the burns on his face, his hair singed short now, the way his arm hung loosely in its socket. Ilya raised their eyes to the angels standing around them and snarled their rage.

"Hello, little one," Jude said gently, lips curving into a sickly smile. "So you are the human that this one has so thoroughly corrupted." He nudged Dee's chin and grinned when Dee flinched away from the burning touch.

Ilya trembled, their eyes fixed once again on Dee. Tears stained their cheeks and wet the gag. Their jaw worked around it and they whimpered softly, all their fury gone and replaced with horror.

"I-Ilya, *no*," Dee whimpered. His body was gripped with cold terror, and he shivered. The angel's blood still seared in his veins. Sweat poured down his back and soaked his shirt.

Dominic stepped forward and reached for the cuffs on Dee's wrists. Dee cringed away from him, ducking his head and whimpering softly. With one touch, the chain on his wrists fell away. Dee threw his head back and screamed as Dominic wrenched his arms forward and passed his hand over the cuffs again. Fire flared through Dee's shoulder as the chain locked his hands in front of him. Still, he sagged, dragging in breath after breath of relief. His shoulder wasn't twisted quite so terribly this way. He swayed on his knees, dizzy and trembling from the pain stabbing through his abdomen.

"Go to them," Jude said gently, nodding toward Ilya. "Go to the one you corrupted, *daemon.* Look into their eyes and see that you have brought them to their death."

Dee's head snapped up. "*No*," he croaked. "No, merciful powers, no, *no*, please, they are innocent, *please*, kill me, not them, please, *please* ..."

Ilya cried out wordlessly and shook their head against Lucas' grip, eyes wide and desperate. Their gaze was locked on Dee, just as he was unable to look away from them.

"The wages of sin is death, little snake," Jude murmured. "You know that. Their life was forfeit the moment they let you into their heart. It is wickedness, to love something wicked."

Dee desperately shook his head. "Please," he breathed.

"**Go to them**," Jude commanded.

Dee and Ilya both flinched away from the thunder of his voice. Dee lurched forward on his knees, but before he could cross the small width of the Trap, Jude kicked him to the floor. He convulsed and screamed, curling around the wounds in his stomach. He cradled his arm, grateful – so, so grateful – that he had his hands again, even if they were still shackled. The command crushed his bones, tugged at his limbs, and he dragged himself forward, sobbing as every movement sent jagged agony stabbing through his shoulder.

He crawled until he could feel the edges of the Trap under his skin like an electric current. He collapsed to the floor in front of Ilya, pressing his face against the cold cement in supplication. He splayed his hand out against the floor, reaching, reaching, fingers going numb as he forced them closer to the edge of the Trap.

"Ilya," he whispered. "*Ignosce me, carissime Ilya –* " [*Forgive me, dearest Ilya –*] He grunted as Dominic kicked him hard. Ilya screamed and thrashed against Lucas' grip.

"K-kill me," Dee groaned, helpless. "I-I will – will take the punishment for my sins. But please … do not punish them. I will – will take the punishment, I will take the knife, just *please*, do not hurt them …" He bit down on his tongue as Lucas threw his head back in a peal of laughter.

"You are not in a position to bargain, little one," Lucas said with a chuckle. "Yes, you will take the pain, you will take the punishment. You have no choice in this. We do the holy will of our Lord. But this one, this precious little thing that you turned away from the path of righteousness and took down the path of evil and sin …"

Dee forced himself to look up. Lucas had one hand fisted in Ilya's hair and the other gently cradling their face. Ilya glared up at him with rage in their eyes.

Lucas smiled gently. "This one will also pay the price. This is the pursuit of true justice, little snake. Sometimes it is fierce. Sometimes it is born through pain. But it is always glorious. 'If thou do that which is evil, be afraid; for he beareth not the sword in vain: for he is the minister of God, a revenger to execute wrath upon him that doeth evil.'"

Dee's stomach dropped as Lucas drew his blade and held it to Ilya's throat. Ilya went still, their eyes wide and brimming with tears as they looked down at Dee in stark terror.

"*No*," Dee sobbed. He could barely form the word past the horror clogging his throat.

"Their life is the price of your sin," Lucas murmured. His gaze pinned Dee to the floor. "And you will watch them pay the cost."

Dee let out a wordless scream of agony as Ilya began to sob.

12

"Ilya," Dee breathed, muscles shuddering as he tried to force himself through the Trap. It was like pushing against an electrified fence, the current jolting through him and locking his muscles into agonizing rigor. He wept sulfurous tears and threw himself against the Trap again.

Ilya was mumbling incoherently through the gag, tears streaming down their face and into the now-soaked fabric. They struggled against Lucas' grip and cried out when Lucas grabbed a handful of their hair and twisted it viciously.

"L-Lucas, *please*," Dee sobbed, pressing his forehead against the floor. "I-I'll do *anything*. I'll ... You can – you can f-flay me, like you said, or – or hang me, or – "

Ilya's scream silenced the words in Dee's mouth. He looked up, stomach heaving, but Lucas was not hurting them – Ilya was staring at *him,* eyes wide with horror. They desperately shook their head. Tears cascaded down their cheeks and onto the floor.

"P-please," Dee rasped. "Lucas ... *please.*"

Lucas smirked. "Beg if you must, creature," he said with a grin. "Beg, scream, cry, but their fate is tied to yours – and their fate is sealed." He looked down at Ilya and reached for the gag. "Confess, little one," he murmured. "Confess your sins before we surrender you to judgment." He pulled the gag from Ilya's mouth.

"*No*!" Dee wailed.

"*D-Dee*," Ilya sobbed, taking in hitching, gasping breaths. "Dee, I'm so sorry, Dee, *no* ..."

Dominic snorted and stepped forward. Dee flinched away as Dominic's boots stopped near his face. "*Dee*? That's what you've been calling it? Dee as in *demon*?" His lips twisted and he kicked Dee hard in the stomach. Dee shrieked and curled into himself, retching against the pain. "What a dark joke to play," Dominic said as he pinned Dee under his boot.

"He's not an *it*!" Ilya shrieked. Their face was flushed red, shining with their tears. They trembled in Lucas' grip, even as Dee tried to force his hand through the Trap again. Dominic kicked Dee onto his back and laughed at Dee's scream.

Jude's lips quirked into a smile. "Oh, it's a *him* now too, is it?" he crooned. He knelt by Dee's side and dragged him upright by his collar. Dee gagged and choked as it closed around his neck. "The human seems to want to treat you as if you were human, too." Jude looked at Ilya, and Ilya shrank back against Lucas, trembling under Jude's gaze. "Just how debauched are you, little one? Did you take him to your bed? Did you love him, lie with him?"

"*No*!" Ilya cried. They wet their lips and glared at Jude. "H-he never wanted that!"

Dee's stomach lurched and he shook his head, eyes streaming as he choked, shuffling on his knees. He could not meet Ilya's eyes. His cheeks would have burned with shame if he had a heartbeat. It was true; all he'd ever wanted – and all Ilya had ever done – was to be held, cradled, soft hands rubbing his back and soft lips resting against his forehead. Acid clawed its way up his throat and he gagged on his panic.

Jude huffed out a laugh. "Well. At least there's *that* small mercy." He drew one finger across Dee's throat and chuckled when Dee screamed and tried to twist away.

Dee swallowed and tasted bile at the back of his throat. "Th-they are human," he heaved, head spinning with the pain. "They – th-they are – are *human*, it's not like with me, th-they are ... Their s-soul is still pure, *please* – "

"Nothing is pure that has love for you," Dominic said with a vicious sneer. He stepped forward and struck Dee across the face.

Dee whimpered as blood streamed from his lip. "P-please, angels, *no*!" he sobbed. "Please, please, l-let them go, h-hurt *me* ... not them ..."

"Some things are unsalvageable, little snake," Jude said almost sadly. "They were lost the moment you arrived in their life. It is regrettable, but ..." Fingers combed through Dee's short hair. "They are damned to the flames."

Ilya whimpered and heaved a broken sob. Dee reached out and gasped when his fingers again hit the edges of the Trap. His shoulder was on fire. He could scarcely breathe.

"At least their list of sins is short," Lucas sighed. He untied the rope from around Ilya's wrists. Dominic stepped forward to help as Lucas forced Ilya's hands together in front of them and tied them, palm to palm. He clutched their hair and forced them onto all fours in front of Dee. Dee thought he would be sick from the terror in Ilya's eyes, the tears that trembled there, unshed. His throat clicked as he swallowed. His lips were numb.

"I-I'm sorry," he breathed. Ilya whimpered. Then he heard a sound, one so familiar that he knew it in his bones. He looked behind Ilya and saw that Lucas had stepped back and uncoiled a whip, letting the end *smack* against the ground. He whined wordlessly, the collar seeming to choke him again. Tears poured down his face. His abdomen flared with pain.

Dominic pulled Ilya's shirt up until it bunched around their shoulders, exposing their back. He tucked the hem of the shirt into their neckline and stepped back.

"This will not take long, little human," Lucas said, his voice placid and calm. "Punishment for the sin of loving the wicked creature in front of you, and then ..." He shrugged. "You will die, and we will continue our work."

"N-no," Ilya sobbed. They reached forward, and their hands passed through the Trap as if it wasn't there. Dee lurched forward and clutched their fingers, knuckles going white. He was shaking so hard he felt like he would fall to pieces. Ilya squeezed their eyes shut.

"No, look at it," Jude murmured. Ilya opened their eyes and stared up at Jude, panting, trembling. Jude shook Dee by the collar. "Look at it. This creature is your downfall, little one. Look into its eyes as we deliver justice for your sins."

Ilya brought their gaze to meet Dee's. Their lips trembled and their mouth fell open with a sob.

The first lash came down, and Ilya screamed their agony.

The sound split Dee in half. He lunged against Jude's grasp. His fangs flashed and his eyes blazed, pupils blown wide with fury. "*Invocabo maledictum super te, damnnatus potestates* – " [*I invoke a curse upon you, damned Powers* –]

A blow snapped his head to the side. He pitched onto his broken shoulder, smashing his head against the cement floor. The room spun around him and he blinked against the ringing echoing through his head. It took him a breath to realize the sound was Ilya screaming.

He blinked, slowly, half-blind with pain. His body felt boneless. He couldn't move.

Jude dragged him up to his knees again and grabbed his face. Dee roared as his skin blistered under the touch, smoke from his own burning flesh choking him as Jude pried his jaw open. Each time he tried to reach up to pull the hand away, his shoulder exploded with pain.

"I thought we told you not to use that language or else we'd cut out your wicked tongue," Jude rasped in Dee's ear. Dee could see Ilya kneeling in front of him, being held back by Dominic as they raged and fought to get to him. He squeezed his eyes shut, willing his head to stop spinning. When he opened his eyes, they still would not focus.

Even under the searing agony of the angel's touch, he felt a trickle of warmth down his neck. He shuddered and froze when the smell of his own blood overwhelmed him. It was streaming from the cut on the side of his head, soaking his hair and staining Ilya's shirt more.

He weakly tossed his head, trying to shake free of the angel's burning grip on his face. He fell perfectly still when the cold blade of Jude's knife pressed down against his tongue. It pricked, and blood welled in his mouth. Jude released his face and clutched his collar instead, keeping the knife in Dee's mouth, almost touching the back of his throat. Dee gagged and winced as it only cut his tongue deeper.

Dee forgot the knife when his eyes finally focused. Ilya was on their knees in front of him, taking deep, gulping breaths, hands bound and braced against the floor. Each exhale was a sob. And Dee could smell their blood – clean, not like his at all. His fangs flashed and clinked against the knife in his mouth.

"Continue," Jude said with a smile. Dee raised their gaze to Lucas. Lucas grinned and wound up for the next swing.

"*N-n –* " Dee coughed as the blade slit his tongue and more blood pooled in his mouth, dripping from his lips.

Lucas brought the lash down, and Ilya's scream tore Dee apart. Dee's tears stung the burns on his face. He sobbed weakly, choking on the collar and the knife in his mouth. Blood streamed down his temple and matted his hair.

Dee felt the next lash as if it had landed on his own back. He wailed with Ilya and sobbed when they met his eyes. Jude braced Dee's head back against his chest and stroked his fingers down Dee's cheek. Dee writhed and burned under the touch.

"This is the price of your corruption," Jude whispered in Dee's ear. "Look at the agony you have caused in this human that thought they could trust you."

Dee screamed against the knife as his heart shattered in his chest.

13

Ilya's back was a mess of blood. It streamed down their sides in rivulets, staining the cement beneath them. Dee's head spun with the scent of it. He gagged weakly on his own blood, and on the knife that Jude kept firmly between his lips, pressing down on his tongue. His eyes burned and streamed with helpless tears.

Ilya wailed as another lash came down. They sagged against the ground, barely able to hold themself up under the whip. They took great, heaving sobs, their head bowed toward the floor.

"Please," they cried. "Please, no!"

"*I-Il* – " Dee gagged on the knife and tried to reach for them with his hands chained together, shoulder wrenching as he did. They raised their head to look at him. He felt shame like a knife to his heart when he saw their tears, the snarl of agony written across their face, the way their bound hands trembled against the floor.

"Almost done, little one," Lucas said softly. "Almost done."

Dee roared his rage and lunged forward against Jude's hold. He sobbed and choked when the knife pressed down harder against his tongue.

Lucas raised his gaze to Dee, his lips pressed together in something that looked almost like *sorrow.* "Just a little more punishment for your fallen friend," he murmured, tilting his head at Ilya. "Then we surrender them to the flames, and continue our work with you."

"N-no, *please*," Ilya sobbed. They trembled in every limb as they looked back at Lucas, wincing as it pulled on the lash marks on their back. "P-please, please don't kill me, don't ... Please don't kill *him* ..."

Lucas tsked and lowered his arm. "Don't worry, little human," he said softly, and hardness found its way into his eyes again. "You will be reunited again – a few decades from now, after we have finished punishing our little snake."

Dee screamed and coughed on his own blood. *Ilya isn't damned. Ilya isn't going to Hell. Even once the angels are finished with me, I'll never see Ilya again.*

"D-Dee," Ilya whimpered. Dee's eyes were wide, black taking up almost the entire iris, fangs bared and flashing in the light. He couldn't look away from Ilya. Blood trickled down their arms, pooling on the floor in front of them. They reached out, flinching and sobbing as the muscles twitched in their back. Their hands slid along the floor, reaching past the Trap and toward Dee. Dee struggled and tried to clutch their hands. They were too far away.

Crack.

Ilya screamed and crumpled to the floor, half in the Trap and half out. Their blood smeared on the ground.

"Come on, Jude, let them be together," Dominic said as he watched Ilya writhe in pain. "The little creature is the human's downfall. At least let it touch what it has broken."

Jude rolled his eyes and slid his knife out from between Dee's teeth. Dee winced as it sliced the inside of his mouth. "Fine," Jude huffed. "But once the human is dead, I want the demon's tongue." He shoved Dee to the ground.

Dee cried out as the bones in his shoulder crunched. He lay motionless on the floor, room spinning, stomach heaving. He cried out and flinched away from a gentle touch on his arm. When he could finally get his eyes to focus, he saw Ilya, sprawled out on the floor beside him, desperately reaching for him with their bound hands.

"Dee," they whispered. Their voice cracked. "Dee."

"I-Ilya," Dee murmured. The sound was slurred, twisted by Dee's bleeding tongue. "I'm s-sorry."

"I l-looked for you," Ilya sobbed. They shuddered and hissed out a breath through their teeth. "We tried to find you, Dee. We knew ... I couldn't let them *h-hurt* you – "

"I'm sorry I brought this pain on you," Dee croaked. "F-forgive me, Ilya, *carissime Ilya, ignosce me ...*" [*dearest Ilya, forgive me ...*]

"N-no," Ilya sobbed. "No, *no ...*"

Dee and Ilya screamed together as the lash fell on Ilya's back again.

Dee shrieked and bared his fangs at Lucas, eyes blazing. He was too weak to stand. He could only lie on the floor with Ilya, their blood mingling at the edges of the Trap. He wrapped one hand around theirs and held tight.

If there is a H eaven like I've been told, and not just a Hell after this ...

He could not bear to think any more.

"Last one, little one," Lucas said softly. "Dominic, put them on their knees again for me, would you?"

Dominic snorted and stepped forward. He fisted a hand in Ilya's hair and dragged them upright. Ilya's hand was ripped from Dee's grasp. Their blood smeared against the floor as Dominic put them on their knees just outside the Trap.

A pit opened up inside Dee like a clap of thunder.

Where a moment ago he'd been trapped, pinned inside the circle by an unseen force, now he could feel the downward pull toward Hell inside him again. He could smell sulfur in his nostrils, could feel the unearthly heat of his home against his skin. He could feel how he rattled around inside the body, hardly tethered to it at all. There was another body here, one with a pounding heart and a pure soul, and his mind cried out for him to leap inside the fresh body so when they both died, he could latch onto them and ride that tether into Hell.

He would become nothing if he died in this body.

Dee trembled, gasping, as the thunder rolled through him again and again. He'd so quickly forgotten how it felt to be free of the Trap. He blinked against the tears that blurred his vision and raised his head, looking for the source of the newfound power.

Ilya knelt in a smear of their own blood, shaking and sobbing, their eyes squeezed shut in anticipation of the final lash. Mingled in with the blood was a streak of the Trap's white paint, moistened and smeared against the floor.

The circle was broken. It was enough.

Dee raised his head to stare at the angels around him. He could not fight his way out, not now. There was no escape. No escape but death. And to escape death now, he had to rend himself from this body and enter Ilya instead. It called to him, a fresh body with only the whip marks to cause it pain, inviting him in to look through their eyes and feel through their skin, a pure soul to tie himself to. He would have to drag them to Hell with him in order to survive.

Dee's stomach lurched. He clenched his jaw so hard his teeth ached. *Never. Never again. Not to Ilya.*

Upstairs, there was a *bang*.

Everyone froze.

Lucas tilted his head toward the ceiling. "Hm. Go see what that was, would you?" he said breezily. Jude and Dominic both nodded and headed for the stairs.

Dee lay still with bated breath, not even daring to look up. If the angels saw that the circle had been broken, they gave no sign. Jude and Dominic climbed the steps and opened the basement door. They disappeared into the silence upstairs.

A scream pierced the air. The house shook in its foundations.

"*Damn*," Lucas spat. He jerked Ilya back by their hair, dragging them backward until they fell against his chest. They clawed at his hand but went still when his knife pressed against their throat.

"*Thy will be done*," Lucas murmured, and pressed the blade in.

Dee shrieked and launched forward with strength he didn't know he possessed. He passed through the line of the Trap as easily as the angels had. He pried the knife away from Ilya's throat, screaming in agony as his broken shoulder twisted. His skin burned like an open flame as he tore Lucas' hand from Ilya's hair, taking whole curls with it. He shoved Ilya behind him and lunged again at Lucas, mouth open, fangs bared, growling like a cornered animal.

"*Tu nolo adtracto eos*" [*You will not touch them*], Dee roared, feeling flames lick along his skin. Drops of blood fell from his lips and steamed when they hit the ground.

Lucas' eyes flashed. His mouth pulled into a wicked grin as he adjusted his grip on the knife. The edge was marred with Ilya's blood.

"*Ego ire necare tu, daemon*" [*I am going to kill you, demon*], Lucas sneered.

"*Tum ego ire adigere tu ad infernum mecum*" [*Then I will take you to Hell with me*], Dee snarled, and lunged forward.

Lucas swiped at Dee, and Dee staggered back. His body was ablaze with agony, every breath, every movement sending fire racing along his limbs. He lunged forward again and gripped Lucas' wrist. He screamed as his hands blistered. Lucas grabbed at Dee's hair, but his fingers slid right through the short strands. Dee snapped his teeth in Lucas' face, inches from tearing skin. Lucas jerked his head back. Dee tightened his grip on Lucas' wrist and forced his hand back with a burst of strength, slicing the knife through Lucas' throat.

Lucas' blood poured over Dee's hands like a fountain. Dee let out a twisted scream as Lucas grabbed his arm with his free hand. Dee's skin blackened, angelic blood streaming down his forearms, burning everything in its path. Lucas stared at Dee with shocked, empty eyes.

Lucas swayed. He looked down at his hands, one holding Dee's arm, one holding the knife covered in blood. Dee's strength was fading. He clung to the angel, half-leaning on him as Dominic's blood still burned through his veins.

There was a whimper behind him, and Dee's heart plummeted in his chest.

Ilya.

Dee glanced behind him, desperate, sick with terror at what he would see. Ilya lay on the floor, wrists still bound, one hand pressed to their throat. Blood spilled out between their fingers. Their eyes were wide with terror and their shirt covered their back once more.

A boot scraped against the floor. A flash glinted in the corner of Dee's eye.

Dee's breath was punched out of him, a half-formed plea on his lips as agony lanced through his chest. He was only vaguely aware of the angel collapsing to the floor in front of him, holy blood spilling out of his body until his eyes went empty and dead.

The cacophony upstairs had ceased, too.

"I-Ilya," Dee croaked, and turned to face them. They were staring at him in horror, tears falling from their chin and streaming down their neck.

They weren't looking at Dee's eyes. They were looking at the knife, buried to the hilt in his chest.

14

Dee's throat worked, again and again, as he stared down at the hilt of the knife in his chest. He felt the blade like a shard of ice buried deep inside him, piercing the heart that lay silent within him. Tears rolled down his cheeks and he took a staggering step toward Ilya. They lunged at him with their hands still bound in front of them, the wound at their throat forgotten, as he collapsed in their arms.

"N-no," Ilya mumbled, eyes wide with panic. "N-no, *no*, Dee, *no* ..." Their hands shook as they closed around the handle and jerked the knife out of Dee's chest. He let out a strangled whine and slumped in Ilya's arms, limp and trembling and cold. Ilya dropped the knife to the floor with a clatter that made them both flinch and did their best to cradle Dee in the circle of their arms.

"No, Dee, *no*," Ilya breathed. Their lips trembled as they looked him over, tears falling freely now, mouth twisted, voice breaking. "No. No no no no. Dee, *no*."

Dee's chest heaved with rattling breaths that took more and more strength with each gasp. He whimpered as he felt the floor leaching his body heat through his clothes until it felt like he was lying on a slab of ice. Ilya's hands fluttered over him, brushing the last long strands of hair away from his face, clutching at his hand, cradling his cheek in a palm stained red with his blood. Dee shivered and looked up at them. They were blurred with his unshed tears and with the fog that was slowly closing over his vision.

A warm wetness soaked his shirt. He blinked, forced himself to focus. Blood was spilling down Ilya's neck and chest from the cut at their throat, unheeded and forgotten in their panic. Dee reached up, shaking, his hands still cuffed together.

Ilya ducked into the touch and his fingers brushed their cheek, but he shook his head and pressed his hand against the wound instead. Their blood felt inhumanly warm, compared to the icy cold of his fingers.

He knew he would feel cold. The blazing heat of his home didn't call to him anymore.

"P-please, *no*," Ilya sobbed. "No, Dee, I'm so sorry, *no* ..."

"Ilya," Dee breathed. "*Carissime Ilya*" [*Dearest Ilya*]. His arm shook as he tried to keep his hand pressed to their wound. "*Fortasse in aliam vitam*" [*Perhaps in another life*].

"Wh-what?" Ilya whimpered. They held him tighter against their chest. "Dee ..."

Dee's eyes rolled back. He couldn't feel his lips. The slice of agony that had pierced his heart was fading now, dulling to a flat, metallic weight in his chest. He whimpered softly, his eyes streaming, as he tried to find Ilya. He could feel their warmth, could feel their arms around him, but that was fading, too.

"*No*!" Ilya cried as Dee's hand grew cold against their neck. "Dee, please don't ..." Slowly, slowly, his hands slid down their chest, leaving a smear of blood in their wake, to fall limp in his lap. His head fell back and he heaved one more tortured, wheezing breath. Then he was still.

15

Ilya folded over Dee, wracked with sobs, and wailed against his shoulder. "*Dee*!" they screamed. Their throat spasmed shut. They coughed and gasped for air. "*Dee, NO*!"

"**Ilya**!"

Ilya was nearly thrown backward by the force of the voice. They looked up, tears streaming, at the figure standing at the top of the stairs, shining like a star made human. They whimpered and cringed away, holding Dee tighter to their chest. His body was growing colder by the second.

The figure dashed down the stairs and screeched to a halt, falling onto their knees in front of Ilya. The light emanating from the figure faded until Ilya could just make out the angel's face.

"Dara!" they shrieked, sick with hope, their heart hammering in their chest.

"Oh, god, *Ilya*," Dara cried, reaching out and brushing her fingers against the cut at Ilya's throat. It sealed immediately, leaving no scar. Ilya blinked and realized Dara's face was spattered with blood. Her clothes were soaked in it. She touched the ropes at Ilya's wrists, and they fell away.

"D-Dara, *Dara*!" Ilya sobbed. They clutched her hand. "Dara, h-help, *help*, Dara, he's ..." Ilya cut themself off with a broken sob.

Dara had gone very still at Ilya's side. Ilya's stomach lurched as they finally got a good look at her face, her light faded enough now that she no longer hurt to look at. Dara was staring at Dee with fathomless sorrow written across her features.

For a long moment, Ilya couldn't speak. They felt cracked open, flayed alive, crushed under the weight of their anguish, looking down at Dee's face as he lay perfectly still in their embrace. His head hung limply over their arm. His eyes were still half-open, his face blank – empty. His body felt ice-cold against Ilya's skin.

"*NO!*" Ilya screamed, rocking Dee back and forth, heart aching at the weight of him in their arms. "D-Dara, please, please, *fix him* ... Y-you, you fixed *me* ..."

"No, Ilya," Dara said gently. Her voice was husky and rough.

"*Please!*" Ilya sobbed, and grabbed her hand. "Dara, *please*, *please*, heal him, h-he ..."

"I can't, Ilya," Dara murmured. She bit her lip as she looked at Dee. "He's ... he's dead. He's gone."

Ilya stared dumbly at Dara. Their skin felt like it was ablaze, save for where Dee felt freezing in their embrace. Ilya's hand shook as they gently cradled Dee's head.

He seemed so *small.* His right arm hung oddly from his shoulder, and his face was marked with burns in the shape of the angels' fingerprints and hands. His hair was almost completely singed away, leaving only a few patches of short, uneven strands – and blood soaked the hair that was left, staining his temple and neck. The fountain of the angel's blood had burned Dee's hands and forearms. The front of his shirt was marked with more blood – his and Ilya's. When Ilya peered closer, they saw that there were holes in the shirt over Dee's abdomen. They stared, uncomprehending, at the tiny rips in the cloth.

Not holes. *Stab wounds.*

Ilya lurched to the side and gagged weakly. Dee slid further onto the floor, and Ilya clutched him tight, holding him in their lap as they sobbed.

"Th-they hurt him so much," Ilya wailed. "Dara ..."

The angel made a strangled noise in her throat. "I kn-know," she whispered.

"They ..." Ilya sniffed, then flinched, pain shooting through the whip marks they had all but forgotten in their desperation. Dara's mouth pinched as she lifted the back of their shirt and passed her hand over the wounds, soothing the pain and mending the torn flesh.

"Th-they told him he was ... was *wicked*," Ilya whimpered. "They t-told him he was – was s-sinful and h-had c-corrupted me ..." They heaved a wracking sob and crushed him against their chest, pressing their forehead against his so hard it hurt. They squeezed their eyes shut and struggled to draw breath. "Th-they were – were punishing him ... for *me* ... and me for him ..."

"I'm so sorry," Dara rasped. The sound cut Ilya to the bone. "I'm so ... so sorry I let them get to ... to *both* of you. I never ... I never could have imagined they would be so goddamned *brazen* ..." She curled her hand into a fist, shaking the house in its foundations. She blew out an icy breath and released her hand. The house settled. "I'm so sorry."

Ilya raised their head and saw Dara with her hand stretched out, inches from Dee's face.

"*NO*!" Ilya shrieked, and clutched Dee tighter against their chest. Dara froze. "No, d-don't – don't *touch* him ..." They swallowed bile and couldn't tear their gaze away from the burns that marred Dee's face.

"He's gone, Ilya," Dara said, the sound barely a breath. "I can't ... I can't hurt him anymore." She reached out and drew her fingers gently across his cheek. His skin didn't blister; it stayed unbroken and whole. Ilya looked up at Dara with confusion furrowing their brow.

"He doesn't live in this body anymore," Dara murmured. Her voice broke, and she cleared her throat. "There's nothing here now that I can hurt."

Ilya sobbed weakly and held him close. "Wh-why is he so cold?" they whimpered.

Tears glittered on Dara's eyelashes. "He was driving around a ... a body, Ilya. A body that wasn't ... alive. What you felt ... the warmth that came from him was – "

"Was his fire," Ilya croaked. They pressed their lips to Dee's forehead, their tears falling into his hair.

"Yes," Dara said softly. She pulled her hand away. Her fingertips were stained with his blood – or from the blood of the angel Dee had killed to keep Ilya safe.

Ilya's gaze strayed to the ring of worn and blistered skin around Dee's throat and wrists, and the iron cuffs and collar that had burned him. Their stomach heaved, and suddenly they could barely stand to look at Dee.

"T-take them off," Ilya croaked, shuddering. "Th-the – the cuffs. And the ..." They rocked forward with a broken sob. "Th-they put a *collar* on him again!"

Dara moved with speed that made Ilya's head spin. She tapped her finger against the iron locked around Dee's neck and wrists. The cuffs and chains fell away and clinked to the floor. Ilya snatched them up and hurled them across the room until they hit the still, silent body of Lucas – the angel who had taken Dee. Rage burned in Ilya's belly.

Dara followed their gaze. Her eyes flashed, and sparks danced across her skin. The earth groaned beneath them, so low Ilya could feel the vibration in their chest.

Another deep inhale, another deep exhale. The earth fell still again.

"I-is he in Hell?" Ilya whispered, tamping down the tendril of hope that dared to swell in their chest.

"No," Dara said with finality. Ilya's eyes fell shut and they nodded, rocking Dee and shivering as their own blood cooled on their clothes. "No, he ... he is truly gone. It has not often happened, but when a demon passes through the veil with no human soul to ..."

Ilya crumpled and muffled a sob in Dee's shoulder. Dara trailed off into silence.

Ilya nodded, over and over, as they held Dee. "They killed him," Ilya croaked. "They *killed* him." Ilya found Dee's hand and squeezed.

Even so, as they wept, they could feel the emptiness of the body. Without Dee inside it, there was no warmth, none of his goodness, none of his life. Without Dee, the body was a stranger to them.

"They killed her, too," Dara growled. "They showed neither any mercy. Just as they showed you. They did not even ... mean to kill her. I don't think they considered her for even a moment."

Ilya's throat bobbed. Every beat of their heart felt like a throb behind a bruise, pain with no relief. They could not bear to let go of Dee, could not bear to feel him leave their arms for the last time.

"Wh-what happens now?" they whimpered. The basement seemed to grow even colder around Ilya.

"We bury him," Dara murmured. The air carried a crackle of electricity, humming with the inescapable current of the angel's sorrow. "We tried to find the human's family when we first found Dee, me and Evangeline." A single, crystalline tear rolled down her cheek. It evaporated before it hit the ground. "We never did. I ... I don't know who she was or where she came from."

Ilya whimpered, and the pit inside them only grew. They held Dee's hand to their face and brushed their lips against his knuckles. His hand felt limp and cold – and dead.

"I'm sorry," they whispered, and crumpled over him again. "I'm so ... *sorry*. I ... I love you, Dee. I love you." Their throat tightened, and they couldn't speak. They knew he couldn't hear them, wherever he was – because he was gone, truly gone, not unreachable but *gone*. Ilya tipped their head back and wailed their grief. Their voice echoed oddly against the cement walls and floor of the basement. When they felt Dara's cool arm around them, they leaned against her and wept into her shoulder.

"Come on," Dara said gently. "Come on, Ilya. Let's get you home."

"Dee," Ilya whimpered, holding him tight. "Dee."

"Let's go," Dara said, a little more insistently. "Eva's keeping watch upstairs. And once we leave, she ..." Dara tilted her head back, as if staring through the ceiling into the floor above. "She's going to fucking *smite* this place from the face of the earth."

Ilya's throat bobbed as they looked down at Dee's face. Ilya didn't know what was worse – the slackness there, the emptiness, or the burns that marked his skin. Slowly, slowly, they closed his eyes and rested their forehead against his temple.

"Okay," they croaked, flat and despairing. "Let's go."

Dara wound her arms around them both, hiding her tears. She closed her eyes – then the basement was empty, save for the knife, the iron, the dead angel, and the smears of Dee's blood on the floor.

16

Dee woke up choking on smoke. He rolled to his side, heaving forward, his lungs aching like they were on fire. He clutched at his chest – and at the knife that had pierced his heart. The knife was gone. And beneath his ribs, a heartbeat thrummed, hummingbird-fast with pain and fear. He swallowed thickly and reached for the collar that he had died in.

Gone. His wrists were free, too.

He blinked ash out of his eyes and scrubbed his face. Tears left tracks in the grit on his cheeks. He shuddered and realized his body was bathed in sweat, oppressive heat crushing his skin and forcing its way down his throat. The smell of sulfur burned his nostrils. He coughed and reached for his abdomen, bracing for the stab of pain through the wounds left by the angel's knife.

Nothing. No pain, no blood, no wounds.

Trembling, he raised his head and dared to look around.

A thunderclap of relief broke over him and was quickly swallowed by terror. He cringed away from the dust that blew into his eyes and blinked against the blinding roar of fire in the sky. He could almost feel his lungs blister from the heat. He gagged and clawed at his throat, whimpering, head reeling with confusion and pain.

"K-Kiernan?" croaked a wavering voice behind him.

Dee cried out and scrambled away in the dust, only just now realizing he was naked. He covered himself, squinting through the smoke at the shadow that stood before him – just a shadow, no flesh, no bone. He swallowed and winced at the sandpaper feeling in his throat. His lips felt cracked, almost too dry to speak.

"Eligos?" Dee rasped.

The shadow flew toward him and he flinched back, throwing his hand in front of his face. Disbelief fluttered in his chest. His shoulder was restored; it was like it had never been broken. For the first time, he looked down at his body, and saw that it was not his body at all.

The last body had never been his either, though.

"Wh-what's happening?" Dee asked before he doubled over in a fit of hacking coughs, trembling on hands and knees.

A touch like a tendril of fire licked over his jaw, his cheek. His eyes watered, but he lifted his head and tried to focus on the shadow in front of him – one that bore a face he knew so well. *Had* known for so long.

"You are corporeal," his friend breathed.

Dee groaned as the heat from the sky above singed the hair on the back of his neck. "H-hotter than I remember," he murmured with an uneasy twist of his stomach. The ground baked against his skin.

Why am I here?

Why am I alive?

"You did not have a body, last time you were here," Eligos whispered. Dee could barely hear him over the hot, screaming wind. "Did you go to Earth, my friend? Did you see the colors, hear the music, eat the humans' food?"

Dee raised his gaze to Eligos' and braced against the memories of the knife, the whip, the holy water. He shivered despite the heat and rubbed at his neck.

The shadow drifted back, and Dee could feel the sorrow radiating off his friend. "You were found," Eligos murmured.

"Y-yes," Dee said, choking on the word. "I was found, and ... and taken. I w-was held." Sweat stung his eyes.

"Where?" The word was barely more than a breath in the wind.

"I don't know," Dee moaned, and he slumped forward, baring his back to the blazing sky. "In a dark place. A basement. By three angels – Powers."

His friend gasped, and Dee felt a touch like fingers through his hair.

"But I was ... I was saved." Dee raised his head. Tears ran from his eyes. "I was saved. A human ... they took pity on me. And ... two Virtues – "

"You were held by *Virtues*?" Eligos gasped. The tendril of touch in Dee's hair retreated. "Kiernan – "

"P-please," Dee whimpered. "Do not ... don't call me by that name. The Powers, they ... they made me ... recite that name, made me say it as they drowned me in holy water ... They carved it into my skin, over and over, then let me heal enough so they could do it again ..." He let out a shuddering sob and reached out toward the shadow that was his friend. "Please."

"I ... I am sorry," Eligos said softly. "What do you want me to call you, friend?"

"Dee," he murmured. His tears evaporated on his cheeks. "Just ... Dee."

Dee swore he caught the flicker of a smile in his friend's shadowy face. "Alright," Eligos said.

"But the Virtues did not hold me," Dee murmured. "They did not ... hurt me. They ..." Dee could barely get the words out past the lump in his throat and the fire in his lungs. He longed to claw the prickling, stinging skin on his back. "They cared for me. But ... the human most of all."

Eligos was silent for a long time. "I have never heard of such a thing," he said finally, his voice desiccated and dry.

"Neither have I," Dee said brokenly. "I had ... I had a few days, at most, in the body I found. And then I was taken."

"Y-you've been gone for *years*," Eligos said gravely. "That whole time ..."

"Most of it," Dee said. "Most of it was ... under their penance."

A sound like the roar of a forest fire tore from Eligos. Dee flinched away, scrambling backward on his hands. "What they do is not *penance*, Kier – Dee. Even their Lord does not call for torture. He calls for death, if he calls for anything." The shadow spat sparks, and Dee squeezed his eyes shut against his friend's sudden anger, shifting to his knees in the burning earth. His friend's anger passed over him like a wall of fire, then flickered, faded.

Dee shivered as Eligos stood perfectly still before him. Then, slowly, Eligos reached out and let the shadow of his hand pass over Dee's shoulders. "You are changed," Eligos said softly.

"I kn-know," Dee whimpered, cowering against the ground.

"No," Eligos murmured, and guided Dee's head up until he met his friend's eyes. "You are ... you are not of this place anymore," he breathed, his touch brushing Dee's face like smoke.

Dee's throat bobbed. He was desperately thirsty. He looked down at his hands, and they were peeling in the blazing heat. He swallowed hard and met his friend's gaze.

"What have they done?" Eligos whispered.

"They killed me," Dee whimpered. "They ... p-put a knife in my heart."

"But what did they do *first*?" said Eligos. His gaze burned Dee's skin. "They have done ... something."

Dee whined softly as he looked into the depths of his friend's eyes. He felt it all, the whip, the knife, the iron, the water, the crack of his own bones –

– the burn of Dominic's blood in his veins.

His hand flew to his throat, but there was no wound there, no scar. He trembled as he remembered how it felt, the fire creeping through his veins and searing him from the inside out.

"They gave me their blood," he croaked.

The shadow of his friend twisted and keened in his shared pain. "*No*," he gasped. "That must have been – "

"Torture," Dee whispered, and shut his eyes. Even his tears burned him. "It was torture."

"And you died with it ... still burning you?" Eligos said.

Dee opened his eyes and looked up. The blazing sky felt imprinted on the backs of his eyes. "Yes," he murmured.

His friend's scalding shadow swiped the tears from Dee's cheeks. "Then," Eligos said, voice quavering, "you know you cannot stay here."

Dee folded forward with a sob. "I know," he whimpered. "But I cannot return to earth, I ..." He clutched at his hair. It was long enough to grab now, curling past his ears and against the nape of his neck. "Th-they will hunt me."

"But you will burn here," Eligos said. Dee felt the too-hot touch encircle his wrist. "See?"

Dee couldn't pull away. The prickling heat of his skin under the touch of his *friend* was too much like the agony of the angels' clutches. He was frozen, staring down at the shadow that held him with a fiery grip. He whimpered and pressed himself lower against the rocky ground. The stones ground into his knees and burned him there too.

"Go," Eligos said with a groan. "Go, my friend. Find the human, or find your solitude. You can live on Earth. But ... carefully. Perhaps in secret." He lifted Dee's face. "This may be difficult to hide."

Dee blanched. He licked along his lips and winced when his fangs pricked his tongue. He had not meant for them to come out, had not tried to show them in his pain or fear – they were there, part of him. He shuddered and swallowed hard.

"Your eyes, as well," Eligos murmured. The shadows around his own eyes deepened. "Still slitted. Like they always are."

Dee whimpered softly. If he looked like what he was, unable to hide even his fangs behind the subterfuge of human teeth, he would end up right where he'd been – or worse.

I had decades more penance to pay. Dee whimpered again, louder. His flesh felt like it was melting off of him slowly.

"Come," Eligos said above the howling wind. "Come. You cannot stay here. The blood that ran in your veins was never meant to last here. It may be why you burn still."

Dee was so, so tired of burning.

He struggled to his feet, blushing at his own nakedness. Even wearing the human woman's body had not made him feel so exposed, but this was *his* flesh, *his* blistering skin.

Still, even the fire of the sky above him and the burning grit beneath him was nothing compared to the agony of the angels' touch, of holy water in his lungs, of angel's blood in his veins.

"Wh-which way do I go?" he croaked.

"I don't know," Eligos said sadly. "I know only fire, and that is everywhere." The sky flared above them, and the shadow of Dee's friend seemed to waver.

Dee reached out and let the shadow touch his palm. "Thank you," he whispered, eyes streaming from the heat and from the sinking feeling in his heart. "Thank you, for – "

A gust of wind and sand that scoured skin from Dee's body swept over them both. Dee cried out and fell to his knees, protecting his nose and ears. The sand felt like sparks falling on his back. The air felt like the inside of an oven. He sweat, and he panted, and he burned.

When the wind faded he stood up, casting a glance up at the inferno sky. He was utterly alone on an empty, blasted plain, swallowed by fire and heat.

He picked a direction, and started walking.

About the Author

Isaac Ryals is the award-winning author of the dystopian series *Honor Bound*. His achievements include Reader Views Literary Awards winner in the LGBTQ+ category, Next Generation Indie Book Awards finalist, Reader's Favorite Awards five-star seal, and The Wishing Shelf Book Awards Red Ribbon award. His short fiction and poetry have been featured in *Erato*, Z Publishing's *Colorado's Emerging Writers* and *America's Emerging Poets*, and *High Grade*. He works at a university and moonlights on an ambulance as a paramedic. He lives in Illinois.

You can follow Isaac online at:

https://whump-tr0pes.tumblr.com/

https://archiveofourown.org/users/whump_tr0pes/works

Hunting Static

Jayde Layne

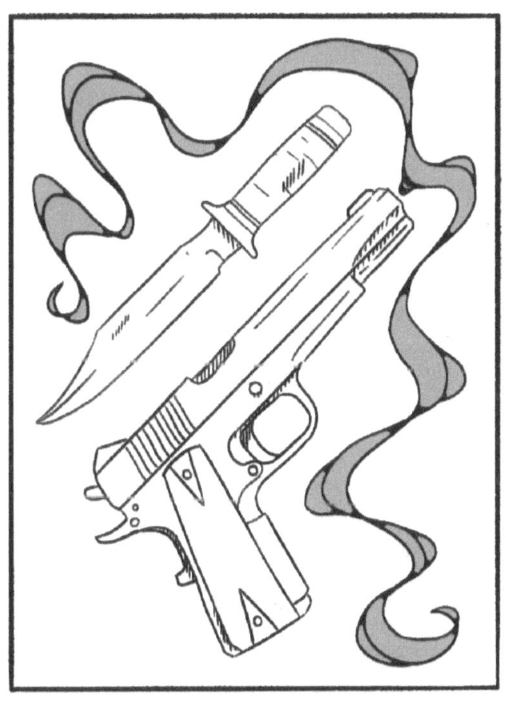

Cover Design by Nicole Alessi

Cover Illustration by Hen Towers

Contents

CONTENT WARNINGS

This story contains the following content:

- Monsters
- Death of parents and sibling (child death)
- Implied/referenced child abuse

If this book isn't for you, no worries! But if it is, we hope you enjoy this story about a monster known as The Creech and the hunters who are trying to stop it...

1

Streetlights

After the bus drove away, the only sound was the crickets in the grass. It was almost eleven p.m., but the air in Tulsa was warm and balmy, decent enough to sleep at the bus station if she wanted to. She wasn't sure if she wanted to. After being on a cramped bus all day, she really didn't want to spend the night on a metal bench.

She slid her phone out of her pocket. The blue light was a stark contrast to the orange of the streetlights that stretched down the dark, desolate road, disappearing onto a black freeway in one direction and meeting the glitter of the city in the other. No one in Shadow Watch lived in Tulsa, if she remembered correctly, but it was worth checking anyway.

It took a moment for her data to connect this far from the city. She sighed, rolled her shoulders under her backpack, and moved to sit on one of the dusty benches. She might be willing to splurge on a motel room if she could find one within walking distance – her whole body ached for a mattress, even a shitty one.

Finally, her phone connected. There were a few people online, scattered as they were across time zones. Navigating to the 'Sanctuary' role, she scrolled through the list of users, checking the cities in their bios. Tucson, Santa Fe, Waco, El Paso, LA, San Francisco, San Diego, Seattle, Portland, Miami, DC, Raleigh, Atlanta, New Orleans, Chicago, Albany, Kansas City, Detroit – as expected, no one in Tulsa.

"Fuck," she muttered. She scrolled idly through the various chats, getting rid of notifications as she tried to make her tired brain think of what to do. In the general chat Sarah had been exchanging knitting patterns with MadHatter; Sarah had lost her husband several years ago to a chupacabra, but her bad hip kept her from hunting, so instead she opened her home in El Paso to other hunters passing through. MadHatter was a nursing student in Albany who taught other hunters how to patch themselves up – they hadn't disclosed much of what brought them to Shadow Watch, just that it involved a vampire.

The other chats were the same as when she checked them a couple of hours ago – quiet. No new updates in the chats for vampires, werewolves, fairies, demons, angels, poltergeists (though she should probably go through that chat and her notebook again, brush up before the job she was scheduled to do).

Her thumb hovered over a chat near the bottom of the list. There hadn't been an update in that channel for months, and for good reason. The damn thing was so elusive, went underground for so long between attacks, and there were only a handful of others in the server who had even seen it. Only one other was hunting it like she was: Corpse Queen, who hadn't been online in weeks.

She shook her head. Now wasn't the time to go back down that rabbit hole. She needed to figure out what she was going to do for the night. Right as she was about to close the app, the circle by Corpse Queen's name turned green, and a message popped up at the top of her screen.

It happened again.

Her breath caught. Her fingers were already shaking as she typed back her bland response: *what.*

Three dots. 'Corpse Queen is typing.'

I saw it.

A second later:

Come to Tulsa.

She let out a strangled, slightly hysterical chuckle. What were the odds?

I'm already here. What's the address?

***

She splurged on a cab to take her to the motel. It was what she expected, a crappy place on the edge of town, like most of Shadow Watch's nomadic hunters preferred, herself included.

She climbed the rickety stairs to the second floor. As she passed door after door, she shoved her shaking hands into the pockets of her leather jacket. She'd never met Queen in person or even heard their voice. She had no idea what to expect, and if there was one thing she hated, it was being unprepared.

Room 216, the same gaudy orange as all the other doors in the lineup. Fluorescent lights buzzed over the doors of the outdoor hallway, little white moths fluttering around them. She watched them instead of the door as she raised her hand to knock. Her heartbeat thundered in her ears.

Shuffling on the other side of the door, the creaking of floorboards. There was a pause, probably as the person on the other side peered through the peephole, then the heavy sliding sound of locks before the door opened just enough for a face to peek around the edge.

It was a thin face, with a strong, curved nose and tightly pressed lips. Their hair was red and spiked, dyed yellow at the tips to look like flames, and a black ring went through one of their eyebrows. They dragged their eyes up and down over her, then asked in a husky voice, "CyberHex?"

Heart in her throat, all she could manage was a nod. They paused for a moment longer, then grunted and swung the door open wide, revealing the worn white tank top they wore and the splotch of red covering their left side.

"Come in, then."

Hex hurried inside and closed the door behind her. The room was like every other motel room she'd been in, except for the large military backpack sitting on the bed and the open first aid kit on the tiny side table. Questions itched at the back of her throat, but for the moment concern won out, and she swallowed them down. There would be time for questions later.

"It got you, huh?" she managed to say, and Queen shook their head as they eased themself onto the edge of the bed with a wince.

"Oh, yeah. Those claws you remember aren't just for show."

She cleared her throat. "Do you – want help?"

Queen grimaced again, as if they didn't like what they were about to say, but still answered, "Yeah, please. I can't quite reach all of it."

With a gulp, Hex set her backpack on the end of the bed. She didn't know a lot about medicine, but she knew how to stitch up a wound. Hopefully that would be enough.

Queen pulled the tank top over their head and dropped it to the floor. They had several scars from hunts and two matching ones under their pectorals, though Hex's eye was immediately drawn to the gouges running down their side, right under their shoulder. There were four of varying sizes, like bloody fingers.

"Shit."

Queen huffed, almost a laugh. "That was pretty much my reaction too."

Hex knelt down next to Queen's legs to get a better look. They weren't so bad up close – bloody as hell, but shallow, a glancing blow. She forced herself to breathe out and backed up to get the kit from the bedside table.

Using that as an excuse not to look at them, Hex asked, "So, um, what should I call you?"

"Cory," they answered quietly. "He."

"Okay." She returned to her previous position, ready to get down to business, only to notice Cory's raised eyebrow. "Oh, um, Hex is fine. She." Cory nodded and finally looked away, letting Hex focus on her task. "This is going to sting."

Cory didn't flinch as she cleaned away the blood. She could see his ribs move as his breath caught sometimes, but no other sound escaped him until he said, "Is it going to need stitches?"

"I mean, I'm not an authority, but I don't think so."

He let out a relieved breath. "Great. That would've hurt like a bitch."

Setting a bloodied alcohol wipe aside, Hex began ripping open packaging for gauze pads and medical tape. She should have waited until the first aid was done, but she couldn't resist anymore – she *had* to know.

"So ... what happened?"

Cory gave a tired sigh, but didn't rebuff her. "There's a suburb," he began, pausing for a wince as Hex taped down a pad. "On the other side of the city. Another family thought their neighbors were casting curses, so I went in to take a look around. Didn't find anything about magic, but when I was going through their basement, I heard static."

Chills rolled down Hex's arms and into her fingers.

"I checked for what could be causing it, but I couldn't find anything. So I said fuck the curses and hid in a closet to wait it out. I was right – a few hours later, the fog came in."

Hex forced herself to exhale. "Did it look the same?"

Cory nodded. His eyes were glazed as he stared at the floor, no longer reacting to Hex as she layered gauze on his wounds. "Yeah," he whispered. "That same gray light." He sat up straight and shook himself. "I followed the static upstairs. The couple who lived there had already gone to bed, and it was in their bedroom, just standing over them, like it was trying to decide which one of them to eat first."

Done with her first aid, Hex sat down beside him on the bed, hanging on his every word. The image in her mind's eye was crystal clear: the tall figure, skin all scribbled-in like a little kid's drawing. She was shaking – she hadn't stopped shaking since she got to the hotel room.

"What did you do?"

"Shot it." Cory dragged his bag over to him, trying to suppress the winces the motions caused. "With a .45. Didn't do anything."

"Didn't do anything?" Hex asked with a frown as Cory pulled on a new shirt. "What do you mean? Did it ricochet or go through it or ..."

"It took the hit, the bullet went in and left a black hole, but it didn't drop. Getting shot just pissed it off. It flashed across the room to me – you remember how it moves?"

Hex shuddered and nodded.

"I dodged, but it still got me a little." Cory reached around to pat the bandages under the new, clean shirt. "But here's where it gets weird. When I smacked into the wall, the spirit box I had in one of my pockets turned on. And I swear to God the thing *flinched*."

Hex's eyes widened. Before she could ask any questions, Cory continued, like he knew that if he let her start asking, she'd never stop.

"It looked at me, looked back at the people it was going to eat, and glitched out. Then the fog lifted and it was gone."

"Holy shit." Hex sat back, running her hands through her own badly dyed black and purple hair. This was the closest she'd gotten to it in twelve years – it had been here, in this city, only a few hours ago. So close, and yet. "What about the other people?"

Cory shrugged. "They still had their faces and were screaming their heads off, so I assumed they were fine and high-tailed it out of there. They'll probably remember it as an attempted robbery and tell themselves the monster they saw was a dream."

Hex's mind raced. There were a million things to check, a million details to examine. She had to get it all in order before her head exploded. "Okay, okay, let's start over."

Grabbing her bag from the foot of the bed, Hex flipped through the various notebooks until she found the oldest one, with its worn cover and duct-taped spine. Scrawled on it in permanent marker were the words, 'The Creech.'

"Wow," said Cory as she dug around for a pen. "I thought you were joking about the notebooks."

Notebook and pen in hand, she turned herself sideways and crossed her legs, not caring that her muddy boots were on the comforter. "Start from the beginning. What was the address?"

Bemused, Cory rattled it off. Hex put a star next to it on the page to remind herself to add it to her map later before moving on. The date matched – the last attack had been eight months ago, when the Creech took a ten-year-old, and the timeframe matched her estimates of how long it could go between victims.

"Who lived in the house? What were their names?"

"Just the two adults. Jessica and Brian Ramirez."

Hex scribbled them down and circled them. She'd need to do some digging, see if they matched the Creech's target pattern. It was likely, with them living in the suburbs, but it was always better to double-check. Underneath the names she started to write down Cory's account, but didn't get far before she felt his curious gaze burning into the top of her head and looked up.

"What? Why are you looking at me like that?"

Cory shook his head. "Nothing, I just – this is why I asked you to come. There's no folklore for this thing, nothing to fall back on, except for you. I knew you'd be able to put it all together. I'm more of a shoot first, ask questions later kind of guy."

"Yeah, well" – she spun her pen over her knuckles – "it's kind of my thing. When your spirit box turned on, did you see what frequency it was at?"

"Oh, uh, 103.9, I think?"

She wrote it down and circled it three times. If certain frequencies could hurt or deter it, they might be able to trap it.

Or kill it.

Going over the data again, a realization pushed the butterflies from her stomach to her throat, and Cory noticed.

"What?"

Her knuckles turned white around her pen. "You interrupted it. It didn't get to feed. It ran away. It's still hungry." She swallowed hard and lifted her eyes from the page. Cory's were burning brighter than his hair. "It's going to hunt again, soon."

Cory's smile was sharp. "Then so will we."

2

Fog Lights

The light was wrong. She could tell even through her closed eyelids that there was something off about it. When she opened them and saw the gray, her first thought was that it was just weirdly cloudy outside. But that wouldn't explain why her dresser wasn't casting a shadow, or why the windowless hallway on the other side of her open bedroom door was as bright as her room.

She sat up in bed with a jaw-cracking yawn. It was Saturday morning. The last thing she wanted to be doing was getting up before noon, but the house was so quiet. Mason should've been pounding on her door by then, or racing up and down the hall like the Tasmanian devil while the voices of her mother and father drifted up the staircase from the kitchen. But there was nothing. Had they gone out without her?

She glanced at her alarm clock, but to her surprise, it was blank. Not flashing, like the power had gone out during the night, but blank, as though it wasn't plugged in, though she could see it was, and she couldn't hear the AC running. Maybe the power was still out?

Uneasiness coiled in her stomach as she climbed out of bed. It was probably nothing, but ...

Her bedroom window didn't offer any answers. The whole neighborhood was shrouded in thick fog, shrinking the world down to just her yard, lined around the edges with the dark, eerie silhouettes of trees. No shadows were cast, and she couldn't find the sun, not even as a dim disk somewhere in the clouds. She turned from the window with a shudder.

"Mom? Dad?" The silence weighed down her words, turning them from a shout to a whisper, and she got no answer. She couldn't hear any cars passing by, though the road that went past their house was usually busy even on the weekends.

With a gulp, she moved towards her bedroom door.

All of the lights in the hall were out. She flicked the light switch a couple of times, but they remained dark, leaving only that weird gray.

Okay, so the power was out, and maybe her family was out too, or still asleep. There was no reason for her to be so nervous. Even if the fog was creepy. She would just go and see if her parents were still in bed, just to make sure.

Her parents' room was the next door down, which swung open soundlessly at the touch of her hand. The bay window across the room cast dim gray light onto the bed below to show the two shapes lying there, side by side, seemingly asleep. That was the confirmation she'd been looking for, so why did the butterflies in her stomach refuse to die?

Those butterflies drew her closer to the bed. Something about the stillness of the forms made her skin crawl – they were as still as the air, as the fog, as the light – she needed something to move. Something alive.

"Mom?" she said, reaching for her mother's shoulder.

There was no answer.

Her mother rolled onto her back as easily as the bedroom door had opened, without the slightest rustle of sheets.

She let out a strangled gasp and staggered back until she hit the wall. Fisting her shaking hands into her shirt, she whispered aloud, "This isn't real, this isn't real, I'm dreaming, I'm gonna wake up."

That was the only explanation for why her mother didn't have a face.

"I'm gonna wake up. I'm gonna wake up. Come on, come on, wake up." She couldn't tear her eyes away from her mother's face, where only smooth flesh remained, only shallow slopes where her eyes and nose should have been. There weren't even any veins showing through.

Over her mother's shoulder, her father's face was gone, too, including his usual scruffy stubble, leaving their bodies to stare at each other without eyes.

She wasn't waking up. Why wasn't she waking up?

Crackle. The sound drew her attention towards the hall – the first thing she'd heard outside of herself since she woke up.

Should she follow it? It might be dangerous, but this was a dream, wasn't it? Dream logic would say that if she played along, she'd wake up faster, right?

So she followed the fuzzy hum out of the bedroom and back into the hall. It sounded like radio static. Was the power back on?

It led her to her brother's room across from her own, growing in a quiet crescendo as she approached. Again the door was ever-so-slightly ajar, and the hinges were as silent as the rest of the house. She felt the butterflies again, crawling on the inside of her skin.

Something stood over her brother's bed. Not a someone – no person was tall enough to have to hunch in half lest their body go through the ceiling, with arms long enough for the knuckles to brush the carpet. It was impossibly thin, its pale skin filled in with black markings like scribbles, some floating outside the lines of its body. It was difficult to look at, the edges of its form flickering and jittering like a glitch on a computer screen.

Despite that, she felt a hint of relief upon seeing that her brother still had a face and was sleeping peacefully. That relief evaporated when the creature moved, reaching an arm towards Mason with long, wicked claws that hooked menacingly into her brother's shirt.

Slowly, the thing bent down, leaning closer, closer, closer to her brother's face.

Mason's eyes popped open. Staring directly into her eyes, both pairs the same shade of green, inherited from their grandfather, he said one word, so much more solemn than he'd ever sounded before.

"Natalie."

A creaking groan like rusty metal. Her brother's face began to blur, melting away like chalk in the rain, tiny particles of color drifting towards the creature's head.

Finally, she got the courage to scream. The sound pierced through the silence like shattering glass, but the creature didn't so much as twitch in response. All she could do was stand there and watch as her brother's face disappeared.

Mason's body dropped soundlessly to the mattress. The lifeless way he rolled, the blank space on the front of his head, made her want to retch.

She wasn't waking up. Even as the thing turned and fixed its pinpoint black eyes on her, she didn't wake up. The dread that had been building since she first saw the fog pushed against the back of her throat.

Maybe she wasn't going to wake up.

The creature jittered. A clawed hand moved in her direction, and it opened a maw full of sharp, strangely realistic teeth. Predator's teeth.

Something in her snapped. Adrenaline flashed through her veins, her skin went hot. Another scream scraped out of her throat, and she took off running down the hall.

The thing itself didn't make a noise. There was only the static, and a moment later a loud crash as it smashed a hallway table.

She nearly broke her neck going down the stairs before darting out into the living room, and knowing the doors would be locked, headed for the back. Her dad had always talked about nailing up the built-in dog door that came with the place, but had never gotten around to it, and now she was thanking her lucky stars for his procrastination.

As she turned the corner, she caught sight of the creature again. It wasn't running to chase her; instead, its flesh jittered within the contours of its body and it vanished into thin air, reappearing ten feet closer.

Well, she didn't have time to process that particular nugget of information. Instead, she focused on vaulting over the couch and scrambling through the dog door. The second she squeezed her skinny body through, she took off into the fog.

Soft grass tickled her bare feet. Outside the air was as suffocating as it had been inside, and nothing cast a shadow on the dew-wet grass. The fog itself was thick, more similar to smoke than mist, and the faint taste of ozone coated her tongue. Trying to ignore all of it, she headed for the barely visible silhouettes of the trees.

The static rose and fell behind her like the tide as the creature stuttered after her. She plunged into the tree line and kept going. She couldn't run forever, there was already a sharp stitch aching across her ribs, and she didn't know how far the fog went. But her only other choice would be to stop and bet that it was all actually a dream, and the longer she was wreathed in the fog, the more certain she felt that this was *not* a dream.

A shape in the fog caught her eye. She slid to a stop on the wet grass; the large oak tree with its many gnarls and branches like grasping hands loomed over her – their favorite climbing tree. The fog managed to make even its friendly presence seem ominous.

Shoving her bare fingers and toes into the familiar spots, she scaled the tree faster than she ever had before, going higher and higher until the branches were too weak to hold her weight. The bark scraped through her tank top when she put her back to the trunk, planting a hand over her mouth to smother her heavy breathing.

Not two seconds later the creature came into view. It glitched from tree to tree, pausing for a moment at each one before glitching to another, giving no indication that it was searching. It went right past her tree, and a few white-knuckled minutes later, vanished into the fog.

She waited until she could no longer hear the static. Only then did she climb down, breathing through her teeth to conceal the sound, and the second her toes hit the grass, she was running again, back towards her house. The stitch in her side burned with every breath, but she kept running. Maybe she could barricade herself inside – could that thing glitch through walls?

She only slowed when she reached her backyard. Her heart was pounding; she could hear it in her ears, feel it in her throat. Her side burned, her ankles itched from the grass, and sweat stuck in the inside of her elbows and knees. God, what was she supposed to do? Her parents were –

Crackle.

She froze.

Slowly, she looked over her shoulder. There the creature stood, jerking from side to side with that horrible toothy grin. Its flesh began to jitter, the scribbles of its skin shifting in a nauseating pattern.

She didn't have the breath to scream this time. She took off again, away from the house, and the static followed.

Where was she supposed to go? The fog seemed to stretch on forever. Were her neighbors gone too, already consumed by the creature? Was *everyone* –

Wait. There, to her left, a splotch of yellow. Yellow light, shining on a patch of grass. Sunlight?

She didn't have time to think about it. She turned, scrambling against the grass, and booked it for the light. From behind her came a loud burst of static, and the creature's claws caught in her hair with a jerk.

She threw herself to the ground and slid over the wet grass. Right into the sunbeam.

It felt like stepping through an old TV screen. It rippled over her skin, made all of the hairs along her arms stand on end, and there was a sharp stinging pain over her scalp as the strands of hair the creature had caught tore from her head.

Light. Bright, blinding light. She squeezed her eyes shut against it and laid there on the grass, panting. The static sound was gone, and the choking fog had disappeared, replaced by the warmth of the rising sun.

When she opened her eyes again, the world had gone back to normal. The sun was in the sky where it belonged, the fog was gone, shadows stretched over the ground, and birds twittered in the trees as though nothing had happened.

Relief flooded in so quickly she felt nauseous. It really had been a dream. There was no static, no taste of ozone in her mouth.

Slowly, she levered herself upright. It was crazy how far she had gone in her sleep and how vibrant the pain in her scalp and her side was, considering they were probably just remnants of her nightmare. Unless she had been sleep-running. If that was a thing.

She retraced her steps back to the house. A quick tug on the back door confirmed that it was, in fact, locked, so she crawled back in through the dog door. She must have done that in her sleep as well. She must have.

But the house was still so quiet ...

She shook it off. It was just a dream. It wasn't real. None of it was real. It couldn't be.

Then she reached the top of the stairs and her stomach twisted into knots. The table the creature had crashed into in her nightmare lay in pieces on the carpeted floor, mingled with shards of blue glass and trampled sunflowers – she could've been the one who broke it, she supposed, but wouldn't her parents have heard the noise?

She came to her parents' door first, and there was a second, smaller dose of relief when she pushed against it and the hinges squeaked.

The bed looked empty. For a moment that was reassuring – they might've just gone out without her – but when she drew closer, the relief evaporated as quickly as it manifested. There were no people in the bed, but peeking out from the covers was the collar of a shirt.

"Please," she whispered to the empty air as she reached out a shaking hand. She didn't know what she was asking for, but whatever it was, she didn't get it. When she pulled the covers back, she found two pairs of pajamas lying on the bed, empty.

She yanked her hand back as if burned, and without pausing to process, spun on her heel and fled back into the hallway.

Her brother's bedroom door was already open. Scored into the wood were four long claw marks.

A desperate sob stuck in her throat. She managed to keep it there until she tore the blanket off her brother's bed and saw his dinosaur pajamas laying there, empty. The T-Rex on the front was rumpled, looking up at her with pity.

The tears burst free as her knees hit the carpet.

It wasn't a nightmare. Why couldn't it have been a nightmare?

3

Dawn Light

Dim orange light crawled between the blinds, casting alternating bars like tiger stripes across the page. Hex hissed a curse under her breath – she hadn't intended to stay up all night, but here she was, her phone at three percent battery and four energy drink cans scattered across the tiny table, courtesy of the vending machine outside.

She had accomplished a lot, though. She placed the suburb on her map, researched the two would-be victims, added the spirit box frequency to her hypotheses list, and updated the Creech chat in Shadow Watch with what they'd learned from Cory's encounter.

The man in question was sleeping restlessly on the lone motel bed. Even in sleep he had one arm wrapped around himself, like the pain from the claw wounds was seeping into his dreams.

With a tired sigh, Hex flipped back to her hypotheses list and stared at the lines. A lot of them had been crossed out over the years, those remaining more like genuine questions than hypotheses.

The oldest, circled and underlined so many times and in so many different colors of ink that it was hardly legible: *Why did I survive?*

Hex gnawed on the inside of her lip. The Creech had attacked numerous times, before and after Hex's personal tragedy, and she had cataloged as many as she could track down.

Only a third of those attacks included survivors. One of her old theories had been that it could keep people asleep, or at least docile, while it hunted, but if that were the case, there would never be any survivors. Unless it couldn't always control more than one person.

Another theory, however, could be that it couldn't affect people like that at all. It could be relying on the benefit of surprise, and people waking up in the middle of its attack was up to chance.

She wasn't sure which idea she preferred. The latter would make it easier to take down, certainly, but the idea that her survival was pure dumb luck made her stomach squirm.

Old mattress springs creaked. When she looked over at the bed, Cory had rolled onto his side and was rubbing his eyes with one hand, the spikes of his dyed hair flattened and disheveled.

"Morning," she said, and Cory jumped so hard he winced.

"Jesus," he grumbled, running a hand through his hair and making it stick up even more. "I forgot you were here."

"Sorry." Hex tapped her pen against the page. She should give it a rest for the day, close the notebook and nap for a few hours before she had to go to her job, but that question glared out at her from the paper, refusing to be pushed down for the hundredth time. Consumed by the thought, she didn't notice Cory frowning at her.

"Did you stay up all night?"

"Huh?" She looked up, processed, and continued, "Oh, yeah, guess so. Trying to put the pieces together."

Cory grimaced as he rose from the bed, but managed a few words through his ground teeth. "And did you – find anything?"

"A little." The rapid pen tapping continued. The pressure of her old, well-loved leather jacket kept her from resorting to bouncing her leg, but only just. All of these years later, the jacket still smelled like cigarettes and was still too big for her. "The city matches the pattern, and Jessica and Brian fit the Creech's menu. Good jobs, good lives, no evidence of addiction or problems with the law. Just a couple of parking tickets."

Shuffling across the room, Cory let himself drop into the chair across the table from Hex without answering. Despite sleeping, the bags under his eyes were bruise purple, and Hex frowned.

"Why did their neighbors think they were witches?"

Cory shrugged, then immediately looked like he regretted it. "The people who hired me live in the same cul-de-sac as they did. One of them didn't get a promotion they wanted, and the other's garden wasn't growing right, so I guess they didn't like the Ramirezs and blamed them. Like any other witch hunt in history."

"Hm." She sat back, her hands going to her jacket pockets. In one of them was the old knife. She wrapped her fingers around the hilt, seeking the reassurance of the comfortable grip.

"I honestly didn't think I would find anything. I figured if these people wanted to pay me to look around in their house and not take anything, I might as well, you know?"

Hex nodded and looked back down at the open notebook before her. That same question sat there, taunting. "We shouldn't go back during the day. If they called the cops, we don't want to be walking around a suburb looking the way we do."

"So we wait for night. Then what?"

"I'm not sure," Hex admitted, biting her lip. "I mean, this is new territory. As far as we know, it's never been interrupted and chased away without consuming at least one person. We can guess that it'll stay in the same general area and try to hunt again as soon as it can, but it's still just a guess."

"Yeah," sighed Cory. Folding his arms on the table, he rested his chin on them, despite the pain the wound must've caused in that position. For a few moments there was quiet, the only sound the roar of cars and trucks as they passed the motel outside. Through the walls a radio played in someone else's room, but it wasn't static. There were words, though too garbled for her to make out.

The question slipped out before she could stop it. "How did you survive?"

Cory's entire body stiffened, but Hex didn't retract the question. She had regurgitated her story dozens of times, on paper, in typed documents, in voice recordings, going over every detail again and again and again, compiling her research on top of it to see what fit and what didn't. The process never got easier, but it was necessary.

Cory, on the other hand, had been stingy with details, and before that was fine – she didn't expect everyone to cope the way she did. Now those details mattered.

"I ..." His fingers dug into his biceps. "I hid."

Hex waited, but Cory was silent, staring through the table like it wasn't there, stuck in a memory too long ignored. Keeping her movements slow, she slid a hand into his line of sight.

"Cory? Where did you hide?"

He closed his eyes, squeezing them shut tight like he didn't want to see what was in front of him.

"Under my bed," he answered in a whisper. "I was just a kid – eight years old, maybe. I woke up in the middle of the night when it should've been dark, but it wasn't. It was gray."

A shiver went down Hex's spine.

"I went looking for my mom. She was in the living room, and that *thing* was – " He stopped short of saying it, picking his head up from his arms and shaking it, as though the motion could make the memories go away. "But it didn't see me. So I ran back to my room and hid, and eventually the fog went away. But I didn't come out. I was too scared. I was under there for – God, hours, at least, until a neighbor came looking."

His eyes opened, staring directly into Hex's like he could see into her soul. "You know what they found in the living room."

Hex fidgeted, but didn't break eye contact when she nodded.

"Just empty clothes," he continued, and his eyes unfocused, glazing over. "Nothing missing, no sign of foul play. They made it a missing person's case that's probably still sitting in a filing cabinet somewhere."

The quiet returned. Hex let him have it, not saying anything until he blinked and zoned back into reality. He sat up straight, with only a little grimace, and squinted at her.

"How did *you* get away?"

Immediately, Hex folded her arms. It was a refuge, the black leather her armor, the knife in her pocket a sword. She felt like she was about to step onto a battlefield, but it was only fair. She had asked first.

"Pretty similar to you," she began with an embarrassing waver in her voice. "I woke up and everything was gray. When I went to my parents' room, they were already …" The image floated before her eyes, faceless bodies that she should've known but were foreign without their features, and goosebumps spread down her arms. She swallowed. "Then I went to check on my little brother, and that's when I saw it. Consuming him."

She shook her head with a wry chuckle. "I was stupid and screamed. It turned and looked right at me. So I ran outside into the forest. I was able to hide for a while, but it found me."

Cory leaned forward, entirely focused on her. Hex held on to his gaze like it could anchor her here, in this shitty motel room, not lost in the fog and adrenaline rush.

"I thought it was going to catch me for sure. But there was a … I guess you could call it a weak spot in the fog, where sunlight was coming through. So I ran for that and kinda slipped out of the fog. Then it was all gone. All that was left was their clothes."

"You busted out?" Cory asked, eyes wide and voice awed. Hex shrugged, instinctively rolling her shoulders, trying to dispel the sensation of something right behind her, catching up.

"I guess? I don't know if I actually broke through or if there was a hole, but yeah. That's how I got out."

"Wow."

Hex took a subtle, centering breath. "Yeah. So, that's a thing. I don't know if that weakness is built into the fog or if it was just that one time, maybe it was hungry or something, I don't know."

Cory's eyes fell to the tabletop. His fingers tapped quickly across the surface to a rhythm. Thinking, but not talking, so Hex pushed herself to continue.

"And from you, we know that it can't necessarily sense people nearby. It can probably track by sound or sight like any creature, but it can't supernaturally tell where its next victim is, even in the fog."

"Or," Cory muttered in a dark tone, "I wasn't up to its standards."

"That's a possibility too," she said, narrowing her eyes at him. The Creech was a pretty picky eater – it usually went after middle to upper middle class families, ones that hadn't had too many negative life experiences. For Cory to not meet those requirements by age eight was ... concerning, and another discussion altogether. Not one for two people who just met in person, one of whom was injured and the other sleep-deprived. "A few answers, but even more questions."

"As usual," Cory snorted.

"Welcome to the life," Hex agreed.

The light through the blinds was growing steadily stronger, morphing from orange to the soft yellow of morning. Hex clenched her jaw to hold in a yawn – she would be crashing soon, no matter what her research brain said about it.

"I keep thinking about the fog," said Cory, still tapping the table. "What is it? A spell or something, or does it just follow this thing around?"

"I've thought about that. I talked to a guy from another online group, that Riddles in the Dark forum, and he floated the idea that it could be a pocket dimension. Maybe the Creech has specific requirements for feeding that can only be satisfied inside the pocket."

"Hm. It's as good a theory as any."

Hex sighed and unfolded her arms to rub her eyes. It was just past six a.m. according to her nearly deceased phone, and she was meeting her client at ten. There was time to steal a nap if Cory didn't want to immediately check out.

As though sensing her thoughts, Cory spoke up. "You should get some rest. Hunting this thing isn't going to be easy."

"I'm supposed to meet someone," she answered with a jaw-splitting yawn. "For a job. At ten."

"I can drive you."

"You have a car?"

Cory smirked at the obvious envy in Hex's voice. "Yeah. It's shitty, but it gets me where I need to go."

"Look at you," Hex teased. "Living the good life."

Cory chuckled, but quickly grew somber again. "So, are we doing this? In it together?"

"Yeah," said Hex. "Together."

4

Flashlights

They pulled in to the suburb a couple of hours after sunset. Perfect cookie-cutter houses extended as far as the eye could see, a labyrinth of cul-de-sacs and sidewalks, lit with bright LED streetlights. Hex had lost count of the number of suburbs she'd been to, all across the country, but they all invariably looked and felt the same. There was variation in regional architecture, differences in the number of parks and the hue of the grass lawns, but all with the same restrictive, reverent hush, the same creeping sensation of being watched by unseen eyes, the same distant barking of dogs.

Hex took a deep, shaky breath. She'd been tracking this thing for years, but always a step behind. She'd never been so close.

Cory killed the engine on his shitty old pick-up and twisted around to grab something from his pack in the backseat. Hex unzipped her own backpack, sitting on the floor between her feet, and produced the same gadget she'd used in the haunted house earlier that day. It would need to be calibrated again before they could hunt.

"What's that for?" asked Cory, gesturing to the detector, and Hex raised an eyebrow.

"It detects radio waves. Haven't you hunted ghosts before?"

Cory scrunched up his nose. "I know what it *does.* But this thing isn't a ghost. So, what's the point?"

"The Creech gives off a signal," she explained as she fiddled with dials and buttons. "It's very specific, and it lasts for years." She'd broken into plenty of places – including her own childhood home – to prove it. "All of this is in the chat in Shadow Watch, you know."

Cory snorted and climbed out of the truck, Hex following a moment later.

"Shoot first and ask questions later, remember?"

"Still," Hex insisted as Cory came around to the sidewalk they were parked along. "I update it every time I find something new."

"And when was the last time that happened?"

The bitterness in his voice pulled her up short. Before she could decipher who that bitterness was aimed at, he came up alongside and nudged her shoulder. "Come on, brainiac. Let's get moving."

They set a quick pace down the street. They didn't want to linger in one place for too long; the neighborhood was fairly nice, and neither of them looked like they belonged, with Hex's ratty jeans and boots, oversized black leather jacket, and faded purple streaks in her hair, and Cory with his eyebrow piercing and flame-colored spikes. He'd donned a long, army green coat, very Constantine, and popped a handful of painkillers before they left for their mission.

Hex kept a sharp eye on the detector and an ear out for static, while Cory studied each house for fog.

After three or four blocks, Cory spoke up. "So, since I've clearly forgotten some important stuff, want to give me a refresher?"

Hex gave a hum of acknowledgement. "There's not a lot that will help us actually kill it, honestly."

The first mention she'd been able to find of it was in 1924, when a husband and wife vanished, leaving piles of clothing behind. Since then it occasionally popped up in newspaper articles in similar 'rapturing' stories, or accounts of people being found dead of animal attacks inside locked homes, or someone going 'mad' and babbling about a monster.

Going underground for months or years between feedings, it worked its way across the country at an excruciatingly slow pace, hitting any suburban neighborhood it could find. Based on that pattern, Hex had predicted it would appear somewhere in the southern Midwest, but with the sheer number of suburbs that seemed to surround every city, it was impossible to say exactly where or when.

That was the worst part. Never knowing where it was until it was too late. Cory interrupting it here was pure dumb luck, and there was no way in hell she was going to let the chance pass her by.

Cory kicked a rock, sending it clattering down the sidewalk ahead of them. "You said you talked to someone on Riddles in the Dark about it, right? Shadow Watch can't be the only group that's heard of it."

"We kind of are," Hex admitted. "I've found a couple of other people online and in person, but it goes so long between feedings that most people who survive slip through the cracks or convince themselves they made it up."

Or are threatened into keeping their mouths shut.

Her shoulders tensed at the thought. She rolled them under her backpack. Cory, with the insane number of pockets his coat and cargo pants had, didn't need his.

Cory took notice of the motion. "What? Did you pick up the frequency?"

"No, I just ..."

Should she tell him? They hadn't come after her in years, but they might if she and Cory started drawing attention to themselves, as they were sure to do prowling around a suburban neighborhood like this.

With a defeated sigh, she asked, "Have you ever heard of Project Chimaera?"

"No," Cory answered, kicking the same rock a few feet further. "What's their schtick?"

"They're basically the Men in Black. They work for the U.S. government. I don't know if part of their job is keeping monsters a secret, but it certainly seemed that way when I met them."

The rock skittered off the sidewalk and into the road. "You met the Men in Black?"

"Man and Woman in Black, technically."

Cory rolled his eyes. "Of course, my mistake. What'd they want?"

"Wanted me to shut up about the Creech." In her pocket her fist coiled tight around the hilt of her knife. Eleven years later and it still pissed her off. "Said if I didn't, they'd throw me in juvie with no way out."

With a shake of his head, Cory responded, "That's fucked up. But, hey, if the feds are killing monsters, it's a net positive, right?"

"It would be, if they were actually killing them. Some people have claimed to see them capturing monsters, but not killing them."

"For God's sake." He kicked another rock that was lying halfway out of its median. "I can't stand hunters who do that. Who cares how they work, they're dangerous and they need to be put down."

"I can see why people want to study them," Hex admitted. All of the windows on this street were dark, the residents all asleep, completely unaware of the danger that prowled in their midst. "Knowledge is useful. But when the U.S. government is doing it, you know that they're trying to figure out how to make ghost bombs or something."

As they walked, she never took her eyes off the frequency detector. Just as Cory opened his mouth to reply, it ticked over to a very familiar number. Hex stopped dead and threw out her free arm to stop him with her.

There it was. Static.

Cory's eyes widened in understanding. Slowly, they both turned to look at the house beside them.

It was the same as all the other houses in the neighborhood. White clapboards, basic roof with only a slight incline, the blue-trimmed windows dark, like eyes staring out at the street. There were two cars parked in the driveway, a truck and a Prius. On the back window of the latter was a sticker with four stick figures, two large and two small, and a little stick figure cat.

With a gulp, Hex dropped her arm and stepped towards the driveway. Cory followed.

Hex's heart was already pounding as they approached the front door. Cory tugged on the handle a couple of times and shook his head – locked. Hex glanced to either side, then tapped Cory's arm and pointed to the gate into the backyard. That one wasn't locked.

It was a well-manicured yard, with a big swath of grass and some neatly trimmed shrubberies and flower bushes. They walked across the grass, wary of the noise if they took the gravel path. Through the glass sliding door was a darkened kitchen; the gray light hadn't arrived yet, but as they approached the door and the static got louder, Hex had to fight to banish the memories from her mind. She wrapped her sweaty hands around the door handle and pulled, but like the front door, it remained stubbornly closed.

Cory tapped her shoulder, motioning with his head when she turned to look. Like most houses in the Midwest, there was a basement, with windows peeking out above ground level, just wide enough for someone their size to slip through. And, lo and behold, the first one Cory tested swung open on stiff, rusted hinges.

After shooting her an excited grin, Cory slid in with a dim *thump* when he hit the basement floor. Hex pulled her backpack off with shaking hands.

God, she hated this fear. She'd been looking for this monster for so long, and now that they finally had it cornered, that's when her brain decided to freak out?

Suck it up, she thought sternly to herself as she pushed her backpack through the window. *We're doing this, whether you like it or not.* Then, with only a moment more of hesitation, she went in after it.

She landed in the pitch darkness of the basement. Cory had already dug his flashlight out of his coat and was shining it around with interest, a thin silver beam in the gloom. The room was smaller than she expected, crowded with old cardboard boxes and broken furniture, with a rickety set of wooden stairs leading up to the rest of the house.

The static filled her ears. Biting her tongue, she dug through her bag until her fingers brushed the cool metal grip of her flashlight and the familiar corners of the spirit box. She pulled out both, but didn't turn the spirit box on quite yet, and left the frequency detector inside.

"When do you think it'll start?" Cory whispered as she shouldered her bag again and clicked on her flashlight.

"Probably not long," she replied, just as the room around them began to grow bright with gray light. She dragged in a strangled breath, tasting ozone – the fog was rising from the floor, pouring from the walls, curling around their legs, and the light was just like it was back then, just as *wrong*, the fog just as thick in her throat, and the static made it so hard to think –

Cory put a hand on her shoulder and made her jump. "Keep it together, Hex," he said, though it sounded like a reminder for both of them. His eyes darted around and his hand shook on her shoulder, but he was, for now, still calm. His fingers squeezed. "Find something different. Focus on that, not on the memories."

Hex forced a smooth-ish breath in and out. "The flashlights," she murmured. "The beams are different." They cut through the fog like silver roads, revealing some clutter in the room. It wasn't much, but it was enough to make her heart beat slower. She shook herself. "Come on, it'll be upstairs."

The wooden stair shifted at the first press of her boot. Hex cringed and froze, but any noise the board made had been swallowed by the fog. Cory prodded at her back, and she kept climbing.

Here the static was even louder. Without saying anything to each other, the two of them followed the sound further into the house, towards an open bedroom door.

The place was quaint, tastefully decorated, with a few too many crosses on the walls, but Hex barely noticed. Her vision was tunneled on their target. The closer they got, the louder her heart pounded in her ears.

When they reached the doorway, she pressed her back to the wall beside it, forcing another steadying breath, and locked eyes with Cory as she held up her spirit box. He nodded and pulled his from one of his many pockets. The static on the other side of the wall swelled.

Now or never.

Hex stepped around the doorframe and into the room.

And there it was. The Creech, standing at the foot of the bed, exactly the same as it had been more than a decade before with its hunched-over posture and scribbled-in skin. The edges of its silhouette flickered and fuzzed like a slowly dying TV set.

This time Hex didn't scream. Now, finally standing in the same room as the thing that had ruined her life, the fear was gone, replaced by a cold, deadly anger that kept her hands steady as she made sure her spirit box was on the right frequency. Clenching her jaw so hard that it ached, she pressed the button.

All Hex heard was a dull buzz under the crackling static of the Creech itself. But Cory was right – it *did* flinch, all the scribbles of its skin vibrating with agitation. It went blurry for half a second as it snapped around to face her. Those pinpoint eyes bored into her.

The Creech's victims, whoever they were, shifted under their sheets but didn't wake, not yet, and for a moment Hex was back in her little brother's room, his body falling lifelessly onto the mattress, until Cory moved in her periphery, dragging her back to reality – or whatever reality existed in the fog – as he flipped on his own spirit box.

To Hex's shock, the Creech recoiled from the second frequency, one of its spindly arms jerking up towards its face. The static pitched higher and dipped, a sound of pain.

It was working, the radios were actually having an effect on it, and Hex saw her opportunity.

Hex grabbed the dial on her spirit box and cranked the frequency up even higher. The Creech staggered, arms flailing, and this time there was something inside the static, something like a long, low groaning that the fog couldn't quite silence.

"Okay," Cory whispered in a hoarse, overwhelmed voice. One of the shapes on the bed shifted again, but neither of them paid attention. "Now you go left, and – "

But Hex wasn't done. High frequencies made it flinch – what would a low frequency do?

She spun the dial down, and immediately knew that she'd made a mistake.

In seconds the groan ceased, the static crackling high and sharp. The Creech glitched out of sight, into thin air, and before she could process that it had moved, a weight slammed into her.

She hit the floor hard. Her backpack provided a tiny bit of cushion, but it wasn't enough to stop her breath from being knocked out of her. Claws flashed overhead and Hex barely reacted quickly enough to roll away as they came down, embedding themselves into the wooden floor, sending splinters flying and a heavy vibration through the boards.

There was a flurry of startled motion and sheets and a high-pitched scream from the bed – they were out of time.

So far Hex had thought that only two sounds could get through the fog: voices and static. Now she learned that there was a third – gunshots. The shot ripped through the air, deafening even in the fog, and the static roared around them like a massive waterfall.

Whether the shot came from Cory or if the homeowner was packing heat, Hex couldn't tell, and it didn't matter. All that mattered was that the time it took for the Creech to glitch out and back in gave Hex the opportunity to crank the dial on her spirit box back up. The monster jerked and shuddered. Another shot went off, the muzzle flash bright against the gray.

Cory grabbed Hex by the arm and hauled her to her feet. "Let's get out of here!" he shouted over the continuing screams of one of the people in the bed, but Hex braced her feet when he tried to pull her away.

"No! It's right there, we – "

Bang!

The Creech's head jerked back as the bullet struck dead center.

But it didn't fall. It made an infuriated noise, an angry *hiss* that crept through the static like a snake through grass, and glitched out of the room.

Both of them froze. Hex held her breath, tension strung through every part of her, but the creature didn't reappear. Instead, the room began to darken as the fog faded, and both she and Cory hissed a curse at the same moment. The Creech was gone, leaving them in a room with a screaming woman in a lacy nightie and a man with a happy trigger finger.

Cory shoved her towards the door. "Run!"

This time she listened, scrambling to find the off switch on her spirit box as they bolted towards the front door. The floorboards vibrated beneath their feet as the man gave chase. He was yelling something, but Hex's ears were ringing too loudly to make out the words.

Cory made it to the door first and went for the lock. Hex glanced over her shoulder at the dark silhouette at the end of the hall; the arm moved, and Hex yanked Cory down just as the gun cracked again.

The glass on the front door exploded, raining shards down on their backs. An alarm started blaring, adding its high and tinny call to the tornado of conflicting sounds that were making Hex's head spin. Finally, Cory managed the chain on the door. He and Hex stumbled down the porch steps and took off across the lawn.

Up and down the street, windows were lighting up yellow, front doors cracking open, curious faces peeking out. Hex ducked her head to conceal her features and ran as fast as she could.

5

Lamplight

It seemed like only a few seconds passed before she was smacking into the side of Cory's truck, but it must've been longer judging by that familiar burning stitch in her side. The houses on this street were dark and quiet, so she tried not to close the door too hard when she climbed into the truck, slinging her backpack off of her shoulder and into the footwell.

The engine stuttered when Cory tried to turn it over. After three attempts, it came to life and Cory pulled away from the curb, shouting, "What the hell was that?"

Hex braced her hands against the dashboard and tried to breathe. The adrenaline still sang in her veins, she couldn't catch her breath, the fog and the light was everywhere, and still Cory was shouting.

"You could've gotten us killed!"

"Sorry," she croaked from a dry mouth. "Wanted to see – if all of them worked – "

Cory cursed and slammed his fist against the steering wheel, eyes wide and panicked. "That was not the time to be conducting a science experiment!"

Hex sat up and tried to lean back into her seat. Sharp pain pierced through the skin around her spine, sending her lurching forward again with a cry, and Cory's voice changed.

"Hex? Are you hit?"

He meant by the gun. "No," hissed Hex as warmth began to soak into her shirt. "Think there's glass in my shirt."

Oddly enough, the pain was grounding. Her thoughts cleared – there was something she was supposed to do when she panicked. Something with counting.

That was it. Counting and breathing. She inhaled as slowly as she could, counting to five, and let it out to the count of seven. It took several repetitions for her breathing to steady, and several more before she became aware of her surroundings: the black plastic dashboard, the AC turned up too high and blowing right in her face, highway signs flashing by the windows.

Cory was still babbling, a mix of curse words and assurances that she would be okay, that they'd get her fixed up, that they were safe now, and despite everything an amused smile curved her lips.

"I'm okay, Cory," she said, stopping the flood of words immediately. "Just hurts a little."

"A little? You were bent over for like ten minutes!"

"That was the panic attack, not the pain." She straightened up, not leaning back, and attempted a smile when Cory's eyes darted to her. "This is nothing. A poltergeist threw an entire standing mirror at me once."

"Jesus." Cory shook his head hard. "Okay. We'll be back at the motel in a few minutes. Christ, you scared me."

The rest of the trip was quiet, interrupted only by Hex's winces when she moved too fast. There was at least one bit of glass lodged in her back and more loose under her shirt, being pressed down by the weight of her jacket. She had about a minute to get anxious about possible damage to the coat before Cory pulled into the motel parking lot.

Cory offered her his arm when they reached the stairs, but Hex waved him off. Her knees may be shaky from the adrenaline rush, but her legs worked fine, and thankfully Cory accepted that without a fuss.

After all the chaos, the dark, quiet interior of the motel room was bliss. Cory left his pack by the door and moved to the center of the room, retrieving the first aid kit from where they'd left it the night before and clicking on the bedside lamp, filling the space with soft yellow. Her shoulders lost some tension – it wasn't the eerie gray light of the fog.

"Come here," Cory said, gesturing to the bed. "Let me look."

Hex shuffled over and slowly sat down on the edge of the mattress. The adrenaline was completely gone and for once she actually wanted to sleep, but that wouldn't be happening for a while yet.

She jolted when hands suddenly landed on her shoulders.

"Just me," said Cory. He pulled the jacket down and off of her with quick, efficient movements.

Once Hex swallowed her heart back down where it was supposed to be, she managed to ask, "Is it torn?"

There was some rustling and two *plops* as Cory tossed both of their coats onto the bed beside her. Maybe she was imagining how the leather cracked like a whip and the polyester snapped with suppressed tension. The tension in his voice was definitely not her imagination when he said shortly, "Looks fine to me."

Hex let out a breath of momentary relief, only for it to catch when the mattress dipped behind her.

"Need help with your shirt?"

Her throat was too tight to answer. She shook her head and reached for the hem herself; the shirt was a size too big for her, which made it easier to wrestle off, but the movement made the glass shift and catch against her skin.

A cursory examination showed that the shirt was bloody but untorn. A blessing – she only owned four shirts.

"Good thing I only wear black," she mumbled, getting a half-amused chuckle from Cory. There was a click from behind her when he opened the first aid kit, and Hex barely restrained herself from twisting around to keep her eyes on him.

It's just Cory. He might be a little pissed, but it's still him. You're fine.

With a hard swallow, she asked, "Do I need to take my binder off?"

Cory hummed, the mattress dipping again as he leaned in. "I don't think so. There's just some glass dust on it." A hand brushed briskly over her back. Hex clenched her teeth and her fists around the shirt in her hands, willing all of her muscles not to move as chills shot down her spine and rippled across her skin.

Cory brushed the back of the binder twice more. "There, I think I got it all. You have some cuts below it and a piece stuck near your neck."

Hex forced her breath through her teeth. The sooner this was done, the sooner they could figure out their plan B. "Just get it over with."

"Alright, give me a sec."

Hex braced herself. It wasn't the pain she was worried about, she could handle pain. It was the proximity, knowing someone was behind her and had the advantage. She couldn't see what they were doing or how much it would hurt and knew that it would be so, so easy for them to plant a hand between her shoulder blades and push her down –

There was a slight, sharp pain, then, "Got it."

Her knuckles were white where they gripped the bloodstained shirt. She knew what was coming next, but she still jumped when the cold antiseptic wipe hit her skin. Cory worked quickly, at least, mopping up the blood and cleaning up the wound, and Hex kept it together surprisingly well, even when she felt the press of his fingers as he stuck a bandage to her skin. Her hands were shaking and she was covered in cold sweat, but she held it together.

Then the wipe returned, this time in the middle of her spine beneath the binder, and before she knew it, she was three steps away from the bed, clutching the shirt to her chest as she shook.

Her chest was heavy. She pressed her forehead to the rough texture of the motel wallpaper and tried to slow her breath, with mixed results.

"Hex?"

She jolted, then immediately scolded herself. *Come on, Hex, pull it together.*

"Sorry," she managed to say in a semi-steady voice. "I just – I just need a minute."

"Did I do something?"

Hex shook her head without turning from the wall. "No, it's not you. I – I'm not – " God, she was so exposed without her jacket, without the baggy shirt to conceal the shape of her body. She couldn't remember the last time she'd let anyone touch her this much, with or without the heavy leather barrier. "I'm not used to this. I'm jumpy."

"Okay." Cory's voice was softer than it was before, so soft it made Hex's chest ache. That could've also been the hyperventilating, though.

He waited patiently for several minutes while Hex tried to pull herself together. Part of her was tempted to say screw it to the bandages and let them heal on their own, but the dripping of blood down the small of her back begged otherwise.

Eventually, she managed to step away from the wall and turn back to face Cory. He was watching her, a blank expression on his face that made more anxiety begin to twist in Hex's stomach, but for now he didn't scold her for making everything so difficult. He waited for her to come back to her previous position, and didn't say anything when she gave a too-obvious shiver at the chills that returned when she turned her back to him.

"Where did you get your jacket?"

All Hex could think to say was a puzzled, "Huh?"

"Your jacket," Cory repeated firmly. Hex jumped at the momentary touch of another wipe, gone as quickly as it came. "Where'd you get it? Tell me."

Oh. He was trying to distract her. Well, she didn't have any better ideas. Might as well play along.

"My third foster home," she murmured. A bandage wrapper crinkled and she tensed in anticipation, but Cory didn't touch her.

He just said, "Go on."

Hex gulped and continued. "The couple running it were taking care of the husband's father. Old guy, Vietnam vet and everything."

Cory stuck on the bandage at the end of her sentence, lightning quick, and Hex stuttered for a second. But only for a second.

"He mostly kept to himself. He had a bad leg so he didn't leave his room much. But he had a whole bunch of old stuff in there, including my knife." The knife that was currently unreachable in her jacket pocket.

Another cold swipe of antiseptic, another bandage, but neither were what made her throat tighten.

"One day, I snuck in there while the adults were taking him to a doctor's appointment. I don't know why, but I took the knife off his dresser."

That was a lie. She knew exactly why she took it.

"It was stupid and obvious, but he never said anything about it. One time, he invited me into his room and I thought for sure ... but he didn't. He just asked if I'd play checkers with him."

The low lamplight of the motel room was so similar to the lamplight in his room as the two of them played, moving their pieces across the board without a word between them.

Another bandage. Hex barely noticed.

"Eventually, the couple decided to stop fostering. He needed more care, and their careers were taking off. So they sent me back." She couldn't quite keep the bitterness out of her voice. It was the same old story, over and over. Even in the decent homes, she was the weak link. The thing that could be easily discarded.

"The day I left, I tried to give the knife back to him. He told me to keep it." She could still feel the rough texture of his hands as he pressed her fingers around the hilt. His rickety voice when he said she needed it more than he did. "Then he gave me his old jacket too. Said he never wore it anymore."

The last bandage went on just in time for the crinkling of the wrapper to conceal Hex's sniffle – she hoped.

"All done," Cory said quietly, and the mattress shifted as he moved back from her.

Hex practically leapt up from the bed. Without looking at Cory, she made a beeline to her backpack to dig out a new shirt. It was just as big as the last one, a black concert tee she'd gotten from her dad, worn soft with age.

Her breath was still shuddering, and at the thought of her dad, her eyes pricked with humiliating tears. She had gone down too many memory lanes tonight. Clutching both of her shirts to her chest, she beat a hasty retreat to the tiny bathroom.

Click went the lock, and for a moment Hex leaned back against the door, using the pressure on the cuts to drag her back into reality.

Surprisingly, once the tears subsided, she didn't feel as shitty as she expected to. The chills were gone, leaving only the drying sweat to mark them, and she pulled the clean shirt on with a sigh of relief – safe at last.

Hex studied her reflection as the sink filled with cold water. Maybe it was the harsh bathroom light or the cloudy mirror, but she looked pale, sick, the bags under her eyes nearly the same shade as the streaks in her messy hair. Hair that needed re-dying, judging by the lines of brown at her roots. She shook it out to make sure there was no glass lingering, and when the basin was full, dunked her bloodstained shirt inside to soak.

By the time she opened the bathroom door, she felt fairly composed. Cory was still on the bed, one hand holding up his tank top as he inspected the bandages on his side. Bandages blooming with fresh red.

"Shit," Hex hissed.

Cory gave her a half-smile, tight with concealed pain. "All the running got the blood pumping again, I guess."

"Why didn't you say anything?" She was already halfway across the room, going for the first aid kit, and Cory didn't stop her when she dropped to the floor next to her bed.

"We were a little busy, and you had glass stuck in you."

Hex pressed her lips into a thin line and batted one of his hands out of the way. As gently as she could, she lifted the bandage away; the wounds beneath were irritated, red around the edges, and sluggishly oozing blood, but to Hex's relief, they didn't look like they were getting infected.

"Not infected," she said, and some of the tension in Cory's body loosened. "Just irritated by the running, like you said. Let me get another bandage."

Cory didn't argue, and said nothing as Hex changed the bandage, but his shallow breathing and trembling gave him away.

"Do you want pain meds? I think there's some in the kit."

"Nah." His voice was breathy, exhausted. "Don't wanna be knocked out if something happens."

"Okay." Hex sat back, letting Cory's shirt fall back over the fresh bandage. Wounds tended to, now would be the time to go over what happened in that house, get the data down, but the thought of it made her stomach twist. There was no avoiding it: she had fucked up, and it nearly got them killed. "Look, about what happened – "

"We'll talk about it later," Cory interrupted. The edge had returned to his voice, but the glow of the lamp softened the hard planes of his face into something almost child-like. "We need to rest."

"Right." Of course Cory needed to sleep. "I'll get started putting that house on my map and writing down what we found out so we can talk it over in the morning." And Hex could apologize.

She stood up, about to go negotiate with the vending machine for more caffeine, when Cory caught her wrist.

"Hey, I said we. As in both of us."

Hex balked. She was tired, sure, but she was used to it. There were more important things to do. "But – "

"No buts. You didn't sleep last night."

"I slept this morning, remember?" She tugged her arm away from Cory's grasp, but his intent stare kept her pinned in place.

"You napped for two hours. That's not nearly enough, and you'll probably be able to think more clearly if you sleep before going over everything."

Something itched under her skin. It was a familiar itch, the buzz of *go go go now now now* that had kept her up the previous night, desperate to sort it all out as quickly as possible so that she could move on to the next clue, the next crumb of information, the next data point.

"We'll probably only have one more shot at this," she attempted. "We need to know everything we can."

Cory snorted at her and slowly stretched himself out on the bed, wincing as the movement pulled on his wound. "You'll be useless to me on a hunt if you're sleep-deprived."

She eyed the other side of the bed warily. Cory raised an eyebrow.

"If you keep fighting me on this, I'll be forced to stake you."

That got a laugh out of her, and some of the tension eased. Enough for her to recognize the validity of Cory's argument, even if sleeping didn't usually go well for her.

"Okay, okay, fine. You're probably right."

"Come on then." Cory patted the other side of the bed with a lopsided smile. "I don't bite."

"I might," replied Hex, only half joking, but Cory just laughed.

Okay, I can do this. She couldn't remember the last time she shared a bed with someone, but it would be fine. It didn't have to be a big deal. So long as she didn't make it one.

Before she could psych herself out, Hex went around to the other side of the bed and climbed on; jeans, boots, and all. For a second she panicked over which way to face – *facing Cory would be awkward but facing away would leave her vulnerable* – until she settled for laying on her back and staring straight up at the ceiling, letting the sting of the cuts distract her.

To her relief, Cory didn't call attention to how weird she was being. The lamp clicked off, plunging the room into darkness.

"Goodnight, Hex."

She squeezed her eyes shut and didn't answer.

6

FLUORESCENT LIGHTS

"Natalie?"

Hex warily looked up from her notebook. It had been more than a year, but that name still left a bad taste at the back of her mouth. The feeling wasn't assuaged by the sight of a red-jacketed school security guard standing in the doorway. He gestured to her, and she reluctantly got up from her desk as the beginnings of anxiety stirred in her stomach.

The last time she'd been called out of class, it was to be chewed out by the principal for stealing (which she totally did not do ... this time), so she wasn't looking forward to whatever new lecture awaited her.

The security guard didn't try to talk to her. They never did – all security did was stand around in the halls, scowl at students, and buy weed off the senior dealers. He just led her down the many halls and staircases it took to reach the main office.

Then he did something surprising. Instead of taking her to the principal's office, he opened a door to an empty room, holding only a table and three chairs.

"Wait here," he said roughly. "They'll be here in a few minutes."

"Who's they?" Hex demanded, but he merely glared at her. So, with great reluctance, she stepped inside. The door closed behind her, and she heard the lock click. Dammit.

With no other option, she sat down in the lone chair on one side of the table. The room was silent except for the buzz of the fluorescent lighting embedded in the ceiling, so much like radio static. She dug her headphones out from her bag and put them in – she didn't play anything, she wanted to hear when whoever it was came for her, but they were enough to muffle the buzzing.

Then all she could do was wait. She'd gotten used to waiting – social workers were incredibly busy, and waiting in various offices had become a fact of life.

The room wasn't anything special. It had the same short blue carpet as the rest of the office areas at the school, with the same yellow wood paneling on the walls. One thing she did notice, however, was the lack of the red recording light on the camera tucked into a ceiling corner. Just as she noticed, she heard dim footsteps, and the door opened.

On the other side were two adults in black suits, a man and a woman. They looked like FBI, with the man's perfectly military haircut and the woman's tight bun, but there were no badges or identification anywhere on them. They came in and sat down, stiff and proper, and the man tucked his briefcase under his chair as Hex pulled the earbuds from her ears.

"Hello, Hex," the woman said in a saccharine voice. It was meant to be friendly, she was sure, but still she felt her shoulders tense. It sounded wrong coming from these people, the woman with perfectly plucked eyebrows and the man compulsively smoothing his tie.

These weren't school officials or social workers. So, who were they, and what did they want from her?

"Who are you?" she asked again, and this time got an answer.

"We represent the United States government," said the man with a smile that was too wide. "A small branch, but an important one."

He didn't say which, and Hex got the feeling he wouldn't if she asked. So her next question was, "What do you want?"

The woman cleared her throat and sat forward, resting her interlaced hands on the table. Hex leaned back in her chair, wanting to be as far away from this strange, perfect-looking woman as she could be. "We'd like to speak to you about your family. What happened to them."

Hex's stomach dropped like she was sitting in the Tower of Terror rather than a normal plastic chair. The missing persons cases for her mother, father, and brother were technically active but had gone cold months ago (because they weren't missing, they were *dead,* and Hex had seen them die). Did these people think they found some evidence? Or ... if they were part of a secret government agency ... did they know about the Creech?

Still, she was cautious. Three foster homes had taught her that. She narrowed her eyes and said, "What about them?"

"It's come to our attention," the man said, "that you believe they were killed by a supernatural creature of some sort."

All of her muscles tensed. Yes, she had told the police what happened, as well as her court-issued therapist and a couple of kids at school who had pushed her, but how did that get all the way up to the feds?

"So? Can't a crazy girl have her delusions?"

The woman's smile grew, straining at the edges of her mouth. "You don't really believe it was a delusion, Hex. We both know that."

Hex snorted and tossed her head. "Isn't that how delusions work?"

The man sighed, exasperated, but that was the exact opposite of Hex's problem. "The thing is, *Natalie*" – ah, there it was – "that we can't have you running around spreading rumors about a soul-eating monster. You could instill a culture of fear in this community, and that wouldn't help anyone, including the police who are trying to find your family."

"What?" She couldn't help her disbelieving chuckle. "No one actually believes me. They all think I'm crazy. No one's afraid."

"All it takes is one person," the woman said. "Next thing you know, we have mass hysteria on our hands, and that gets incredibly messy." She was still smiling. Didn't her face hurt?

The man was smiling too, but not as ferociously as the woman. "Whether or not you think people believe you, we need you to stop telling that story."

"Stop telling the truth, you mean," Hex snapped back. "Screw you. I have freedom of speech, don't I?"

The man leaned back and folded his arms. "Of course. Just not about this." He smiled wider, flashing his painfully white teeth. "We have different rules than most agencies."

"Bullshit."

Abruptly, both of their smiles dropped. The woman turned, staring coldly into her partner's eyes. He nodded and sat back up, very obviously clenching his jaw, and loosened his tie a smidge.

"Now, listen to me, you teenaged brat." Hex's already tense muscles coiled like a snake, but he didn't stop or slow. "You have two options here. You can agree to ditch the insane story about a glitching monster and keep living your insignificant life as you have been. Or you can be a stubborn idiot and wind up in juvenile detention."

Her breath caught. The man smirked, but Hex couldn't help the obvious fear that had filled her. She'd seen other kids who had come out of juvie in the system, and the stories they told were full of horror and abuse even worse than the homes.

The woman tilted her head and chimed in, "And you know how dreadfully slow the courts are these days. Who knows how long it would take for your case to be processed. Years, probably."

Hex shuddered, shoulders hunching around her neck. She couldn't go to juvie – in there, she wouldn't be able to keep track of the Creech. Wouldn't be able to figure it out, find it ... kill it. She had to stay on the outside.

So, even though it tasted sour, she said the words. "Fine. I won't talk about it anymore."

The fake smiles returned. "Excellent," the woman said as the man retrieved his briefcase and opened it on the table. "We knew you were a smart girl."

Hex scowled at her.

From the briefcase, the man produced a piece of paper and a ballpoint pen that he set down in front of Hex. It was a contract, written in legal typeface, with the tiniest font she had ever seen in her life.

"This is an agreement that stipulates that you will no longer speak of this creature to anyone," he said, holding the pen out to her. "It also rules that should you break this agreement, you will be arrested and detained until such time as a judge can rule on your case, however long that takes." His eyes, reflecting the fluorescent lights above, held a warning. So, with a shaking hand, Hex took the pen.

I don't need to talk about it, Hex thought as she signed on the dotted line. *No one believes me anyway. I can find it myself.*

The man whisked the paper and pen away, back into his briefcase, and shut it with a decisive *snick.* "There, that wasn't so difficult, was it?"

Hex shook her head and muttered, "Can I go back to class now?"

"Of course," the woman responded. "It was a pleasure to speak with you."

Hex bit her tongue to avoid saying anything snarky. The two stood up and left, just as confident as they had come in, and as the door shut behind them, the red light on the camera blinked back on.

It would take several days of research and downloading Tor, but eventually Hex managed to find a few places where people were talking about encounters like hers, and she finally had a name to fit to their bland faces.

Project Chimaera.

7

Moonlight

The Creech was in the motel room.

Hex laid there, ice in her veins as the gray fog filled the room and the static filled the air. She could feel Cory beside her but dared not look. She couldn't bear to see him faceless.

It leaned over her. The shifting pattern of its scribbled skin was nauseating, but she couldn't look away. Couldn't reach for her jacket where her knife lay in the pocket at the foot of the bed. Ozone tinged her tongue.

Was this what it felt like for Mason? Were these the last few moments of her little brother, having to stare into the maw of the thing that was going to consume him?

It kept leaning closer, its strangely realistic teeth gleaming in the gray. Her mind spun off into frantic side thoughts – *why even have teeth if you don't eat flesh* – until the raising of its clawed hand snapped her back to full awareness. Maybe it was a trick of the light, but she could've sworn she saw Cory's dried blood on those claws. Cold sweat dripped down her back as the hand rose higher, higher, higher.

It plunged downwards and Hex woke with a strangled sound. She scrambled off the bed and planted her back to the wall, but when she actually opened her eyes, the room had changed. There was no fog, no gray light, no monster. Just pitch darkness, the tiny green light of the smoke detector on the ceiling, and the soft sounds Cory was making in his sleep.

Fuck. *Fuck.* Hex pressed the heels of her hands to her eyes until she saw swirling colors and held her breath. She was not going to cry over a nightmare like a little kid. She refused.

After a minute or two, the urge to cry retreated behind the veil of exhaustion. Hex dropped her hands and peered at the clock through blurry eyes; its red numbers said 3:03 a.m. She cursed under her breath.

Well, she gave it her best shot, but as usual, sleep failed her. Might as well get something done before morning.

Hex circled the bed to the side table and clicked on the lamp. Cory stirred, a sharp jerk of his head, but didn't wake.

Even in sleep he was tense: clenched jaw, balled fists, furrowed brow, all of his muscles pulled wire-taut. He jerked again, another muffled sound escaping from between gritted teeth.

Hex frowned. Some people didn't like being woken from nightmares, herself included, but –

His whole body went stiff. His nails gouged into his palms and his chest stilled as he held his breath. Before she could overthink it, Hex grabbed his shoulder and shook.

At first, he didn't react. She added a call of his name to the mix, and on the next shake his eyes flew open.

For a long moment, they stared at each other. Hex could feel him trembling, noted the way his eyes flickered as they tried to adjust to the light, and didn't move a muscle. Eventually, he blinked and let out his breath, deflating like a balloon. She waited another second before taking her hand away.

She didn't know what to say. What are you supposed to say in situations like this? After a few awkward seconds, she folded her arms over her stomach and asked, "Are you okay?"

Cory slowly levered himself upright and rolled his shoulders with an uncomfortable grimace. "Yeah. Just a nightmare. Didn't mean to wake you."

"You didn't." She rubbed her arms, bare without her jacket. "I had one too, that's what woke me up."

"Oh." He gave her a quick once-over, then asked, "Was yours about the Creech too?"

"Most of them are." Hex perched herself on the edge of the bed to dismiss the feeling of looming over him as the creature had loomed over her. "Except the one with the angry banshee. My ears still ring after that dream."

Cory mustered a chuckle. He looked more haggard than when he went to sleep, his hair spikes flattened and mussed, exhaustion heavy on his shoulders like a physical weight. "That one based on reality?"

"Oh, yeah. She shattered every window in that house."

"I don't work with ghosts much," he said, fingers picking at the duvet. There was a hint of cold sweat on his forehead. "I prefer the monsters that go away when you kill them."

It was Hex's turn to make herself laugh. "They're not too bad. Most of the time, the place isn't even haunted and I just have to sprinkle some holy water and chase the raccoons out of the attic."

"Still," Cory insisted. "The real ones are so hard to get rid of. How do you kill something that's already dead? Freaks me out."

Hex shrugged. "They are hard to get rid of, but most of the time, you don't even have to kill them. Most are just scared or confused or angry about something that happened to them. It's almost like being a therapist."

"I would be a terrible therapist," scoffed Cory, and this time Hex's laugh was genuine.

"Me too. But ghosts just make sense to me, I guess." Maybe because she had so much in common with them. Maybe because the girl Natalie had died the same day as her family, and Hex was the ghost who rose in her place, with no future ahead of her beyond *kill the thing that killed you.*

Dammit, it was too early (late? Where was the cutoff?) for her existential crises. She stood up from the bed and reached over to grab her jacket. "I'm not going to be able to go back to sleep. Want anything from the vending machine?"

Cory pushed the blankets back with a sigh. "Whatever has the most caffeine."

"You got it."

***

"Huh."

Cory raised his head from where it was resting on the table. "Huh what?" He was bleary-eyed and weary, but resolutely took another gulp of his energy drink and sat up straighter.

Hex twirled her pen over her knuckles and tapped the end of it against her notebook page. "I found the house we were in. It's a few blocks south and west of where you first saw the Creech."

"Okay," said Cory with a long blink. "Which means ...?"

"It's still trying to follow its pattern." She flipped to a different page in the notebook and spun it around to face him. Glued to the page was a basic map of the United States, cities and towns the Creech had visited marked with stars and dates, a line in red ink connecting them all with arrows indicating the direction it was taking. It was moving west, jumping from city to city, suburb to suburb, but only in the last decade had it started heading south after hitting a place in Canada. "It can't get very far hungry, but it's still trying to go in the same direction."

Cory perked up. "So we'll only have to patrol the streets to the southwest of the last house we were in."

"Exactly."

"And," he added as he leaned in to get a closer look at Hex's scribbled notes, "it only made it a few blocks last time, so it probably won't be able to make it out of the neighborhood."

Hex hummed, tapping her pen. As she had so many times before, she pondered the Creech's path. Except for once in Canada, it had stuck inside U.S. borders. Always moving west, pinballing from north to south.

"Hex? What are you thinking?"

"Nothing," she said, pushing the thought away. Cory was so practical; why should they care about why and where it was moving if that didn't matter for killing it? She leaned back, stretching her back over her chair until it popped, doggedly ignoring the sting of her cuts. "The sun will be rising soon."

Cory leaned his cheek into his hand, propped up on the table by his elbow. "We should be able to get some sleep once it comes up. My nightmares aren't as bad during the day."

"Naps are safer," Hex agreed. The words on the page before her and the satellite images of the house they'd broken into on her laptop screen blurred together, her vision going double for a moment before focusing again. Her next words slipped out by accident.

"This really sucks."

Cory snorted. "Tell me about it."

She didn't have to. The bags under Cory's eyes said he knew perfectly well all the ways that they had suffered because of this monster. Killing the Creech wouldn't bring their families back, wouldn't take the nightmares away, but at least if it was gone no one else would go through the same thing. The call and cause of every hunter that had ever lived.

One of her fingers moved idly around the trackpad on her laptop, a digital fidget, tracing the roads on the map further south, towards the edges of the neighborhood. There wasn't much there aside from the rows and rows of houses, but at the southern edge was a square of green and a symbol of a tree. *Howard Johnson Memorial Park.* Two clicks later, she was on the official city website for the park.

Hex scanned the page. She was barely absorbing any of the information, but the light and the pantomime of reading was keeping her eyes open just that little bit longer.

At the bottom of the webpage was an event calendar. There was something scheduled for that night. A high school graduation party.

Hex stared at it for a few seconds. Then she sat up straight, her heart beginning to race as she turned the screen towards Cory.

"Look," she said, jabbing a finger at the calendar. "There's a party happening in the neighborhood tonight."

Cory's eyes narrowed as he squinted at it, then widened again when he made the same connection. "A bunch of happy, successful people with good lives, all crowded together in one place."

"Like a buffet." She frowned. "But as far as we know, it's never attacked this many people at once, and usually it waits for the victims to be asleep. This doesn't fit the pattern."

"It's starving," countered Cory. "A desperate animal will do anything to survive."

"You're assuming it acts like an animal."

"And you're assuming it acts like a ghost, stuck in an infinite loop."

Hex bit the inside of her lip. Cory had a point – it clearly needed to eat, therefore it would feel the pressure of starvation – but even in this situation it was following its pattern as much as it could.

She planted her head in her hands with a frustrated groan. "God, if we could just figure out what the hell it *is*." A demon, a monster, a ghost, some cursed kid's drawing come to life?

"Is that what you were trying to do last night?" Cory's voice was almost flat, but there was a current of tension threaded through it that had Hex's muscles tensing. She raised her head to find him glaring at the surface of the table, picking at a scrape in the varnish with his fingernail.

So he was still pissed. Great.

"You could've gotten us killed, you know," he continued, still not looking up. "And those two people. Do you get that?"

Hex folded her arms over her chest, squeezing herself tight. "Of course I do."

"Then why would you – "

"Because I wanted to know. If high frequency hurt it, maybe low frequency would do something else that could be helpful."

"We knew enough." Cory's eyes finally darted up to meet Hex's, full of anger that had been simmering for hours, and she braced for whatever was going to come next. This, at least, was familiar territory. "We had it right where we wanted it. We could've killed it, right then, and all of this would be over!"

"We don't even know what kills it," Hex countered. "Bullets don't work. The frequency just seemed to stun it. What was your plan, whale on it with a bunch of different weapons until something stuck, hoping that the victims wouldn't wake up?"

"Something would've worked eventually – "

"Yeah, and that's what I was trying to figure out!"

There was a pause, a moment of quiet while they both tried to formulate their arguments, and Hex bit the inside of her cheek until it hurt. Cory was the one who invited her here, specifically because of her research and her knowledge, but now he was angry at her for exactly what he had valued her for.

"Look, if you don't want to do this, then – "

"Oh, fuck *off.*" Cory shoved himself away from the table and got to his feet. Hex flinched, just the smallest bit, then curled her fingers into the biceps of her jacket and squeezed herself tighter. "What, do you think I'm here for kicks? That thing killed my mom just like it killed your family, and I am *sick* of seeing it in my fucking nightmares!"

With the anger came a rush of adrenaline that made Hex's hands tremble. There was a war in her hindbrain, seesawing between fight, flight, or freeze. This time it landed on fight.

"I don't just want to kill it, Cory," she spat back at him. She had her head tilted down to hide her eyes behind her hair, glaring at that spot on the table Cory had been picking at rather than him as he stood next to his chair, chest heaving. "I want to understand it. I want to understand why this happened to me, and to you, and to all of those other people."

"Why the hell does it matter?" asked Cory, waving his hands in the air. This time Hex didn't flinch, but she tracked those hands from her periphery.

"Because what if there are others?"

Cory paused, dropping his hands and his voice. "I thought you tracked all of its attacks."

"I did, but – I don't mean another Creech, exactly." One of her hands uncurled from the leather and began to pick at the skin around her nails. This idea had been brewing for a while, but she pushed it to the back of her mind, trying to stay focused on her real target. Now the words came pouring out. "I mean other creatures like it. Think about it. The Creech has no folklore, no origin point. It just popped up in 1924, practically out of thin air."

Cory shoved his hands into his pockets. "You don't know that," he said through gritted teeth. "Newspapers weren't as common before that, and – "

Hex couldn't help rolling her eyes. "They had newspapers for centuries before that, Cory. And I've been in libraries and archives all over the country, scouring reports from across the world, and there is no mention of it until 1924."

Out of the corner of her eye she saw Cory's mouth open, and the rest of her words came out in a rush, like a river breaking a levee.

"So, how did it get here? And, more importantly, are there other things like it that don't kill in such a distinctive way? Artificial things made of graphite and static with no origins?"

Cory mimicked her pose, crossing his arms and choosing a spot on the carpet to stare at rather than Hex's face. "It could've evolved from something else – "

"Then what? If it evolved, then it had to have an ancestor and others of its kind. So where are they?"

Cory didn't answer. He just stood there, arms folded, a battle raging on his face. Hex pressed on.

"What if this is part of Project Chimaera? What if there are more monsters out there that they're trying to cover up?"

"Okay," he said gruffly. "I get it."

Hex sat back with a shaky breath. "Listen, I am sorry for last night. It was the wrong place and the wrong time and I could've gotten us killed. I get that. But I'm not sorry for being curious."

There was a long silence. Cory stood there in deep thought, drumming his fingers against his bicep, and Hex waited in growing anxiety. This was how it always went for her, always screwing up somehow, always ending up on the outside. She wouldn't be surprised if Cory decided to go and kill the Creech on his own. Upset, but not surprised.

But when Cory met her eyes, the anger was gone, replaced by exhaustion.

"Fine. Apology accepted. Just don't do it again – I'm too young for a heart attack."

That coaxed a quiet laugh out of her, and Cory gave a tiny, tired smile. Whatever his line was, Hex hadn't gone too far over it ... yet.

With a huff, Cory let his arms drop and turned away. "Well, I'm giving up and going to sleep. You?"

"In a minute," said Hex, pulling her notebook back to her. "I want to update the chat with what we found out." And maybe start a new hypotheses list.

Apparently too tired to keep badgering her, Cory gave her a thumbs up and staggered over to the bed. He collapsed onto it face-first and let out a pained grunt when it jostled his wound.

A fond smile grew on Hex's face.

8

Neon Lights

At four p.m. the dive bar was practically empty. Outside was bathed in orange afternoon light, but in the darkened interior, the neon lights hung in the windows cast bright puddles of pink and blue across the floor.

Going out had been Cory's idea (he hated being cooped up, and Hex had been able to stand his pacing for approximately an hour before breaking), but it was Hex that made them come to this place in particular – right across the road was the park the party was going to take place at.

She watched it through the window as they sat together, wound up, leg bouncing incessantly, watching for fog and straining her ears for even the faintest hint of static. This was a gamble, and if they bet wrong, they might never find the Creech again.

Cory frowned at her leg. "You're going to shake your chair apart."

"Sorry," Hex muttered, twirling a purple strand of hair around her finger. "Can't really help it."

"Do you get like this waiting for a ghost too?"

Hex shot him an unamused look, dropping her voice to a conspiratorial whisper. "No, but a ghost didn't kill my whole family."

Cory's smile was lopsided. He had redone his hair spikes before they left, now sharp enough to pop a balloon, Hex suspected. She was surprised that he carried around the extra weight of hair products, until he reminded her that he had a car and not just whatever he could fit in a single backpack.

"It could be a ghost. We don't know, remember?"

She gave him a light punch on the arm. "Smart ass."

"That's me, I'll be here all night."

"How are you so calm?" She expected another joke, another brush off, but instead, Cory's expression grew solemn.

"I'm not," he said and held out a hand. "Look." It was trembling. "Just good at pretending."

Strangely enough, Hex found that reassuring. At least she wasn't the only one freaking out.

The bartender stopped in front of them. She was pretty, with dark hair and big brown eyes. "Can I get you guys anything? You're a bit earlier than the usual crowd."

"A beer, whatever's cheapest," said Cory.

"Just soda," Hex said when the bartender's eyes turned to her. "Root beer, if you have it."

Once the bartender walked away, Cory quirked an eyebrow at her. "Don't drink?"

Hex just shook her head. She'd seen what alcohol did to people. She had no interest in being one of them.

The bartender returned with their drinks. They were both a few sips in, sitting in companionable silence as other early-comers filtered in through the doors, when a thought occurred to Hex that had her setting the drink down on the bar.

"Hey," she began, keeping her eyes glued to her fingers as she picked at her cuticles. "I just want you to know – I mean, I don't know if it's relevant, but just in case – I don't date. Or – anything. So, if this was – if you wanted – I don't."

For a second Cory stared blankly at her. Then it clicked, and for the first time since she met him, Cory looked mortified.

"No, that's not – you're nice, but I'm not really into girls."

"Not really a girl," Hex corrected, yet she smiled. The twist of anxiety in her gut (at least the one associated with Cory) unwound.

"Still. This is a strictly platonic root beer, I promise."

The front door opened. A square of orange light from the setting sun fell across Hex's face before the door closed again. They had a while before dark and the party.

A dim hum took up residence in the room as more people entered, filling up the space with idle words and the background sounds of the various sports being played on the wall-mounted TVs. Hex tapped the toes of her boots against the bar and tried to keep her nervous leg-bouncing to a minimum, going back to picking at her nails instead.

It was anticipation, yes, but there was something else that was getting to her. Something that got under her skin and made the hair on the back of her neck stand on end. She closed her eyes and listened: to their left someone was complaining about the brand of beer the bar had even as he drank it, in the back corner was a couple speaking in tense whispers, down the bar someone called for the volume of a TV to be turned up. But none of it was – there! The low, mechanical crackle of static.

Hex went cold all the way to her tapping toes and shaking fingertips.

"Cory," she whispered between her teeth after making sure the bartender was out of earshot. "Do you hear that?"

Cory paused in sipping his beer to listen. For a moment he tensed up, then glanced down the length of the bar and relaxed again.

"It's just the radio." He tipped his bottle towards the other end of the bar, where an ancient-looking radio was sitting against the wall, but Hex wasn't convinced. She knew this static, knew it in her bones, and her fears were confirmed when the bartender went over to the radio and cranked up the volume to hear the tinny weather report. And still the static buzzed in her ears.

Cory slowly set down his beer. His eyes flickered, counting off exits as he raised his hand to get the bartender's attention.

"It doesn't make any sense," he hissed, completely unnecessarily. Hex knew it didn't make sense. It was the only thought swirling in her mind. A dive bar wasn't exactly a place for the Creech's favorite snack of well-off, well-adjusted people, and they were too far from the park for the static to be this loud if it was manifesting there.

"Hey," the complaining man yelled at the bartender, "what's with the static? I can't hear the game!"

Hex pulled her backpack into her lap.

Before she could unzip it, the constant pink-blue-yellow glow of the neon lights in the windows dimmed. Cory was still trying to get the bartender's attention so that they could slip away, but his other hand rested on the bar, curled into a white-knuckled fist. From the corner of her eye Hex saw the fog leaking in through the cracks in the windows and doors.

"Cory," she murmured urgently, tasting lightning in the air. "Screw the tab, we need to go."

He dropped his arm, the hand instead diving into one of his inner pockets, probably for a weapon or his spirit box. The fog suddenly billowed across the floor, as though being blown by a stiff wind, clumping around the legs of chairs and tables.

"What's all this Halloween shit?" muttered the man at the bar as he glared down at the fog. "It's not even September."

Hex and Cory got up from their seats. Her fingers gripped the zipper of her backpack, ready to go digging for the spirit box at a moment's notice. They didn't even get that much time.

With a sudden, deafening burst of static, the lights and TVs in the bar all blinked out like extinguishing stars, filling the bar with that horrible gray light. And there, in the middle of the room, stood the Creech, its pinpoint eyes staring right at them.

There was stunned silence save the static. Then someone shouted, "What the fuck?!" and the scribbles in its skin began to shift.

Hex grabbed Cory by the lapel of his trench coat and yanked them both sideways, toppling to the floor as the Creech glitched forward. The wooden bar splintered and screams erupted from the other patrons. There were so many other people in the bar and yet the Creech turned to continue its assault, locked in on them like a heat-seeking missile.

Cory made it to his feet first and hauled Hex along with him by her wrist. Hex's head was spinning – this was so far out of pattern, they didn't have time to coordinate with spirit boxes or weapons, and it was still so focused on them, like it was –

"Hex, move!" Cory shouted in her ear, giving her a hard shove towards the door. She ran, Cory on her heels. If the Creech was so dedicated to pursuing them, the other people in the bar would be safer if they fled – right?

They burst through the front door and ran out into the parking lot. The sun was gone, the fog was thick, everything was gray, the taste of ozone in her mouth, Hex's literal worst nightmare come to life, and the plate glass window shattered as the Creech glitched through it in pursuit.

They both instinctively went for Cory's truck. Hex threw herself into the passenger seat just as the Creech glitched to where they had been standing a second before.

Cory cranked the engine, yelling over the static, "Where do we go?"

"Look for light!" Hex shouted back, then twisted around to look out the back window, scanning the flat gray for that late-afternoon orange. She found it behind one of the hedges that blocked the bar from the noise of the main road. "There!"

Hardly had the word left her lips when the passenger window exploded in a cloud of glass shards. The Creech's spindly arm was long enough to reach across the entire cab if it wanted, but instead, its claws went for Hex with lethal intent. She dove sideways, letting herself slide off the seat and into the footwell. Most of its claws slashed into the leather to reveal dense foam insulation. Pain erupted under her left cheekbone and red shone on the shortest of its claws.

"Cory! Go!"

The truck lurched into reverse. Hex smacked back into the seat, leaving a red smear, but was more interested in how the scribbles moved over the Creech's skin as it glitched away from the moving vehicle, writhing against the gray like black maggots.

She felt the impact as Cory hopped the curb and barreled through the hedges. From her position Hex couldn't see outside – all she could do was brace her arms against the sides of the footwell and try not to hit her head.

Orange light spilled across Cory's face. The relief only lasted for a split second before bright white broke through it and Cory yanked the truck to the side, throwing Hex into the wall. A long horn sounded as Cory just barely avoided a collision.

His chest heaved. Warm blood sluiced down Hex's cheek and onto her shirt and jeans – more goddamn bloodstains for her to worry about – and she was vaguely surprised to find that even through the mad dash she still had her backpack.

"Hex?" Cory asked tersely. His eyes were glued to the windshield, his knuckles white around the steering wheel. "Are you okay?"

She took a breath. She felt fuzzy, the pain of the new cut and all the old ones filling her brain with buzzing, her fingers cold, all of her limbs shaking. But she still had her face, so, "Yeah. I'm good. I'll pay to get your seat fixed."

Cory barked out a harsh, slightly hysterical laugh. "As if that matters."

The wind whipped through the broken window. Heart rabbiting in her chest, Hex pulled herself back up onto the passenger seat, disregarding the chunky pieces of safety glass strewn all over it.

"It was hunting us." Her voice sounded distant even to her own ears.

"Looks that way," agreed Cory, mouth pressed into a grim line. He turned his head a little, just to get a glance at her, then did a double take. "Jesus, Hex, your face."

"It's nothing." She stared blankly through the windshield, brain spinning so fast it was a miracle they weren't smelling burning rubber.

The Creech recognized them. It recognized them, remembered them, followed them, and it went in for the kill, disregarding the opportunity to feed in favor of removing them as a threat.

"You were right," she murmured. "It's not just a pattern."

"That's great, I feel very vindicated." Cory slowed at the next light, glancing anxiously in the rear-view mirror. "How long do you think it would take for that thing to catch up with us?"

"I ..."

She had no idea. As far as she knew, it had never done this before. In all the cases she'd studied, if it got interrupted, the Creech would just leave, as it had the night before. She'd never seen an instance where it chased someone. How did it track them down? Was it some sort of energy they gave off that it could follow the same way it found its victims, or was it simpler than that, just following sight or sound like a wolf?

"Hex." Cory snapped his fingers. "Hello, Earth to Hex?"

"I'm thinking," she snapped back.

"What's the shortest time it's ever waited between two manifestations?" he asked. He was driving mostly legally, but pushing the upper limits of acceptable speeding. Like he feared the fog would catch up to them. For all they knew, it would.

"This is. Less than a day between last night and now."

Cory muttered a curse. "We don't know when it decided to look for us or how long it took to find us, so, worst case scenario, it's following us right now and it'll catch up as soon as we stop."

That sparked an idea. Reaching for her backpack, Hex rummaged through it until she found her radio wave detector, already tuned to the Creech's frequency. As soon as she turned it on, it began to drone.

Now it was her turn to curse.

"Any ideas, brainiac?" Cory asked.

Hex chewed on the inside of her unsliced cheek, her chest tight. "It's not acting like it's supposed to. It's never been this aggressive before."

"It's also never been this desperate before. It knows we're coming after it, so it's lashing out, like a cornered wolf."

This entire time she'd been seeing the Creech as a force of nature, like a hurricane – a hurricane didn't feel desperation when its plans were foiled, it didn't pursue certain people, it just went where the wind blew and the conditions were good. It seemed inexorable, bouncing from town to town, moving slowly year after year, decade after decade, too slow and strange to draw much attention to itself.

But it clearly had needs and, if it really was trying to kill them for being a threat, fears. If it had needs and fears, it could be manipulated. And there was one pattern it was still following.

"The fog still came," she said, slowly, like she was afraid of scaring the thought away. "The fog and the static and everything still happened. It changed when and where it manifested, but it couldn't change how."

"So we'll know when it's coming." A sharp, wolfish grin spread across Cory's face. "We can trap it."

9

Headlights

They drove out of town, into the rolling hills that surrounded the city. The air was cool and humid, streaming in through the shattered truck window, blowing Hex's hair back as they searched for a suitable place to lay their trap.

They found it soon enough – an open field of green grass, surrounded by sparse woods. Cory pulled off the road and trundled a few feet into the clearing, the truck jarring and jostling. All the way, the radio wave detector in Hex's lap kept up a soft drone.

They had worked out a plan on the way over. Now all there was left to do was put it in motion.

Cory parked a short distance from the road. He left the headlights on, beaming out into the trees on the other side of the clearing, casting long, deep shadows.

Hex's hands were shaking as she dug out her supplies. Spirit box, flashlight, the humming frequency detector. Cory, handing over his own spirit box, noticed.

"Do you want to be the one in here? I can – "

"No," said Hex, tightening her grip on the little radios. "I want to do this."

To her relief, Cory didn't fight her on it. He just nodded and methodically began loading his pistol to have at the ready. Bullets wouldn't kill the Creech, but they could at least be distracting.

With a final, bracing breath, Hex peeled her jacket from her shoulders. "Look after this for me?"

Her life was one thing, but she wasn't about to risk her most precious possession to the Creech's claws. Cory nodded, hard determination in his eyes.

Hex tossed it into the backseat, where hopefully it would be safe, then before she could think twice about it, climbed out of the truck. Her boots sunk into the soft grass, like it was trying to stop her, hold her in place. The cicadas in the trees were deafening, the crickets loud in her ears, and the dried blood running down her cheek cracked into flakes with every motion of her jaw.

She strode forward and took up a position on the edge of the light, flittering with little insects revealed by and drawn to the beams, turning the spirit boxes as high as they could go. The last of the sun disappeared behind the hills and the moon shone down silver, sliced through by the artificial beams of the headlights.

Cory sat in the truck with the driver's side door open, just as tense as Hex as the minutes passed, the frequency detector trilling louder and louder. She was prepared to wait as long as she had to – ghost hunts were an exercise in pointless patience – but it didn't take long before the lights on the detector were flashing red.

Hex switched it off and let it fall to the grass next to her feet. She kept her shaking legs braced, a spirit box in each hand, thumbs poised over the buttons. The timing had to be perfect. Too soon and the Creech might call off the attack and vanish again. Too late and ...

Fog spilled out from between the trees. It crawled across the grass like malignant hands, grasping at blades of grass to haul itself forward, and the silver light of the moon began to shift into dull gray. It reached Hex's feet, swirled thick around her ankles, and still she kept herself in the same spot. The consuming fear that had devoured her before was nowhere to be found. In its place was determination, braced by the chill of adrenaline in her veins and the taste of ozone on her tongue.

The shadows had vanished with the gray light, making it easier to see the movement behind one of the trees. Familiar, jerking movement that vanished and reappeared behind another tree.

For a second she went back – rough bark against her palms, the stitch burning in her side, the monster jumping from tree to tree as it stalked her – until she latched onto the dim, washed-out glow of the truck's headlights and hauled herself back to reality, just in time for the Creech to glitch into existence before her.

She didn't freeze. She didn't hesitate. The Creech came in swinging and Hex ducked under its arm, jamming her thumb against the power button on her spirit box. The sound that came out was painfully high-pitched and loud enough to send any dogs within five hundred yards running.

The Creech's body jerked, the scribbles on its skin writhing. Silently, it raised its clawed hands again, but Hex was already dropping the spirit box to the ground and diving under its next strike. She stumbled, one knee hitting the ground before the momentum carried her another few staggering steps.

A sharp *crack* rang through the clearing, and the Creech made a sound like nails on a chalkboard. Cory, giving her time to get to the second spot.

She made it there on her knees, slammed the button on the second spirit box, and let it fall to the grass. When she looked up, the Creech was standing over her, the markings on its skin practically vibrating, the edges of its form jolting and jittering like it was trying to move and couldn't, and Hex's hands shook with hope.

The plan was working.

The Creech vanished for a split second and came back facing the truck, and Hex cried out to Cory over the cacophony of static.

"Turn it on!"

Cory hopped back into the driver's seat. Even more noise came pouring from the vehicle as he cranked the volume, the radio set to the same frequency as the spirit boxes.

The Creech's body blurred with the speed at which it was trying and failing to get away. A low groan reverberated out from it, in stark contrast to all the shrieking radios – the ominous creak of metal slowly giving way to great pressure.

Leaving the spirit box in the grass, Hex pushed herself back and out of range of the claws, then staggered to her feet. She couldn't believe it – it actually worked!

Then the Creech reached out with its long arms, its movement stuttering like a storyboard sketch, and with surgical precision, smashed the second spirit box to pieces with its claws.

Time seemed to stand still as the sound cut out in the broken box. Those pinpoint eyes locked on Hex, who stared back with her heart threatening to choke her.

Of course, said the little voice at the back of her mind as she stood there, her boots glued to the ground. *If it's smart enough to hunt, it's smart enough to break something it doesn't like. Stupid, stupid –*

Crack!

The Creech jerked and Hex's head snapped around. Cory was standing in the headlights, the only thing casting a shadow in the gray void, the barrel of his gun trained on the Creech. He pulled the trigger again, making Hex nearly jump out of her skin, before the Creech let out a metallic grinding sound and glitched ten feet closer to Cory.

Nauseating adrenaline suddenly ignited into fury. The image of Mason, helpless in the monster's grip, burned away the fear keeping her feet pinned.

She wasn't going to lose anyone else.

It took only a few seconds to close the distance. The blade of her knife tore into its scribbled skin with a sound like ripping paper. There was no resistance to its flesh; the knife went through it so easily, tearing a ragged wound clear across the Creech's back. And on the inside there was ... nothing. It was hollow.

The Creech's huge hand slammed into her side, knocking Hex to the ground with a hard *thunk.* Pain radiated from her ribs in a starburst and she couldn't tell if it was from the impact with the hand or the ground, but what did it matter? It was looming over her with that grin full of wolf's teeth and for a moment she was frozen, just like in her dream.

There was a dim shout, muffled by the ringing in Hex's ears and the fog that sat so thick in the air and in her throat. Then, with a flash of green and orange, Cory threw himself bodily into the Creech.

It almost seemed like it would topple over. At the last second it went incorporeal, letting Cory hit the ground and roll, before reappearing over him with a burst of static.

It looked so much like it had that day in Mason's bedroom, all bent over, skin squirming like it was alive, leaning down closer for its meal. She could've lost herself again if it weren't for the pain: in her side, on her back, on her face, in her knuckles where she gripped her knife like it was welded to her skin.

Hex grabbed a fistful of grass and hauled herself upright.

Cory, ever prepared, twisted until he could pull a slender blade of his own from one of his pockets and plunge it into the Creech's side. It tore the skin just like Hex's knife had, and the creaking groan returned as Cory slashed at it again and again. The back of Hex's shirt was soaked with dew and cold sweat.

In three steps she was behind it. It saw her coming this time and vanished.

She spun around just in time to duck beneath its claws. The wounds Cory had left across its abdomen were already knitting themselves closed again as it had with the bullets, but through the connecting strands, she still saw nothing but air and the white of its skin on the other side. Like a monster made of paper mâché, some kid's Halloween craft project gone wrong. So terribly, terribly wrong.

"Stay down!" Cory shouted. A second later Cory's knife spun over her head, aimed at the Creech's chest. She expected it to tear right through and keep going, but to both of their surprise, the blade struck something and ricocheted off, a dim sound like a ringing bell reverberating from the strike.

This was her chance. Hex sprang upwards, aiming her knife at the same spot. It went through the skin just as easily as before, only to stop with a jarring impact she felt all the way up her arm.

The Creech froze. Its expression didn't change, but Hex imagined she could see shock in the squirming lines of its body.

Bracing her other hand on the hilt, Hex slowly twisted the blade around the obstruction, carving through scant paper resistance. And the Creech just stood there, craned over her as if in a trance, with a new sound spilling out of its hollow throat – a long, low keen, crackling in a staticky death-rattle. The fog flickered, and Hex glimpsed stars overhead.

With one final burst of strength, she wrenched the metal object from the Creech's chest. It thudded into the grass at her feet, leaving behind a gaping hole with black edges. Edges that were rapidly spreading.

Hex and the Creech both stared at each other as the black spread like spilled ink on paper, climbing and branching through the fibers of skin, engulfing its signature squiggle marks that, for the first time, were perfectly still. The dark spread down its arms and coated its claws, up its neck and over its teeth, its eyes vanishing under its onslaught, all while it stood there, unmoving. For a moment it stood, a stark black statue against the gray light.

Then the Creech folded in on itself like a house of cards. The black particles fell around her, leaving black smears on the backs of her hands and her bare arms. The gray light faded and fell away.

The monster was gone.

10

Sunlight

Unmuffled by the fog, Cory's ecstatic whoop rang across the clearing. "We did it!" he cried, throwing his arms into the air. "We killed it! We actually *fucking killed it*!" He spun in a circle, his trench coat flaring out and raining stray pieces of grass, and when that wasn't enough, took off at a sprint, cheering all the way.

Hex didn't move an inch. She stared down at the pile of dust, the buzzing in her skull even louder than the truck radio and the remaining spirit box somewhere in the grass. She half expected the pile to start moving, to piece itself back together and call the fog back, but everything was still. Goosebumps pricked up her bare arms. The stillness was almost worse.

The shine of the headlights caught something in the grass between her feet. Slowly, smothering winces at the pain that was making itself known as the adrenaline faded, she knelt down to retrieve it.

It was the thing that she carved out of the Creech's chest.

She stood up, turning it over in her hands. It was about the size of her palm, made of cool metal with tiny dents and divots. When she held it up to the headlights, its shape became clear: it was a little metal heart, imperfectly cast and covered in rust. Hex could feel the questions rising, held back only by the fog of pain and broken dissociation, but before she could fall down the rabbit hole, Cory came sprinting back up to her, a wild grin on his face.

"We did it!" he cheered again, and threw his arms around her. He probably would've picked her up and spun her around if she hadn't let out a choked cry.

Immediately he let go and stepped back, his expression flipping to concern in less than a second. "What's wrong? Are you hurt?" One hand was still on her shoulder. Hex reached up and grasped his wrist while she tried to get her breath back enough to answer, the metal heart secure in her other hand.

"Ribs. Might be broken."

"Shit, sorry," Cory hissed. "How's your breathing? Can you talk?"

"Y-yeah, I can breathe, just hurts."

"Okay, here. Let's get back to the truck."

"Wait," she said, balking, staring at the pile of ashes. "What if it's not dead? What if it regenerates or something – "

"Hex. It's a pile of dust."

"Still – !"

Cory turned and put his other hand on her shoulder, making her meet his solemn, firm eyes.

"Listen to me. You're holding its heart in your hand." He smiled again, blindingly bright, and if Hex wasn't mistaken there were tears in his eyes. "You avenged them. *All* of them."

Her little brother's face flashed through her mind. Her parents' bed, occupied by empty clothes. Suddenly, she felt like crying too, and before she could stop them, the tears fell, leaving warm trails in their wake and stinging across the slice on her cheek.

"We did," she managed to croak out.

Cory made a sympathetic sound and squeezed her shoulder. "Come on. Let's get out of here."

***

The diner was on the edge of the city, one of those classic places trying to emulate a time long past, open 24/7. Bandaged and bedraggled as they were, they surprisingly didn't get any comments from the waitress when she directed them to a booth next to a window. All she said was, "I'll be quick with that coffee," and winked before rushing back to the kitchen.

Thankfully, Hex's ribs were bruised, not broken. If they were broken, she would've had to go to the hospital and answer too many questions. As it was, she just ached, the fresh bandage on her cheek pulling when she moved her jaw. Maybe she could bum a couple more painkillers off of Cory before she moved on.

That thought made her stomach twist, but she resolutely ignored the quiet dread beginning to form. Having someone around had been nice, especially when she didn't need to watch what she said around them as far as hunting went, but she always knew it wasn't going to last. Cory needed her to hunt the Creech and that was it. An alliance of convenience.

"Here we are." The waitress had reappeared with a full coffee pot and filled their cups generously. "What can I get ya?"

Cory ordered a mountain of pancakes. Hex went for French toast and downed two cups of coffee before the food even made it to the table. Neither of them said a word as they ate, but Hex's brain never slowed down.

She still had questions that needed answering, a few hypotheses to chase, but first she needed to go back to her regular hunting – this little sabbatical had put a serious dent in her meager funds. Maybe she could convince Cory to drop her off at the nearest bus stop, or even better, a truck stop. Her hair could use a wash, and she had black smears of Creech dust on her hands like charcoal.

Once the food was gone, Hex's hand found its way back to the metal heart. She held it under the table, memorizing every dent and streak of rust. Somewhere under the buzz of bottomless coffee and barely-held-back dissociation, there was a hint of frustration – *they'd finally killed the damn thing and still it left more questions* – but she passed it back and forth between her hands, unable to let it go.

Cory was the picture of contentment as he sipped his coffee, watching the cars rush by and the stars slowly retreat from the dawn threatening the horizon. His fingers tapped against the table, probably eager to get back on the road, back to life now that it was all over.

Hex felt staticky. Too many emotions crackling under her skin.

With a little shake of his head, Cory opened his mouth. "Hey, I've been thinking – "

Something buzzed. Cory made an annoyed sound and dug his phone out of his pocket. His glare faltered when he saw the caller ID.

"Sorry, I should probably answer this." He slid out of the booth and headed for the front door. Hex kept watching the dawn.

She needed to get a grip. The sleep deprivation probably wasn't helping. She rubbed her eyes, scrubbed her hand over her face, bringing the smell of the rusted metal heart with it.

Cory came into view, pacing the length of the diner as he talked. He smiled at something the person on the other end said, then laughed.

Hex was perfectly happy being on her own. She'd been alone for a long time and she was used to it. It shouldn't be hard for her to say goodbye to Cory and hop on the next bus to wherever another ghost (or family of raccoons) was plaguing someone's home.

So why did the thought of parting make her throat tighten?

She sighed and tucked the metal heart into her pocket. Cory was so happy that the Creech was dead – he probably wouldn't want her around if she was going to keep going after the mystery. Like he said back in the hotel room, he just wanted it to be over, and it was. So they were too. She looked away, plastering a neutral expression on her face, and started looking up bus routes on her phone.

Eventually, Cory came back to the booth. Hex didn't ask, just glanced at him, but he answered the unspoken question. "It was a friend of mine who lives in Southern Texas. He was saying that he'd heard rumors about a neighborhood having a chupacabra problem."

Hex snorted. "Classic Texas."

"Yeah," agreed Cory, but his eyes were serious when he looked up. "He also said his daughter saw a ghost walking around in the desert. Scared the crap out of her."

She swallowed, fighting to keep her tone light. "Sounds pretty serious."

Don't get your hopes up.

"It's kind of perfect, because I was thinking" – Cory fiddled with a tiny plastic container of creamer, rolling it back and forth across the table – "maybe we could stick together for a while? I mean, we worked pretty well together, and I think we could both stand to diversify, so to speak, and that way we could get more jobs, and you wouldn't have to take buses everywhere. So, you know, just a thought."

The static calmed, and a smile grew over Hex's lips.

"I'd love to."

Cory let out the breath he'd been holding. "Thank God. I don't think I could stand singing Bon Jovi to myself for another road trip."

That pulled a laugh out of her. "Don't worry. I have plenty of recommendations that were written this century." Relief was light in her stomach like helium, and Cory looked at her with shining eyes. The life of a hunter was such a lonely one, after all. Maybe Hex wasn't the only one who felt it.

"So, partners then?" he asked, offering a fist across the table. Hex bumped it with her own.

"Partners."

Acknowledgements

I owe my sincere gratitude to my friends, Athena and Alika. Without Athena's help this book would not exist, and without Alika, neither would Hex.

About the Author

Jayde Layne is an ASU graduate, now living in Flagstaff, Arizona. Her work focuses on horror and dark fiction.

The Windows to a Shapeshifter's Soul

Booker G.A. Feniks

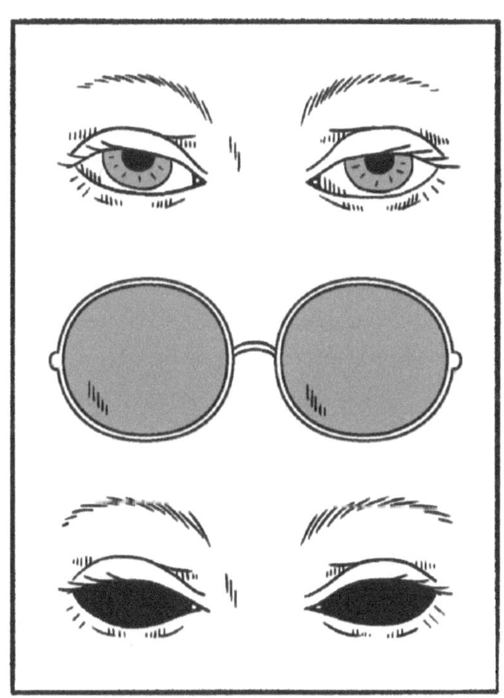

Cover Design by Nicole Alessi

Cover Illustration by Hen Towers

I dedicate this book to my family, and to my grandmother who never got to see me grow into the man I am today, but without whom I never would have gotten where I am today.

And I dedicate it to myself because, through it all, I always stayed true to who I was, and if I can't be proud of what I have accomplished, no one else will.

Contents

Content Warnings

This story contains the following content:

- Captivity
- Restraints
- Dehumanisation
- Torture
- Character Death
- Death of parents

If this book isn't for you, no worries! But if it is, we hope you enjoy this story about a magizoologist and his new job ...

1

Josef, Brooke, and Vanja

He felt their eyes watching him, multiple pairs that bored into the back of his head. Tracing his steps through the apartment, homing in on him wherever he turned. He moved with slow, languid steps, weaving between piles of discarded books and haphazardly placed furniture. All the while they watched him, those piercing eyes. Following him, moving through the empty space he left behind him, silent footsteps echoing in his mind.

Then she pounced, and Josef crashed to the ground with a resounding laugh. His cackle joined the excited yipping of his three-headed dog. His small, rustic apartment was filled with the sounds of their combined joy.

"Spot, Spot!" He pushed at the three great maws yawning over him, dripping hot saliva onto his freshly pressed shirt. The central head, with its little pink bowtie, whined and pushed at Josef's arms, trying to smoosh itself under his hands. The left head, with a bright red bow snuggled between its ears, was snuffling at the side of Josef's head, drooling incessantly in its excitement. The right head, with a purple bow attached to its right ear, was licking her master's face, while her tail was trailing a streak of fire through the air as it wagged and wagged.

"Stop it," Josef breathed out, trying to grab some air. "You'll set off the fire alarm again, silly pup." With a great push and many whines, he managed to dislodge Spot, trying to pet all three heads at once with only his two human hands. She was bouncing around him, barking in three deep, baritone voices, her coal-black fur soft under his touch.

"I was just getting you your food," Josef admonished her, pressing his finger against the warm, wet nose of the central head. Her coarse tongue darted out and almost swallowed his entire wrist whole, leaving hot slobber to cool on his shirt cuff. The glasses he lost in the kerfuffle he found under the coffee table. He gave the dark lenses a cursory dust-off and inspected the thin, metallic frames. They sat securely atop his crooked nose, hand-made specifically for his face, hiding from the world his russet eyes. Without the second set of eyelids his full-blooded dragon kin had, he found the world painfully bright, and his eyes were sensitive to almost everything. His apartment stayed dark, with dimmed lights and pulled-down curtains. Luckily, Spot was also used to the darkness, still dancing around his legs, rubbing her thick body against his abdomen. He could only hope the fur wouldn't show on his black slacks.

He set about feeding Spot her morning portion of hot coals and bison flank. She had three bowls made of iron, decorated with little coloured symbols corresponding to each head. Whenever Josef slept in late, she would grab all three bowls and jump on him, hanging them over his head as he tried to rub the sleep from his eyes. She loved those bowls, handcrafted just for her, the way they clanked and thunked. It was the very first thing his uncle taught him about cerberi: they had sensitive hearing, and they loved sound-based toys.

There was a picture on the mantelpiece, right above Spot's bowls, that featured his uncles. Brooke Ryan and Josef Braun were a handsome pair: a six feet, two inches, hairy, Irish blacksmith, and a five feet, six inches, nerdy, German dog trainer. They met through his mother, Brooke's long-suffering twin sister.

Uncle Josef had been the most famous magizoologist of his generation and the owner of an award-winning show cerberus. It was on Josef's own birthday that his uncle gifted him Spot II, the descendant of a long line of show dogs. Alongside her came the three metal bowls, Uncle Brooke having worked on them for weeks. Josef still remembered the way his uncles stood together, arms around each other's waists, heads pressed against one another. His mother had called it love at first sight, love until the very end. Watching them stand over him, Spot in his arms, they looked like the happiest pair of people in the world. Josef had felt honoured when he was asked to help design their gravestone. Love like that only comes once in a lifetime.

Spot bumped against his legs, her bowls already empty, pulling Josef out of his reverie.

"Shit, I'm gonna be late!"

In record time he had run a brush through his curly, auburn hair, dug out his house keys from the deepest recesses of his couch, and left the house in a dress shirt still covered in drying cerberus slobber. *I'm so not getting this job.*

2

THE FACILITY FOR THE CONSERVATION OF MAGICAL CREATURES

The Facility for the Conservation of Magical Creatures (known as the FCMC amongst the common rabble) loomed above Josef like an omen. The Behemoth of dark metal glinted in the morning sunlight, its many windowed eyes staring down at the man approaching it. The massive double doors were an unwelcome invitation into the belly of a beast that burrowed deep beneath the earth. The weaving tails of corridors and hallways that stretched beneath the small city were only rumours, but each rumour held a grain of truth within it. The corporate, metal Behemoth was just a taste of the beast that was the FCMC, and Josef willingly approached it. He felt like a knight of old approaching a dragon, in the days where people still thought of dragons as mindless, brutish beasts. He felt like Sir Thaddeus the Dragon Friend, the first man to ever study his scaled foes. The very man who brought the world of humans out of a dark, deadly, terrified age, into the age of enlightenment and knowledge.

Sir Thaddeus' face was plastered upon a plate made of gold hanging above the double doors of the entrance. His handsome, almost kingly profile was turned towards the profile of another man, his expression severe. The smiling, handsome face of Charles Young contrasted with the stern face of his ancestor, both of them framing a ring of black metal inserted into the golden plate. Both grandfather and grandson, the first man to study a dragon and the man behind the genius of the FCMC, stared at the curling body of a snake biting its own tail.

Every time Josef looked at the old logo of Limbo Laboratories, he couldn't help but shiver. Why anyone would incorporate the symbol of such an organisation, old and dead as it was, into their own signage was beyond him. How much they differed, with the FCMC striving for the protection of all magical beings. The Limbo Labs, meanwhile, were better off forgotten in the annals of history.

Josef walked through the double doors of the FCMC building. He pushed his glasses further up his crooked nose and ran a hand through his curly hair once more. He caught a glimpse of himself in the reflection of a bell at the welcome desk. His dark, olive skin stood out against the bright blue dress shirt he wore. His skin-toned lips were turning red from where he was worrying away at them with his teeth, picking at the dry skin there until he could faintly taste his own blood. His cheeks were pleasantly round, but he noticed that his collarbones stuck out too much. His mother's funeral, he realised for the first time in weeks, had taken far more out of him than he had anticipated. He supposed that he'd needed to see the effect for himself to believe it, despite all the times his sister Vanja and his father pointed it out to him.

Out of the corner of his eye he saw the glint of metal, and he focused his attention on a statue placed in the centre of the room. The tall, looming presence of Sir Thaddeus was much more appealing than his own visage, with its broad shoulders and thick chest. It was mounted upon a base bearing a plaque with his name and was held up securely by the steel cords attached to its back.

"Can I help you?" The receptionist appeared behind the welcome desk before he so much as leant towards the bell. Maybe just looking at it was enough to summon the clearly bored, possibly underpaid young woman with a drawling, accented voice. She scratched the corner of her red lips with an equally red, manicured nail, and the motion made her very shiny, very golden hoop earrings swing. Josef wasn't sure what was more glaring about her: the almost eye-bleeding shade of red that she seemed to prefer or the far-too-overgrown horns growing out of her head. He didn't even think to mention the horns; he doubted that she didn't know. Still, poor girl, had the money for a manicure but couldn't even find a good buccicure place in town.

"I'm here for a job appointment." He coughed, fumbling with his wallet and managing to not drop his ID when giving it to the receptionist. She didn't take it, didn't even move her plump hand away from her mouth, just took a cursory glance at the thin, plastic rectangle, and then looked back at him.

"Right, nephew of the hellhound trainer, yes?" She quirked her red lip up into something that almost resembled a smile, and Josef wondered if Vanja, if she were there with him, would like her.

Then he realised what she had said and felt his cheeks flush hotly. "I, uh ... "

"It's your name; it gives you away." She giggled, and it sounded melodic, almost tempting. "Not that it's not a nice name, but certainly not very common. Not the whole combination, at least." She added the last sentence after a moment of silence, in which Josef tried his best not to choke on his quickening breaths. He pushed his glasses further up his nose, bunching up the fabric of his slacks with his fist.

"Nice eyes, though. Got a dragon in your family?"

He swallowed and let out a breath. "Yes, actually. Adopted great-grandfather, passed on his genes through the paternal line."

"Explains the lack of wings," she added, her grin only growing wider. "I'm a satyr, hence the horns. Full-blooded, but most people don't really get to see the hooves."

She didn't seem to mind his little snort or his shy smile. "Always nice to meet someone else with non-human ancestry. We seem to gravitate to each other, almost."

"It is nice, isn't it? You'd think we'd be more widespread by now, what with it being the twenty-first century. You know, with the internet and all." She sent him a wink, and he realised that her eyeshadow was of a similar shade of red as her lips and nails. "That why you're interested in working with magical creatures?"

His smile became more earnest. He could feel his eyes crinkle at the edges, slightly lifting up his glasses. "No, actually. You see, I originally wanted to be an athlete like my mother, but right before her death she told me I didn't need to be like her to make her proud and ... "

"Uhu ... " She breathed out slowly, giving him a look he couldn't quite place. He held his breath for a moment, looking at her through the dark lenses of his glasses, fiddling with a stray thread from his trousers.

"My sister gave me the idea, inspired by my uncle. The hellhound trainer one," he eventually said, breathing out each word slowly and deliberately. She gave him a nod, no longer smiling at him, no longer softly gazing at him with slightly closed eyelids, a finger pressing gently against the corner of her lip.

"Well." She coughed, looking back to her computer. "Hate for you to be late, talking to me like that. I'll let the guide know you're here."

"The guide?"

When she looked back up at him, it was with a blank look. "The tour guide."

"I'm sorry, I came here for a job interview."

"No." She kept staring at him. "You have an appointment."

"Where does a tour factor into this?"

"You'll be joining four other interviewees. You'll be touring around the facility, being introduced to the magical creatures you'll be working with." She paused, and when Josef didn't respond, she continued, "It's how Mr Young wants it done. He wants hands-on interviews, not just a conversation behind a desk." She turned back to her computer, her blank stare unwavering but her head swivelling downwards and to the side. Josef rubbed at his temple, trying to make sense of it. He felt as if he was going mad, as if this were something he obviously should have known.

Vanja and he had done research. It was true that the job searching website had mentioned a 'job appointment' as opposed to a 'job interview', but Josef had assumed this was a mistyping, an intern who made a mistake, nothing to focus on, not really.

The receptionist with the red … everything waved him over to the elevator and told him which button he was supposed to press. His stomach clenched when the elevator jerked and began moving, and he wasn't sure if it was just the locomotion or if he was making one big mistake.

3

Galaxies in Your Eyes

He arrived at a room with five other people already waiting for him. He went to open his mouth, bumble out an apology, but he was silenced by a sharp-looking woman sitting at the head of a meeting table. She waved him into a seat next to a man, about his own age, with a blue tie and a diamond earring. The only thing Josef could think about as he sat down next to him was just how much those two accessories clashed.

"As I was saying," the woman at the front said with a voice like the beginning of an earthquake, and a severe expression that terrified Josef, "here at the Facility we value hands-on work above all else. In your job working with the endangered animals we keep at the Facility, you will come in contact with beasts that you won't find in a regular zoo. Many of them are dangerous; some of them are even deadly. Very few of them are peaceful or harmless, but even with such creatures you must ensure that you act accordingly. That is why the Facility does not conduct regular interviews. All of you already possess knowledge of, and even experience with, working with magical creatures of some kind. The thing that will set apart those who will and those who won't get the job is the ability to adapt and make split-second decisions. We need to ensure that you are prepared to work with the creatures entrusted to us, and today you will do so in a contained environment. If you do well here, you may look forward to further training and a bright future in the conservation of magical creatures. Now, are we ready to head down to the veterinary level?"

All four of the people around the table nodded, and Josef followed suit only a few seconds later.

During the tour guide's lengthy speech, he had a good chance to look at who he was competing with. Out of the four, the person he sat beside was the only other man in the group. The other three interviewees were women, one also his age, another that looked barely out of college, and one who looked older than his mother.

The youngest, although looking to be barely eighteen, must have had relevant experience, meaning she was most likely very confident in her skills. She was dressed in a pink skirt and a black shirt that reminded him of something one of Vanja's exes would wear, with pentagram earrings reminding him of a completely different ex.

The oldest woman had silver shot through her blonde hair and wrinkles in the corners of her eyes. Out of them all, he expected her to be the most likely to get a job. With her age came experience, and Josef could only imagine what sort of experience this woman had.

The last woman, the one more his age, had freckles and wine-coloured hands. The scales that travelled from her fingertips to the edges of her wrists were striking in colour, and their particular pattern upon her palms made him think that she was a demon. And yet he was second-guessing himself. The work of a magizoologist required patience and focus, traits demons weren't known to possess. She had an ace up her sleeve, he could feel it.

The fourth person in the room, the man with the diamond earring, was handsome, even despite the blue tie. He had scars all across his fingers and his wrists that stood out starkly against his dark skin, and Josef could immediately tell he was a former mage vet's apprentice. The scar over his right pinkie was shaped like a baby cockatrice beak, and the burn across his left wrist was most likely the work of an egg-bound phoenix.

I'm not getting this job, Josef thought to himself again.

***

He felt their eyes on him, countless gazes boring into him, watching from behind thin bars. They trailed after him as he meandered between the medical equipment strewn about the many emptied-out rooms. He was stuck at the back of the tour group, surprised that they weren't being introduced to any other vets or caretakers.

Up ahead, the tour guide was talking in short, clipped sentences, things Josef couldn't quite catch. He knew one thing: no one was allowed to touch anything, not until they were authorised. Later on, they were each supposed to be assigned a creature, something small and harmless like a golden goose or a rainbow fish. They were supposed to show their knowledge of handling magical creatures, but Josef wasn't thrilled about it. He would have preferred a basilisk or maybe a sprite but knew he would probably end up explaining to the tour guide the science behind jackalope fur resembling that of a common deer.

He was also told not to pay too much attention to any of the animals around him. Many of them were shy and got nervous when people looked at them. From the brief glimpses he allowed himself, he found a veritable menagerie. All the animals were in cages of different shapes and sizes. They had blankets and food bowls, plastic water bottles hanging off the thin bars. Some had IVs, others wore visible bandages, while most just seemed lethargic or tired. Josef felt his heart hurt at the sight of them. He noticed a larger cage with a sickly-looking unicorn without its horn, and he had to bite down on his knuckle to keep from crying. In another corner he found himself enamoured by a three-headed viper bearing the scars of a fight upon its glistening, scaled body.

Then there was the kitten. A small, black, thin kitten. It was in an impossibly tiny cage on wheels, being moved by three different scientists. They carried it past adolescent draconids, a tank holding a kelpie, and a giant, monstrous wolf the size of a car. Its black, bottomless eyes managed to catch his gaze, unblinking as it scrutinised him. Josef felt a chill run down his spine, a hand jumping to his throat where he was struggling to swallow. The tiny kitten wore a tiny muzzle that linked to a chain attached to the top of the cage. The chain was long enough to let it lay down but not long enough to let it walk to the edges of the cage. It scratched at the floor with mindless abandon, staring at Josef all the while. It was as if he couldn't look away, as if he was being hypnotised. This was a creature he didn't recognise, and yet he felt as if he knew it. Inwardly, in another plane of existence, he knew it, but the words weren't there to describe it.

"Mr Ryan."

Josef bit down on his tongue, swivelling around to the rest of the group. The tour guide was looking at him, her mouth forming a thin line and her eyebrows downturned.

"Yes?"

"I would be very happy if you stayed with the group," she hissed through clenched teeth, "and didn't look at the creatures like I had asked you to. Especially not in the Dangerous section."

Josef gulped and nodded, hanging his head and returning to his spot at the end of the line. He looked back, and the scientists carrying that thing were already gone. As he walked, listening to the droning words of the tour guide, he couldn't get his mind off it. The chain, the muzzle, the eyes. The little tag at the bottom of the cage read Subject-20-465 and nothing else. No species, no age, nothing that he noticed on all the other animals. And those eyes.

As the group turned the corner, Josef looked up and saw a corridor lined with doors, each one with a name plaque at the top beneath a small window. These were offices, and as Josef walked past one, he saw a poster hanging up on the other side of the little window. The poster was of a pink and blue nebula against a black and starry background, and it was in that moment that Josef knew.

The kitten had eyes that reflected the stars.

4

Expectations and Firebirds

"Brooke, come sit!" Vanja's lilting voice brought Josef out of his thoughts, her pale face lit up and her slender arm pointing to the seat beside her. Her long, black hair was put up into an elaborate braid she had, very likely, done herself, and her dark blue lipstick was perfectly contrasted with her pale greenish-blue eyes. She had a slight accent as she spoke, trilling out her Rs in a way that Josef always liked the sound of. It was as if she was purring every time she called him Brooke.

Jozić Vanja had been a Croatian painter in her youth. By 'youth', she really meant that she had won a few art competitions at school at the age of five. In actuality, she was his adopted younger sister, Spot's favourite person in all the world, and the daughter his father, Dante, had always wanted. She spoiled the three-headed pup, and Josef never knew where she got all the money to buy her so many treats. Josef thought she never paid rent and sold her art online to fancy art critics for way more than it was worth. And she had enough free time on her hands to find him a job. Uncle Josef would've been proud.

"We've been coming to Déjà Brew a lot lately. Who caught your eye this time, Rus?" The smell of fresh coffee wafted out of the door to the quaint coffee shop they sat outside of. A few tables down from them, a teenage couple was making googly eyes at each other, holding hands atop the little plastic tables that looked like they had been carved out of wood, legs and all.

"New cashier fell into my eye. He's so cute, breath of fresh air after my ex." She giggled as she sipped her decaf, trailing a long, black nail over the edge of the coffee cup. She was wearing a low-cut, black dress and cord bracelets. Her earrings were the most casual thing about her, plain silver studs.

"So, he emo or goth?"

"Goth!" Vanja squealed, squeezing her fists and shaking them in excitement. "I waited to bring out my goth clothes since Julia moved back to Poland."

Josef nodded, picking up the foam cup Vanja bought for him before he got there. "He from around here, then?" He pushed his glasses further up his nose, then traced his eyes over the scene inside the café. He didn't see any cashier that looked even remotely goth.

"I don't know. Yet! I will find out, you just watch. But enough about me, how did job interview go!"

The coffee suddenly became too bitter for him, and he had to set it back down with a pronounced grimace. "Doubt I'll get it." He swiped at his mouth with the back of his hand, and let his glasses slide down his nose to look Vanja right in her black-rimmed eyes. "Although I doubt any of us will get the job."

"Why? What happen?"

"Oh, I let my curiosity get the better of me and broke the rule of not looking at the creatures." When Vanja gave him a blank look, he cleared his throat. The next five minutes were taken up with him explaining, in detail, exactly what he knew about the weird interview structure at the FCMC.

"Make sense, yes."

Josef hadn't touched his coffee since he began explaining, but in that moment, he didn't need it to choke. "They could have at least told us in advance! I wore my best shirt for this interview."

"It have Spot slobber on it, can't be best shirt. One of best shirts, I would understand, but not best shirt." Vanja took a sip of her drink, staring down at him over the rim of her cup. The little shrug she did had Josef's blood pressure rising.

"Will you let me finish explaining?"

"Go ahead." And then she smiled, and he could no longer make himself feel mad.

He cleared his throat once more, took another sip of his coffee, and carried on, "Well, we eventually ended up in a medical room. I was on thin ice already at that point, and I didn't have high hopes for what was to come. We were to go alphabetically, however, and I ended up being last, so I had the chance to see how well the other four people did. The handsome guy with the diamond earring was given a jackalope to handle. Turns out, he knew absolutely nothing about non-avian monsters, and I had to show him how to hold the poor bunny. The tour guide recommended that he go work for a magical aviary instead."

Vanja let out a twinkling giggle, and her eyes went blank for a few seconds. *Artists.* Josef shook his head. She always drifted off when thinking too deeply.

Then, when she came back to the world of the living, she ripped a small notebook out of her purse and began sketching in it. Josef gave her a few moments to get her thoughts out onto the paper before he carried on with his story. With each tale he had to give her a pause, time to commit her imagination to a physical form, before he could move on again.

"The one that reminded me of your exes ... "

"Pink skirt and pentagram earrings."

"Yes, thank you. She looked the youngest but turned out to be older than the rest of us combined."

"Ooooh, really?" Vanja's eyes were twinkling as she looked at him. Her elbows were firmly stuck to the table, and her chin rested in her open palms.

"Yes, she's actually a fairy. Out of the five of us, she's the most likely to get the job. Well, maybe. Fairies, or fae-folk, are beings of pure magic, and the most sentient of the fae species, and the only ones able to take on a human size and shape. They don't get along well with other fae species."

"What did she get?"

"A brownie."

"What?"

"Remember when I told you about the domovoy?"

"Oh! Little house helpers!"

"Yes. I had to calm it down for her, because the two kept on screaming at each other in the fae tongue." At the reminder of that he reached up to massage the bridge of his nose. His migraine was returning, and he doubted it would leave anytime soon.

"We live in nation of UK, does FCMC get many fae?"

"Too many for a fairy to comfortably work for them."

"Tell me of demon lady next."

"Yes, well. As I told you previously, demons are known for their impulsiveness, like fairies are known for their egos, humans for their competitiveness, dragons for their greed, h—... "

"Lecture me later, carry on with story, Brooke." She gave him a pout and her lips looked like a blueberry. Over her shoulder, Josef saw the young couple standing up and leaving. He didn't even notice how he was forlornly looking after them, until Vanja was snapping her fingers before his eyes.

"Sorry, right. Ahem." He slipped his glasses off his nose before continuing, "The demon lady, I think you would have liked her. She wasn't impulsive at all, and actually was the calmest of us all, I think. Her downfall was her, well ... her hydrophobia."

"Her ... fear of water?"

"Yes. I know, an elemental creature, sort of weird to have a fear of one of the elements. But humans can have mechanophobia and we're the ones that make the robots, so anything is possible, really. Anyway, they gave her a hippocampus. She burst into tears."

"Poor dear. You know I am half rusałka, I adore water. Is perfectly safe, really." She flashed him her pointed teeth, and he bared his own fangs back at her. His weren't nearly as noticeable or impressive, but the burst of smoke from his nose easily did the trick.

"That's why phobias are irrational fears, Rus," he explained over Vanja's laughter. "She was so scared, I had to come over to help her calm down. You know how I always carry a coal in my pocket for Spot, so I gave it to her to fiddle with and she really ended up liking setting it on fire and extinguishing it. I even let her keep it."

"Aww. You're sunshine, Brooke. What about last person?"

"Ah, the woman who seemed older than my mother. She was another human, like the diamond earring guy. I thought she would have gotten the job; I was so sure. Someone who has lived that long surely would have a lot of experience."

"What happened then?"

"Well, she was given a baku."

"Cute dream eaters with little elephant trunks."

"Yes, the one you drew me a picture of for my twenty-ninth birthday. It had eaten a dream that didn't sit right with it and needed help expelling it. The woman didn't ... she didn't know how that works."

"Let me guess: she thought baku give her bad dreams?" She had that cheeky smile on her face again. Those rusałka genes came out the strongest when she smiled. Her pale, blueish gums were pulled back to further elongate her sharp, pointed teeth. Her light greenish eyes were the colour of the moss that grew along the riverbanks, and they crinkled at the edges when she grinned.

Josef took another sip of his coffee and hummed thoughtfully, messing around with his glasses, moving them from one side of the table to the other. "Mhm, which isn't at all how these creatures function, after all. They only eat dreams, and they especially like eating nightmares to help people. They don't give people nightmares."

"So, she didn't understand basic of how baku even work?" Vanja was sounding gleeful now, replacing her chin atop the little bridge she made with her intertwined fingers, her bony elbows resting atop the table.

"No, and that was when we found out that she applied for the wrong job." Josef's eyes flitted between Vanja and the waiter who had exited the café while they talked, hands full of packed trays and a pleasant smile on his tanned, bearded face. "She wanted to apply for a secretary job, but something went wrong, there was a glitch in the system. I ended up helping the baku instead."

"Aw, poor dear. Did she get transferred?"

The waiter dropped the trays off at the only other taken table, before a skeletal young woman. "The tour guide said she would talk to HR about it, but that the woman shouldn't count on getting an interview. She had multiple chances to correct the mistake and didn't take them." Josef watched out of the corner of his eye as the woman unhinged her jaws to a ridiculous degree, before swallowing the food presented to her right before the waiter. It took her only a few seconds, and once she was done her skin was flushed, and she had gained a healthy chubbiness to her cheeks. She gave the waiter a pleasant smile, and he gave her a knowing one back, before picking the trays up. However interesting the snake demon was, it was the waiter, as he was leaving, that held onto Josef's attention. The leg braces he wore over his work boots were shiny, and his eyes were a pleasant shade of purple.

"True, true. Oh, but Brooke! How did you do!" Vanja's yell brought him back to his own table and back to his long-since-cold coffee.

"I was given a raróg."

Vanja's eyes began to shine. "Song raróg or flame raróg?"

"Song raróg, the small ones. I don't think they would have let us handle a fire bird at this stage, even a docile one."

"But they let you handle hippocampus!" Her smile turned into a pouty grimace again, and she crossed her arms over her chest.

"Yes, but hippocampi, like the rest of their horse-hybrid cousins, such as the unicorn or the pegasus, have a higher intelligence level than most species of fire birds. They are less unpredictable than a bird that can literally set itself on fire."

"True, I suppose."

"But yes, they had me deal with a raróg. The poor thing had lost its voice and couldn't bring happiness to people anymore. Turns out that it had, quite literally, lost its voice on the wind while flying. The tour guide took the li'l guy back from me and passed it on to an actual employee. I would have loved to go hunting for a raróg's voice, but that was the end of the interview."

Vanja had a thoughtful look on her face, her painted fingers gently massaging her pointed chin.

"Penny for your thoughts." Josef hummed, reaching his hand out teasingly to rest between them. Vanja grinned again, shooting him a wink.

"You're so silly, Brooke," she laughed. "How could you not get hired? You're perfectly fit for it!"

Josef let out a huff and a puff of air that dislodged a lock of hair from his eyes. "Yes, but I already told you, I broke the rules before the interview even started. And I'm sure they get plenty of people applying for the job, they are the FCMC, after all."

That sweet, little pout was back on Vanja's face, and she wagged a slender finger right before Josef's nose. "Brooke, Brooke. You don't know people at all. You don't even know yourself. If I, Oh Great Vanja, tell you you're getting job, you'll get job. Trust me, Boo." Her fingers wrapped around his wrists, and she turned their hands so that Josef's were resting in hers, palms up to the sky. He had very little in him of a dragon, but the hard, almost scaled skin upon his palms was one of the very few traits he had from his great-grandfather.

"If you say so, Oh Great Vanja. I didn't know rusałkas could tell the future."

Vanja flashed her sharp teeth at him in a smile.

"Nothing like that, Boo. Just woman's intuition."

5

Hot-Blooded

Josef's father, Dante Rubino, was a tall, powerful-looking man, the husband of the late, famous Olympian, Elspeth Ryan. He stood a head taller than his son, who was already above average for a human. Dante had far more of a dragon in him than Josef, with his scaled hands and his sharp teeth, his warm body and his muscular frame. He had olive skin darker than his son's, and dark brown hair that contrasted with Josef's Irish genes almost viscerally. His mother had the same red hair as Josef, and when Dante and Elspeth stood together they looked like a princess and her prince, but each pulled from a different fairytale. Josef, the perfect little mix of Irish and Italian genes, with a German first name and an accent like an Englishman, never really fit into the perfect little picture that his parents made. Not him, not the little black sheep. Or the little white dragon, as his father always said.

Dante never really healed after Elspeth's death; Josef could see that. He seemed depressed, he was shedding at an unhealthy rate, he was barely eating. And yet he was managing, somehow, to put on a brave face for his son. Dragons bonded for life; Josef knew he didn't have long left with his father.

"How are you managing, hatchling?" Dante's voice was always soft, gentle like a warm breeze in the summer. He always called Josef 'hatchling', even long after Josef became an adult. It was a dragon cultural term of endearment between a parent and a child, but it only ever reminded Josef of the fact that he was too human to really be a dragon. Not like Vanja or his father, not like the fairy and demon women from the interview. He was too far removed from it all.

"I'm good, dad. I'm job hunting still." Josef was drinking a coffee again. It was two weeks after his interview; they were at the same café he and Vanja went to, drinking the exact same coffee as last time. His father didn't really drink coffee. He preferred the tiny, bite-sized pastries instead.

"Do you need help?" Half of the pastry platter was long since forgotten, his father's appetite clearly leaving him already. "If you're struggling with rent, I could help."

Josef smiled at him and looked his father in the eye over the top of his glasses. His father had red eyes darker than his own, with the identical slits in the centre and the clear, second eyelids that Josef lacked. Unlike with Josef, people could tell that Dante was part dragon long before they looked him in the eyes.

"I'm fine, dad. I have a lot saved up from when I did weightlifting. And you know that Uncle Sef and Uncle Brooke left me almost everything." Josef saw the wobble of his father's lip, and he steeled himself for what was to come.

"Wouldn't you like the cottage, hatchling?"

"Dad, no. Uncle Brooke left that to you and mom, and mom left it to you. I'm fine in my apartment; Spot has enough space, Vanja is my neighbour, it's close to my dream job, and the queer club is right down the street from me."

Dante seemed dejected at that. His face fell, and Josef didn't know how to read that.

"If you're sure," he mumbled, picking at his pastries once more.

Josef took another sip, holding the warm cup between his calloused hands, focusing on all the little points alongside his fingers where he could feel the spikes of heat. "Are you sure you wouldn't just like me to move in with you?"

Josef's father shook his head. "No, hatchling. You have your own life here, you're right ... "

"Dad." Josef wanted to say more. He wasn't sure *what* exactly he wanted to say, but he wanted to say *something*. That was when his phone rang. The vibrations against his thigh made him jump, scrambling for the little, black rectangle.

"Yes? Hello?" Dante focused on his pastries again while Josef turned his head to face the other way. He cupped the phone against his ear.

"Is this Mr Joseph Brooke Ryan?" said the voice on the other end of the receiver. Josef cringed, swallowing thickly.

"Yes, can I help you?"

"I am calling on behalf of the Facility for the Conservation of Magical Creatures to let you know that you have been accepted into the role of a Junior Caretaker." The voice was prim and proper, soft and lightly high-pitched. It spoke so casually, so matter-of-factly, that Josef didn't fully comprehend what it said at first.

"Alright, thank you," he mumbled.

"Your starting date is next Monday, on the twenty-seventh. You are to go to the office on the first floor to receive your worker ID before you do anything else."

Josef nodded along dumbly. "Thank you. Bye."

When the phone clicked off, Dante was staring at Josef again. He just stared back at his father, not knowing what to say, what to think, how to even react, what facial expression to wear.

"Josef? Son, what is it?" Dante's gentle, rumbly voice seemed to have a magical effect on Josef. He immediately snapped out of it, jumping out of his seat with such force that he tipped over his chair and almost upended the table.

"I got the job!" he shrieked, his entire body shivering in excitement. Dante, much more calmly, stood up and walked over to his son. Josef was immediately enveloped by his father's giant, muscular arms. They were both smiling, Josef showing so much teeth that he felt almost ridiculous. And his father ... Dante's shoulders were shaking.

"Dad?"

"I'm so happy for you, hatchling," he said with a voice choked by tears. He said that, and yet it was hard for Josef to believe him.

"Thank you." They stood there for a few more moments, and when they parted, Dante excused himself.

Interlude 1: Not My Name

His skin rippled beneath his fur.

"Darling, come here." The velvety, cold voice had his ears standing at attention. Darling felt another ripple tear through his body. It was painless, perfectly safe, and yet each time he did it he felt disgusted with himself. He felt the long, doe-brown fur along the entire length of his massive, soft body retreat into each individual follicle. His legs elongated; his joints cracked and snapped, rearranging themselves beneath his toughening skin. His face snapped back into a flatter shape, and the hair atop his head shot out to cover the two long, sensitive ears. Darling spat out a glob of mucus that tasted like hay, aiming right into the bin that sat beside Charles Young's desk.

He scratched with elongated claws at his exposed stomach. Young fed him too much in his rabbit form, but the weight looked lovely on his humanoid body. Darling also ran a hand through his long locks, untangling any stray hairs that often ended up as knots post-transition. Young didn't brush him, and his less-than-gentle stroking often left Darling's fur an absolute mess.

"Darling," Young hissed out. The man crawled on his hands and knees towards his master. His claws scraped at the linoleum floor of Young's office, and he felt his tail tickle the skin over his bare buttocks.

"Good boy." The perfectly manicured hand that descended from Young's desk scratched under his chin, and Darling wanted so badly to spit at him. The slight wetness underneath his thick beard made the fine hairs on the underside of his neck tangle, and Young seemed absolutely oblivious to the fact that it pulled at

Darling's delicate skin. He hated having his scent glands scratched. He wasn't a dog.

"Wear this." Young dropped a shirt onto the floor before Darling. The shapeshifter grasped at it. His fingers were long and slender, but his thumbs were shorter and pulled too far back for him to comfortably grasp the shirt. It was white, standing out starkly against his long, auburn hair, and dark brown, lightly furred body. He left it unbuttoned; his fingers couldn't wrap around the hem of the shirt well enough to even attempt to button it. It didn't cover anything up, anyway; Young was a good head shorter than him and considerably leaner. His tail still brushed against his bare skin; his long, flat-footed legs stood out like wings on a fish. The shirt wrapped around him far enough to cover his breasts, but not enough to cover his large, soft stomach.

"Darling, stand up," Young cooed, brushing over Darling's velvety ears. He hated that name, but he had no other. Not like Shark.

He was a bit shaky when he stood up onto his legs. His large, furry feet stood firmly on the slippery floor, but his knees wobbled from the unfamiliar position, and his hips protested from the sudden straightening. Young didn't steady him, didn't help, just kept on staring into his computer.

Charles Young was a handsome man of a little over thirty years. He had a profile that could only be described as 'royal', with an aquiline nose, a rounded, dimpled chin, and a broad forehead. Face-on, he was even more handsome, with lips that looked sculpted out of rubies and amethyst pupils set into almond-shaped eyes. He had high cheekbones and a blemish-less face, with pearly white teeth and skin so fair that even Snow White would be jealous. And hair, hair so dark it reminded Darling of a black hole, brushed into a stylish swoop over his forehead. Darling didn't look at him for long.

"We're going to meet with my favourite subject today." Young smiled and it was blinding. There was nothing kind nor happy behind that smile. It didn't even reach his eyes.

***

Darling trotted after Young as they travelled through the Beneath, meandering in the halls of the HEL Facility. The Health Evaluation Laboratories, situated somewhere within the roots of the FCMC Behemoth, housed the newcomers. Each and every magical being that came in recently and was yet to have a treatment plan decided upon.

"Hold it down, don't let it bite you!" Young screamed at the young nurse that grasped at Darling's flailing limbs. Darling was spitting and hissing, and Young just stared at him with so much hatred in his eyes. The grip upon his left leg was inhuman; Darling could feel the bones shift and crack as he tried to buck, kick him off, do something.

"Darling, don't fall behind," Young hissed.

Darling hid his face beneath his long lengths of hair, ripping his eyes off the examination table covered in claw marks and deep grooves. Why it was still there, he would never understand.

The guards at the door nodded at Young. They had batons and tasers, dressed in thick garments and bulletproof vests. They each also wore protective talismans upon their persons, horseshoes and silver, and whatever else they thought that week would prevent them from being mutilated by a pissed off minor god.

"Sir." The guard on the left, a broad-shouldered man with a thick, white scar marring his dark cheek, nodded at Young. The other guard, a blond-haired woman with perpetually downturned, angry-looking eyebrows, leered over at Darling. Her smile showed too much teeth, too many fangs that made her look ravenous. The man to her left didn't skip a beat either, appraising Darling beneath the thin cotton shirt that he wore. He tried to pull the shirt tighter around himself, but he could still feel their eyes stick to his thick, naked thighs.

Once Young was through the double-barred doors and Darling was still outside with the guards, he let himself grunt at the two of them, thumping his feet in warning. The man just chuckled.

"Are you angry, little bunny?" the woman cooed, reaching out to stroke his head. She didn't even have time to get up onto her toes before Darling dipped through the doorway and attached himself to Young's side.

A wash of cold air greeted him, seeping underneath his skin. Young was grinning at him. His arm snaked around Darling's waist, while his hand rubbed the side of his neck. He hated the fact that the petting felt good, that Young's body against his was warm.

"Did those two guards scare my little Darling? Don't worry, I'll deal with them." The purr in Young's voice was almost tangible, and Darling felt as if his skin was being coated in a film of something slimy and sticky wherever Young touched him.

"Oi, hands off him, you creep." The new voice was loud and reverberated within the small room, penetrating Darling to the bones. Young immediately snapped to attention, pulling himself away from Darling with something that could almost be called disgust.

"Subject-20-465, you're awake." Young placed his arms behind his back, straightening his spine and pushing his chest out. The grey button-up did very little to hide his body, although there really wasn't much to look at. Young was a thin, gangly man with the physique of a teenager but the appetite of a geriatric dieter. He was neither very tall, nor very broad, nor very muscular. Physically, he wasn't imposing at all, no matter how he carried himself.

"Young," hissed Shark. The emaciated figure within the cage was pressed up against the bars. Their pale skin was going red from where the bars dug into their chest. Their ribs stood out horrifically, and their sunken-in face upon a long, bony neck always had Darling shivering beneath his fur. Their unblinking, endless eyes stared right at Young, stuck within a frame of sunken-in eye sockets.

"How are you feeling today, Subject-20-465?"

The being behind the bars was almost like a twisted, mirror reflection of Young. They both had skin so pale it was almost translucent, and long, black hair that seemed to suck in all of the light around it. They both had high cheekbones, a dimpled chin, and perfectly sculpted ruby lips. Young was smiling with his pearly white teeth, while the other had their lips pulled back in a snarl that showed a mouth full of shark-like fangs. And their eyes ...

"That is *not my name*!" the figure roared, and the lights above them blinked and flickered.

Young carried on smiling, his eyes perfectly still as he stared into the eyes of the figure. "Would you prefer Shark, then? Isn't that what some of my workers have started calling you?"

Shark's lips pulled back so far that Darling could see all of their grey, blood-less gums, a serpentine tongue flickering out to lick at their cracked, dry lips. Their eyes were open so wide that Darling thought he should be able to see the entire universe within them.

"That is NOT MY NAME!" The next roar shook the very foundation of the room, and bits of plaster rained down upon his and Young's heads. Darling covered his head with his arms, pressing his ears tightly against the sides of his face. He could still hear the roar reverberating in his head, bouncing off the walls of his ear canals.

"Well, you have to pick one or the other, my dear," Young continued, completely unaffected. "You know that you can't intimidate me into saying it. I own you, Shark. Your body, your soul, your power, and your name."

Shark grasped at the bars of their cage with their long, clawed hands. "How's Thlayli doing?" Their voice went soft, so quiet that Darling wondered if Young actually heard it.

Young's smile dropped, his small, manicured hands bunching up the fabric of his dress trousers. "His name is *Darling*." This hiss was not a warning, as all the others were. This one was a promise.

Shark pulled their lips away from their teeth in something that almost resembled a smile. "That shirt suits you, Big Guy." Their black, endless eyes were trained on Darling, and he felt the cheeks of his human form grow warm. He, cowering behind the much smaller, much weaker, Charles Young, could no longer look at the one person within this facility he could trust. Because he knew that Shark could not trust him.

"Subject-20-465, I see that the wounds from your previous punishment have already healed. I think you won't mind another one."

Darling was shaking but not from the cold, digging his fingers into the thin fabric of the trousers. He couldn't look at Shark but knew that their eyes were still on him. Those eyes always stared, always looked, never blinking. They saw right into his soul.

"Sure. Bring it on, Charlie."

Darling was already at the door, ready to run out through it, back to the safety of Young's office, when he heard the almost imperceptible whisper meant for his ears only. "I'll see you later, Thlayli."

6

Red and Gold Horns

On Monday, the twenty-seventh, Vanja dropped Josef off at the FCMC building for his first day at work. Vanja agreed to have Spot stay over; she worked from home, after all, and Josef even managed to persuade her to drive him around every so often. It was a deal that largely only benefited him, but she didn't seem to mind.

Inside the building, the receptionist from his interview was still there, her perfectly red nails still scratching at the corner of her perfectly red lips. When she noticed him, she almost jumped out of her seat.

"Josef! Welcome back!" She gave him a big smile and her brown eyes crinkled at the edges. Her blonde hair was braided into a pair of plaits that were wound around the base of her horns, and the rest of her horns were decorated by golden bangles. He realised that her plump cheeks were naturally rosy without the use of makeup; the lipstick and eyeshadow seemed to work perfectly with her olive skin.

"Nice jewellery," he huffed, feeling the air within his gullet growing warmer.

"Knew you'd like it, dragon-eyes." She giggled, giving him a wink. Josef coughed, huffing out a little burst of smoke.

"Dragon-eyes?" He pushed the glasses further up his nose.

"Oh, I'm just messing with you." She giggled again, and Josef had to wonder what changed between his last meeting with her and his current one. He didn't even know her name.

"You knew I would be in today?" he asked, trying to change the subject. Her cheeks went even more rosy.

"I've access to all the timetables." Her voice was soft and quiet. The blush only deepened. Josef decided to drop the subject, asking, instead, where he was supposed to pick his ID up from.

"First floor, office 4A," the receptionist trilled, and just as Josef was about to leave, she shouted after him, "My name is Phoebe, by the way!"

"Nice to meet you, I'm Josef!" A whine escaped his throat. *She knew that already!* He quickened his steps, tripping as he threw himself into the lift. This was going to be a long day.

***

Josef clipped the worker ID onto his lanyard, then spun it around so that no one could see his photo. They never let you wear glasses for your ID photos, and he never really understood it. What was the purpose behind it? To prevent light glares? He wore sunglasses; his glasses quite literally were there to prevent light glares. It annoyed him so much that ...

Josef felt his shoulder hit something, and a small man bounced back with a grunt.

"Oh, sorry."

Josef found himself face to face with a short, thin, handsome man. His dark hair was perfectly styled to fall gracefully across his forehead, his purple eyes shimmered like gemstones, and his lips, pulled down in a frown, were so red, naturally crimson, that they looked delicious. Josef felt himself blush and internally kicked himself for being so careless.

"Be careful where you walk. I don't tolerate daydreamers."

In that moment, Josef felt the fire within his belly extinguish itself. With cold, hard eyes, Charles Young looked up at him. His boss, *that* Charles Young.

"Sir! I'm so sorry! I didn't mean to! If I knew it was you, I would ... "

Mr Young thrust a hand up in front of his face. "Who are you?" Mr Young's perfectly manicured hand hovered before Josef's eyes as he gasped for air, trying to recall a single word within his scattered brain.

"Josef Braun. I … I mean, nephew of Josef Braun. Josef Brooke Ryan, the new Junior Caretaker. Sir!" His back shot up; his shoulders pulled back. *What am I doing? I'm not in the damn army*, Josef admonished himself. In moments like these he was thankful that he was just enough dragon to not sweat.

"The new Junior Caretaker? Perfect!" Mr Young's handsome face immediately dropped the frown, and a beautiful smile replaced it. It didn't quite reach his shining eyes, but the curve of his red lips twisted above his perfect teeth had Josef feeling hot in ways that he didn't quite mind.

Mr Young turned on his heel, and Josef realised with horror that he couldn't take his eyes off his boss' shapely backside.

"Come along, nephew of Josef Braun. If you are working for me, you must have learned a thing or two from your uncle, right?"

Josef's long legs tangled beneath him as he tried to catch up to his boss. "Yes, sir! My Uncle Josef is the reason I decided to pursue magizoology."

Although Mr Young was a full head and some shorter than him, Josef felt minuscule. When Mr Young smiled at him, looking down at him from beneath his long, black lashes, his dragon flame grew so big within him that it began burning at the edges of his gullet.

"How quaint, being named after your famous uncle." A perfectly white canine bit into the succulent flesh of Mr Young's bottom lip. Josef wanted to kick himself.

"I'm actually named after both my uncles." When Mr Young turned away, Josef smacked himself on the forehead, twice or so before Mr Young looked back at him.

"So you're Josef Jr?"

Josef nodded quickly, feeling as if his brain was bouncing around in his skull from the force of it.

"Then I hope you are his junior in more than just name."

Josef didn't even notice when they began climbing down into the depths of the FCMC building, descending staircase after staircase, the blinding yellow lamps above them hanging on thin cables. They swung like trees in a storm, and the further down they went, the more Josef registered the gentle shivering of the earth, the quakes that tested the foundations of the rooms they were passing through. With each storey they descended, Josef also noticed a buzzing in the air, a continuous noise whose source he could not place. It grew louder and louder, until it was so loud that Mr Young handed him a set of bright orange ear plugs. Putting them in, Josef noticed the clear pieces of plastic sitting, almost invisible, within Mr Young's ear canals.

"Now, Josef Braun's nephew," Mr Young began at a semi-yell— the buzzing was getting so loud already— "what I need you to do is employ some of your uncle's disciplinary tactics! I am sure you have worked with naughty and rambunctious hellhounds before. This will be no different, I assure you!"

Josef's brain was running a mile a minute, turning towards his stores of knowledge. It was an automatic response, and yet a part of his brain was rebelling, asking 'why?' A part of him wanted to know what this was about, why Mr Young was in need of disciplinary measures of all things. Who or what was he to discipline?

"Ready, Mr Ryan?" A door stood before him, Mr Young's hand placed on the handle. It was thick and double-barred, made of something that smelled like gold but was harder than steel. Above the door, Josef spied the words 'Health Evaluation Laboratories, Level 5 Containment Chamber' written in a bright, but fading, white. Standing there, the orange earplugs uncomfortably squished into his ears, the buzzing had become a roar. A literal roar, Josef realised, the continuous angry howl of a beast. Whether it was a roar of fear, anger, or pain, he couldn't quite tell.

"I'm ready, Mr Young." The door opened, and Josef felt a piercing cold escape through the door. The walls were covered in a thick layer of frost, and the five guards standing in a star shape in the centre of the room were dressed as if they were about to embark on a journey to the farthest reaches of Antarctica.

Josef stepped into the room and brushed a snowflake off his shoulder. It melted into a puddle the moment it made contact with his skin, only to freeze again before it even hit the floor. He noticed that the five guards in the centre were frozen to the floor, unfrozen only from the waist up.

They each held a larger version of a catchpole, the loops overlapping upon the body of an emaciated being. The being had black fur that seemed to eat up all the light around it. It was half upright, with digitigrade legs and a tail like a crocodile, its front paws extending from a barrel-like torso. Josef could count each of its ribs beneath its fur. Its face reminded him of a horse, but with a mouth full of three rows of shark-like teeth, and bloody-red horns burst out of its forehead. It was no creature he had ever seen before, and yet when it twisted to face him, he thought he recognised it. From its jaw dripped down saliva swathed by a freezing mist, like liquid nitrogen, and clouds of warm air were puffing out from its flaring nostrils. Its eyes were endless, black with swirls of purples and blues and speckles of white, as if he was looking into the sky above his uncles' cottage.

Those were the same eyes he saw on the kitten.

"Mr Ryan!" Mr Young placed a hand on his shoulder, his velvety voice rising above the crying of the beast. "Now is the time for you to use your skills!"

Josef nodded, not paying much attention to what Mr Young actually said. The hand on his shoulder pushed him forward, and Josef took a tentative step. The beast was panting, and yet also howling without pause. He saw long welts across its back when it twisted and turned, trying to rip itself out of the metal loops binding its body. There was a loop around each of its legs, one on each of its paws, and one wound tightly around its neck. Only its tail was free to swing wildly, following the motions of its body like a pendulum.

"Loosen the bonds!"

The guards all turned their heads to stare at him, each wearing an identical look of incredulity, noticeable even beneath their balaclavas.

“Do as he says.” Mr Young’s voice cut through the howling, and his warm breath ghosted over Josef’s neck. The guards relented, each loosening the loops with shaking hands. Once free, the beast ripped the catchpoles off itself, tossing the instruments across the room to shatter into minuscule shards of ice.

Josef took the opportunity while it was distracted to pull a piece of coal out of his pocket. He tossed it between his hands for a few seconds, making sure that it was sufficiently extinguished, before he knelt and rolled it across the floor. The beast turned when the little, black ball stopped by its feet. The beast’s endless, starry eyes focused on the coal, and Josef was shocked to learn that the coal’s light didn’t reflect off of them. It was as if those eyes held the actual stars within their confines.

Josef could feel the guards all holding their breaths, and Mr Young at his back was all taut like a spring. He was the only one who was relaxed, watching as the creature before them bent down, poking at the coal with one big claw. A harder push sent the coal tumbling back over to Josef, who caught it with the inside of his shoe. The creature waited, poised, and Josef didn’t disappoint when he kicked the coal back over. Josef and the creature passed the coal between each other like a football, until the little ball had rubbed off almost completely on the floor. The ice separating them was covered in a large, black smudge, and the remains of the ball crumpled when Josef tried kicking it back again.

The creature was no longer looking at the remains of its toy. Its eyes were pointed right into Josef’s own. He knew it wasn’t possible, but, in that moment, it felt as if that penetrating, endless gaze could look straight through his glasses and right into his soul.

He didn’t know how long he held that gaze, how long the creature before him tore him apart from the inside, judging every little bit that made him *him*. He came to at the moment that the connection was broken, those starry eyes disappearing from his field of view, taken over by an open, pinkish maw full of rows of sharp teeth. A second later, Josef heard the scream, and this time knew that it was one of pain. He saw an arc of lightning race through the air, dimming the glaring, white lamps above them.

"Wait! Stop it!" It was his voice that spoke, but he didn't recognise it. It was his body that moved towards the convulsing, foaming-at-the-mouth creature, but he didn't register the movements until he was already by its side. Its claws made deep grooves in the floor of the chamber, its giant tail flailing madly as it beat dents into the metallic surface.

Josef felt a hand on his shoulder, and a firm grip pulled him backwards. "Very well done, Mr Ryan," Charles Young's voice purred in his ear, and it had him shivering.

"Why are you doing this?" The tears choked him; he felt his throat clench around words he didn't know he was brave enough to say. There was something in Mr Young's expression that he couldn't place, a quality to his frown that Josef wasn't good at discerning.

"Believe me, Mr Ryan. I want this about as much as you do. But there are sacrifices I must make for the safety of my staff and of all the other subjects at the facility. This is an unfortunate unpleasantness that we just have to live with." He said it with such conviction, his voice so calm and steady. His amethyst eyes were twinkling prettily, and Josef forgot where he had left his voice.

"I believe you," he choked out eventually, when Charles Young wrapped his small hand around Josef's bicep and began leading him away with a smile.

"Of course you do, Mr Ryan. I'm your boss, after all."

7

Starlight Pollution

Josef didn't go to see Vanja when he got home that day. When she didn't reply to his text that he was on his way, he figured she was already asleep, and Spot not far behind her. Instead, he climbed up to the roof of his apartment complex.

From the roof, he could see an endless black void yawning above him. The light pollution from the city streets was cruel, only allowing the grinning moon to pierce through the darkness above. Back in the cottage where his uncles lived, the stars were like spotlights shining down onto the earth below. Here, in the city, the spotlights came from far off streetlamps and office buildings. It often made him think— imagine that they were alone. The denizens of Earth, abandoned by the universe, unaware that they were the last beings in existence, that it wasn't just the glare of streetlights that made the stars disappear from the sky. In the dead of night, when most people were asleep, all the shops were closed, and only the occasional car ran past his hanging feet, Josef imagined that he was the last being in existence. Sometimes, he even started to believe it.

"You're back late." Vanja's voice was thick with sleepiness, but it still managed to startle Josef out of his daydream.

"I'm back on time," he huffed, taking her hand and helping her sit down. "You just fell asleep early." Her lipstick was smudged, and her eyes were blurry.

"Spot is very energetic, she had me running around all day." She hid a yawn behind a dainty, pale hand.

"Do you miss the stars?"

"Silly question, Brooke. I don't miss stars. I miss their reflection in water, in lakes and rivers and seas."

"Right, rusałka blood."

"Yes. Water creature, not sky creature like you dragon types."

"You still miss it, don't you?"

"Yes. Boo, are you taking my attention off today? I want to ask how today went."

"It went ... fine."

"Tell me, Brooke."

"Why do you always call me Brooke, Rus?"

"Because you are as much Brooke as you are Josef. I am making up for all people who only see you as Josef, nephew of Josef Braun. You are also Brooke! Son of Elspeth Ryan and Dante Rubino! Nephew of Brooke Ryan! Brother of Jozić Vanja!"

"You don't have to shout, Vanja, I can hear you." He laughed, throwing a hand over her shoulders. Her head thunked against the side of his neck and it hurt, but they were both laughing so it was okay .

"You are Josef Brooke Ryan, not just one or other. And Josef Brooke Ryan just got his first proper job, so tell Oh Great Vanja all about it."

"My weightlifting *was* a proper job." He pouted. "But, anyway. I fell in love with my boss after falling *into* him, and then had to 'discipline' a creature I have never seen before, because it was acting out."

"I ... what?"

"I had to 'discipline' ... "

"No! You fell for your boss? Brooke! You are worse than me!"

"I didn't know he was my boss, at first! And— and I don't even control who I fall in love with!"

"Oh, Brooke, Brooke. Diamond earring guy not good enough for you?"

"I didn't end up getting his number ... And it's not like I'm going to start dating my boss! Just ... quietly crushing on him."

"Boooooooo. I need to get you boyfriend. Maybe take you to some event, have you meet people."

"Vanja."

"What?"

"Shut up."

"Ah, you're grumpy because you're lonely. Don't worry, Oh Great Vanja will help you."

"I'm leaving."

"Wait! Don't leave me on edge!"

"On the edge, Vanja!"

"That what I said!"

"Ugh."

INTERLUDE 2: THE MAN IN THE GLASSES

Young didn't leave him alone often. Sometimes, Young would need to be present Above. Above the roots of the FCMC, he had an office, he had workers, he had to be present. Darling wasn't allowed Above. Only the most senior of staff could come down to the trailing hallways Beneath that Darling was allowed to occupy, and all the other workers never crossed his path.

The man with the glasses was the first one in years whom Darling did not recognise. He didn't know the names of all the workers, but he could recognise them. Their voices, their smells, to some degree the way they looked as well.

The man with the glasses smelled like the firebreathers Young kept in the deepest parts of the underground. He had a gentle voice, and he was handsome in a way that Darling didn't see often. He was new, completely and utterly new. And yet Darling saw him trotting behind Young like a lovesick puppy, descending into the bowels of the Behemoth. They were heading towards Shark.

Whenever Young was gone, Darling refused to stay in his rabbit form. He was a simple woodland shifter, a forest nymph in possession of only two forms, both of which he felt comfortable wearing. However, the lack of thumbs proved annoying, even if his great bulk made it easy to rifle through Young's desk. He never knew what he was looking for; he never really looked for anything specific. Reading didn't come easily to him, so files and memos were useless to him. With a lack of reading skills, he didn't need to look for writing utensils either. He was fed enough, and Young didn't leave any clothes in his office.

Darling liked pictures. Young often had pictures in his desk, hidden in the folds of white sheets of paper. There were photos that had Shark on them, photos of other subjects, front-facing photos of different workers.

Young was predictable, and Darling knew how to read him well. There, beneath pages upon pages of scrawls that Darling couldn't read, he saw the photo of the man with the glasses. Except he had no glasses, and his intelligent, reddish eyes glared up at Darling from the photograph.

Darling grasped a piece of paper, a slip that Young wouldn't miss. He pressed it against the first word he saw, standing out in bold, black letters above the photo of the man with the reddish eyes. He used his nail, instead of a pen, to scratch the word into the paper, tracing it over the black letters he could just barely see beneath the white sheet.

Then he returned to his rabbit form. His thick, furry dewlap functioned as a pocket, the small slip of paper pressed between his chin and the sack of fat.

***

The Beneath was completely underground. There were no windows, and the lights from the walls were a glaring yellow and hanging off chains. But there was circulation of fresh air throughout the entire labyrinth of rooms and hallways. The vents that allowed for said circulation were too small for a human to crawl through, big enough for something smaller to crawl through, but screwed tightly to the walls. Darling had the opposable thumbs to unscrew the vents and the smaller, fluid body that let him crawl through them, dragging his belly over the metal floors. All the vents were connected in a network that spanned the entire length and width that the Beneath covered, letting him reach anywhere within the building that he wished.

The room that Shark lived in outside of 'testing' was somewhere within the centre of the entire network but situated on the lowest floor of the entire complex.

The air within the room was cold but crackling with energy. Through the thin grate of the vent, Darling could see Shark. They were leaning against a wall in the large room, barred off from a massive, crackling generator. A single, thin cable reached over from the sparking arcs of lightning and the blue, cold light of the bulbs, snaking its way across the floor. It slipped through the bars in the centre of the room, trailing a path up Shark's leg, up their naked body, to the collar digging into their pale throat.

Darling began scratching at the grating, long claws letting out clanking sounds against the thin metal. Shark's eyes shot open, and the galaxies within them settled upon the vent. Gently, slowly, Darling pressed his chin against the grate, pushing with his shoulders until he could feel the slip of paper rest between the plates of the grating. He finished pushing it through with a gentle nudge of his nose.

He saw the paper fall in dancing arcs, gently cascading down onto the floor. It suddenly went careening towards Shark, fluttering with such fervour that Darling feared it would rip. But it slowed, and it rested softly between Shark's legs. They snapped the paper up, licking their lips with a forked tongue.

"His name is Brooke, then." The smile upon their lips was almost sweet, their eyes softening at the mention of the man with the glasses: Brooke, as Darling now knew to call him.

"You did well, Thlayli, my friend." Their eyes met through the grate. "I think, with him, we might have a chance." If only Darling believed it. Shark had said the same thing so many times before, so many plans they had created. And yet they were still here.

"Go back now. Before Young catches you."

***

The return journey was faster than the first trip, Darling no longer having to worry about losing the slip of paper squirrelled away into the folds of his dewlap.

He got back to the office just in time to screw the vent grate back in place, tossing the screwdriver into the mounds of pillows and blankets that functioned as his resting area. Then, with a quick step and his head held high, Young marched into the office.

He didn't say a thing to Darling, didn't even look in his direction, as he fell into his desk chair with a sigh. His entire body went boneless, and he puffed out a breath of air to relocate a lock of hair that had hung before his eyes. These were the moments Darling hated the most, the moments where Young acted the most human, reminding Darling that this wasn't a robot that he was trapped with, programmed to cause pain and fear. This was a human, with a premeditated want to hurt him. He had feelings, emotions, he knew exactly what he was doing to Darling.

"I can't stand them," Young huffed, and Darling felt the need to hide himself. "What a damn annoyance. They work for me, *me*! Not anyone else. They're supposed to listen to me! I *own* them, for fuck's sake! And now they're defying my orders and overloading the generators again! If I didn't need them so much, Welei would already be dead! Stupid creature, getting in my fucking way! How am I supposed to get those drake skulls to that jeweller *now*? How am I supposed to transport the damn unicorns to the butcher? Don't they know how much energy it takes to trap those damned cockatrices for those stupid cock fights? They're ruining *everything*!" Young burst out of his seat, his voice rising until it was painful to listen to. Darling wanted to hide even more, digging his claws into the linoleum floor, his ears standing at attention. That name, it felt wrong, like something he wasn't supposed to hear, something he shouldn't know.

That name was what he needed. He didn't know how he was supposed to get it, but he needed it.

Young dug into his desk, pulling out a small, black rectangle, pressing a button on the side of it.

"Reminder." His voice was unpleasantly husky as he spoke into the small recorder. "Up the dosage of Subject-20-465's tranquillizers while in the generator cell. Until the new trainer works out how to subdue them, it's best they're kept on a higher dose, fuck the fact it messes with their energy levels."

The recorder returned to the desk, and Darling felt his heart sink.

They would never get out.

8

The Beginning of the Universe

The next day, Josef woke up with a spicy taste on his tongue. Vanja had treated him to a late dinner of curry. She didn't make it, thank the ancestors, and they were able to have a nice chat over reheated curry leftovers before Josef had to nod off after a long day at work. Since it was a Tuesday, and Josef didn't have to work, they had breakfast together, taking Spot out for a long walk near Déjà Brew. Their conversation eventually fell upon the creature Josef had to deal with the day before.

The creature still eluded him. No mythical being he knew lined up one-to-one with the curious amalgamation he had met the day before. Vanja had no ideas, other than one.

"Maybe it is old god? Lots of old gods were shapeshifters who took on animal characteristics. Egyptian gods had heads of animals. Norse gods and Greek gods could shapeshift into animals."

Josef replied with a sigh, "But we haven't found any proof for the existence of old pagan gods. If any existed, they were most likely wiped out long ago. And what gods do you know of that can create ice, but also have eyes like a galaxy and the head of a horse?" She didn't have a response to that, and they moved on to different topics.

***

On Wednesday, Josef arrived at the FCMC building and immediately went to say hi to Phoebe. She wore gold again and smiled at him so widely that it made him feel odd.

"Busy day today!" She giggled as he swiped himself in. "Mr Young wants you down below again. It seems that you have made an impression on him, dragon-eyes."

Josef pushed his glasses further up his nose, looking away from her. "He wants me downstairs? Really?"

Phoebe nodded, her grin even wider, her eyes trying to catch his through the slivers between the frames and his face. He nodded at her politely, gave her a kind smile, and marched towards the elevator.

He met Mr Young at the second to lowest level. Mr Young looked as radiant and handsome as ever, and yet the smile he gave Josef still didn't reach his eyes.

"Mr Ryan. This way. After your performance on Monday, I'm sure you will be glad to know that you are on your way to being promoted to Senior Caretaker. I'm sure this is a shock to you, this only being your second day, but I've been looking for someone like you for years. Years! Someone who knows how to deal with all manner of beings, who can so easily calm down a raging beast. Our little issue has stumped hundreds of other trainers, but *you* are a *natural.* I don't care how you did it, but if you can work your magic again, I'm sure there is more than just a promotion waiting in your future." Mr Young didn't let him get a word in, although Josef had nothing to say in the first place. A promotion. Already. Based on a single day of work and a single show of skill. A promotion.

"Thank you, Mr Young," he mumbled, trying not to stumble either over his words or over his feet.

"Don't thank me. Thank them." The same double-barred door from Monday opened before him. The 'them' Mr Young referred to, as they both stepped into the cold room, was an emaciated, skeletal figure with pale, translucent skin, sitting behind a set of bars bisecting the room. They had their back turned to him and Mr Young, but Josef could still see their long, black hair trailing down from their shoulders; the digitigrade legs were covered in a layer of black fur that they sat upon. They didn't turn, and Mr Young didn't say anything to them.

He turned once more to Josef. "Think of them as a particularly intelligent dog, like a hellhound. I want them eating out of the palm of your hand and walking at your heel as soon as possible. Have I made myself clear?"

Josef nodded, watching Young do a half pirouette and begin to walk out.

"Oh, and Mr Ryan. *Don't* listen to what they say. They're very gifted in mimicry."

And then Josef was alone with the being.

"Hello, Brooke." Their voice was melodic and velvety. They turned their face towards him, and a pair of black, bottomless eyes stared back at him. Their mouth was full of shark-like teeth, just like before. Their face was intersected by two long, bleeding slashes, carved into their thin skin in an X shape, and their neck was wrapped in a thick, leather collar.

"You know my name." Josef swallowed, taking a step back from the creature. He had heard of beings capable of reading his mind and of those capable of mimicking human speech. Something wasn't adding up, however. Josef knew, from dealing with harpies before, the more beastly cousins of sirens, that a being capable of mimicry did not possess humanoid vocal cords. Their voices never sounded quite right.

"Yes. I do. My name is ... I go by Shark. There, now we're even." Their smile was handsome, even if their raised lips twisted the scars upon their face. That velvety, melodic voice spoke with a resonance unique to humanoid vocal cords, something his ancestors had meticulously evolved within themselves. Something that no mere mimic could replicate. Something no mere hellhound trainer had any right to know. Josef knew the shame of having knowledge above his station, and yet ...

"Does that hurt?" He approached Shark, taking steady steps towards them. Young was a businessman; Josef was sure he was simply provided with incorrect information about how to care for this creature. He could fix that, he *would* fix that.

Shark fluttered their eyelashes, leaning more heavily against their bars. "It's excruciating." Josef thought that he saw a star falling within the depths of Shark's galaxy eyes. He noticed that they were shivering, but he wasn't sure if it was from the pain or the cold. He knelt either way, shrugging his blazer off his shoulders and placing it around Shark's prone form. He had to stretch his arms through the bars that separated them, reaching over with the sleeve of his dress shirt to wipe, ever so gently, at the whispers of blood that dripped from their face.

"I don't know why I'm here," Josef began when he realised that Shark wasn't going to speak, "but I want to help you." He could feel the fire within his belly growing warmer.

"I love your eyes." Shark's voice was so quiet, Josef wasn't sure if he heard them right. Something, however, compelled him to reach up, putting his dark lenses away into his pocket. His eyes met the endless reach of Shark's galaxies, and he felt as if he was falling.

"I love yours too."

Shark's nose scrunched up as they smiled, and the corners of their eyes crinkled. Their lips were a dark, juicy red, and they reminded him of Mr Young's lips. That was when he realised that Shark looked nearly identical to Mr Young.

"This face is my own, believe me, Brooke." The sincerity of their voice, the only sound that Josef heard anymore, took his breath away.

"I believe you."

Shark seemed to catch their breath, their chest stuttering with their words. "Thank you. I'm glad someone does."

Josef swallowed thickly, his head growing fuzzy, and all that he could say was, "Yeah." His limbs felt leaden, refusing to obey him as he was compelled to move forward, enraptured by the swirling stars within Shark's eyes.

"Kiss me." He pressed himself against the bars, and they reached out through the bars to grasp his hands to steady him, and their hands were *freezing*. Josef leaned over until his face rested against the bars. The cold metal between them was a buffer, but the warmth of their shared mouths was sweet and comforting. Their lips were as soft as he thought they would be. Josef could feel the tension escaping from Shark's shoulders, travelling up their throat and escaping through their open mouth. In a distant part of his brain, he worried about the wrongness of this, the fear of Young finding them overpowering the haze within his mind. But even as his eyes cleared, he leaned further into the kiss, finding comfort in another warm body, in being *wanted* for what felt like the first time in years.

Their kiss was short but meaningful, and Josef believed, for a moment, that this was the end of the world, that this was everything there was in the universe, and that when they separated, everything would end. But when they did, he realised that the universe had just begun.

He held onto that feeling for the rest of the day.

9

Treasured Time

Josef worked twelve-hour days, from 6:00 a.m. to 6:00 p.m., Monday, Wednesday, and Friday. That sort of schedule suited him very well. It gave him time to take care of Spot, hang out with Vanja, read.

It gave him a lot of time to read.

***

When he came in to work on Friday, Phoebe wasn't there. He didn't even notice it, with his nose stuck to the pages of a book, until he was almost at the elevator and the receptionist hadn't beamed at him and told him 'Hi'.

Unobstructed by small talk, although slightly dejected at Phoebe's absence, he descended in the elevator with his face pressed into his book.

"What'chu reading, Cookie?" Shark hummed as Josef made his way towards the barred-off half of the room.

"I told you not to call me that, Shark," he grumbled, still not pulling his face out of the book. "Just because it rhymes with 'Brookie' doesn't make it not sound ridiculous." The shapeshifter giggled, and the sound was melodic. It almost sounded inhuman, inorganic. Like a windchime dancing with the wind as a bird sung from the branches above it. The shiver it elicited from Josef made Shark grin, and when he finally put the book down, he saw that grin only widen.

"You're reading up on old gods. Have you become religious, Brooke?"

Josef knelt before them, sliding the book to the back of the room. Their hands immediately encircled his neck, pulling him down further and squishing his face against the bars. His glasses discarded, they kissed, and it was even better than the first day.

"I'm just doing some research, *mi tesoro*." The pet name seemed to go down well, if the fireworks in Shark's eyes were anything to go by.

"Tell me all about it."

And he did. For countless hours, Josef talked. He talked so much that his throat hurt by the end of the day. He told Shark everything, from his research to his favourite pastimes, to his Uncle Josef who instilled a love for magizoology within him. And all the while, Shark listened, tracing their hands up and down his body, exploring him and loving him.

Josef talked, and his hands were busy with a small first aid kit he had snuck in. He swiped the antiseptic cloth over Shark's face with gentle strokes, bestowing kisses upon their face every time they flinched. And still he talked, and he explored their naked body. Each bruise, he kissed; each bleeding wound, he patched up. Each time he came upon a new wound, Shark's body froze within his grasp, their chest hitching and their eyes slamming shut. Each time he swiped the antiseptic wipe over these new wounds, rubbed cream into a yellowing bruise, or placed a plaster over a cut, Shark melted into his grip, their muscles becoming pliant beneath their taut skin.

Eventually, they were both sitting sideways against the bars, their shoulders pressed closely together. Shark wore Josef's coat, snuggling into it despite not needing the warmth. Josef had taken off his shirt on Shark's earlier behest and was sitting with his chest on full display, the scars and the freckle-like scales that dotted his skin being peppered by kisses.

"You wanted to ask me something when you first came in." They already knew how to read him, and he had no clue how. Their voice was thick with sleepiness, but it was still a good few hours before Josef had to go home. He hadn't even noticed the time, not when Shark began telling him about their life prior to the FCMC. A cottage in the Scottish countryside, fresh milk every day and their own little vegetable garden.

"I ... meant to ask you what you are." It seemed silly, now that he had said it out loud.

"Well, what are you, Brooke?"

"I'm two-quarters Irish, human. One-quarter Italian, also human. And one-quarter German, but this time dragon."

Shark hummed, and their fingers traced over the scaly skin on Josef's palms.

"Your beautiful eyes, they're from your dragon half, aren't they?" The glasses made by Uncle Brooke were somewhere on the floor between Josef and the door, and his russet eyes were staring right at Shark.

"The only part of me that gives it away, really." The laugh that came out of him was needlessly bitter, but he didn't seem to know how to stop it. "I'm ... too human for dragonkind, but too dragon for humankind. I don't fit in anywhere."

Shark's dark hair brushed against Josef's bare shoulder, and the weight of their head was almost comforting. "You're enough for me, fit in perfectly," they mumbled sleepily, pressing another kiss against a reddish scale beneath his collar bone.

"Fit in? Where?"

"With me." They pulled their head back up and their smile took Josef's breath away. "I don't fit in with humanity, or with all the humanoids like your rusałka friend Vanja. I ... I come from a planet in a different solar system, and the closest things I resemble on Earth are the fae. But I'm not fae, I'm an alien, born from a comet that came to Earth. Although, I'm not really an alien anymore. I've spent my entire life on Earth. I've spent the past forty-three years on Earth, since the day of my birth. Where do I fit in? Nowhere. Nowhere but with you." They reached their arm up and placed their palm against the bars. Josef did the same, and their skin was wonderfully cold compared to his perpetual warmth. His hands were bigger, broader, with longer claws he had always struggled to trim. Their hands were delicate and slender, but their thumb was considerably shorter than it would have been on a human, and their pointer finger was longer than their middle one. It was humanoid enough that you couldn't tell at first glance, and yet completely alien to him.

"You're perfect," he whispered.

"So are you." And this time, they did more than just kiss.

***

At 4:00 p.m., two hours before Josef was off work, his company-issued walkie-talkie buzzed.

"Shit, Shark, my coat!" Josef jumped up onto shaky legs, scanning the floor on his side of the room for his trousers. Shark was crawling and rolling across the floor, trying to get to the long-since-discarded coat.

"My body feels like jelly," they whined, their knees making 'thunk, thunk' sounds against the floor as they quickened their pace. The walkie-talkie flew across the room when Shark finally retrieved it, buzzing all the while. It perfectly missed the bars and landed in Josef's grasp as if deposited there purposefully.

Phoebe's voice briefly rang out from the walkie-talkie before the connection switched over to his cellphone, stuck up on the ground floor of the building. He hadn't expected anyone to call him at this hour, but he was glad the FCMC had ways to get around the lack of service down Beneath.

"Hello? Who is it?" Josef briefly cursed himself for not asking Phoebe what the number was.

"Hatchling? It's your father, how are you?" Dante's voice on the other line made Josef cringe. Not only because of what his father had interrupted, but also because of the weak, breathy way he sounded.

"I'm sorry, Dad, I was busy and don't have good service at my workplace." Out of the corner of his eye, Shark was shoving the coat back through the bars, their hands shaking slightly.

"Oh, should I call later?"

"No! It's okay, I just finished as you called." His hand flew to the microphone on his walkie-talkie when Shark burst out laughing, hoping that his father didn't hear it.

"Oh, is that Vanja there with you?" Dante sounded so hopeful, and Josef's heart broke. His father loved Vanja; she was the daughter he had always wanted. When his two children called together, it almost seemed to breathe new life into Dante.

"No, it's my ... my partner."

"Oh, hatchling, I'm so happy for you!"

From the middle of the room, Shark was beaming, their little, pale face pressed against the bars. Dante sounded as happy as Shark looked, and Josef's heart ached.

"Hey, Dad, would you like me to visit you?" Josef met Shark's eyes, and wished he had his glasses in that moment.

"Oh, no, it's alright. Spend time with your partner, hatchling, you're still young."

"Dad, you don't sound alright. Are you sure you don't want me to come stay with you at the cottage?"

Shark's face fell. Josef's heart beat an uncomfortable rhythm when he realised he couldn't tell what Shark's expression meant.

"I'm alright, hatchling. You don't have to come visit me at all."

"If you say so, Dad. I'll call you later, though, okay? And I'll remind Vanja to do the same." He smiled even though his father couldn't see him. Dante said a weak goodbye, and the walkie-talkie clicked, but Josef didn't pull it away from his ear for a long while.

"My love ... " Shark's arms were around him when he sat back down, their face pressed into his neck.

"I don't know what to do, Shark. I just don't know what to *do*."

Interlude 3: The Mistakes of the Pitiful

It was Sunday, and Darling was alone again. It was rare that Young would leave Darling by himself twice in one week. Brooke had to have made an impression on the cold, inhuman man, but Darling didn't care to find out what linked them.

Instead, he took the reprieve that Young's absence gave him. He went to visit Shark.

"Thlayli, I think I'm in love," Shark sighed, leaning against the nearby wall in a faux faint. "I've missed the touch, the presence of another sentient being. I missed the connection, this feeling. He fell into it so easily too, but now he holds me of his own volition! What a man ... "

Darling scratched at the grate of the vent, showing Shark that he was still listening. Shark's eyes seemed brighter, almost, as he watched them move around their cell. The reddish, angry wounds upon their face were almost fully healed already. There would be no scars.

"Saying it like that, maybe I'm just desperate for the contact. But, Thlayli, he understands me! He is struggling, and he has tough decisions to make, but he is so kind, so sweet." Shark was pacing their cell again. Darling wanted to scream, make some sort of noise, something between frustration and annoyance. Shark was walking, they were being active again, and yet the both of them were no closer to getting free, not even with the human man's help.

"He has something within him, I can feel it. He's the one, Thlayli, he is!" In that moment, Shark collapsed against the floor, and the door to the generator room burst open. Young marched in, holding a taser in one hand and a whip in the other. His eyes swivelled around the room, up the walls and across the ceiling. Darling curled up behind the grate, suddenly feeling his body freeze, as if paralysed. Why couldn't he move? Why couldn't he run away?

"What did you do, you fucking bitch?" Young yelled, and it was the first time in a long while that Darling had heard him raise his voice. He felt his heart thumping against his ribcage so fast, he was scared it would jump out of his chest.

"'Bitch' still isn't my name," Shark hissed from the floor, their body in a boneless sprawl. Their hair tastefully rested against their skin, hiding their most intimate parts beneath curtains of black tresses.

Young's face was red, and his lips were pulled back in a snarl, appearing thinner than normal. His cheeks weren't as defined beneath his reddish skin, his nose now shorter and flatter, his chin dimple-less. He raised his hand and the skin over his fingers was coarse and calloused, his fingernails jagged and torn.

The whip fell, the crack piercing Darling through the heart. It landed upon Shark's bare stomach, leaving a red valley that parted their white flesh. Their shriek was ear-piercing; the small whimpers coming from their clenched lips were animalistic. Another blow fell, and their hands tore at the metal floor of their cell, their legs going taut as they tried to push against the pain. Another blow made them choke on a sob, and the fourth one had them smashing their head against the floor. Another sob fell, followed by another whimper, and the four cuts on their abdomen wept. The blood stained their pale body, like painted, white roses, and they lay prone upon the floor for all to see them.

"Darling, to my office, now!"

The roar kick-started Darling's heart, sending him into a frenzy of flailing paws. The sound that he made as he galloped back through the metal vents was deafening.

***

Young already waited for him in the office. A kick to his soft belly had him rolling across the floor, flailing around as he tried to get his feet back under him. Young said nothing, but his face was back to its handsome state. His perfectly manicured hands grabbed Darling by one of his ears when he was done shifting. The pull against his scalp was excruciating. It was as if the very skin upon his head was being ripped open.

There was no shirt waiting for him when Young dragged him to his bed, forcing him to crawl on all fours across the floor. Another kick to his side had him curling up into a tight ball, pressing his hands against the tender spot. Young still didn't say a word. He never did, all punishments doled out by his own hand perpetually silent.

The next kick forced the air out of his lungs, and Darling could already feel the bruises forming. His throat burned and his eyes stung from the pain.

Young never hurt him too bad; he could take it. A few kicks and then he would be apologetic, that's always how it worked between the two of them, like an abusive relationship, like they were lovers that just couldn't stay away from each other at the end of the day. Darling took it obediently.

Young's eyes burned like dual, purple flames. Darling remembered hearing once that blue-purple flames were much, *much* hotter than a regular fire. And these purple flames were scorching, burning away at his resolve.

Another kick forced out of him a choking gasp. A thin stream of air sounding akin to a train whistle, forced out between his large front teeth. He couldn't breathe, his chest felt like it was about to cave in, his shuddering ribs rattling beneath his skin. His throat kept burning, like he was choking on shards of his own ribcage alongside the strangled air his lungs couldn't quite expel.

He looked up at Young through the curtain of his hair hanging before his darkening eyes. The long tresses tickled his flat nose and the edges of his jaw, and it was something other than the pain that he could focus on. The corners of his vision were already black, and he was looking at that man through a pinprick of light. If he focused on the tickle of his hair against his skin, he could hang onto consciousness for a while yet, however precarious his connection was. Young stared down at him, his body slack, his eyes completely blank, almost glazed over. Darling didn't break eye contact, even if he couldn't be sure that Young actually saw him.

This little rebellion was his secret, his only reprieve; he was determined to hang onto it.

"Oh, Darling." Young's voice was barely above a whisper. He bent over, and Darling was sure that he could hear the way his breath rattled in his chest. A soft, manicured hand reached out and stroked over his ears. The little sigh which accompanied that action was almost euphoric, and Darling felt the urge to yank his head back.

"Poor thing, I won't hurt you."

You already did, he wanted to scream. Scream, cry, yell, even whisper. He wanted to tell Young exactly what he did, in a language he would understand.

Young scooted over, suddenly kneeling right before Darling's face. His gangly, thin arms wrapped as best as they could around Darling's Flemish bulk, and Darling let himself be guided. The man wanted Darling's head pressed against his collarbones, low enough that the tip of his ear brushed against where Young's heart should have been. The top of his head was pressed firmly, near painfully, against Young's chin. He could feel that pinprick of pain shoot through his spine, making his tail wag and tingle, and he wanted so badly to thump, to warn even *himself* of the danger he was now in.

Young's hands brushed over Darling's head, over his silken ears and down to the base of his neck. "I know you didn't mean to, my poor, little bunny," Young cooed. "That horrible, horrible creature brainwashed you, forced you to visit them. Completely against your will." Darling wanted to scream. "But you must understand, I'm only trying to protect you. Things of that kind can hurt you so easily, but I can tame them, I can force them to behave. I *will* force them to behave, eventually." Young's hands trailed down over his shoulders, smoothing down the ruffled fur on his back, going lower and lower. Darling stayed still, silent, when Young began fondling his tail, stroking up the entire length of it, as if it was something else he wanted to stroke. Darling felt sick.

"Shhh, I'll keep you safe." The breath on the back of his neck was warm, leaving tingling pinpricks wherever it ghosted over him. "I'll keep you safe from that monster. I'll make sure Welei never touches you again. You're mine, Darling. Mine!" His hands left Darling's body in the blink of an eye, and cold air attacked him. Young was moving away from him, leaving him on the bed to shiver and shake. He was just an animal, after all. You don't touch your animals in that way. Not even Young would stoop that low.

Young left him alone in the office, still gasping for air. There was a click, and the buzzing static assaulting Darling's sensitive ears disappeared. He curled up around the little, black rectangle, its cold, plastic body warming up swiftly as it lay there, pressed against the side of his chest. He could feel his bones grating against each other as he breathed, and he realised with horror that something was broken.

He couldn't shift anymore.

10

GHOSTS OF OUR ANCESTORS

Josef came into work the next morning to Phoebe beaming. She was dressed, as always, in all red, but the golden accents she had taken to wearing had increased. She even had a golden nose ring in, and Josef wasn't sure if he remembered her wearing one previously.

"Not much for you to do today, dragon-eyes!" She beamed right up at him as he swiped his ID card. He let the ID swing free on its lanyard and looked at her with a quirked eyebrow.

"Not much work? I thought I was meant to be downstairs today again."

Phoebe's smile faltered a bit, but it was back on her face in seconds. "Well, Mr Young has different plans for you today. I heard that he personally changed your timetable." She fluttered her eyelashes, painted black, the only part of her makeup that wasn't red.

"Personally?"

"Yup." She popped the P as if she was popping a bubble gum bubble. "Which means you've got a free afternoon, dragon-eyes." Her facial expression changed. Her beaming smile turned softer, she angled her head downwards to look at Josef from beneath her eyelashes, her red lip caught between her small, pretty teeth. Josef noticed with a professional interest her lack of canines and how the rest of her teeth were even and uniform.

"I suppose I do," he mumbled, playing idly with his ID. Maybe he should call Vanja, have another meet up at Déjà Brew.

"So ... " Phoebe began, twirling a lock of blond hair around a red-painted finger, "I happen to have the afternoon free too."

Josef blinked, realising that she was still talking to him, so he smiled at her. "That's nice."

"Would you like to go out with me?" She blurted it out with such force that Josef took a step back. She leant over her desk, coming almost completely face to face with him, her cheeks burning almost as red as her lipstick.

"Phoebe ... I'm not attracted to women." He took another step back from her, not looking in her direction. She sank back into her seat in the corner of his eye, and her face seemed accepting, although maybe it was just sad.

"I'm sorry, I thought you liked me back." She sounded dejected, and Josef's head shot back up to look at her. He slipped his glasses off his nose, reaching around the computer at her desk to hold her hand.

"But I *do* like you, just as a friend. I'm sorry if I gave you the wrong impression, Phoebe. I'm autistic." She had pretty eyes. He could see them much better now without the blockade formed by his dark sunglasses. Those eyes were slightly wet, but they crinkled at the corners and Josef realised that she was smiling.

"Oh, it's not your fault, dragon-eyes. I'm like that too, and I don't always know how to take the hint." She was laughing now, wiping at her eyes as she let out small, wet chuckles. Josef squeezed her hand tighter.

"Learned how to flirt off the TV, huh?"

"Yeah, I did." They were both laughing, although Josef would have rather called it 'giggling madly'. It was early in the morning and there weren't many people moving in and out of the building at this hour. Even so, he had a slight notion in the back of his mind that if anyone walked in on them at that moment, they would have thought both him and Phoebe mad.

Once their giggling died down, Phoebe squeezed his hand back, before releasing it and rubbing the pads of her fingers together.

"You know, if you want to go out still, we can." Josef returned his glasses to his nose and smiled at her as she blushed. "It won't be a date, but you can meet my best friend and sister, Vanja. There's this great café near here where we always hang out. It's called Déjà Brew."

Her blush didn't die down, but a smile returned to her face. "I'd like that."

"Great, see you there, gold-horns." He turned on his heel and made his way towards the elevator. He smiled when he heard the little squeal of delight coming from the front desk.

***

Mr Young had two offices, one in the Behemoth tower where he spent the majority of his time. It was his office for the new hires, people who weren't allowed to move between the main building and the hallways belowground.

His second office was situated within the roots of the facility, where only employees with the correct level clearance were allowed to visit him. Josef had the right level of clearance, courtesy of Phoebe the day before. She had printed him out a new Senior Caretaker ID before he even knew he was fully promoted. Uncle Josef would have been proud of him, he was sure of that.

He stepped into Mr Young's lower office following a polite knock and a calm response of "Enter." That early in the morning, Josef knew he wouldn't find Mr Young in the Behemoth. And yet he felt as if he had stepped into a slightly darker version of his office up top. Both had linoleum floors, minimal decoration, and mahogany desks presented in the very centre of the circular room. There were no windows here, but the chandelier hanging from the ceiling gave off a bright, white glow, and Josef was grateful that he always wore his dark glasses.

There was something that resembled a mural on his left, a stone relief featuring Young's ancestor, Sir Thaddeus. It was identical to the one in his other office but was lit up with wall-mounted spotlights from up above. Sir Thaddeus was a handsome, kingly man, with gentle blueish-violet eyes. His hair was somewhere between chestnut brown and dirty blond, falling across a broad forehead. He was clean-shaven, with red lips below a flat, broad nose.

Mr Young was at his desk, writing something, and didn't even look up when Josef came in. So Josef waited, familiarising himself with the office from where he stood in the doorway.

"Close the door, Mr Ryan."

Josef jumped and did as told, shutting the door with a click that sounded far too loud. Mr Young still refused to look up. Josef wandered closer, shuffling his feet. In the corner of the room (or what functioned as a corner), situated behind Mr Young, Josef spied a dog bed, and upon it, a furry creature. The creature had chestnut brown fur and appeared to be the size of a human, maybe slightly shorter than him. It had its back to him and Mr Young, and Josef imagined that it was sleeping.

"Mr Ryan, what brings you here." Mr Young still didn't look up at him, and his words were more of a demand than a question.

"Oh, um." Josef cleared his throat. "I just wanted to make sure that my timetable was correct, sir. There have been a lot of changes recently, and ... " He was cut off, Mr Young bringing his hand up to silence him. In the corner of the room, the furred creature stirred.

"Your current timetable is correct. You will be aiding the other Senior Caretakers in preparing the halcyon chicks from last winter for release. Then you are free to go home." Mr Young finally looked up at him, but Josef was no longer paying attention as he smiled disarmingly. "But don't worry, Mr Ryan. You will be paid the full rate you are owed, and on Wednesday, you will be back to your regular timetable, from 6:00 a.m. to 6:00 p.m."

The creature behind Mr Young had shifted, twisted around atop its bed so that it could face them. It was a humanoid rabbit, Josef realised, with the flat, pinkish nose, the three lips, and long ears hidden beneath a head full of brown curls. Its eyes were massive, with wide, round pupils and brown irises that were so dark they almost looked black. The eye whites were but slivers at the edges. Josef noticed that it was holding its arms close to its chest and that its breathing was laboured and thin.

He made a move to step towards it, but Mr Young thrust his hand out to stop him. "Where do you think you're going, Mr Ryan?"

Josef didn't know where his voice went when those purple eyes penetrated straight through him.

"To help," he squeaked. "It's hurt."

"Darling had an accident. He was already looked at, and the vet decided that he simply needs to rest."

Josef was convinced. After all, would Mr Young lie to him? Could eyes so beautiful be capable of lying? His head felt fuzzy, and the more he looked into the depths of Young's eyes, the more he was starting to forget what he came here for. Why was he arguing with his boss in the first place? Maybe he should step back, maybe go ask Phoebe for a painkiller. He was starting to get a migraine again.

He said his goodbyes to Mr Young and, with one last look at Darling, left the office.

The farther away he got from Young's office, the more his headache seemed to recede. The fuzzy spots in the corners of his vision slowly melted away, and yet Josef was still struggling to remember the conversation. His mind began to wander as he meandered through the halls of the FCMC.

Josef remembered only snippets of his childhood. His parents were often at work, and his uncles were busy despite working from home. But there were moments that he remembered vividly. Sitting on his father's lap, listening to ancient dragon bedtime stories, curled atop his stomach that glowed like burning coals. The days where his mother would take him out into the backyard, teach him how to shoot a bow. Before his birth she had been an Olympic-level athlete. Her arms were almost as thick as Dante's, her fingers were covered in callouses, her hair was cropped short at her chin, and her cheek was marred by a horrid scar from her training days. She was the most beautiful creature young Sef had ever seen.

"Strength, Josef," she used to say, "is not a substitute for kindness. Without strength, a kind man cannot change the world. Without kindness, a strong man does not want to change the world. A man who is both strong and kind, he will know how to change the world, even if it's just to change the world for one person."

Josef could overpower Mr Young; how could a scrawny human ever measure up to him with his years of weightlifting and his dragon might? But he didn't, not in that moment. He didn't, and couldn't, help Darling. He couldn't be kind and compassionate to that creature that looked at him with sad, forlorn eyes. What good was his human compassion if he couldn't act upon it?

Josef remembered how his uncles would sometimes sit around the fireplace, simply talking. Uncle Josef would tell him about all the animals he worked with, from the smallest of mischievous pixies to the colossal, sea-faring leviathans. Uncle Brooke would smile, and the fondness within that smile always stuck with him. Uncle Brooke, like Elspeth, seemed wise beyond his years to his favourite nephew.

"Firecracker," he used to say, "why are you sad?"

"Because those people were mean to you and Uncle Josef."

Uncle Brooke would smile, picking little Sef up. "Don't be sad for me, firecracker. Be sad for them."

"But why, Uncle Brooke?"

"Because they are sad people. Happy people do not hurt others. Happy people do not act rude or mean towards others. Sad people do that, and those sad people deserve our compassion." Uncle Brooke had a crooked nose and two large front teeth, he had thin lips and squinty eyes, and he had a smile that Josef believed could scare away the mightiest of storms. "Be kind to others, Josef. Be kind, because there are sad people in the world who do not understand kindness. Be the one to teach them how to be kind."

I failed you, Josef thought. *I cannot be strong right now. I want to be kind, but I cannot. Something is stopping me.*

His headache returned, but his head had never felt clearer. He took a deep breath, standing before the doors of the elevator, and began to replay the interaction within the office again. Every time, he came back to Darling's crossed arms. His breathing was shallow, his ribs had been broken. He wouldn't have wanted to hold himself where it hurt the most.

And then it struck him; the rabbit had something within his grip. And he was looking right at Josef, maintaining constant, unbreaking eye contact.

11

Barista Guy and Receptionist Girl

After hours, Josef decided to approach Phoebe.

"Are we off, then?" she asked, already packing up her bag.

"Yes, I suppose so." He swiped them both out, returning the ID card to Phoebe but keeping his in hand, playing around with it. "Can I ask you something?"

"Anything. We're friends after all, right?" Her smile was disarming.

"I made friends with Vanja the first day we met, so I'd say we are."

"What did you want to ask me?"

"Does Mr Young have any pets?"

Phoebe stopped, her red backpack hanging in her loose grip. Now that he could see her fully, not hidden behind her desk, he thought of her as very beautiful. She was slightly fat and a bit curvy. She was dressed in a pencil skirt and a suit jacket, both of them the same shade of red, that accentuated her round figure perfectly. The blonde hair atop her head was matched by the striking shade of gold on her furry legs, and her hooves were decorated by red ribbons that almost reminded Josef of the straps of sandals. If he was attracted to women, he very well would have gone out with her.

"He has a rabbit. Flemish giant; big, fluffy bugger who's called Darling and lives in his office." She was eyeing him. He didn't really understand what that look meant, but he came closer to her and whispered in her ear.

"Does he have a human form?"

Phoebe jumped back from him as if he had shocked her. Her eyes flew wildly around the lobby, her ears twitching slightly despite them being perfectly human-looking. She made a zipping motion over her mouth, and he handed her a slip of paper he had previously prepared.

"Your number?"

"And address. We'll talk about this some other time."

She nodded, and when he smiled at her, she smiled back. Arm in arm, they exited the lobby, climbed into her red car, and zoomed off.

***

Josef was the first one out of the car. He manoeuvred his way around to the other side, opening the door for Phoebe as his gaze wandered. It landed on the table taken up by Vanja, dressed now completely in her goth outfit from five years ago, and a dark-haired, bearded person wearing makeup twice as heavy as hers and a shirt that showed even more of their ample cleavage than Vanja's usually did. Josef never thought he would see the day where one of Vanja's partners managed to out-goth her, not Oh Great Vanja herself.

"Rus, hey!" he called out to her, and the rusałka turned her head with a flip of her long locks. *What a show off*, Josef thought to himself, *a damn endearing one, unfortunately.*

Vanja and her new partner both stood up when he and Phoebe walked up. The new person wore golden contact lenses and had Doc Martens that reached their knees, with leg braces made of black leather and a dark type of metal caging in their legs.

"I like your shoes." Josef smiled.

The new person smiled back, and Josef felt pleased with himself. "Thank you. I'm Murphy, by the way, Vanja's boyfriend."

Then it clicked for him, just as he was taking Murphy's hand. "Hey, you're the new barista guy!"

Vanja was cackling at his side, and Murphy was trying to hold her up when her knees buckled.

"Yup. I'm way tamer in my work clothes." Murphy had perfect white teeth, surrounded by deep red lips framed by his carefully styled facial hair. He had dark brown hair and skin that was naturally tan, paired with a wide, flat nose. He looked like no one that Josef knew, and yet something about him seemed so oddly familiar.

"I almost didn't recognise you in all of that makeup." From behind Josef, Phoebe was standing with her hands behind her back, awkwardly looking between him, Vanja, and Murphy. Her tone of voice wasn't unkind; however, something told Josef that she didn't mean it as a compliment.

"Phoebe Oikonomou, I never thought I would see you again." The hiss of contempt that Murphy let out took even Vanja by surprise, if her open-mouthed expression was anything to go by. "Still working for that cunt, are you?"

"Murphy!"

Phoebe was seething, Josef could feel it from where she stood at his back. "I have no choice, you Mean Girl-ass bitch!"

"Phoebe, that's enough." He could feel the tension rising, he could feel it like he could feel the heat of the sun beating down upon his face. Phoebe was still behind him, as if using him as a shield. Or a fence, to stop herself from making the wrong move. He wasn't sure which was worse.

Murphy was holding onto Vanja with both hands, shaking from top to bottom. His features were melting, twisting and shifting. His left eye was pinched inwards, and his right arm was undulating weirdly as it visibly shortened.

Then they both threw their hands up into the air and left, Phoebe disappearing into her red car again and Murphy limping, with one leg shorter than the other, towards his black motorbike. Josef and Vanja were left alone, standing on either side of their favourite table at Déjà Brew.

"Takeout?"

"Absolutely."

***

"I'm gonna go broke if I have to buy three puppuccinos every time I get out of the house." Josef took out an earbud just in time to hear a loud, wet gulp that came from Spot's direction. Vanja giggled against him, laying atop him on his sofa, her head pillowed on top of his stomach.

"She's happy, can you blame her?"

"I guess I can't." They fell into a comfortable silence again, him listening to music on his phone while Vanja was busy reading a book. From where he lay, he couldn't quite read what it was, but he knew for a fact it wasn't English, German, or Italian. It did, however, feature a haygriff on the front cover, the leporine cousin of the griffon and hippogriff. It had the back end of a ptarmigan, with its rabbit-like paws, and the front end of a snow hare, long ears and all.

"What do you think that was about?" he asked her after she had leafed through five more pages. Her bookmark was a feather shaped out of metal, made by Uncle Brooke for her thirtieth birthday. She slotted it into her book and set the book down, turning so that she was laying on her stomach, her chin digging slightly into Josef's belly.

"I think Phoebe and Murphy are exes," she said bluntly.

"Did he tell you that?"

"No, he has not texted me yet."

Josef scratched the side of his face, his glasses forgotten somewhere on the coffee table. "How much do you know about him?"

"Well, he is Murphy Young, age thirty-nine, goth since age thirteen. He work at Déjà Brew, but he prefer photography and modelling. He has website where he post his photographs, they are very good. He is ... "

"His name is Murphy Young?"

"Yes? It common name, is it not?"

"What colour are his natural eyes?"

Vanja gave him a little pout before she put on her thinking face again. "Purple. Very pretty colour, I wanted to make painting of his eyes, but we are both so busy that I haven't finished it."

"He's related to Charles Young?"

"Maybe? If he is Young, and his eyes are purple, does it mean he is definitely family to your boss?"

Josef paused, resting his hand atop Vanja's head. Her eyes fluttered shut, and she snuggled deeper into his gut, chasing down the warmth of his dragon fire.

"He reminds me of Young, that's the problem. And I saw his eyes before, they're the same shade."

"He look nothing like Young beside eyes."

"No, but something in his face reminds me of my boss."

Vanja opened her eyes again, trailing them across the living room. "We can ask him. Murphy is so kind, he tell me everything I ask of him. We have no secrets. He know I am part rusałka, and my mother ran off with selkie man to have my sister, abandoning me in England. He know your family took care of me when I was searching for my father. He know how much you mean to me, he would tell you everything, if just to make me happy."

"Thank you, Vanja. Tell me, what was that about his body going all ... "

"Melty."

"Yes."

"Ah, Murphy is shapeshifter."

"Oh, really? Huh, that's exactly like Shark."

"Your boyfriend." Her cheeky, sharp-toothed smirk was pissing him off.

"No! Not my ... Vanja! I can't date someone who is being held captive in a facility for non-sentient magical animals!"

"You have to do something about that."

Maybe the sigh he let out was overly dramatic, but he didn't really care. "But what? What can I do? I wasn't even allowed to see them today."

"Don't know. Talk to Murphy. Talk to Phoebe. Maybe Murphy knows. Phoebe might know, she work there. And when you have plan, I will help you."

"Thank you for your wealth of wisdom."

"I, Oh Great Vanja, am pleased with your thank you."

12

When Knowledge is Power

Phoebe met him at the front desk the next time he came into work. She was, as always, dressed in an all-red get-up, but her golden accents seemed more toned down that day. She still gave him a smile, although it was no longer the beaming, bright thing from before when she still crushed on him.

"Dragon-eyes, hey."

The ID scanner beeped loudly when Josef scanned himself in. Phoebe's lithe fingers were click-clacking over her keyboard, and she wasn't paying as much attention to him as she used to.

"Are you alright? What happened two days ago was ... "

She cut him off, snapping her head around sharply. "It's not your fault, Brooke, but I'd rather not talk about it." She turned back to the computer, and he could hear her chewing on something as he thought.

"Would you tell me where you knew Murphy from, or does that count under 'it'?"

"We used to be best friends, college roommates," she said after a moment of silence. "We fell out because I was offered a job here, at his uncle's company, some six years ago. It was either that or having to move back to Greece to live with my parents." Josef hummed as he listened, and Phoebe's ears were twitching again with each new note.

"I didn't know you were Greek."

A grin brightened up her face, and she turned to look at him again with those shining eyes of hers. "Of course not. I grew up in the UK, living with my auntie. But finding satyrs outside of Greece is kind of hard, no? We are indigenous to that part of Europe."

He was nodding along, and with each nod his glasses slipped further down his nose, until he was scrambling to catch them in mid-air. That got a laugh out of Phoebe, and Josef felt compelled to join in with her. He was, deep down, annoyed that she wouldn't tell him more, but that little spark of anger was overshadowed by his joy at seeing her happy, at knowing that they would be alright after all.

"Would you like to go see a movie with me tomorrow? As friends, no Vanja or Murphy, just the two of us."

Phoebe had the sort of smile that could light up a ballroom, and she gave him such a smile right then. "I would love to, dragon-eyes. How about that new superhero movie? The one with the underwater kingdom."

"Great, it's decided! See you then."

"Bye!"

***

He got in touch with Murphy through Vanja a week and a half later. He debated with himself (and with Spot) whether it was rude to text a complete stranger without said stranger even knowing that he had their number. In the end, he was the one being invited to the complete stranger's apartment, so he supposed that it evened out.

"Make yourself at home, Brooke." Murphy waved his arm out in an arc, presenting to Josef his very clean, and yet very cluttered, apartment. Josef smiled and stepped in, thinking how Murphy must have picked up the 'Brooke' thing from Vanja.

"Thanks, I appreciate you inviting me over."

Murphy was milling around, a cat with two tails trailing in his wake. "Of course! You're, what, Vanja's brother, right? Even if not biological. It would be weird if I purposefully tried ruining our relationship. I want to be friends with my future brother-in-law."

Josef's eyes snapped up from the nekomata that was making biscuits on the blanket-covered sofa and zeroed in on Murphy. Here, within his own home, Murphy was dressed far more casually. His makeup was toned down, although he still wore black mascara, and his lips were a dark shade of burgundy. He wore an oversized hoodie with the logo of a band Josef didn't recognise, and a pair of jeans, both of which gave him a much more masculine silhouette than in the coffee shop. His hair was still styled the same way, and his facial hair was still immaculately groomed.

"Whoa there, brother-in-law? Haven't you and Vanja been dating for, what ... "

"Two months. And don't sweat it, Brooke! I don't even have a ring! I'm just thinking ahead." The nekomata meowed in protest when it was scooped up, only to immediately settle back down when Murphy placed it in his lap.

"Murphy, man, Vanja's never been with anyone for longer than half a year, what makes you think you'll last that long?" The sofa was covered in a thin layer of cat fur, and both of the armrests were covered up by photography gear, yet Josef managed to squeeze himself in next to Murphy, sitting shoulder-to-shoulder with him, both of them gently petting the two-tailed cat.

"Because she told me." His voice dropped an octave, and he stared right at Josef. In that moment, without the golden contacts, Murphy's eyes were so brilliantly purple that they didn't seem real. The shape of those eyes, too, was the exact same almond shape as Charles Young's.

"She told you what?" Josef had to fight the lump in his throat and mentally scream at himself not to just ask Murphy, then and there, about his uncle.

"That she never felt like anyone truly understood her. Except for me. Because I understand what it's ... what it feels like to be estranged from your family, to feel other in a country you weren't born in, and to always look for that one person that understands, never to find them." Those purple eyes were covered in a sheen of tears, and Josef moved to wrap his arms around Murphy on instinct. He wasn't sure how long they sat there, him just holding onto Murphy as the other wept. He didn't know when he himself started crying, and when his tears twisted within him into full-out sobs. At some point, Murphy was hugging him back, trying to wrap his short arms around Josef's broad back, lending a bony shoulder for him to cry into.

"Your uncle," Josef began, and he could feel Murphy's body tensing, "is holding someone within his facility that understands me in a way you and Vanja understand each other."

"I'll help you."

Josef immediately pulled back, although he didn't dislodge Murphy's hands that still rested on the small of his back. It was comforting, it felt safe, and he needed that safety.

"I don't want your help, Murphy. I can't ask that of you. Just ... tell me everything that you're able to about your uncle."

The nekomata danced and leapt from Murphy's lap to his just as its owner was getting up. Murphy paced, and he paced a lot. All day, for hours as Josef listened to him talk, Murphy paced. He wore braces upon his legs even indoors, metallic cages that made his legs rigid, caused him to limp. And yet he walked, and paced, and jumped around the room with every burst of emotion, even when it began to hurt.

And this is what Josef learned from him: Charles Young was one of the oldest shapeshifters in existence. No one knew his true face, his true age, or where he even hailed from. He was a direct descendant of Sir Thaddeus the Dragon Friend, but no one knew when the shapeshifting gene was introduced into their blood. Murphy always wondered if such a perfect replication of human and animal genes alike was even native to Earth in the first place. Young was no werebeast, skinchanger, or nymph, capable of shifting only between one human and one animal form, much like Shark.

Charles Young was a greedy man. He used his ancestor's good name to start up a company that made him rich, while everyone outside of the Young family saw him as a philanthropist, an altruist. The FCMC, in all its glory up Above, was made with only money in mind down Beneath.

A good ten, maybe fifteen years ago, Murphy's uncle showed up to a family gathering with a new face. A dimpled chin, round lips as red as blood, skin as pale as snow, and hair as dark as a black hole. That's when things stopped adding up. That was when the energy bills stopped being paid, but no energy company could safely say that Young was partnered up with them. Murphy had been the black sheep of his family ever since he came out to his parents as genderfluid, but not even his homophobic, Bible-thumping aunt could say that she hated Murphy more than she hated Charles. And the family dug. They dug deep.

"More security?"

"So much more." Murphy was taking a sip of gin and still pacing, seemingly uncaring that he had work tomorrow. "Too much for a simple veterinary practice, unless that's not all that the FCMC is. Have you ever seen hundreds of guards working at a zoo?"

"No, and I worked at two zoos in uni." Josef was nursing a whiskey with Coke, Hissitis the nekomata (named that because she was a very hissy kitten, apparently) rubbing up against his leg as he pet her fuzzy head.

"My family also dug up proof that Charles was constantly employing and then firing different animal behaviourists, trainers, et cetera. People who knew how to discipline creatures, more or less."

Through the fuzz of the whiskey, Josef was putting all this information together. Slowly, the puzzle pieces were beginning to fit. "I'm a trainer. My uncle trained hellhounds and I did an apprenticeship under him almost twenty years ago."

"And that's why you got to meet ... "

"That's why I met Shark. Cause I could discipline them. So Young could control them better." The whiskey was discarded upon a stack of books that functioned as a coffee table. Josef stuffed his face into Hissitis' fluffy belly, feeling the gentle rumbling from her purrs. Curse his dragon genes, he was such a lightweight.

Murphy finished off his gin and reached over for Josef's discarded whiskey, clearly assuming that the man wasn't planning on finishing it. "And now, Charles has probably figured out that you became friends with his super powerful alien-cum-power generator, and will restrict your access to them as much as he is able to."

"Why's he not just fire me, then?"

"Because you're the only Braun left, Brooke. The only one who has your uncle's knowledge. The only one Charles can still manipulate to do his bidding." Murphy seemed to want to leave it at that, and Josef was almost ready to let him. But then there was the question:

"How do I get Shark out?"

"I don't know," Murphy said with too much honesty for Josef's taste. "That's for you to figure out."

13

When Power is Corruption

It was a few weeks before Josef was allowed to see Shark again. It was disconcerting for him, and he found himself bunking with Vanja more often. Nightmares of Shark's bruised and bloodied corpse haunted his dreams, with images of his father's dry husk spliced in every few nights.

The one positive of his off days was the ability to come up with a plan. Neither Phoebe nor Murphy knew why Shark was being kept at the facility, barring the obvious energy source. Neither knew how to free them exactly, but the fact that Phoebe was willing to talk to him about it was a start.

"I'd love to help out, Brooke," she said during one of their café excursions, "but I don't have anywhere else to go. If Mr Young finds out I helped you, or if freeing Shark makes the FCMC collapse, I have nowhere else to go."

Josef was chewing the end of a croissant, his glasses perched at the very tip of his nose. "Not even Greece?"

"I'm not going back to Greece." And that was the end of the conversation that day.

It took him another two weeks to get the information out of her, although reluctantly on her part.

Vanja was there, playing tug with Spot in Josef's living room while he and Phoebe were on his sofa playing a game of chess. He didn't quite remember how the conversation started, but it ended with Phoebe spilling her heart out:

"They want to marry me off," she sobbed, and her king tumbled off the playing board. "To some billy twice my age, so that he can teach me how to be a 'proper woman'." Maybe it was Vanja's presence that finally did it, maybe it was the cosiness of a shared dinner and warm blankets for the three of them to hide under. Something finally made Phoebe crack, and Josef's heart broke for her.

"You are proper woman, no?" Vanja approached her with a cup of hot chocolate, and Spot nosed at her knee.

"I'm too autistic, apparently. They sent me to live here in England with my aunt, but she's not much better than me."

Josef wrapped an arm around her, piling another blanket around her shaking shoulders.

"I can't return there, I can't!"

The day ended with them curled underneath a blanket fort, empty mugs discarded across the floor. Josef lay upon his back, Phoebe and Vanja curled up on either side of him within the crooks of his arms, their heads weighing down his chest. He fell asleep last, listening to the cars outside of his window and watching the starless sky yawning endlessly at him.

***

He got to visit Shark on a Monday, when Phoebe welcomed him at the front desk and told him that he was needed down below again. He went immediately.

The penetrating cold from the rooms Beneath fought against his naturally high body temperature. The room he usually met with Shark in was empty, so he followed the whispers of ice crystals and cold air until he came upon a room dominated by screaming and roaring.

Within the centre of it sat a large pillar, sparkling arcs of electricity dancing around it madly. Shark was in the corner of the room, behind another set of bars, a collar wrapped tightly around their neck and their face melting and moulding into that of a black-furred panther.

"Enough! Get out of here!"

The guards within the room, two of them exactly, dropped their batons and their poles, slamming the door shut behind them as they went. Josef's voice echoed off the walls of the small room, barely audible above the sparking of the generator. There was a gate left swinging open in the centre of the room.

"So, this is what Mr Young keeps you here for?"

Shark's face collapsed in on itself, before reforming into their usual handsome, yet gaunt, features. "Yes. I'm an energy source. Without me to power this building, Young would have no hope in controlling all the beasts he sells and butchers. I make him money, and make sure the other things he makes money off of don't escape. And as long as Young has my name, I am his to do with as he pleases." A heavy pause hung in the air between them. "You left me, Brooke." It was as if one of the ice crystals from the air had been shot at him, piercing him through the heart.

"I didn't mean to," he begged and took a step towards the gate. "I wasn't allowed back here." Shark took a step in tandem, meeting him halfway. It was the first time they were allowed to touch each other without the bars, without the eyes of other people upon them. Shark's arms wrapped tightly around Josef's neck, and his arms went to the small of their back.

"Show me that you didn't mean it, my love."

So he did, despite the crackling of the generator that drowned out their words and despite the collar that wrapped around Shark's throat until their skin went purple. He touched them and caressed them and spent all the time he could proving to them just how much he had missed them.

***

They lay on Shark's side of the room, with the gate swinging freely upon its hinges, touching each other as much as they wanted to. Shark's arm was thrown across Josef's stomach, and Josef was pressing kisses against their neck with such fervour, as if it was as necessary to him as breathing.

"Do you really think this is love?" Josef breathed into the crook of their neck. It wasn't the question he wanted to ask, but it was the only one that felt right in that moment.

"It's a feeling," Shark rested their lips against the crown of Josef's head. "And love is also a feeling. Does it have to be love, this early on? Can it not just be a connection, maybe one borne of lust? The want of another warm body against yours, bringing you pleasure?"

Josef trailed a kiss up their long, sinewy neck, until he reached their lips. "Would you mind if it ended up being love at some point?"

"No," they said, kissing him back, "I wouldn't. I like you. Your kindness when we first met. I like your beautiful eyes. I like how perfectly imperfect you are. I like that you're not scared of me, that you don't see me as something to study, something other. I like that you stayed. I'm sorry for influencing you." Their lips brushed against his again, and Josef tightened his arm around their waist.

"I'm other too. I don't fit in, not as much as I'd like to. I guess I didn't fight against the mind control all that much because of it. Because I was lonely too."

"And I love you for that. And for the fact that you stayed and came back for me."

Josef pulled back and stared deep into the depths of Shark's eyes. He saw the galaxies swirling in a vortex of fantastical colours, like a pot full of different coloured paint as it is being stirred for the first time.

"I'll get you out of here, *mi tesoro*."

Interlude 4: Time Falls

Darling rarely kept track of time. Each day felt identical within the confines of Young's office. It harkened back to the days when he was still a kit, unaware yet of the wider world, living each day as if it was to be his last. The forest had a day and night cycle, and the four seasons left him with a reminder of how many years had passed, but weeks and months meant nothing to him. The birds didn't need to sing of Mondays, and the foxes didn't understand the concept of weekends. The rushing river didn't know that it froze over in January, and the trees weren't aware that they lost their leaves in September.

Each day that he spent curled up around the recorder atop his bed, stuck within Young's office, all he could do was think. He wasn't taken out, he couldn't shift, his ribs were still healing. And the days stretched out longer and longer, and the recorder was forever cold against his skin.

Then, one day, Brooke arrived again. The last time he had seen the man in the glasses, there was no recognition within his russet eyes. This time, Brooke purposefully dipped down his glasses and gazed at Darling with pity.

"Mr Ryan, what brings you here?" Young was at his desk as always, busy with paperwork that Darling couldn't read. There were notes scattered around the tabletop, reminders that couldn't quite replace his lost recorder.

"Mr Young," Brooke began, and his voice was a deep, pleasant rumble, and Darling could, just for a moment, imagine perfectly why Shark loved this human so much. "I want to bring to your attention that your ... how do I say this?"

Young waited, and Brooke fumbled, and Darling wished he could speak up in a language they would both understand.

"Mr Young," Brooke began again, "you must free Shark." The air grew still within the room. Darling wasn't able to see Young's expression, but he commended Brooke for holding his gaze for so long, letting the tension grow with each passing second.

The little clock upon Young's desk ticked away. Darling's heartbeat fell in line with its tune.

"My dear Mr Ryan," Young finally said, his words slow and elongated, "I know that Subject-20-465 seems sympathetic, but we are keeping them here for their own good."

Darling watched as Brooke's resolve crumbled, as his hands began to shake and his shoulders fell forward.

He wanted to say something, he was opening his mouth and about to speak, when the walkie-talkie upon Young's desk interrupted him. Young barely used it, and when it clicked awake Darling jumped in his skin.

"Boss, need you on level +5, ASAP." It clicked off again, and Young excused himself, leaving him and Brooke alone. They stood there like that for what felt like hours, neither wishing to move, neither wanting to break the silence and the stillness.

Brooke's eyes were on him, and Darling had to wonder how much Shark had told him, how much he truly knew and was willing to do to free them.

That was when his phone rang. He picked it up with what amounted to a smile.

"Hello? How can I help you? Hmm? Yes, I'm Josef Brooke Ryan, who's calling? My father? Is everything alright with him? He's ... but are you sure? I called him last night and he was still walking and doing fine! A stroke ... I understand. Yes, I ... How long does he have left? Oh. Oh. Alright. I'll be there tomorrow. Yes, that's fine. I'll stay with him however long it takes. Thank you for letting me know. What's your name again? M'kay, thank you for the information, Sue. I'm glad someone like you is taking care of him. Thank you again. Goodbye."

With each word he spoke, Brooke's face fell, and his voice hardened. With each beat of silence that followed, his demeanour crumbled, until he was sobbing into his hands. He didn't even wait for Young to return, he simply left.

Darling realised then that he was alone. Utterly and completely alone. As in the days of the forest, when it was just him against the world, he was completely alone. Brooke, his father clearly on his deathbed, wouldn't help them after all.

When Young returned to his office sometime later, Darling lay with his back to the door, the recorder pressed against his bare skin. He listened as the man wandered around his office, mumbling and muttering to himself as he went. He paid no mind to Darling, and Darling was fine with that.

He just waited. The passage of time meant little to him, but he knew when the sun rose and set. So he waited. Until night fell.

14

The End of the Universe

"Are you sure about this, Brooke?" Murphy was driving the car, a black Kia that didn't attract attention. From the back seat, sitting next to a napping Spot, Josef was staring up at the starless sky, his glasses put away in his coat pocket to let him see better.

"I'm sure, now drive."

Vanja looked back at him from the passenger seat, her eyebrows downturned and her lips pulled into a pout. He hoped he hadn't sounded rude.

"But what about plan, Brooke?" she asked, still looking at him.

"I'm sorry, Rus, but we don't have time for that." Murphy had switched the radio off some time ago, and Josef bemoaned the lack of music to distract himself.

"We'll just ... improvise," Murphy added, his voice wavering.

"We will. And at least Phoebe promised to help us," Josef said as the car pulled up outside the FCMC building.

She met them right at the entrance, wearing a muted red suit in such stark contrast to her usual attire. She looked scared, worrying away at her bottom lip, refusing to meet his or Vanja's eyes.

"Where's Murphy?"

"He's staying in the car with Spot."

Her expression didn't change, but she reached out to grasp his hands. "Think this through, Brooke. Are you sure you want to do this?"

"You don't have to help," Vanja cut in, getting in between Phoebe and Josef. All three of them were buzzing with energy, and the tension in the air was palpable.

"I dismissed the guards. The building is empty. I'm coming with you." Phoebe reached out and grasped Vanja's hand. She was still holding onto Josef with the other.

"You have this much power?"

"No, I just know how to hack the company's systems."

"Girls, later." Josef extracted himself from Phoebe's grasp and began making his way towards the elevator. Phoebe and Vanja, still holding hands, trailed behind him. Their eyes were on the back of his head, boring into him, tracing every one of his steps as he navigated the empty space of the Behemoth's ground floor. The waning light of the moon filtered through the glass windows, creating scattered crystal-like lights across the floor and walls.

The elevator ride was silent, the creaking and gasping of the mechanisms reverberating in Josef's ears. The lower they went, the less light there was.

"I lead now." Vanja's voice was barely a whisper, a breath against the back of his neck as her slim, fluid body brushed past his elbow. Her eyes, so pale up Above, seemed almost bioluminescent in the guts of the Behemoth. Josef felt Phoebe's much shorter body press against his side, the faint clip-clopping of her hooves the only sound audible within the penetrating darkness of the Beneath.

"Follow the cold air."

The silence was horrifying. The buzz of the electric lights, the distant cacophony of scientists working, the marching of the guards, all were gone. The cold, metal walls beneath his fingers were still; they forgot to vibrate now that only a fraction of the usual population of the Beneath existed. Josef wanted to pull his hand away, wanted to exist without touch, without sound, suspended within the darkness. The simple action of brushing his fingers against a bruise in the wall's shell was overwhelming, shooting electricity through his entire body. But he had to hold onto something, he had to know where he was going. He still existed, even if the world no longer did. The universe could have ended outside, and he never would have known that he was the only thing left alive.

"Brooke, talk to me." Phoebe's lips were pressed to his shoulder, the highest place on him she could reach. Her quiet, vaguely accented voice sent a shiver down his back, and the golden hoop earrings she had worn since his first day at work were sparkling faintly in the corner of his eye.

"I'm here, Phoebe, I'm here."

Her hand was pressed into the side of his stomach, her hooves were still clacking against the metal floor of the passageway, her breath was tickling his neck. Vanja was up ahead, and she was turning around now, every so often, her pale blue eyes the only point of light within the consuming darkness.

And then Josef felt a soft, warm hand wrap around his wrist. He felt fur lining the palm, and the thumb was placed lower on his wrist than he would have expected, gentle pinpricks from claws digging into his skin.

"Darling."

"What? Who? Brooke, there other person here?" Vanja asked, her head swivelling around wildly.

"It's Darling. He's Shark's friend." The warm palm travelled up his arm, from his wrist to his bicep, until it rested upon his shoulder. With the combined pressure of Darling and Phoebe's bodies against him, Josef felt real again. He felt alive again.

"It's getting very cold. We must be on the right track," Phoebe muttered, and Josef wondered if her words were meant for the rest of them or not. Darling let out a chittering tooth grind, what Josef assumed to be in agreement.

"This door, yes? Generator?" Vanja's trilling accent reached Josef through the darkness again. There was silence from the other side.

He went in, Darling close on his heels. The lightning that danced in arcs around the generator lit the room up blue. The contorting shadows on the walls almost reminded him of the reflection of water seen through a sheet of glass. They undulated, gyrated, melting into each other and then falling apart like scorned lovers.

There, lit up by the blue light, their eyes reflecting each galloping bolt that raced through the air, was Shark.

"I knew you would both come for me." Shark's smile was pressed against the bars of their cage. Darling rushed past Josef, throwing himself at Shark. He wore only a shirt multiple sizes too small, his hands trembling as he passed a small, black recorder over to Shark.

"Thlayli, you clever, clever thing!" Shark was looking at Darling ... at Thlayli with so much admiration. Josef forced himself to stop. He had moved up to the doors of the cage, pressing his lips against the lock and blowing bursts of hot air over it, puffing and huffing until the lock began to glow red. And he stopped himself, right as the metal reached its melting point, to watch Shark and Thlayli. Shark's arms were stuck through the bars, grasping at the short fur on Thlayli's back. The rabbit man was holding gently onto Shark's head that rested against his shoulder. Seconds passed, and they weren't separating; minutes passed, and Josef noticed that Shark had started crying. Thlayli's eyes didn't water, but he looked distressed with his blown-wide eyes, his perked, rigid ears, and the way his fur stood on end across his entire body.

Finally, they separated, and Shark reached for the recorder. "*I'll make sure Welei never touches you again. You're mine, Darling. Mine!*"

The voice reverberated through the small room, drowning out the crackling and spitting of the generator. Although only for a moment, as the generator began to whir louder. The lightning became more frantic, more wild. It sparked and danced, and it shot out, hitting the walls, the floor, the ceiling. Josef threw himself at Thlayli, pressing him against the bars of Welei's cage. A bolt shot past Josef's cheek, lighting up the terrified look upon Thlayli's face. Another bolt struck him in the back between his shoulder blades. He felt the underdeveloped muscles of his wings clench and constrict; his coat and shirt burned away, and the stench of burned flesh filled the room. The generator grew brighter, whiter, the arcs transforming finally into a singular bolt. With a deafening crack it shattered the door of the cage, and a moment later, the entire thing collapsed in on itself. Bits of metal pelted Josef's exposed back.

"Brooke, Thlayli, are you alright?" Welei's voice was frantic, their lithe body shooting through the door and over to them both. Thlayli was terrified but unharmed, and he threw himself at Welei the moment he was free from Josef's grasp. His dragon genes were strong, but Josef still felt the pulsing ache in his back. The wound burned and pinched as he shed himself of his coat and shirt. The shirt he threw over Thlayli, covering the tiny garment he had most likely stolen from Young. The light orange button-up reached to just above the middle of his thighs, and the sleeves reached to his wrists. The coat he wrapped around Welei's much smaller frame, buttoning it up to the very neck to hide the hideous hole in their throat that the collar had left.

"My hero." Welei's hands were immediately on Josef's bare skin, tracing across a pair of scars beneath his pectorals, then down to a set of claw marks on his side, reaching back upwards to wrap their arms around his neck. They pressed a kiss to another scar on his shoulder, their gentle hands brushing over the burn on his back. They kissed him, and the burn cooled in seconds beneath their touch.

"I love you, *mi tesoro*. Welei."

They smiled with a mouth full of shark teeth, and it seemed like the most beautiful thing Josef had ever seen. "I want you to say my name again, Brooke. I want you to own it, willingly. Say it again."

"Welei."

"Who do you think you are, Braun's nephew? Stealing my pets from right under my nose!"

15

Strength Without Kindness Proves Nothing

Josef had scooped Welei up into his arms. Vanja and Phoebe were on either side of Thlayli, keeping him upright. The two women had burst into the room right after Young. There was a pause in which they had all looked at each other, before Phoebe rammed her horned head right into Young's back. There had been a crack, but the five of them didn't wait long. They had reached the elevator long before Young recovered.

"Phoebe, run to the car immediately. Tell Murphy to come here with Spot, she's big enough to carry Welei on her back." Josef's words were frantic. He could feel his voice draining out of him with every moment that passed. "Vanja and I will hold Young off as long as we can. Hurry!"

She ran out of the room before he was even done talking. Vanja was helping Thlayli rest against the statue of Sir Thaddeus in the centre of the room, while Josef threw himself at Phoebe's desk, hiding Welei there behind the solid wood. He noticed, out of the corner of his eye, that Vanja took a fire extinguisher to a water fountain, and he ran up to help her. He grasped the fountain with both hands, feeling the skin upon his back ripping. With a pull, the metal body of the fountain came away, and the water splashed across the floor. Vanja was muttering something in Croatian under her breath, her hands waving wildly over the spurting water. With a breathed-out curse, the water pressure increased, and the water shot up to the very ceiling.

Murphy had arrived in that moment, and Spot was leaving spots of sizzling, hot slobber in her wake. Phoebe was right behind him, her hand resting on his shoulder.

"Murphy, get Shark to the car. Phoebe, help Vanja get Thlayli to safety too." As he said that, he heard the elevator ding.

Young was a man of short stature, and yet it wasn't hard for him to seem intimidating. His bubbling, purulent face was enough to stop all of them in their tracks. His eyes were even brighter than before, and a steady flame of hatred burned within them. His hair had grown lighter, his face rounder. The gums inside his mouth were receding as he bared his teeth; his nose collapsed back into his face and his chin smoothed out.

"Filthy, thieving scum," he shrieked, moving towards them with jerking movements. "You use your uncle's name to get ahead in life, and now you insist on stealing my energy source too. Has anything you've ever done been your own idea, Josef? Have you ever done anything for yourself and not because some other person had the idea first? You're weak, Josef Brooke Ryan. Weak!"

Josef was aware that his hands were shaking. He was aware that the shiver was travelling up his arms and overcoming his torso, until his entire being was shaking. Maybe Young was right. Maybe he was just doing what everyone around him wanted him to do. He became an athlete for his mother, then turned to magizoology for Vanja. He studied hellhounds for Uncle Josef and dragons for his father, Dante. He had freed Welei and Thlayli because it was what they wanted, what they expected of him. He needed an entire ensemble of people to help him with the rescue. He wasn't even brave enough to visit his own father, not when Dante kept telling him he didn't have to.

"Brooke, don't listen to him! He lies, he's always lied to you!" Welei's voice cut through the silence that encroached upon him. Their face was peeking over the top of Phoebe's desk.

Everything happened so fast. Young launched himself at Welei, but Thlayli bodied him halfway to the desk. They fell, twisted around each other. Young's foot came down onto Thlayli's leg and a crunch followed. His hands wrapped around Thlayli's throat. A shrill, ear-piercing scream caused the windows to shiver, and Thlayli's teeth dug right into Young's cheek.

Vanja was by the statue of Sir Thaddeus, and the stream from the water fountain was shooting right at Young's back on her behest. He and Thlayli were right below the statue, flailing and writhing but refusing to let go of one another.

"Spot, get 'em!" Murphy's voice cut through the screaming. With a growl, a bark, and a whine, Spot lunged at Young. One of her heads grabbed him by the throat, another by the waist, and the third was snapping at his face as he attempted to keep her hot, slobbering maw away from him.

"Brooke, do something!" Phoebe and Murphy were with Thlayli; Welei was still behind the desk and Vanja was suddenly by them. Spot and Young were still by the statue. Josef approached it.

Josef pushed, and he could feel the muscles tear beneath his skin. He pushed, and he felt the burn on his back protest. He pushed, and the fire within his belly burned, feeding on his organs. He pushed, and his vision grew blurry, smoking billowing out of his nose with every pained huff.

There was nothing but the statue, the pain. The cacophony of screams was drowned out by his heartbeat drumming away in his ears. The light of the moon was but a pinprick, resting upon Young's struggling body. The statue was growing hot against his skin, Sir Thaddeus' handsome profile looking down at him with scorn. Young's mangled, and yet still beautiful, face was zeroed in on him with gnashing teeth, but Josef no longer saw him, nor the statue, nor anything but the blinding whiteness before his eyes. He just pushed.

He pushed for Shark who loved him despite his DNA. He pushed for Vanja who saw him as more than just the nephew of Josef Braun. He pushed for Phoebe and Murphy and Thlayli who saw him as a friend. He pushed for his father, Dante, who was always so proud of him. He pushed for his mother, Elspeth, who taught him to use his strength for good. He pushed for his Uncle Josef who taught him about his heritage. He pushed for his Uncle Brooke whose legacy had always been kindness and compassion. He pushed for himself, because he knew that he could, because he knew that he had to.

He pushed to prove Young wrong. He pushed to show Young that he was better. He pushed to show Young that he wasn't weak. He pushed and felt the rivulets of blood cascade down his back.

Josef Brooke Ryan pushed with a roar that echoed through the entire building, shattering the glass in every window. He pushed until the steel cords snapped and the statue tipped, teetered on the corner of its pedestal. Young barely had time to turn his head before it collapsed atop him. He didn't make a single sound. He simply smiled at Josef. And that smile reached his eyes.

Spot was at his side before his knees hit the linoleum floors. There was pain, a series of searing hot slashes across his back. The steel cords had left his skin shredded, the tension when they snapped shooting them backwards towards Josef and the statue. He felt as if his body had been filled up with acid that coursed through his veins, burning him from the inside. His hot blood burned; the lashes burned. He didn't even notice when his vision was going grey at the edges.

"Brooke, talk to me." The soft, melodic voice was paired with a delicate hand against his cheek. He couldn't place if that was Vanja or Welei.

"Talk to us, dragon-eyes." The familiar nickname had come from behind him, but he was in too much pain to turn his head.

"I'm alive," he whispered, his voice hoarse and his throat burning. When he swallowed, the fire within his lungs only worsened, scorching his throat further.

"You're alive, my love, you are." And this time Josef knew that it was Welei that was whispering into his ear, and it was their cheek that pressed against the side of his face.

He was alive, he was real, and the world hadn't ended after all.

16

Saying Goodbye

He woke up in the car when a pothole jostled him, and his entire back became bathed in ice. When the icy cold eased up, it burst into flames, and each small movement would interchange between cold, freezing pain, and a burning like that of the sun.

"Brooke, you're awake!" His hiss of pain had alerted Vanja, now in the driver's seat of Murphy's Kia. His vision was blurry, tears were streaming down his face, and yet he would've recognised her anywhere.

"Man, I'm so glad you're okay, Brooke." Murphy's voice was barely above a whisper, thick with sleep. He was pressed up against Josef's shoulder, and that was when Josef realised that Phoebe was the one in the passenger seat instead of him. His head hurt, pounding incessantly, and his back was tearing itself apart with every gentle jostle of the car.

His throat was thick, burning him as he tried to speak. "What happened?"

"The police arrived." Phoebe didn't elaborate, but she turned around in her seat, staring at him. Her earrings were dangling and catching glimpses of light that the moon outside cast upon the car. It was a welcome distraction from the pain.

"They miraculously let us take you away instead of calling an ambulance for you." Murphy's hand was outside of Josef's peripheral vision, and it hurt every time Josef tried turning his neck, but he was doing *something* with that hand.

"Said that we'd take you there ourselves. But we're hoping your dad's nurse might be able to help out with that."

"Murphy turned into Young, and Phoebe helped him talk to police." Vanja's voice was also thick with sleepiness, and he had to wonder how long they had been driving, if they would make it, if all of this had been in vain or not. "We explained that statue of Sir Thaddeus fell and you got hurt."

"But ... what about Young? Couldn't they see his body?" His body, the body of a dead man, the body of Charles Young. By the ancestors, there was a body, there was a dead man. Josef had killed someone.

"There was nothing there, Brooke," Murphy mumbled into his shoulder. "Just dust." But dust that was once a body, was it not?

"You saved them, dragon-eyes."

He had killed a man. He was a murderer. Murphy's gentle hand grasped the back of his neck, ever so slightly moving his head until Josef was looking down. There was Spot laying across his feet, her three heads resting on the seat between him and Murphy. Then there were two rabbits, one doe-brown giant with lop ears, and one pitch black, skinny thing. They were curled up together in his lap, their tiny heads resting against his stomach.

"You saved them, Brooke."

He had saved them. These helpless, hurt beings who had been tormented by a cruel, inhuman man for years. They were safe because of him. He would have the scars to prove it, and the pain would forever be a reminder.

***

Sue met them at the door with a scream. Josef refused to have his back looked at. He rushed through the house, the others following behind.

"Are these your friends, hatchling?" Dante was uncomfortably pale, his skin taut over his face. He was cold to the touch when Josef reached out, and his eyes were completely white.

"Mhm. Vanja's here," Josef said, and he heard his voice as if on the other side of a tunnel. Dante's face lit up when his daughter came over to grasp his other hand.

"This is Murphy, my boyfriend." Vanja's voice was a whisper.

"This is Phoebe, my friend from work." Josef picked up from there. "That's Thlayli, with the long ears. And this ... this is Welei, my partner."

"Hi, dad," Welei said, hovering over Josef's shoulder, watching Dante smile. Their hand was pressed against Josef's elbow. They had eaten in the car and already seemed so light on their feet. Now they were there to catch him were he to fall.

"Oh, hatchling." Dante's voice grew weaker with every word. "I'm so happy for you. So, so happy." His warm breath created clouds of smoke before his face. The smoke eventually disappeared.

"He waited for us, Brooke," Vanja said. Her voice was barely there.

"He did. He held on for us, Vanja." Josef looked at her. They hugged. Over her shoulder he saw the last of the stars in the night sky blink out of existence.

***

In his will, Josef's father left him the cottage and another sum of money that he put away in a fund alongside the money his uncles left him. Over the coming days they settled in. Phoebe, Murphy, and Vanja left them after a week. Murphy had decided to 'inherit' the FCMC from his uncle, and Phoebe was ready to help him with all of the paperwork that entailed. No one had to know that Young was dead, they just had to think that he was bequeathing everything that he owned to his nephew and moving to an island somewhere to live out the rest of his days. Vanja had never been more on board with anything in her life, and Josef wasn't sure if he should have been worried about that.

That left Welei, Thlayli, and him. The cottage had been furnished in a rustic style Josef always had a soft spot for. There was a master bedroom he shared with Welei, and one of the guest bedrooms was given to Thlayli. Spot had her own mini-bedroom in the walk-in closet of the master bedroom. His father had thought of everything.

17

Healing After The Storm

Healing was difficult. At least for him. Welei seemed to heal in such a short time that it was almost hard to believe.

"My love." Welei always talked to him when changing his bandages. The lacerations over his shoulders and arms had left him with permanent muscle damage, and the lashes that covered almost his entire back would ache until the day he died. And each day, as they peeled away the bloodied strips of cloth, careful not to cause any tearing, they whispered sweet nothings into his skin. Each day, as their lithe, alien hands worked and massaged a healing balm into his skin, they would hum and sing little songs they had heard on the radio or made up themself. Each day, as they rewound the bandages around his torso, tying the knot off into a perfect, little bow, they would call him 'love', and 'darling', and 'sweetheart', and 'my hero'. Josef liked that last one, he could hardly deny it. When the pain had his knees buckling, when it stopped him from falling asleep at night, 'my hero' made him remember why he had done it. When the amethyst eyes of Charles Young invaded his sleep, and the black sky outside pierced through his nightmares, 'my hero' kept him going. It was a decision he could hardly regret.

"*Mi tesoro*," he would mumble into the crown of Welei's head at night, the bags under his eyes heavy and dark, "I would kill for you again." It terrified him how much he meant it.

That was it, then, wasn't it? That was love. Over the coming months, they had made it from 'feeling' to 'love'. From simply a 'connection' to an intimacy they could never share with anyone else. But it wasn't at night when Josef loved them most. It wasn't in the throes of pleasure when Welei doted upon him, still bed-bound as he was. It wasn't in the bare-skinned hold they would have on each other, each time one of them woke up from a nightmare. Their nightmares often shared similarities, but it wasn't that which made Josef's heart burn, the dragon fire within his belly spreading out across his entire body until his whole being was engulfed with the overwhelming feeling of Welei.

It was in the day that he loved them most.

"I bought us chickens," they said one day, before Josef even had the time to notice they were gone all morning. Their hair was up in a long braid, and they were dressed in embroidered overalls, carrying a pair of chickens, one under each arm. He was sitting at the kitchen table with his glasses discarded (he never wore them around the cottage), shirtless and without any bandages, as the cloth tended to make his fresh scars itch.

"Weren't you supposed to be in bed, Shark?"

Welei let out a melodic giggle at the nickname, flashing Josef their shark-like teeth. Their lips pressed against his brow, and one of the chickens let out a loud cluck in protest.

"I was, but I felt bored. Vanja said she'd meet me at the farmer's market in the nearby town." They were beaming as they set the chickens down in the middle of the kitchen, cooing at the birds and listening to them cluck. Josef almost regretted getting them a mobile phone, until he noticed the healthy flush upon their cheeks and the way their face was rounding out with every day that passed. Their skin no longer looked translucent and was even tanning gently from all the time they spent in the garden. He might have still been semi-bed-bound, but Vanja was giving them a run for their money. And they loved it. Moments like these reminded Josef of why he loved them so much.

The daytime love eventually bled into their nightly activities. When he lay in bed with them at night, their arms no longer felt fragile wrapped around his neck, their body no longer promising to slip from his fingers like smoke. Their body was still cold to the touch, but he made up for it with the fire that burned in his belly. They didn't need intimacy anymore to love each other, they didn't need bodies to show one another that they mattered. Not when the sun rose in the morning and made Welei's skin glow in a way that took Josef's breath away, or when the stars peppered the night sky and Welei could see their own galaxy reflected in Josef's russet eyes.

Love was a feeling, but very few feelings truly compared to love.

"What if we bought a goat?" Josef reached out and pressed a finger against Welei's cheek. They let out a snort that was just as melodic as the rest of their laughs, even if it made them sound like a little piggy.

"Really? You mean that? Brookie, I love you!"

"I love you too." And that was the easiest thing Josef had ever done: chosen to love Welei with his whole heart.

***

Thlayli mostly stayed up in his room during the months he was healing. Three times a day Welei would bring food up to him, juggling the responsibility of helping him and helping Josef. Maybe it was because they were an alien that they never seemed to run out of energy.

Thlayli didn't need his bandages changed like Josef did, but his broken leg healed slowly, aggravated by the shifts he was forced into during the night. Welei tried, on multiple occasions, to bring him and Josef together into one room, to let them recuperate together. In the early days the pain made Josef loopy, barely conscious of anything that was going on around him. Thlayli simply preferred being alone.

However, when he was able to, he would do exercises. Welei would pull him up and off the bed, slowly walking around the room with him. He would let out silent whimpers in the first few months, scrunching his face up with pain. And yet he kept at it, and soon was able to walk on his own again. Soon, he was walking to the master bedroom with little steps. He would sit with Welei, watching them go through exercises with Josef, getting some movement into the muscles of his massacred back.

"I'll never move my arms normally again," Josef would often bemoan, regurgitating the hurried words of the nurse, Sue. Thlayli would scooch up to him, dislodging Welei from their spot. He would press his cold nose against Josef's side and watch with glee as his arms flailed wildly.

"I dunno," Welei would respond with merriment, "you're doing great, if you ask me." That was in the later months, however, of their healing.

In the early days, when unable to move from the bed, Thlayli loved reading or being read to. He had a copy of *Watership Down* on his bedside table and would force Welei, and later Josef as well, to read it to him. Welei knew it off by heart by the time Thlayli first ended up with Young but would still indulge him by pretending to read off the page. Welei couldn't count the amount of times Thlayli had fallen asleep on their shoulder as they read to him. They could only hope he dreamt of his own Watership Down.

In the later days, Thlayli would often visit Josef when Welei was away. They would sit together for an hour at a time, Josef teaching him hand signs. First finger spelling, then simple words like 'eat', 'drink', or 'sleep'. By the end of his stay, they were having entire conversations. Josef, bed-bound as he was, thought the world of Thlayli whenever he came over to his room to visit. Thlayli, once he knew how, would not stop thanking Josef for indulging him. Welei would often watch on as they signed back and forth, simply smiling.

Their conversations eventually led to Thlayli asking to go home.

Interlude 5: Josef, Welei, and Thlayli

They were standing at the edge of the forest, a few miles from the Ryan-Braun cottage. Shark watched as Thlayli undressed, handing each article of clothing to Josef. He stood there for a few heart beats, his short fur standing on end from the light breeze. The shift took but a few seconds, preceded by him bringing his hand up to his face. With a flat palm pressed against the tip of his chin, he moved his hand in an arc away from himself. Then, once he was back to his rabbit form, he disappeared into the brush.

Josef took a step back, moving into Welei's awaiting arms. He was shaking, not from the cold but from something else.

"Are you sure this is right?" Josef watched Thlayli disappear beneath the protection of the trees. Welei smiled at him, bringing their face closer to his neck, soaking up his warmth.

"It's what he wants, Brooke," Welei whispered against his collarbone, their wide, endless eyes tracing the path Thlayli took through the underbrush. "He'll be back. No matter how many times he told me he wouldn't return, he always did. We'll see him again."

"And when we do," Josef added, his voice growing thick, "he'll be happy again."

"He will, my love. He will. And so will we."

About the Author

Booker-Garet August Feniks (known under the penname Booker G. A Feniks) is a queer, disabled writer of fantasy, comedy, & poetry. He writes stories that pull directly from their experiences growing up trans & autistic in a foreign country. Originally from Poland, Kielce, Booker writes primarily in English, & has a passion for linguistics & storytelling as a whole. He is young, ambitious, & optimistic about the changing future, although not unfamiliar with activism & the more difficult aspects of growing up marginalised.

Never, Never

Callie Taylor

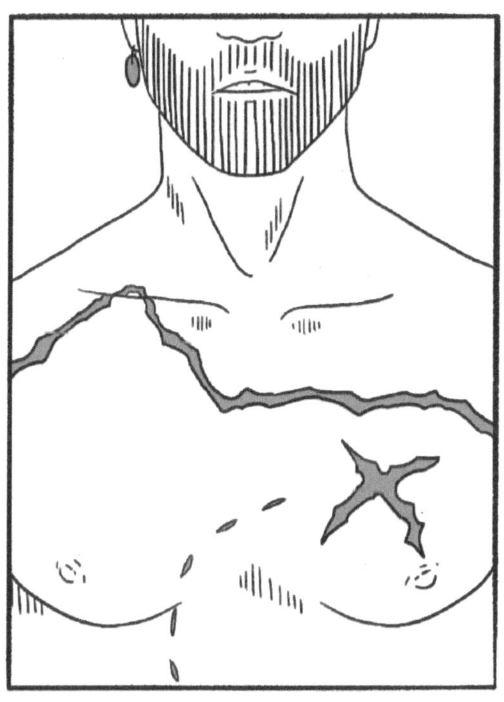

Cover Design by Nicole Alessi

Cover Illustration by Hen Towers

Dedicated to Elli, whose endless enthusiasm and encouragement for this story helped me to see it through.

Contents

Content Warnings

This story contains the following content:

- Heavy gore, including amputation and torture
- Restraints
- Captivity
- Nonconsensual drug use
- Begging for death

If this book isn't for you, no worries! But if it is, we hope you enjoy this story about a very unfortunate captain ...

1

Left

"Pick a hand."

James eyed his captor, sullen and silent. For two days, he'd been a prisoner in the brig of his own ship. No food, no water, kept bound in the same bent position by rough rope. No idea if the men still loyal to him were even *alive*.

His body ached, his head was pounding, his mouth felt swollen, and here was Peter, first mate turned mutineer, giving him stupid orders.

"*Pick a hand*," Peter said again, sounding annoyed.

"Why?" James spat out, his voice rasping. "Why should I do anything you ask of me?"

Peter clicked his tongue. "Well, now, you don't sound like someone who wants a drink of water."

James scowled. So this was how it was going to be. He'd have to play Peter's games, cave in to his demands, just for the pleasure of keeping himself alive. *Fine.* His life was worth more to him than his pride.

"Left," he said, and Peter's face broke into a smile.

"There we go!" he said, producing a small flask from his hip and unscrewing the lid. He pressed it to James's mouth, and he drank, unable to grasp it himself with his hands tied behind his back. It was taken away too soon.

"Now, you said your left hand?" Peter asked, moving behind him. James tensed as his former first mate cut the hand in question loose in such a way that the other was still tied firmly in place. Traitor or not, Peter was skilled in rope tricks. He gripped his wrist tightly, and James winced as his arm was straightened for the first time in days.

Even with one hand freed, the rest of his body was practically immobilized. Trying to fight at this point would undoubtedly fail. His best hope was to entertain Peter's whims until the traitor let his guard down.

"*Left hand, left hand*. Good choice," Peter said, tracing a finger along James's palm, something wild in his eyes. "Now, will you let me cut it off?"

James clenched his jaw. Even though he'd suspected this was the way things were headed, the words were a shock. "*What*?"

"I want to cut off your hand," Peter said. "But only if you tell me to. Will you?"

What kind of game was he playing now? "No. Why would I?"

"Okay!" Peter said brightly, suddenly releasing his arm. James watched him stride out of the room, flexing his fingers. Was that it? Was Peter just trying to mess with his head? He took a shaky breath when the other man returned a few moments later, carrying what looked like a small anvil.

Of course not. Peter's games are never so simple.

The anvil was placed a few feet to James's left, and he felt a shudder run through him when he saw the metal cuff welded to the top. Where had Peter come by such a thing? Had it been the last time the crew made port? He wouldn't know. As a young captain, it seemed a poor choice to mingle with his crew on a friendly level. Better to command respect and leave the befriending to the first mate, he'd told himself after taking the helm of *The Scarlet Merry*. Only now could he see what a mistake that had been.

James was too weak to pull away when Peter seized his hand and could do nothing as he was dragged from the wall, body stretched as far as his restraints allowed, left wrist locked into place atop the anvil.

"I'm going to ask again," Peter said, and his voice wasn't harsh or threatening, just matter-of-fact. "Can I cut off your hand?"

James's heart pounded in his ears, worsening the headache that had nestled between his temples the first day and refused to leave. Should he just say yes? Get whatever Peter had in store over with? Or would he really be spared if he denied the request? He squeezed his eyes shut, thinking of climbing the rigging, steering the ship, engaging in battle. All things better served with two hands intact.

"No," he said at last.

"Alright then," Peter said cheerfully, drawing a small knife. Its edge was polished, razor-sharp, and its hilt was shaped in the likeness of a crocodile, scales rippling gold in the dim light of the brig, twin rows of teeth pulled apart to let the blade spill out, as if the beast were breathing fire. James felt his blood run cold as Peter brought it down to trace the outline of his hand, the dead metal eye of the creature watching him without pity.

"That means I get to convince you."

***

Peter started with the ring finger. One long, deep cut along the inside of it, a few more around the circumference, and he was able to set to work on removing the skin.

No amount of begging or threatening would stop him; James found that out within a few minutes. He'd tried to clench his hand into a fist, but Peter struck him against the knuckles with the hilt of the knife and threatened to take an eye if he made this difficult, so he'd given up on protecting the hand and took to screaming instead.

"*Cut it off, cut it off!*" he howled as the finger was reduced to bone and muscle, and then not even that as Peter began to slice away at the tendons.

Peter responded in a calm, friendly voice as he dug the point of the knife into the first joint and began to pry it away, "It's too late for that. You can only tell me to cut it off when I ask you if you're *ready* for it to be cut off."

And so James could only wail helplessly, straining against the bindings that held him in place until his skin burned and bled wherever the rope touched it. He would have been sick if his stomach had anything to give up.

Peter hummed as he carried on, removing more and more of the finger until it was down to the knuckle. He paused then, looking at the bloody space thoughtfully, and for a moment, James dared to hope he was done.

But then Peter jammed the point of the knife into the wound, and James's vision went white with pain. For a blissful few seconds, he knew nothing, *felt* nothing. But when the world came back to him, Peter was holding his thumb.

***

He didn't know how long it took as the process was repeated, the slow filleting of each finger, the piece-by-piece removal of bone. James's mind felt like it had melted into the pain, each new excruciating stroke indistinguishable from the last as he faded in and out of consciousness, barely able to do more than whimper as his body shook and his hand was *taken* from him one slice at a time.

Eventually, he opened his eyes to see everything gone, the remains of his hand sitting amid discarded flesh and gore, blood weeping from hollow knuckles with every thump of his heart. Peter was carving the skin off his palm, still humming a carefree tune, paying no mind to the scarlet that coated his hands, his knife, his clothes. The mouth of the reptilian hilt was red through and through, like the little metal beast had just messily devoured something. In some twisted way, it had.

James let out a sound that was something between a sob and an animalistic whine, and Peter's gaze flicked down.

"Ah, you're awake!" He lifted the knife, twirling it between two fingers. "Now, I hope you remember the rules, because it's your turn again."

His turn. As if they were playing cards. James couldn't speak, couldn't even nod. It had to be over. He couldn't take any more of this slow slicing. *It had to be over.*

"I think you know what I'm going to ask you," Peter continued in a singsong voice. James only stared up at him. His vision was swimming. He had to stay conscious long enough. He had to be able to say the word, just one word.

"*Can I cut off your hand*?"

2

Clarity

Asleep and awake interchanged so quickly James no longer knew which was which. Both were dark and foggy and full of pain. He began to dread even those short bursts of true unconsciousness; they only meant he'd have to come back to awareness and get used to the agony all over again. His limbs ached endlessly, his body shook, his arm was on fire. All he wanted was for it to stop, to crawl out of his skin and never come back, but nothing would even so much as take his mind off it. His whole world was pain, the pull of the ropes, the memory of Peter's sadistic little smile. The only freedom he could imagine was death, and even that was beginning to sound sweet.

In his moments of clarity, James found himself wishing Peter had seen fit to kill him in the battle that lost him the ship. Wouldn't that have been easier? Wouldn't that have been kinder? Better to die unbound, on his feet, a sword in his hand. Better to die as captain.

James had no conception of how long it had been since the little golden knife had first left its sheath. And how long had it been since he'd been able to glimpse the horizon, the blue of the sea? Time didn't matter anymore, had no consequence. There was no time, there was only the fever of sleep and the haze of wakefulness. He cried for water, for morphine, for someone to shoot him and be *done* with it. The latter two requests were ignored, and so he continued the cycle, now and then rising into moments of awareness, only to be swiftly pulled back under the waves.

After one such spell of peaceful nothingness, James woke to find himself in a bed. Well, sort of a bed. A mat had been placed between him and the wooden floor, a blanket draped over him to form a barricade between his body and the cool sea air. Whoever had done it even had the decency to untie him. Between his next bouts of unconsciousness, he was aware of bandages being changed, the abrasions from the rope being cleaned, water being poured down his throat in a trickle.

Somewhere deep beneath the fog of delirium and pain, this scared him.

Peter was trying to keep him alive. *Why* was Peter trying to keep him alive? The thought added dread to his waking moments and turned his fever dreams to terror. In them, Peter would cut into him again. His leg, his throat, or most often, his hand. Only this time, it kept growing back.

***

Gradually, the fire that enveloped his arm began to cool, his thoughts becoming more lucid. The next time he was visited by whoever had taken to caring for him, he was awake.

Esme Jedediah, Jeddy to the crew of *The Scarlet Merry*, swung the door open, a bowl in her hand and a roll of bandages tucked under her arm. Soft sunlight falling down the stairs from the deck above cast her in an almost ethereal light, setting a glow to her dark skin and turning her tight curls into a halo. The picture of an angel of mercy.

Or destruction. Keeping him alive at a demon's bidding.

She seemed surprised to see James staring at her.

"Looks like your fever's broke," she said in a low voice, dropping to one knee and setting the bowl on the ground next to him.

"How long – " he tried to say, but his voice wouldn't work, his throat creaking with the effort. He tried again. "How long has it been?"

She shrugged, staring down at the bowl. "Somethin' like a week. The captain did a number on you."

His heart sank at her words. *The captain*. He liked Jeddy. Quiet but competent, serious about her job as master gunner. She'd lived practically her whole life at sea. He hadn't seen her during the initial scuffle and had hoped she'd escaped, hoped she hadn't been one of those ready to betray him. But here she was. Calling Peter 'captain.'

She turned her attention to the stump of his left arm, unwinding the stained bandage. He winced as it pulled at the skin, doing his best to choke down a whimper.

"Glad you're finally awake, though," she said as she bunched up the soiled dressing. "I was gettin' tired of listening to your weepin' and moanin'."

James dared to cast a glance at his now-unbandaged arm, his stomach twisting. Crude stitches holding together reddened flesh, blood oozing between them.

Jeddy saw him staring. "Peter left you with a hack-job," she said, dipping a cloth into the bowl beside him. "I had to clean it up after he was done. Slice off the tatters so I could patch it up nicer – "

James was rolled over on his side, dry-heaving, before she could finish. *Slice off the tatters*, just a few more cuts, a few more pieces *removed ...*

She eased him back onto the mat. The effort had left his head swimming, tears streaming down his face as concern lined Jeddy's.

"Easy now, just breathe and you'll be alright, cap – " She caught herself, glancing back down at the bowl. "Mm. You should probably have somethin' to eat," she mumbled, wiping the wound with the doused cloth. Whatever was in the bowl, it stung, and James found himself suppressing another whine.

His stomach twisted again at the mention of food. He was hungry, outright *starving*, but he didn't know if he could keep anything down. Unbidden came the memories of dinners with the crew, celebrations after a successful raid or a good trade, tables full of fish and bread and wine, sometimes fruit, sometimes sweets, always laughter and loud, jovial voices. He'd always taken so much care to be a part of it while maintaining a bit of distance. If they saw him as a friend, a peer, how would he ever maintain order? Respect?

Now it seemed those things hardly mattered. Peter had always sat among the others, laughing with them, sharing stories. He'd been with the *Merry* a scant two years, and yet it seemed the crew would follow him anywhere. Why hadn't James *seen* that they would follow him anywhere?

Jeddy finished cleaning his arm, rebandaged it with deft fingers, and produced a waterskin. "Drink," she said, and he did. The fingers of his right hand were too weak to keep a good hold on it, but Jeddy seemed to anticipate this and helped him keep it steady, tilting his head up with her free hand.

He felt like an infant, frail and helpless. He hated it, but his body betrayed him. It needed the water, the helping hand. His base instincts insisted he try to survive. Jeddy re-stopped the waterskin once it was apparent he could drink no more, pulling aside her worn leather jacket to hook it back onto her belt.

"Keep awake a while longer. I'll bring you some soup," she said, pushing herself up from the floor. James nodded, trying to sit up, but finding himself too weak to even lift his head. Jeddy saw this and knelt back down, helping him into a seated position and moving him so his back was supported by the wall.

The motion made his vision swim. He felt *hollow*, carved out of something far more delicate than flesh and bone. Jeddy laid his mutilated arm on his lap, and the limb throbbed with the shift in position.

"Now, as I said, keep awake." She stood again, making to leave.

"Wait. Jeddy." As much as he dreaded the answer he was about to seek, James couldn't let himself stew in the unknown any longer. He took a breath to steel himself. "Why is he letting you help me? Why ... why am I not *dead*?" He didn't know what he wanted to hear; there didn't seem to be a good outcome. Expertise or an execution in front of the crew, neither would be pleasant in Peter's hands.

Jeddy fixed him with a grim look. "I thought you'd figure it out on your own," she began, turning the door handle. It opened with a soft creak.

"Peter ain't done with you yet."

3

Playing Games

A week went by, at least as far as James could tell. A week of gentle wooden creaks as the ship bobbed on the waters, of straining to hear the voices above deck, of dark air that only ever brightened when the door to the brig swung open. James filled most of his time with sleep and, on the rare occasion the pain in his arm dulled enough for him to think, tried to distract himself with memories. Only the good ones, when he could help it. He tried to recall days of his youth, sailing aboard a merchant ship, long before he'd turned pirate. Sun, storms, and hard work; learning the ins and outs of a ship and earning his place aboard it. He'd been nineteen when he abandoned *King's Joy* for *The Scarlet Merry*, back when Greyson was still captain and James was only a deckhand. Years turned him to second mate, then first, then at last to captain when Greyson decided it was time to retire. And now he'd gone from captain to prisoner, faster than a person could sink to the bottom of the sea.

His memories were tinged with bitterness by the fate he now found himself in, but they brought him less pain than his body did, at least temporarily, and were better than fearing the future.

In his time of rest, Jeddy was his sole visitor, bringing water and a thin soup, checking his wound and changing the bandages daily. When the pain had ebbed enough, James was able to take a more thorough stock of his situation.

His ankles were still cuffed together, a small link of chain between them, connected to a longer one that spanned several feet and was bolted to the wall.

As if he could *stand* on his own, much less try to run. The fever and lack of food had incapacitated him as well as any binding could. If the ship were docked and every restraint removed, James doubted he could even make it to the door.

Jeddy didn't speak much during her visits, only ever commenting on his condition. He didn't dare ask what Peter had in store for him, and even if he did, he wasn't sure she'd be able to answer. Peter was unpredictable. It was impossible to pin down what he might be thinking at any given moment.

Even the mutiny had come out of nowhere. There had been no preamble, no murmurs of discontent. The traitors aboard *The Scarlet Merry* had simply sprung, outnumbering the loyal few, quickly overpowering their former captain and tossing him below.

If only he'd had just another instant of awareness of the plot. He could've fought back harder. They could've killed him, he could've escaped the pain, the *dread* he was currently stewing in.

The food Jeddy brought did little to help him regain his strength, and he couldn't even look at his arm without wanting to empty his stomach. He could feel the ghost of his left hand, nonexistent wounds still being dealt to the nonexistent appendage.

He was blinking away sleep when the door opened, but this time it wasn't Jeddy standing at the entrance.

It was Peter.

The false captain strode into the room, stopping to loom over James, who glowered up at him. Afraid as he might be of what came next, he couldn't find it in him to cower before his captor. To beg for mercy, for release, for a swift death. Not yet. If a threat presented itself, if Peter started cutting into another part of him, James didn't think he'd be able to stop himself from begging. He knew he wouldn't survive a repeat of his hand, and didn't care to die screaming.

"I'm glad to see you up," Peter said, crouching next to him. James did not reply, but his former first mate didn't seem to mind, taking hold of his arm and rotating it so the stump was facing him. James held his breath as the other man began unwinding the bandage.

"Hm," he said, tracing his finger along the stitching. James flinched back, but Peter's grip only tightened.

"*Shh*, no, no," he said, voice barely above a whisper, a mockery of soothing. "Don't try and pull away. Remember what I said would happen if you made this difficult." He closed one eye. "Remember?"

James nodded, feeling his resolve crumble away.

"Say it. Tell me what will happen."

"You'll ... you'll take an eye," James said, his voice like still water, like the slightest ripples could set Peter off.

"That I will," Peter said, grinning. "I wonder how long I could make that last. What do you think? Will you let me put it out right away? Or will I have to cut out a few pieces first? I've seen the inside of an eye before, but never a live one. I wonder how many layers I can cut off if I'm careful. I wonder how much it will bleed – "

James's chest hitched, a sob escaping and cutting Peter short. He could imagine it. He could *feel* it. The golden crocodile sinking its teeth into the socket, biting and chewing and eating as his vision went red, then disappeared. The heat of tears trailed down his face.

"Shhh, don't cry," Peter said softly, wiping away the tears with a gentle hand. His thumb lingered under James's right eye, pressed in lightly. "Does that mean you'll let me do it?"

His chest felt like it was freezing over. "If ... only if I'm difficult. You said – "

"Yes. If you're difficult. Will you let me cut your eye out? I'll let you pick which one." He pressed his finger deeper when James was silent. "*Say it.*"

James nodded, more tears spilling onto his cheeks. In that moment, they felt like blood. "If I make it difficult. I-I want you to put out my eye."

"There, that wasn't so hard," Peter said, pulling away. He stood, letting James's wounded arm drop onto the wooden floor. The pain shooting up from the stump was *nothing* compared to the fate James felt he'd only barely avoided.

"Now, aren't you curious?" Peter said. "Have you been wondering why I did it? Surely you have." He nudged James with his boot. "Yes? No?"

James swallowed, waiting until he was sure he could steady his voice. "Yes," he said. He *was* curious, but he was already anticipating another torturous 'game.' Peter rarely did anything without some sly plan in the works.

"Guess why," Peter said.

"I don't know," James replied.

"Well, *obviously* you don't, but I want you to guess."

James stared up at him, silent as his mind scrambled for whatever answer Peter would deem correct. Peter smiled down at him. Closed one eye.

"You – you got bored," James said quickly, and Peter tapped his nose.

"Good guess! Good, and *almost* right." Without warning, he brought his foot down hard, stomping on the remains of James's left arm and dragging a scream from his throat.

"Almost isn't good enough," Peter continued. His tone was conversational, like they were talking over tea. "Would you like to guess again?"

"*Hnng* – no." James clutched his arm. The stump where it now ended throbbed horribly. Some of the stitched skin had broken, blood trailing down toward his elbow.

"Alright then, suppose I'll tell you." Peter cleared his throat, spread his arms in a grand gesture. "*The fountain of youth.*"

That was enough to cut through the pain, if only for an instant.

"What?" James said.

"I knew you'd think it mad," Peter said. "And I knew you'd say no. You'd say it was a myth. A fairy tale."

"It *is*," James hissed.

"And I'll chase it forever if that's what it takes," Peter said.

James couldn't help but wonder if this was yet another game, a trick to quicken the loss of his sanity. The fountain of youth. It was a myth, *only* a myth. *The Scarlet Merry* would rot in the water before such a thing could be found.

"I hope you're not disappointed," Peter said. "You didn't think the mutiny was about you, did you?"

"If – if it wasn't, then why – ?"

"Why cut off your hand?" He grinned. "Well, it's like you said. I was bored."

James pressed his back into the wall as the other man leaned down, willing it to break and spill his body into the sea. Peter leaned over him, brushing a strand of dark hair out of his face.

"Now, you'd better get some rest. I believe I'll be bored again quite soon."

4

A Form of Surrender

"Why you?"

Jeddy visited him a few hours after Peter had gone, to tend his arm and help him eat another bowl of thin soup. The conversation with his former first mate had left him shaken. Beyond the threat of further mutilation, it had been made clear that he had only been left alive on a whim. To him, that meant he could also be *killed* on a whim and tortured whenever Peter was struck with inspiration. And if he stayed chained down here, such a fate would only be a matter of *when.*

Jeddy raised an eyebrow at his question, wordlessly asking what he meant. James swallowed down another spoonful of his meal.

"You're a gunner, not a nurse," he said. Not just a gunner, but the *Merry*'s master gunner. Quick behind a cannon, quicker to sort any problems that arose during combat and issue the commands to turn the tide of the fight. A soft-spoken woman whose voice hardened and sharpened in the heat of battle, whose eyes came alive when she was protecting her ship. A fighter.

Jeddy shrugged at his question. "The doc jumped ship when the fightin' started. I know my way around a wound, so I volunteered after ... " She pressed her lips together tightly. "After we heard the screamin'."

James nodded, silent. He knew it was stupid, the shame that rolled through him at her words, but the thought of his crew – his *former* crew – listening to him wailing, crying, *begging* for it to end ...

He elected to change the subject.

"Peter said he's after the fountain of youth. He ... he just needed a ship and crew to get there. Are you with him on that?"

She shrugged again. "Dunno. I go where the *Merry* goes."

"No matter who's at the helm," James said. She didn't answer at first, stirring the bowl of soup and staring into the whirlpool of broth she'd created until the liquid stilled.

"You were a good captain," she said at last. "I was sorry this happened, but Peter has too strong a sway over the others, and I won't leave this ship." She didn't look at him, hands tightly wound around the bowl. "But as I said, you were a good captain. I can get you something to help. Morphine. Scale. Rum. Something to put you out of your wits until it's over – "

"No," James cut her off. "For the pain, *yes*, but if you only want me to be lost in myself ... no."

"Peter can be cruel, we both know it," Jeddy said. "I'd surely have nightmares if I knew what else he had in store for you."

He was tempted for a moment. How easy would it be to surrender himself to substance, to die a little less painfully? It might even spite Peter. The other man wouldn't glean so much joy from hurting him if he wasn't even coherent enough to know where he was.

Yet it *would be* surrendering. Giving up on any hope, any chance of catching his captor off-guard and escaping. As small as that spark of hope was, it was still there, and he didn't want to lose a chance to fan it into a flame.

He clenched his jaw, placing his right hand on Jeddy's forearm.

"If you want to help me, bring me more food. Bread. Meat if you can." He was well past the fever, but still kept on the brink of starvation by the scant amounts of soup. No doubt part of Peter's plan to keep him weakened.

Jeddy frowned. "The captain won't like it ... but I can try."

And for the next few days, she did. Chunks of fish hidden within the broth he'd been surviving on, biscuits smuggled in with the bandages. He found it almost touching that she'd risk trouble for him. Hells, she'd asked to care for him in the first place. Before she'd admitted to volunteering, James had assumed she was only tending him on Peter's orders. If she hadn't offered to care for him, would Peter have sent someone crueler? Now that his former first mate's true colors had flown, James had no doubt there were cruel men to be found onboard. At the last port, Peter had hired on new hands, *strangers*, and like a fool, James had trusted his judgment.

The realization that it could have been so much worse sat sour in his gut, and despite where he was and how hopeless it all seemed, in that moment he was endlessly grateful for Jeddy, mutineer or not. It wasn't about Peter for her. It was about the ship. She'd already been a crew member when James had inherited the *Merry* from her previous captain, and she'd been aboard longer than even he had. So in a way, he could understand. Jeddy wasn't a traitor; her loyalties would always lie with *The Scarlet Merry* herself.

***

On her next visit, Jeddy's expression was grimmer than usual.

James thought of asking her what was wrong, if there was some kind of trouble on deck, but pushed the questions away. If she wanted to tell him, she'd tell him.

She handed him the soup bowl, followed by a hunk of bread. Missing hand aside, his left arm was healing steadily, and he'd regained enough strength to sit up on his own. He'd even been working on standing, taking small careful steps around the room, as far as the chains would allow him, when he was sure he was alone. Feeble preparations for an escape opportunity that may never present itself, but each footfall was a small victory, proving to himself that whatever torments Peter dreamt up, he could still stand tall.

The soup of the day was thicker than usual, a hearty mash of beans and bacon. It was probably the best meal he'd had in weeks, and though he did his best to eat slowly, his attempts to savor it didn't last long.

Jeddy said nothing as he ate, which was far from unusual, but something in her gaze weighed heavier today. Hesitant. Regretful.

James gave up on his earlier resolve not to question her.

"Jeddy? What's the matter?" The words came out strangely slurred, his vision wavering as he raised his head to look at her.

Was ... was he getting sick again? But what would be the cause? His thoughts strung together lazily, hardly making sense.

He *couldn't* be sick. There was no plague aboard the ship, and ... no.

No.

He grasped the bowl, clumsy fingers already half-numbed. The scant remains of the soup coating the curved wooden edges of the dish shimmered as they caught the dim light, reflecting back in shining greens and blues.

Sailors called it scale. It was said to be made from mermaid tail and the skin of fish from the southern seas, but for all its supposed rarity, it had no problem circulating the waters, clouding minds, turning men to addiction.

"No," he said aloud, and the word came up garbled, distantly furious that the drug had even found its way aboard his ship. Who'd brought it on? How had Jeddy known? The anger quickly dissolved as a pleasantly cool feeling began to spread through his core, leaching into his limbs.

"Sorry capt – 'M sorry," Jeddy was saying, her figure shifting like a mirage as the walls of the room seemed to warp and melt around her.

His mind felt fuzzy, his thoughts seemed to shimmer before his eyes. The pain – in his arm, his joints, his stomach – was *gone*, replaced by a dizzy giddiness, and he almost laughed in relief.

Maybe he did laugh in relief. It was hard to tell.

Jeddy was standing up, walking or sliding or floating toward the door. He was angry with her. Was he? Why was he?

It was nice, *good*, to not feel the ache, the hunger. To not be afraid. Why *had* he been afraid in the first place? He was on his ship. He was *home*. It was good.

Jeddy was looking down at him, and she was so very far away, yet he could see every detail of her face. An impassive expression betrayed by tears that streamed like black oil. He couldn't tell if they were real or just another product of the scale.

"Peter's comin'," she said as she seized the door handle, and her voice grew, echoed, doubled and doubled until it was like a rhythm in his head.

Peter's comin'.

Peter's comin'.

5

Compass Rose

James felt like he was underwater.

Everything was muffled. Sound, sight, feeling, all dampened by the flow that consumed him. It was like floating facedown, staring at the ocean floor, but somehow still being able to breathe. The room around him distorted and rippled as if each plank of wood was being pulled by the tide, each bit of scant light dancing with the motion of the waves.

It was beautiful.

He couldn't remember the last time he'd felt so content, so *peaceful.* If he'd ever felt that way at all, unbothered by the pitch and roll of the world, it would have been when he was very young. A child, unaware of the kings and governors who would dictate his life, of the ships he would flee to in order to be free, of the weight of responsibility that would settle on his shoulders in time. In that moment, nothing mattered. Nothing, save the feeling of floating and the shifting shape of the room.

Peter swam in eventually, a funny-looking fish if there ever was one. James almost laughed at the notion. But when Peter came, he brought the fear along with him, trailing behind like a shadow, laughing all the way up to where James lay, though his face was unmoving. Was Peter cheerful or angry? James couldn't tell. Both were equally bad, he knew, but his dread felt like a whisper. Drowned out by the waves all around him.

Peter said something, but he was too far away to hear. James felt his arms being lifted, folded together and placed above his head. Peter produced a rope and began weaving it around his wrists, his forearms, his elbows, binding it tighter and tighter until James's shoulders were straining. It *burned*, but was swiftly cooled by the water around him, and he found himself relaxing in spite of the distant ache.

Peter drew his knife, the little polished crocodile that had taken his hand, and a spike of fear shot through him like a rock tossed into a pool. Was the monster here for his other hand or would it devour something new today? James tried to move away, but his body wouldn't listen. Panic washed over him, but the cool peacefulness pushed back. Ebb and flow. Push and pull. His body grew cooler still as Peter tossed aside the blanket that covered his legs and held the sharp-mouthed reptile to his chest, letting its teeth cut through his shirt before pushing back the fabric to better expose his bare torso.

James's heart thrummed in time with the waves as the other man traced down his ribcage with the tip of the knife. Peter's smile seemed to surround him. No matter where he looked, he couldn't escape it.

"We're in uncharted waters now, James," Peter said. "We're almost there."

Almost there. Almost where? He couldn't make sense of any of the words. *Almost to shore, almost to port, almost to the bottom of the sea to raid sunken cities.*

The knife rested on his sternum for a moment, then moved down over his abdomen, his navel, crossing his waist and coming back up.

"I found it on a map, you know," Peter said. "An old map. A *treasure* map. I was overjoyed. I wanted to show you, but then you'd know. And you couldn't know, not if I wanted the ship."

James opened his mouth to ask what Peter meant, but words wouldn't form. No more than a groan came out, and Peter hushed him.

"But now I *have* the ship," Peter said, pressing a finger to his lips. "And I have *you*. And I'm very excited to show you my map."

The knifepoint – tooth of the crocodile – slid down to balance on his hip, gentle as a pinprick for all of a second before Peter began pressing down. James was vaguely aware of pain blooming as the little golden monster bit into him, of the resulting blood trickling down his side. He flinched as Peter dragged the knife into his flesh, pulled it out, and crossed the mark with another line.

"This is where we are," Peter said. "Or at least our general direction. This..." he brought the knife up, placed it over James' sternum – no, his *heart* – and cut another X. "This is where we're going."

He smiled as James writhed, trying to escape the crocodile's bite.

"But of course, our destination is inland," Peter said. "Now hold still."

James probably screamed. It was hard to tell under the effects of the scale. He certainly *felt* like screaming, as Peter dug the knife into his side, under his collarbone, across one shoulder. Tracing out the ridges of a land mass.

"There's said to be mountains surrounding it," Peter said, carving jagged lines across his chest. "A smaller island too. We'll be sailing around that." A wavering circle cut into the skin over his stomach. "We'll dock in a cove here." An angled cut into the right side of his ribcage. "The path of travel is fairly straightforward ... " A dashed line, crossing his torso, connecting one X to the other. "And we can't forget to give you a compass rose." Meticulously carved into his left hip; a hot coal plunged into the waters James was floating in, sinking to settle on his flesh.

He tried to remember how to *breathe*, doing his damndest to keep his eyes on the ceiling, not on the dead-eyed knife, not on the bloody ruin of his chest.

It had been nearly bearable at first, with the scale granting him distance from the pain. But now the biting sharpness was starting to draw nearer. James didn't know if the effects of the drug were already wearing off or if it was all the doing of Peter's knife. He could only gasp like a fish pulled from the water as the feeling sharpened, Peter's map radiating agony with every breath.

The other man stood, surveying his handiwork, and James thought it might be over. Blood ran freely down his chest, soaking into his pants, pooling on the mat, and all he wanted to do was curl in on himself. Hide under the blanket and try to sleep, try to sink back into the cool, calming waters, just for a little while.

He was becoming aware of other pains again. His shoulders burned from the strained position his arms had been bound in, and his throat felt ragged. An ache had begun in his temple, like there was ice forming on the inside of his skull, and he squeezed his eyes shut in a bid to relieve the pressure.

When he opened them, Peter had knelt back down. Knife in hand.

"See? Now we each have a map," he said, his blade hovering over the first X, the one on James's hip. The blood there had begun to clot. "And I'm going to make certain that yours doesn't fade."

James knew it was coming before the knifepoint touched him.

"No, no, n – *AUGHH*!"

It dug in as deeply as before, piercing the already-damaged skin. Without much pause, Peter repeated the process with the X over his heart. James tried to force himself to breathe, though he already felt dizzy. He could only hope he was rendered unconscious soon.

Because Peter still had the mainland. The mountains. The island. The cove. The path of travel. And the compass rose.

6

CHANCE

James faded into unconsciousness halfway through the mainland's retracing and awoke shivering, a headache brought on by the drug's aftereffects sitting frigid in his skull.

He was still bound tight, unable to move for fear of dislocating his shoulders, with the ache there steadily growing into an agony he couldn't ignore. It almost rivaled that of his torso. The bloody map had dried. A mess of blacks and browns and reds covered his chest and abdomen. He hardly dared to *breathe* for fear of reopening the wounds.

Jeddy made her appearance some time later, when the layers of pain over pain had become almost unbearable, and he'd fallen to quiet whimpering. She cut the ropes first, slowly uncurling his arms, placing them down at his sides when he couldn't move them himself, then began to clean the cuts. She wouldn't meet his eyes.

James wanted to yell, to ask her what in the seven hells gave her the *right*, ask her if she realized she'd taken away one of his last freedoms, that she'd taken the sanctity of his own *mind*, but he didn't.

He didn't have the energy. And perhaps more than that, he didn't want to risk driving away the one person who was showing him any kindness, no matter how misguided.

Well-intentioned betrayal was still betrayal.

He sucked in air through gritted teeth as she washed the wounds on his chest. Gentle as she tried to be, there was no way to make such a thing painless, and he could either suffer through it or die of gangrene when the wounds soured.

She'd brought two bowls for the wound tending. The first was warm water. The second … Though he knew it was necessary, his stomach roiled as Jeddy dipped a cloth into it. She looked down at him for all of an instant, a silent apology on her face as she brought the brandy-soaked rag toward his hips. James only nodded, clenched his jaw, squeezed his eyes shut. It was like being set ablaze, like the map was being retraced a third time in acrid, stinging flames.

When it was done, when he lay there shaking, Jeddy gathered the supplies and left. She came back moments later, another bowl in hand. Knelt by him. Offered a spoonful of soup like there was nothing *wrong* –

"No," he said. "I – I can't."

"You're gonna have to eat somethin'," she said. "This one … this one's fine. Nothin' hidden in it."

"I thought the same of the last one," James said, eyeing the bowl, looking for the telltale shine of the drug. But it didn't have to be scale, did it? She could do the same with another substance, perhaps something he'd never even heard of.

"It's not. I swear it."

"How do I know you're being truthful? Where did you *get* it? I don't allow scale on *my ship.*" His voice rose, sharpened by the sting of the cuts, and she bowed her head.

"I *am* sorry for it. I only wanted to help. The last time almost killed you, and – "

"I understand that, but I said *no*. Jeddy, I told you not to. How do I know you won't go against my wishes again?"

"You – " She sighed. "You'd rather starve then? Rather than risk it?"

Yes. No. *He didn't know*. Denying any food would take away the chance of escape just as quickly as giving himself up to the scale, but that wasn't the point. He already felt so helpless here, to the point that refusing a meal was one of the few things he had any power over. No matter how he pleaded, he couldn't stop Jeddy from drugging him again. The choice really *was* to give in to the possibility or starve, but how many more times could he consume the drug before it consumed *him*, before he was lost anyway?

The silence between them was broken as Jeddy suddenly seized the spoon, plunging it into the bowl and taking a bite herself.

"There. There, how about now? Will you eat?" she said, pushing the spoon back into his hand. The way his head was swimming, it took a moment to understand what she'd done, to fully grasp the display, the assurance that he could trust her, at least this time.

James nodded, his fingers curling around the utensil's handle.

"I'm sorry for it. I am," she said.

"No more," James said. "Not again. Whatever Peter does ... whatever piece of me he decides to cut apart or break, I can take it."

"Not again," she agreed, and he could tell that she meant it.

***

Peter came up with a new torment in the week that followed, one that didn't require him to lift even a finger. Beatings.

Men who had been a part of his crew not even a month prior would throw the door open to beat the living daylights out of James, opening his wounds, leaving him groaning and gasping for breath. The bursts of violence never lasted long – Peter didn't necessarily want him *dead*, after all – but they came unannounced, never at the same hour twice. Morning, noon, or night, he couldn't anticipate their arrival. He couldn't run either. Couldn't fight back. Could barely do more than lie there and attempt to shield himself.

The first time, he'd thought it was Jeddy opening the door, only to be met with two of the brutes who worked the sails, barely giving him time to register what was happening before a kick to his stomach had him curled into a ball, waiting for the blows to end.

That seemed to be his stance on life lately: close his eyes and hope it would be over soon. The only pleasant thing he could scrounge from this new situation was that he hadn't seen Peter in days. Jeddy still made her rounds, thankfully, often coming by right after the men left to clean up whatever mess they'd made of him.

James gave up on taking the beatings stoically after the first four or five or six times. What good was pride anymore, except as a drain on the little energy he had? He'd whimper, he'd cry, he'd beg for it to *stop*, but he'd spite them all by continuing to live.

Injuries have a tendency to layer on each other, James mused as he stared at the wall, cheek laid on the cool wooden floor. Was it that? Or had they just been particularly vicious this time? It was difficult to tell. One blow tended to merge with the next, and it wasn't as if he were counting them all.

How many times would Peter send them in? How much more could he take before he lost himself completely, before he became a shadow of a man? It already felt like he was on the verge of giving up. Of begging Peter to *just kill him already*. Of asking Jeddy for the scale after all. Anything to escape the pain he lived in.

He coughed, the movement turning into a wince as pain spiked through his ribs. The half-healed map Peter had cut into his chest throbbed where boots had come into contact with the careful red lines. His right eye was all but swollen shut, and he was almost certain some of his teeth had broken but was too tired to even poke around with his tongue and find out. Everything hurt, the combination of exhaustion and pain heavy enough that he could lie in the muddle, half-conscious, and pretend he felt nothing at all.

The sharp inhale Jeddy made when she swung the door open was enough to tell him that he looked as bad as he felt. She knelt next to him, warm brown hand coming down to rest on his shoulder, the only kind touch he could hope for anymore.

"Are you ... are you awake?"

James wanted to say yes, but all that came from his throat was a pitiful whine. She grimaced, then set about cleaning the cuts on his abdomen. There wasn't much else she *could* do. The only true medicine for him was rest, and he wasn't about to hold out hope for that.

"I can't stop them," Jeddy said as she washed the wounds. "I wish I could. Ain't right, beatin' a bound man. But they do as Peter says, and even if I were able to knock 'em back, he'd only send more."

"Would ... " James cringed, sucked in air, forced out the words. "Would *you*? If Peter ordered you to, would you ... " He let the question trail off, not wanting to even bring the words into existence. *Would you hurt me? Would you add to my torment on an order?*

She pressed her lips together, not answering at first.

Did he want her to? If she said yes, or worse, if she said *no* only for her actions to speak otherwise, would he have anything left but despair? In this state, he had no chance of escape. If he could hold out, if Peter got bored but left him alive, there was a *chance*, but that couldn't happen if he didn't have someone who cared at least a little. Enough to bring him food. Enough to tend his wounds, even in the dead of night. He couldn't bear the thought of losing Jeddy, of her gentle touch turning to harm. The sole ill she'd brought upon him was the scale, and even that had been done with good intent.

"I don't know," Jeddy said at last. "The *Merry*'s my home, I can't leave her. But ... " Her eyes trailed over his body. The bruises and weeping cuts that clouded his flesh, the remains of his left arm. "But I can't hurt you neither."

Something in him – a twist of anxiety in his gut that he hadn't noticed until now – uncurled, sending a feeling of relief sweeping over him. One person still cared whether he lived or died. And that was enough, *had to be* enough.

"Thank you." The words were a whisper. He wasn't lost, not just yet. It would take luck and a lot of holding on, but there was still a chance.

He still had a chance.

7

In All of Her Glory

For a few days, James was granted a reprieve. No blows, no Peter, just stew and rest.

A brief period to heal, likely so his captor could send some new torture crashing onto him, but James refused to look a gift horse in the mouth. He was alive. For a day, and then another, he was alive.

He spent most of his time asleep, his body struggling to recover. On Jeddy's third visit since his last beating, James was able to sit up again, to feed himself again. Wounds began to seal themselves, bruises yellowing and clotted cuts turning to scabs with fading edges. Strength seeped into him like sunlight pushing its rays through an overcast sky, and James did his best to savor it. He did not want to think of the storm on the horizon.

The day the clouds blackened came all too soon. Peter's men tramped down to the brig with a footfall that rumbled like thunder. James curled up at the sound, awaiting the pain he was certain they'd bring. But this time, no blows followed the creaking of the door, only hands that held him in place as his chains rattled and the manacles that bound him fell away. They were taking him from the brig.

The notion of leaving the room, of breathing sunlight and clean air, should've been a joyous one, but it was weighed down by a sudden dread. They wouldn't take him above deck without reason. *What did Peter want?*

His body was stiff, his legs refusing to support him as he was dragged up the narrow wooden staircase. James's heart pounded as they grew closer to daylight, closer to whatever cruelty Peter had laid out for him. Perhaps the day had at last arrived for James to die. Perhaps Peter wished to be rid of him once and for all.

The thought of death was softer than James had imagined it would be; a simple end to the torment, a stop in the path. Hope was a draining thing, death was rest. Knowing Peter, the treacherous man would drag it out, turn it into a nightmarish spectacle, but then it would be over. What followed the end was a mystery, but surely it was a kinder unknown than the one he would face if he lived.

Jeddy entered his thoughts then, sudden as a gale, and a feeling akin to guilt washed over him. And why? This was *his* life, *his* torment, had he not the right to wish for an end to it? Why did welcoming the reaper feel like spitting in her face?

She wanted him to live. She had hope. Perhaps that was why it felt wrong to lose his grip on his own so quickly.

James was nearly blinded as they reached the deck, sunlight touching him for the first time in weeks. He blinked away the light, trying to savor its warmth as he waited for his eyes to adjust to the shift. Once they did, he allowed himself to forget his sorry lot for just a moment as he looked around, taking in *The Scarlet Merry.*

To Peter's credit, she was still in top shape, deck practically gleaming, blazing red sails standing out beautifully against a blue sky. If he were to die today, at least he could see her in all of her glory one last time.

The water surrounding the ship was a fine turquoise. Far ahead, he could see a mountain range that seemed to rise out of the sea, and just ahead of that, a smaller island that seemed to have more rock than shore.

The cuts on his chest throbbed.

They'd made it. Peter's island.

"Welcome back!"

And there was Peter himself, cheery as ever, the sun gleaming in his auburn hair. He let out a sharp whistle, and the sailors around them ceased their work, coming to stand in a half-circle around James.

Weeks ago, he might've called them together in a similar manner, to plot a raid or divvy up loot. Weeks ago, he'd not an inkling it would ever come to this. He doubted he much resembled the man they'd once called captain. Beaten, starved, cut to pieces, in too much pain to stand unassisted.

James tried to keep his head held high, eyes fixed on the horizon, pretending they weren't there. Pretending it *was* weeks ago, and he was still the captain, still someone they held in respect. Pretending they'd never had to listen to his *screams.*

"Now, don't look so *morose,* James. Haven't you missed your old crew?" Peter called out, striding into the circle to face him. James met his eyes, only his eyes. He didn't need to acknowledge anyone else, didn't want to see what shame or pity or *apathy* rested on their faces.

"Well?" Peter gestured widely, spreading his arms in the direction of the distant shore. "What did I tell you? Almost there. Exciting, isn't it?"

James inhaled, exhaled slowly, let the quiet grow for a moment. "Is that why I'm up here, Peter? To see your island?"

"Yes. Well, partly." He walked around to stand behind James, prompting a flinch as he set his hands on his shoulders. "I thought you might be lonely. Life's a little dull when you're on your own down below, hm?" He began to apply pressure, maneuvering James into a kneel. James tried to keep his breathing even as dread seeped in, choking his thoughts, making it difficult to think about anything but what came next, what new idea Peter had for him.

"I think we should play another game or two, don't you?" Peter said when the silence dragged on too long.

Of course. What purpose did James serve anymore, besides amusing a sadistic man? Why should he hope for anything besides pain when Peter decided to show his face? The other man moved back around, smiling down at James for a long moment, staring like a child about to pull the wings off an insect.

"Can I cut off your hand?"

The tension snapped like a twig, a consuming wave of nausea and panic surging through James as he looked right through his former first mate, staring at nothing as he tried to remember how to *breathe.*

No, no, no, he couldn't. Not again, he *couldn't.*

He was looking away from Peter, he was facing the deck, he was *falling*, he was being hauled back to his knees by the two men on either side of him, blood rushing in his ears.

He was below again, tied up. He was trying not to look as Peter dug out another joint, started flaying another strip of flesh, made the first cut.

"James," Peter said, his voice singsong. "I asked you a question."

"*No –* "

"No? So you want it to be an especially *long* game like last time – "

"Please. Please, don't ... " He drew a shaky breath that didn't quite reach his lungs, the words spilling out like blood from a cut throat. He was aware of the stares from the crew. Pity. Horror. Disgust. He didn't care, couldn't care, *couldn't breathe.*

"*Please* don't, please no, not *again, please.*"

"Aw, James, you're confusing me. You don't want me to cut it off? Or you don't want to play the game?"

"D-don't ... th-the game." He barely got the words out.

Peter's smile widened. "So you do want me to cut it off then?"

"Yes."

"Say it."

"C-cut it off. *Please* just – just cut it off."

"What a shame," Peter shook his head. "I wanted to try and get more pieces this time. Maybe saw through a bone. Scoop out the marrow. Are you *sure*?"

James could only nod, frantic, tears streaming down his face. "Please. *Please.* I don't – I *can't* – just cut it off. Please."

For a while, there was nothing. James could see nothing but the *Merry*'s deck, blurred with tears, his heartbeat pounding in his head like a gallows drummer.

Then Peter began to laugh.

"Why, James, I was only joking," he said, leaning down to ruffle his hair. "We've already played *that* game."

James slowly began to lift his head, his body still shaking, choked sobs still wracking his chest, painfully shifting his bruised ribs.

It was a joke. *It was a joke.*

He could taste his relief.

"I'd still like to do *something,* though," Peter continued, but James didn't care.

Anything. Anything but *that.*

For the first time, as if emboldened by his escape from the knife, his gaze reached past Peter to take in his former crew.

Cotts, the boatswain.

Fiver, the cook.

Jeddy.

Not a single sailor was looking at him. Grim expressions fixed on the deck, the bow, the sea. They didn't want to see this, didn't want to watch Peter's cruelties play out. But no one moved to stop it either.

He allowed his head to drop once more. Peter crouched in front of him.

"As fun as it was to watch you snivel, I think I'm ready for the next part now," he said politely. From his belt, he drew the polished little dagger, the dead-eyed devouring *beast.* Set it on the deck before James. Stood for a moment, and was handed something else, which he laid next to the knife.

It was a coiled whip. A cat-o'-nine-tails, the lead at the end of each thin leather braid glinting in the sunlight.

Peter tapped a boot before the items. "I want you to choose," he said. "I want *you* to pick what you want to happen next."

James swallowed, his gaze darting back and forth.

Whip. Knife. Whip. Knife.

Each implement spoke of pain, but the sharpest of his fear had bled away with the threat against his hand. It had been replaced by a numb distance, the sort that used to settle onto him when he was poring over maps by candlelight, wits dulled by lack of sleep. He regarded the items before him with the same eyes that would stare at strait and landmass, tiredly seeking the smoothest course.

A flogging would be brutal. A flogging could drag away what little life he had left in him. But the knife held uncertainty.

What would Peter do if he chose the knife? Cut off something else? Make good on his threat to take his eye? Carve another picture into his back?

A flogging would be bad, yes, but at least he knew what would happen if he chose the whip. A flogging was better than losing an eye.

A flogging was better than the painstaking removal of his remaining hand.

With a shaking finger, he pointed to the whip.

"That one, huh?" Peter said. "It's nice to know what you want, James. It really is. Makes things more fun if you participate, right?"

He stood up and wordlessly walked into the crowd of sailors. It wasn't the end of it. James knew by now that it was always more than threats. There was always something coming.

Peter came back, not a minute later, Jeddy following after him. He gestured down at the items.

Knife. Whip.

James was frozen in place, dread bubbling up all over again as he tried to keep his jaw rigid, tried not to cry.

"How about you, Esme?" Peter asked Jeddy. Her eyes were downcast. Her face stony. "What game should we play with our dear friend James?"

8

His Own Ship

She chose the knife.

One of the men holding James clamped a hand over his mouth on Peter's orders, so he couldn't sway her decision. And she chose the knife. He let out a muffled cry as Peter picked up the blade and pressed it into Jeddy's hand. *Not her, not her.*

"Are you an artist, Esme?"

"No, sir." Her voice was flat. Emotionless.

"What about writing then, do you know your letters?"

"I do, sir."

Peter left her standing there and wrenched James's right arm away from his side.

"Hold him down."

James was forced onto his stomach, one of the men digging a knee into his back. He cried out at the sudden pressure on his ribs. Peter's fingers tightened around his wrist, pulling until his meager strength was overcome and his arm was forcibly straightened. Peter knelt on his palm, his weight driving James's knuckles into the unyielding wood of the deck. One hand remained on his wrist, further ensuring the arm would not move.

"There we are," he said. "Now, Esme, I'd like you to write your name."

"My name, sir?" Her voice was like still water, a careful surface seeking to appease a ship's captain.

"Yes." He smiled. "I want you to carve it into his arm."

James thrashed, though he knew it was pointless. Peter held the power here. He could do whatever he wanted, including shatter one of his few remaining solaces.

The stillness shielding Jeddy seemed to ripple, and she staggered back a half step. "Sir, I-I can't."

"I'm sure you'll find that you can," Peter said. The pressure on James's hand let up for a moment as he stood, clapping Jeddy on the shoulder in a gesture that mocked friendliness. Encouragement. "Now, go on."

Another of Peter's brutes took his place, seizing James's arm and holding it against the deck. From the furthest corner of his vision, he could see Jeddy's face, nothing to betray her feelings but a slight crease between her brows.

"Sir – " She stopped short as Peter leaned in.

"It's going to be either your name or mine, Esme. And only one of those choices ends with you still onboard. Do you understand?"

Jeddy's jaw tightened. "I ... I understand."

She knelt beside James, as she'd often done before. Only this time she wasn't helping him to eat or drink, wasn't cleaning a fresh wound, all soft touch and soothing words. This time, she was the one who wielded the knife.

He understood, he *told himself* he understood, though his chest hitched and he squirmed under the weight of the men in a weak attempt to get away.

It would happen either way.

It would happen either way, and at least this way, only one person had to hurt. Only him. *But why did it have to be her?*

Her hand came to rest on his forearm, palm warm and familiar. A part of James wanted to relax under her touch, for how many times had she steadied him to dab at a cut? But in her other hand, she held Peter's hungry little beast, not linen scraps. The point of the blade pricked against the soft skin of his forearm and she pressed in, making the first line –

"Deeper," Peter said. "Or it won't scar right."

Jeddy nodded, silent as ever, and James tried to hold back from making any sounds, more for her sake than his.

Compared to Peter's other ideas, this is tame, he told himself. It wasn't his hand, it wasn't a terrible pain. He would be alright, he'd suffered worse in the days behind him.

But no matter how he tried to insist it was so, he knew it wasn't about the pain. Jeddy had been the one to nurse him through the worst. To see her on the other side threatened to break something in him. He could hide from the truth, he could pretend it wasn't her doing the damage, pretend it was only Peter –

"James, open your eyes if you'd like to keep them."

And so he did, a gasp escaping him as she began a second line. A third, a fourth. A bloody 'E' cut into his wrist.

The shine of tears in her eyes was the only thing that betrayed her neutral expression. The sight of them stirred a mixture of feelings within him. A great relief that she did not want this, that all her weeks of care *were* care, not simply following orders. A greater sorrow for her own pain. And under them both, speaking to him with a liar's tongue, betrayal. It wasn't her fault. Here, she had no choice, but he couldn't silence the sick insistence.

If Peter ordered you to, would you?

He breathed through each slice as best he could, unable to look away as she carved each crimson letter, the razored teeth of the knife almost gentle in her hands.

E-S-M-E

He wanted to tell her it was alright. That he could not blame her for the obedience that kept her safe, but he couldn't open his mouth. Couldn't form the words.

She stopped after that, bloodied knife laid on the deck beside her, hands clasped in her lap. Head down, eyes not meeting his. Peter said nothing as he knelt to examine James's arm. It hung limp as he seized the wrist and lifted it, angling it this way and that as if to let the new wound catch the sunlight. He let go of it suddenly, allowing the limb to fall back onto the deck.

"I don't like it," he said.

"Cut it off," he said.

Cut it off. The skin or the hand or the arm? What did he mean? Would she obey?

The image came to his mind, Jeddy gently sawing through his wrist with that same stony expression, eyes glistening even as her hands held him down, sliding the knife back and forth and back and forth until it slid through his skin. It was all he could do to hold back a sob.

"Captain ... " Her voice was quiet, the single word sounding like a plea. Who was it for? For Peter to show mercy? For James to forgive her?

"*Esme*," Peter replied in the same tone. "Will you do it?"

She shook her head, and Peter clicked his tongue, bending down to pick up the bloodied knife. He wiped the beast's scarlet mouth on his pants and tucked the blade into his belt.

"That's alright," he said, then bent down to take the whip in hand. Letting it uncoil as he stood.

"It's time for James's pick anyway."

***

He'd felt the bite of the whip once, years before his days aboard the *Merry*, and though it hurt, the welts had healed swiftly, having not even broken skin.

But that had been only five lashes, and not from a cat-o'-nine.

James didn't struggle as they bound him to the mainmast, the rope digging into the fresh cuts on his forearm. He could not dredge up the energy to feel frustrated at the trick, and even if he could, there was no point in wasting it. Peter had known what he wanted from the start. No matter the choice James or Jeddy made, he'd been destined for both torments the moment he was dragged onto the deck.

James tried to keep his breathing deep and steady, though it was difficult with the tension on his torso. Breathe through the pain, through the dread, through the knowledge that this could be the end. He closed his eyes, not wanting to see his former crew standing around him, waiting for the spectacle to begin; not wanting to look back and see whether it was Peter or Jeddy or some other crewmember who would be the one to swing the whip.

He could hear it drag behind him, lead bits scraping along the wooden deck as it drew nearer.

"Do you want to hear the rules of this game, James?" Peter's voice came from a few feet over his shoulder. "Because if you win ... " He trailed off. "If you win, I'll let you go."

Let him go. James would've laughed had he the breath to spare. Let him go *now*, shamed and broken. If Peter meant it in earnest, did that mean he'd be dropped at the nearest port, to die of gangrene or starvation when he could not find work? Or did Peter mean it in a literal sense, to be released from the *Merry*, to sink to the bottom of the sea?

Of the two, the ocean seemed the kinder fate. A soft ending in the arms of the one who had carried him so long.

"Well?" Peter said, and his voice was a step behind him. "Aren't you going to ask what the rules are?"

"Wh ... what are the rules?" James mumbled, resting his forehead against the mast. His arms were already beginning to lose feeling from being strung up. Perhaps it was a mercy; one less layer of pain.

"If you can stay awake through a certain number of strikes, you're free. Doesn't that sound fun? *Free.*" Peter leaned in close to murmur in his ear. "So, how many will it be, James? How many do you think you'll make it through?"

Free, free to be drowned or abandoned, and yet it was still better than his own ship, the home that had turned into a hell. James knew Peter's play. Too low and he would laugh afterwards, say he didn't quite *earn* his freedom, condemn him to weeks more of torturous *games*. Too high, and his body wouldn't stand a chance against the whip. If Peter was feeling particularly cruel, he'd call any number too low, forcing him to raise the count until he bled out right here. An ending, an avoidance of further torment, and yet he found his spirit rebelled at the thought. If he were to die, it could not be here, it could not be to Peter. Surrendering to the sea felt more like a choice; even being abandoned at a foreign port left his fate in his own hands. He would not die strung up like an animal.

"Ten," he said through gritted teeth, hoping it was enough to satisfy Peter, enough to let him survive for just a little longer.

"*Ten*," the other man repeated, sounding surprised. "I would've wagered five! But I like your pluck. Ten it is."

James's heart sank. Chances were, Peter would say that no matter what he chose, but it still felt like he'd duped himself. *Ten.* More blood from him to be stolen, but perhaps it could be the last. Perhaps after this, he'd never have to look up on Peter's cruel smile again.

"Let's begin."

The whip came down, its whistle through the air the only warning before the first strike. It hit right in the center of James's back, pain spiking through his body with the brightness of lightning. He didn't even have time to cry out before the next one followed it, striking him in the side, lead tips colliding with his bruised ribs, and this time he *did* scream, a horrible, ragged sound.

A third. His head was already swimming, and he clenched his jaw. Seven more. Such a small number and yet it may as well be infinite.

"Hh – *Aughh*!" Four.

Five. His vision was splotched with white. *Stay awake. See it through.*

"Halfway," Peter sang out. "And just think, that could've been the last one if you weren't so *ambitious*."

The sixth came down, dragging out another hoarse scream.

Seven.

Eight.

His vision was fading in and out, his body shaking with pain and fatigue. *Hold on. Just hold on.*

Nine. His back had been set ablaze, lines of fire carved in his skin, spreading, reaching up to take him ...

Ten. His body jerked under the final stroke, the only sound escaping him a choked whine. Over. It was over it was over it was over. He was conscious only by the most base definition, seeing but not aware, hearing but not understanding. Feeling the pain roll through him like the tide. Nearly unbearable, threatening to smother him, *drown him*, but he fought it, no matter how much he wanted to sink beneath its waves and cease to know the world around him.

"Well done!" Peter's voice rang around him. "Didn't think you had it in you."

Hands reached up, cut the ropes, let his body hit the deck limply, his eyes staring emptily at the horizon.

"You've impressed me, James." Peter and his smile were over him, silhouetted in blue. "I think you deserve more than freedom. I think you may even deserve to be captain again."

Captain? James thought, the word spinning in his head. No, no, that was nonsense. Peter would never step down. He wouldn't allow things to be as they were, and even if he did, nothing would ever be the same. James couldn't leave behind the last weeks, couldn't bury it all. His hand would never return to him, and the wounds inflicted by knife and whip would plague him the rest of his days. What sort of captain could he be, in this body Peter had twisted to his whims? Even if he were to undo every injury, his crew would never forget how he'd groveled and begged after one whispered threat. He was no longer *fit* to be captain.

"What do you think? Captain of your own ship again."

Of his own ship.

James winced as Peter grabbed him by the hair, lifted his head just enough so he could see the crowd part for a pair of men carrying a large barrel. It took him a moment to truly see it, and another to comprehend it. He took in the broomstick tied to the barrel, a mockery of a mast, the bit of canvas that stood for a sail.

"Beautiful, isn't she? About to take her maiden voyage." Peter released James, and his head dropped.

He'd been brought up to die after all. A mocking death to be sure, but it would end with him wrapped in the waves, sinking under, never to be touched by Peter again, never to shrink from the gleam of his knife. He let his eyes drift closed. Let them throw him overboard, let them have it over with.

"And what's a captain without a first mate?"

His eyes flew open, and with all his remaining strength, he lifted his head to see the crowd make way once more, heads hung, eyes downcast.

Jeddy was brought forward, one of Peter's brutes on either side of her, tearstains on her cheeks.

"S-sir, I don't – "

"You don't what?" Peter said, and his voice was measured. Cool. "You don't think I know everything that happens on my ship? You don't think I know the signs of scale use?"

No …

"You've shown yourself to be a liar and a coward," Peter said, his voice rising. Not in anger, nor in indignation, but in something that resembled theatrics. It was nearly jovial. It was all just a show for him; one more game.

"I gave you the chance to redeem yourself, to prove your loyalty, but you threw it away. You have no place on this ship."

Jeddy's shoulders shook. "Please. Captain. Don't make me leave her."

"Leave her?" Peter folded his arms. "You ought to count yourself lucky I didn't throw you in the *brig* when I found out."

"Peter … " James's voice came out, more whimper than word. "L-leave her be."

The other man shook his head, putting a hand on Jeddy's shoulder in such a way that it almost looked friendly. The false anger had drained from his face, replaced with his careless grin. "Don't tell me how to run my ship. You can call the shots once you're aboard your own," he said with a wink, waving on the men with the barrel.

"Now *heave-ho*, boys. We have a ship to launch."

9

Many Times Over

Peter at least had the courtesy to throw the barrel overboard first.

James was quick to follow it, hands lifting him up, rolling him over the side, letting him fall into the waiting arms of the sea.

He must've blacked out when he hit the water, salt burning into the whip marks with such a fury it shut his mind down. He was screaming when the black had faded, screaming into the brine, drawing in no air, just the salt, just the *sea*. He couldn't tell which direction would lead him to the surface, but he knew he was sinking, and even the primal creature within him that still sought to survive couldn't find the energy to fight the pull of the deep.

An arm curled around his waist before the black could claim him again, lean and strong, hauling him through the waves until his head broke into air, and he was choking, coughing up seawater, his back feeling like it was *blistering*, though the water was cold.

Jeddy.

She seized the barrel by the rope twisted around it and wound it around his arms in such a way it would keep his head above the water when she released her grip on him.

Far above, on the deck of *The Scarlet Merry*, James could hear laughter, hear Peter saying something but couldn't focus on the words.

He closed his eyes.

Just for a moment, he thought, but when he opened them again, the *Merry* was a silhouette on the horizon, set aglow by the setting sun. Jeddy's arms were on either side of him and she was kicking into the waves, guiding them toward the rocky little shore that stood between them and Peter's island.

James watched it grow closer, little by little, with vision that was hazy and blurred. He couldn't tell how far they had to go, didn't know how long he'd been in the water, only that he was dizzy and cold and *weak*.

Shadows cast by the dying sun gave the rock face the appearance of a grinning skull.

How fitting, James thought, before allowing himself to slip back into the calm unknowing of unconsciousness.

***

When he awoke, the side of his face was pressed into the sand and his legs were being lapped at by a gentle tide. James shivered, trying to lift his head and look around, not even making it an *inch* before giving up.

Where was Jeddy?

His head pounded, his back was numb, his body leaden. All he wanted to do was sink back into sleep, but he knew if he let that happen, he would never wake. The thought should've filled him with peace, but instead it only brought dread. *Not yet*, pleaded a voice within him, *not yet.*

James shifted his right arm, moving it up bit by bit until his fingertips were in line with his eyes. He grit his teeth and tried to lift his head again, this time with an arm to support him. It took far more effort than it should've, but he managed, turning his head to look down the other side of the shore. And there she was.

Her knees were tucked into her chest, arms hugging them tightly, eyes fixed on the horizon. The barrel that had carried them here sat a few feet behind her. She had to be exhausted, but her back was too straight for her to be asleep.

She was grieving, James knew. The loss of a ship, of a *home*. For him, leaving the *Merry* meant escaping Peter and the tortures he dreamt up, but what had Jeddy escaped? She was here because of him. She'd lost *everything* for him, and she deserved a chance to mourn that.

But right now he was sure he was dying and could barely even lift his head. He'd need her help once more, despite having taken so much of it already.

"J ... eddy," he croaked, his voice hoarse from thirst, from screaming, from swallowing seawater. She gave no sign she'd heard him.

"Please," he tried again. "Please ... Jeddy," and the words took so much *effort*, but she moved. She pushed herself up from the sand, her expression serious as ever, though there were tears drying on her cheeks. Soon he was being rolled onto his back and lifted, the pressure on the scourge marks cutting through the numbness he felt and making him whimper. The pain threatened to send him under.

He fought it. He had to stay awake.

Had to stay awake.

Don't leave her alone.

Jeddy carried him away from the moonlit beach, the air around them growing darker – or was that just his vision?

Was he fading? No, he couldn't. *Stay awake.* But no matter how he tried, it was an impossible task. The moments came in flashes as James slipped in and out of consciousness.

The sting of sand being washed out of his wounds with saltwater.

A warmth on his face, the glow of a fire, broken splinters of the barrel.

His arm tended, wrapped in strips of the mock sail.

ESME.

He flinched back when he came to then, away from Jeddy, who was bent over his right arm again –

But she didn't have a knife.

No knife, no Peter.

It was safe.

Safe, he thought, as he let himself slip under.

He was being given water, but where had the water come from?

He could smell cooking meat, but hadn't the island been desolate?

After far too long a time, James awoke with enough strength in his blood that he felt he'd be able to *remain* awake. His back throbbed, but it was more a distant ache than the fire it had once been. And while his bones had an ache of their own and his stomach twisted with hunger, it only felt like being alive.

Jeddy noticed him, his feeble attempts to sit up, and propped him up against her, wordlessly handing him a piece of cold fish. They were in the mouth of a cave, facing out toward the open sea. The sun was just beginning to rise behind them, casting yellow light onto the water. Had it only been one night since they'd come ashore? Or longer?

Looking around, James guessed that it'd been a few days at the least. Enough time for Jeddy to set up a makeshift camp. He was laid on a torn piece of canvas, and that seemed to be laid over some kind of vegetation, a layer of protection between him and the sandy stone of the cave. The dying embers of a fire glowed nearby, and next to that, the barrel had been broken apart, the one remaining end turned into a bowl of sorts and filled with water.

She'd done it all alone, with him as nothing more than a burden, an invalid to be worried about while she tried to survive.

"S-sorry," James said. It hurt to talk. "S'my fault you're out here."

Jeddy only shook her head, her brown eyes sad. She brought forward the waterskin she kept at her hip and held it out to him, and he drank.

"I'm sorry," he said again when he finished, and again she said nothing, only tapping the piece of fish in his hands. He took the hint and began to eat.

"Where'd the water come from?" James asked, and Jeddy gestured to the cave behind them. So they were lucky enough to have some sort of spring.

"The plants?" he asked, and she pointed to the ceiling, bare stone. It took a moment to realize what she meant, that there had to be some sort of foliage growing on the rocks far above them. How long had it taken her to climb there? Had she been afraid of falling, of breaking a leg or hitting her head while she was alone on the cliffs?

"And ... you've been able to catch fish," James said, more in an attempt to curb his thoughts than anything else. Jeddy nodded, pointing to the far side of the cave, where a net he hadn't seen before lay on the ground, twisted from the ropes that had circled the barrel.

It didn't seem like she wanted to make conversation, and he couldn't find fault in that. She was still mourning the loss of the ship, a home taken from her because of him. "I'm sorry," he said again. "For ... for all of this."

"Ain't your fault," she replied in a quiet voice. It was the first time he'd heard her speak since the *Merry*. "Nobody's fault but Peter's."

James wanted to argue, say if only he'd drowned, if only he'd bled out on the mast, if only he'd died *weeks ago*, she wouldn't be here, wouldn't have to suffer so much.

But she was right.

It was all Peter.

"I'll kill him," he said, and it felt ridiculous to make such a statement in the state he was in, but he *meant* it. What else could he do for her? What else did he have to offer in return for all she'd done for him?

"I'll kill Peter if it's the last thing I do. I'll kill him, and you can go home."

There was something like surprise on Jeddy's face. "C-captain – " she began, but James shook his head.

"Not anymore." He took a breath. "Jeddy ... I owe you my life. Many times over. And that is not something I'll ever be able to repay, but I need to ask for one more favor. Help me get well. Help me take back my strength, and I will give you back the *Merry*." One more fight, against an enemy that had taken everything from him, for someone who deserved all he had left to give.

"And what about you?" she asked after a moment.

He sucked in air through his teeth. "That'll be it for me, I suppose."

"Sir – "

"James," he corrected her. "Even ... even if I survive Peter, there's no use for me on a ship like the *Merry*. She's an adventurer." He managed to smile. "Better served with two hands intact."

Jeddy was silent for a long moment. Did she want this? He couldn't tell if she was happy, sad, angry, or some mix of them all. He felt the same. Weak as he was, the thought of standing again, of facing Peter, of striking his tormentor down, filled him with a mixture of joy and terror. He couldn't think of anything he wanted more in the world than to take Peter out of it before he could hurt anyone else.

Before he found the supposed fountain of youth and became able to inflict his miseries *forever*.

"Alright," Jeddy said at last. "I'll help you take on Peter. But only on the condition that you *do* survive him."

James looked up at her, puzzled, and was surprised to see the shadow of a smile on her face.

"It's as you said. I saved your life many times over. Ain't about to have that be for nothin'. You survive Peter, and you stay with the *Merry*. Swear it, and I'll help you."

"Jeddy – "

"Swear it."

James clenched his jaw. What good would he be aboard? Even if removing Peter was enough to reinstate him as captain, who would follow a man that couldn't tend the ship properly? Who would obey the orders of a man they'd seen *beg*?

"James."

He met Jeddy's eyes, and her expression was intense.

"I ... I swear it," he said, swallowing. "I'll fight him to the death. And I'll win."

10

Fairly Straightforward

Their skull-faced island was a lucky one, it seemed.

Though barren and foreboding at first glance, it had proven to hold its own treasures. It was larger than James had initially thought, with deep caves and a proper forest on the side that faced the mainland. He wasn't much help with collecting firewood or looking for food, but did his best to tend the fishing net and the fire with his one good hand. Jeddy brought in fish and fruits the likes of which James had never seen before, and once he'd regained enough strength to walk, she showed him the spring, just twenty steps past the mouth of the cave.

It took several days of good rest and food to get James back on his feet, but Jeddy was patient. The first time he stood, it was with her arm around him, and he'd leaned on her heavily as they made a small circle around the cave. It grew easier from there. Because he now had a goal, a reason. Because he owed it to Jeddy to see her home.

His strength grew a little each day, and he learned ways to move around the pain rather than through it. His ankles were scarred from his time spent in chains, and the still-healing wounds on his back kept him sleeping on his stomach, but he was adapting to the new shape of his body, spirit emboldened by sunlight and the absence of Peter's smile.

"What has Peter told you about this place?" James asked one evening. By his count, it had been two weeks since they'd been cast off the *Merry*. The smaller island provided them with all they'd needed thus far, but the land for which Peter had turned to treachery remained a mystery to him.

"Hm?" Jeddy looked up from where she'd been mending the net, tying and retwisting the bits of rope that had broken apart.

"The island," James said. "Peter's not a man of quiet excitement, and I'm sure he had plenty of stories to go around, myth or true."

Jeddy nodded at his words. "That he did. Can't say I listened to 'em all, but he had a good few." She put the net aside and set to sharpening her makeshift knife, formed from one of the metal hoops on the barrel. Her ingenuity never ceased to amaze him; she could turn something meant to mock them into the tools that may well have saved his life.

"He called it the neverland," Jeddy said. "A place where magic still runs wild, where the fae and the merfolk play wargames and the animals are clever as people."

"And do you believe any of that?"

After a moment, she nodded. "And mind you," she said, "I'd normally be as much a skeptic as I imagine you are, but this morning ... " She drew up her waterskin and began to remove its stopper. "T'was almost empty, so I figured I'd wash up with what was left. And when I started pouring it out, it ... well." She turned it upside down, and James watched as it flowed from the skin to the ground, soaking the sand. And it ... *kept* flowing. The water kept pouring from the mouth as if it were a natural body, long after the small container should've been emptied. Once she was sure she'd made her point, Jeddy righted the skin and replaced the stopper, handing it to James.

It was still full.

"What ... ?"

"I dunno. Dunno what it is or why it is, but Peter said there was magic, and after that ... " She took the skin back, tucking it at her hip. "I think I believe him."

James sighed, watching the water she'd poured on the ground begin to dry up. There was magic here, he no longer had room to doubt it. But did that make every legend true? The fountain of youth, Peter's true destination, sat heavy in his mind, darkening it with the thought of Peter staying young and healthy forever, causing any harm he wished until someone managed to strike him down. It had been long enough since their arrival that he might've already found it.

No matter, James told himself. If stopping Peter from reaching the fountain was out of the question, he'd just have to stop him from leaving the island. He'd kill him if he could, but if his treacherous first mate managed to come out on top, he'd need a plan in the reserves, a way to trap him here.

The *Merry*.

The fountain was inland. Peter would have to dock her, and if James and Jeddy could reach her before his expedition returned, they could take away his only means of leaving this place. One way or another, James would make sure Peter never got a chance to spread his cruelties.

"Y'aren't strong enough yet," Jeddy said when he brought it up, shaking her head. "Even if we cobble together a raft to get there, I don't want you falling overboard."

And so they waited, eyes always on the horizon, anticipating the day when *The Scarlet Merry* journeyed out to sea again. Should that day come before James was ready, he'd have no choice but to take up a weapon and go.

Weeks passed with no sign of the ship. Or Peter, for that matter. In the moments between watching for her red sails, James spent his time walking for as long as he could, then running when simply taking the next step no longer posed a challenge. Jeddy helped him massage the scar tissue on his chest and back to prevent it from bunching his skin too tightly as it healed, and at her insistence, he practiced simple tasks one-handed.

Sharpening the knife and laying out firewood, mending the nets and gutting the fish, foraging and even swimming. It was all done carefully and painstakingly slow, but he worked at it all the same, Peter's smug grin in the forefront of his mind.

It was all for Peter. Once his enemy was gone, he could stop, he could let himself fade away, but right now he had to grow strong, adapt, if he wanted to stand a chance at bringing the other man down. That was the thought that drove him, that pushed him to run until he was on the verge of passing out, to tread water until his limbs were burning with exertion. To wake up every morning.

The thought of vengeance, and more than that, the thought of justice, of doing right by Jeddy. And beneath even those, in a part of his mind James refused to acknowledge, there was the thought of what would happen if he lost.

If he faced Peter, but wasn't strong enough to beat him. If Peter won, but didn't kill him. If the little golden crocodile came back to rest its teeth on his flesh.

Can I cut out your eye?

It wouldn't happen. He wouldn't *let* it happen. He'd die first, fighting Peter to the final breath.

***

"Y'think they might be lost?" Jeddy asked one morning, several weeks after their last sighting of the ship. "Or dead?"

"I don't know," James replied. "They may be. I'm sure we'll find out soon enough."

The two of them had begun to build a raft, gathered branches and grasses woven together an inch at a time.

"And what if they sailed around the island? Disappeared into the eastern seas?"

James shrugged. "Maybe." Not if he could help it. What would they do if *The Scarlet Merry* and her crew were nowhere to be found? There would be no way off the island, no way back to familiar waters. Jeddy's home would be lost. She knew it too. He could hear it in her voice.

"I'd wager Peter's still exploring," he said, in an effort to ease both her worries and his own. "You heard his stories. Why leave his neverland so *soon*, whether he's found the fountain or not?"

Jeddy nodded, frowning as she twisted another bundle of grasses into place. "Say it all goes well then. Say we find the ship, and no one's aboard. We can't sail her with only two, can we?"

James cursed under his breath. If it had been months ago, if he were still whole, maybe they could manage it. But as it were ...

"We don't know she's empty. Peter may have left some to keep watch," he said. "How many of the sailors aboard would be willing to abandon him?"

Jeddy sighed, running her fingers over their work. "Many were ready for an adventure into uncharted waters when he first started talkin' about the neverland," she began. "But once he took command ... once they heard what he'd done with you, seemed a lot of 'em regretted that choice."

"Didn't do much about it," James muttered, turning his attention back to his work, steadying the rushes between elbow and knee and tying with his hand. His one hand. The crew could've stopped it at any time. Staged a mutiny of their own to save him from the torment, but it had only ended at the command of their new captain.

"They were afraid," Jeddy said. "If one man tried, if no one else was brave enough to stand up with him, would he be tortured for his insubordination? No one wanted to chance it."

No one. No one, except ...

"You did," he said softly, and she went silent for a moment, her fingers stilling, gaze lingering on the mat.

"Wasn't enough," she replied.

"It was," he said. "I'm alive, am I not? I'm only here now because of you."

She seemed to grow bashful at his words, shifting in place, a smile pulling at her lips. "Suppose that's something."

The quiet grew between them for a long moment before she continued, her hands suddenly setting back to work on the rushes. "Afraid or not, I don't think any of the men are bound by loyalty to Peter."

"And what about loyalty to me?"

"Y'hear any cheers when Peter was whippin' you?" she replied. A twinge of pain went through his back, as if his body was trying to recall.

"I think we can get a few," Jeddy continued, and James nodded along, staring down at his side of the raft and trying to push away memories.

"We'll go to the *Merry* first," he said. "If anyone's aboard, we'll try and convince them, and if not, I suppose we'll go ashore. Look for Peter."

Get rid of him once and for all.

"How do we find him?" Jeddy asked. "M'not even sure we'd be able to find where he's docked the ship."

James looked up at her, unable to keep a grin from crossing his face as the realization struck him.

"I am," he said, straightening his back. He pushed the raft away and placed a finger over his heart. Over the X.

"Here's the fountain. There's said to be mountains surrounding it." His fingers traced the jagged ridges that had been cut into his chest, now nearly healed to scars, raised on his skin. "They'll drop anchor here," he said, moving his hand down to point at the angular cove that had been cut into his ribs. He traced the line upward from there, the path Peter had carved in flesh and blood.

"And if we don't find anyone at the *Merry*, the path of travel is fairly straightforward."

11

Do or Die

After sunset, once stars began to scatter the sky, they set off for the neverland. With only a raft, it would take hours before they reached the cove, but it would be worth it even just to see the *Merry* again. They brought their supplies along: fruit and cold cooked fish, the net, Jeddy's endless waterskin and makeshift knife, and a few sharpened sticks.

And one more thing.

"Made this for you," Jeddy had said, just before they pushed off. She'd pressed something into his hand. Metal and wood and leather. *"It's a lousy replacement, I know, and I don't think you can put much weight on it, but I'd say it's better than nothin'."*

James fiddled with the end of the device as he sat on the raft, testing the leather that secured it to what remained of his left arm, giving him something that could stand for a hand: a makeshift hook.

The remnants of the barrel hoop had been shaped and twisted, held together by wood and hardened by fire and connected to strips of leather that Jeddy must've cut from her own jacket. It was almost comforting to have its weight at the end of his arm, a feeling like a memory.

The air around them grew cooler as the hours passed, the water shining with the gentle light of the moon. Little by little, the shore of the neverland crept closer as their raft bobbed on the waves. And then all of a sudden, there she was. *The Scarlet Merry*, silent and cloaked in starlight.

James could've wept with joy. *She was still here.* Their plan could work. He looked over his shoulder and saw Jeddy, staring up at the ship with shining eyes, and he reached down to squeeze her hand. She gave him a nod, determination setting in on her face. It was time to act.

They got the raft up to the hull, close enough that he could touch the wooden planks that formed her if he wanted, and Jeddy stood, reaching up to take hold of a gunport. He watched her scale the side nimbly, agile as a cat, then waited, holding his breath until she lowered a rope for him.

Something ached inside him as he took hold of it, a voice that mourned what he'd lost. Once upon a time, he'd have no problem climbing up on his own. He could've even matched Jeddy's ascent.

And Peter took that from him.

Anger rose within him at the thought, but he pushed it back, thinking instead of the weeks behind. He'd learned to gut fish with one hand, to swim and mend with one hand. He could learn to climb too. He just needed to survive Peter.

James wrapped the rope around his hook, seizing it tightly with the other hand and giving it a tug to let Jeddy know he was situated, then he simply held on while she slowly, slowly raised him to the deck. All was quiet as he climbed over the side, no movement aside from Jeddy tying the rope in place in case they needed a quick exit. It would serve them to escape the *Merry* herself, but once aboard the raft they'd be slow in the water. It was do or die now.

Together, he and Jeddy moved about the ship, checking each cabin and finding no one.

"She's empty," he muttered. "We'll have to follow their path ashore."

"Wait," Jeddy replied, changing her direction suddenly. Heading for the brig, he realized, and followed.

James made it nearly halfway down the stairs before suddenly finding himself frozen, unable to move forward or back. The memory of the last time he'd been here – dragged up to the deck by cruel men, half-dead, wishing someone would finish the job – caught in his chest like a fish in a net.

His heart pounded, blood thrumming in his ears, making his head spin, his breath catch. His knees threatened to buckle, and he had to flatten his palm on the wall to keep from toppling over.

Stop it, he told himself. *There is no danger here. Peter isn't here.*

He felt like a fool, cowering from memories, but pushing them away felt like trying to slow the tide with a hand. They just kept washing back over him, threatening to drown him.

"James ... ?" Jeddy's voice came from the bottom of the stairs, and he gave her a jerky nod when she cast a backward glance.

"Let's get on with it," he said.

She pushed the door open, and he could hear something shift on the other side, the scrape of chain on wood. The sound sent a chill through him, and he once again fought to keep his legs.

"James?" Jeddy's voice drifted up to him again. "I'm gonna need your help with these locks."

It took a moment for her words to register, for him to realize that he'd need to take another step down the stairs, to sink deeper into his old hell. When he tried, he found his body was rigid.

Go on, move, he scolded himself. *It's nothing. You're letting yourself be spooked by shadows.*

But even when he managed to take those downward steps, he couldn't keep the sick dread away, couldn't silence his mind as it spoke against all sense; *if you go back in, who's to say how long it will be before you're let out? Will you ever come out again?*

He clutched the doorframe, leaning heavily on it. He tried to breathe deeper, to still the rising fear, but even just the smell of the place was sickening.

"S'wrong?" Jeddy asked, and James couldn't find the words to explain.

How could he say he was afraid of a room? He just shook his head. Gently, without another word, Jeddy took his hand and gave it a small squeeze.

"It's alright," she murmured. "Door's unlocked. We'll leave it that way."

Door's unlocked. James took a shaky breath, nodding with more vigor. *The door's unlocked, the chains are gone. You're standing and stronger, and Jeddy is beside you.*

Still clutching her hand, he stepped into the brig, its walls dimly lit by the glow of a lamp Jeddy'd taken from topside. The room seemed foggy and unfocused. It took another moment of silence, another moment of breathing, before James could take in what his former prison now held.

On the floor, chained ankle and wrist, sat Fiver, the cook, and Scrap, the boatswain's apprentice. Neither looked too worse for wear, and both seemed very surprised to see him.

"Captain?" Scrap said, chains rattling as he moved to stand up. "You're ... you're alive."

Captain. Maybe he could be. Maybe.

"Where's Peter?" James asked, kneeling by Fiver and getting a look at the cuffs that bound him. They could try picking the locks or just break the hinges outright, both options he hadn't had the luxury to consider during his own time down here. He wanted to break them. Smash them apart and throw them into the sea, set free two more prisoners of Peter.

"Went back to explore," the cook replied as James set to work on the locks, doing his best to keep his focus on the words, on the metal in his hand.

"Back?"

"Aye, he locked us down here not two days ago. Said he had more to see," Fiver replied.

"And why did he lock you two away?" Jeddy asked. Both men were quiet, exchanging a brief look.

"Peter found the fountain – " Fiver began carefully.

"He killed Cotts," Scrap cut him off. "He wanted to see if the water could raise the dead, so he killed her." A fierce gleam came to his eye as he continued. "I tried to fight him, Fiver too, but the others held us back and now we're here."

"I'm sorry to hear it," James said. "Cotts was a good sailor." For a moment, the only sound was the clink of metal. He meant it, that he was sorry. The feeling of betrayal lingered, the knowledge that his entire time down here, neither man had tried to help him, but he understood. Peter was a man to be feared, and carrying on as if nothing had changed was the simpler path. The safer path. He could neither praise nor fault them, but they were here now, enemies of his enemy.

"Is everyone else with Peter then?" Jeddy asked once she'd removed Scrap's restraints.

The sailor nodded. "He made it clear. Those loyal to him could drink from the fountain. Stay young forever. Those not … " He shrugged, gesturing to the room around him.

James finished working Fiver's chains and helped the cook to his feet with his good hand. His hook had been surprisingly helpful, able to keep the cuff still while he worked.

"We can finish this conversation topside," he said. "I'm sure you two would like to eat something." And James didn't want to spend another second down here. If everything went according to plan, if the *Merry* were to be his once more, he'd lock the doors of the brig for good. The tension within him ebbed away as they climbed the stairs, the constriction in his chest fading, allowing him to breathe deeply once more.

"What've you seen on land?" Jeddy asked as they went. "Were the stories true?"

"Most, from what I could tell," said Fiver. "Even caught a glimpse of the fair folk once. Peter's been speaking with 'em."

"Can't say that's good news," James replied. If the fae were anything like the folktales made them out to be, they'd make a powerful enemy. With any luck, he'd never have to deal with them.

Jeddy took the lead, opening the galley doors and rummaging around for a bit before coming back with hard biscuits and dried meat. While the men ate, James made his way inside. Toward his own cabin.

The last time he'd set foot inside it, he hadn't an inkling of what Peter was planning. It felt strange returning to it now, like stepping into a memory. James wished he could. Travel back to the night before the mutiny and warn himself, throw Peter overboard, stop the violence before it even started.

But that was only wishful thinking. He was where he was now, body carved by Peter into something broken, mind shaped into something that found fear in sounds and smells and spaces, so that he couldn't breathe easy in a room on his own ship. Nothing could be done to change what had happened. All he could do was find a way to mend, to put the pieces back where they belonged to the best of his ability. A feat he'd already begun on the skull-faced island, helped along by Jeddy. His body would never again be what it once was, but it was no longer as broken as Peter had left it. He still had room for healing, body and mind.

His cabin was largely unchanged, save for a few of Peter's things strewn over the narrow bed. James popped the lid on the trunk in the corner, sifting through his belongings until he found clean clothes. Replacing what he had on proved a bit difficult with one hand, but he managed after a few tries with help from his hook. He was struck by how good it felt to be wearing a shirt again, to replace his ragged trousers and slip on a pair of boots.

He hoped Jeddy's things were still onboard and untampered. She'd probably appreciate a change of clothes as well. In case she couldn't find her own, James pulled a linen shirt from his chest to give to her after he finished dressing. He clumsily added a belt and cutlass to his waist, then opened the door to leave.

Dawn was breaking outside, coloring the sky a pale pink. James scanned the deck until his gaze landed on Jeddy. She was oddly still, eyes wide and urgent. It wasn't until he'd begun to walk forward that he saw the man crouching behind her, the point of his knife resting on the side of her throat.

No ...

James looked about wildly, taking in Scrap and Fiver by the bow, kept motionless by the daggers at their necks. His fingers loosened, the new shirt slipping from his grasp to land in a heap on the deck.

Three sailors that he could see, all of them barely more than strangers, men they'd picked up at the last port to help tend the ship. Men that had no reason to listen to him.

Seven hells, why couldn't he have just a touch more luck? He'd been so close, why did things have to fall in Peter's favor?

Only three, but the others were unarmed. If he tried anything, it would only get their throats cut.

"Let them go," he said, his voice low and hard.

The sailors answered his demand with broad grins and snickers, and he saw Jeddy shaking her head, saw she wasn't staring at him, but past him. *Above him.*

Laughter came from somewhere far overhead.

"Give me one good reason why I should, and maybe I'll consider it."

It was Peter.

And he was flying.

12

Steel on Steel

"I'll be honest, James, I thought I'd seen the last of you."

Peter had touched down on the deck and was now strutting around, the only person aboard who dared to move. His little polished knife was drawn, the crocodile engraved in its hilt seeming to taunt James with a grin.

You almost had it all. Don't you feel the fool?

"Coming back to the ship too? *Exciting*. Were you going to steal it?" He laughed. "I've been far from bored here, but if I were, leave it to you to keep things interesting."

"Are you going to kill us?" James asked. He'd had enough of Peter's theatrics. With Jeddy and the others under threat, he couldn't rush in and attack, and if he were to die without even getting the *chance*, he'd prefer to die before Peter began another soliloquy.

"Kill you? Hm." Peter tapped his chin with his free hand. "I suppose I could. But I also could not. What do you think? Should I?"

James felt his upper lip pull back into a snarl at the other man's careless tone, agitation and fear spinning as one within him. Was this a trap? Another game? If James said no, how long would he – *they* – suffer for it?

"You're hesitating an awful lot for someone who seems hell-bent on survival," Peter said. "Do you want me to kill you or not?"

"I ... " James grit his teeth, clenched his muscles to keep from trembling. If he said yes, Peter would waste no time in cutting Jeddy's throat. If he said no, it could mean worse things, *terrible* things. There was only one way out of this. Only one way that gave him a chance.

"I want to play a game," James said.

Peter's eyes lit up. "Oh?" His smile grew wider, his hand tightening around the little knife. "What sort of game?"

"A contest. Between you and me. A fight," James said, straightening. A game where he wasn't tied down, where he had a weapon, where he wasn't facing impossible odds.

"A fight!" Peter seemed delighted with the idea, his feet not even touching the deck as he closed the distance between himself and James. "If you win, you'll want your ship back, I suppose. No matter. I've found I like this island quite a lot. I'm not sure I'll ever leave. And if I win – "

"If you win, you live," James said. It felt so *good* to cut him off. "Did I not mention? This fight will be to the death."

Peter seemed caught off-guard at his declaration, but a moment passed, and a different sort of smile crossed his face. Something dark, something that almost made James regret his words.

"To the *death*? Alright."

"Feet on the deck," James added quickly. "No flying." He lifted his chin. "To ... to keep it interesting."

Peter nodded, thoughtful. After a moment, he held out his hand for James to shake. *Left hand.* James thrust forward his hook, undeterred.

"I accept your challenge."

***

Peter kept the knife. There were other weapons onboard, James knew, but Peter kept the knife.

Was it overconfidence? Or was he trying to get in James's head? He felt unsettled already, with the shadowy mischief on Peter's face, but with the addition of the knife in his hand ...

He stopped himself. It was cutlass against knife, and he had the advantage. Peter was giving up both reach and power, and for what? To *taunt* him? It would be his downfall.

Jeddy and the others were now seated on the deck, sidelined while Peter's men stood sentinel to ensure they stayed that way. Blades in hand, James and Peter circled each other, watching and waiting to see who would dare to make the first move.

Cutlass against knife, James reminded himself. Victory was in reach, and then he'd knock that horrible golden beast into the sea and throw its master after it.

Peter lunged, quick enough that James was hardly able to sidestep him. So far, he was keeping his word. So far, he wasn't flying.

He darted forward again, and this time James parried with the cutlass, sending the knife gliding harmlessly past him with a satisfying *shting*.

He could do this. He wasn't in the brig, chained and helpless. He was on his feet, and he was *stronger*.

Peter was easily bored, and James was patient. If he could avoid attacks until Peter wore himself out, he'd be certain to win. Even if the other man backed out of the deal and tried to run, James could chase him. Hunt him down while he was weakened by exhaustion. End this.

He dodged another swipe from Peter. His opponent seemed to be growing frustrated, though the half-crazed grin remained planted on his face.

"What are you waiting for, James? This is your game. Won't you come play it?"

He'd have to act carefully. Ignore Peter's calls until the other man grew reckless, but engage him before he grew bored and started playing dirty.

"*James*," Peter sang. "Did you hear me?"

Another viper-quick strike, another parry from James.

And the next time Peter darted in, James followed him back out, swinging his weapon with a practiced ease. Peter managed to block each slice with his knife, the sound of metal striking metal cutting through the hush of the waves, the breaths of the men.

Even with just one move on the offense, James could feel himself tiring, the scars that covered his body pulling at him, aching with the movement. His time in the brig would not be so easily forgotten. But neither would his time on the island, and neither would his goal.

He pushed forward again, arcing the cutlass overhead, cutting into nothing as Peter tumbled out of the way. His enemy regained his footing, rushing him from the side only to be diverted with another flash of James's blade.

The blows came in a flurry then, strike after strike, steel on steel, the metallic sound ringing through the air like a sort of music.

Before the mutiny, before he'd had his strength stolen and had to rebuild it from the ground up, James had been the better fighter of the two. Now they were more closely matched. James's skill and power hadn't faded, only weakened, and stepping back into combat was like stepping into a dance he knew by heart. Still, Peter was quick, every movement fluid and agile, and James couldn't quite manage to land a blow.

He was slowing. They both were, really. Breathing heavy, taking longer pauses between each strike. James knew he had to end this soon. His endurance couldn't hold up to Peter's, not anymore.

He surged forward, swinging with a sort of frenzy, summoning all the energy he could. Overhead, left side, sweep the legs, slash at the stomach –

At long last, a stroke hit home, a shallow cut across Peter's ribcage that his opponent had been too slow to dodge completely. The sight of the blood welling up from it filled James with a renewed vigor and he stepped in, landing another hit, *another.*

Small cuts, but victories nonetheless.

Peter was wearing down.

The smile had vanished from the other man's face, his knife nearly a blur as he parried all he could with the little blade. He was all defense now, nothing able to be spared for an attack, but James refused to slow.

He half expected Peter to turn tail and flee, to take to the skies once it was apparent he could not win, but to his credit, he remained grounded. *Playing by the rules of the game.*

James poured his remaining strength into his attacks, backing his opponent into the railing of the ship, knocking the little knife from his hand, and finally, finally delivering a fatal strike.

The cutlass swept across Peter's throat, leaving a trail of red in its wake. Blood flowed freely from the wound, soaking into Peter's shirt. James took a step back as his opponent's chin dropped, letting his cutlass fall to the deck with a clatter.

It was over.

Exhaustion was already beginning to overtake him, leaving him lightheaded as he tried to catch his breath.

It was over.

"James ... " Jeddy's voice came from across the deck, and it sounded like a warning. She and the others were still seated, the sailors guarding them showing no signs of moving. *Seven hells*, he hoped he didn't have to fight them off as well –

"*James*!"

His blood ran cold as he heard a wooden creak behind him. He hardly dared to turn, but he did, and there was Peter.

Blood poured from his mouth, from the gaping wound in his throat, but he was smiling, like some horror from beyond the grave. James could only watch as he pulled a leather flask from his belt, unstopped it with his teeth, and drank.

Water mixed with blood to leak from the wound. Slowly, the gash on Peter's throat began to close, flesh and cartilage knitting together as James looked on, frozen in terror.

It was over. It was over, it was over, *why wasn't it over?*

Peter replaced the flask at his hip, and James dropped to his knees as the other man picked up the little knife. Unable to fight, unable to even flee.

Why couldn't it be over?

A sob escaped him as Peter moved to stand over his bowed form, twirling the little knife between his fingers.

"It's a funny thing," Peter said, his voice thick, muddled. He coughed, sending droplets of blood to the deck. "When one hears tell of the fountain of youth, one doesn't always *anticipate* the other gifts the water can give."

James could barely hear him over the blood rushing in his ears. It had been a fight to the death. Peter could still kill him. Peter had to kill him, *he had to.*

"After all, what good is it to be young forever when you're fragile? A reckless game can shatter a person, keep them from ever playing again or end them forever, and that's no fun." He smiled. "The neverland understands that."

"Please," James whispered, and Peter cocked his head.

"What was that?"

"Just ... just kill me. Please, you've won, so get on with it." He hoped to *God* that was enough, that Peter would see the game through, that he wouldn't have to live through more of the torments the other man dreamt up –

"No," Peter said, and the word was as good as any killing blow.

"*Please* – " James was doubled over now, unable to see past the tears blurring his vision.

"I haven't won yet. You only win a fight to the death when someone is dead."

"So kill me!" James spat out, but he knew it was no good. Peter's mind was made up.

"When the time is right," Peter said matter-of-factly, the little knife spinning round and round and round in his hand.

James lunged forward blindly, past Peter, past the knife, fumbling for the railing, throwing himself over. Better to drown. Better to die on his own terms, to hope that Peter couldn't be bothered to dive in after him –

But he never hit the water.

Arms circled his waist and he was *flying*, the ship and the water a blur below him. He jammed an elbow backward into Peter's stomach and was released, free to sink like a stone toward the sea. The impact with the water was crushing, driving the air from his lungs, but even that wasn't enough. He felt a hand around his wrist, pulling him toward the surface, back into the air, back into the sky with a disorienting speed.

As if for good measure – either to teach him a lesson or to force him into compliance – he was dropped into the water a second time, pulled out again moments later, coughing up seawater, the rapid rise and fall beginning to blacken his vision at the corners as he was carried up, up, up.

The last thing he saw before sinking into unconsciousness was *The Scarlet Merry*, far, far below.

13

X Marks the Spot

James was bound again. Arms and legs wrapped in thick vines, curled up in the middle of Peter's camp. Not secured to anything, not yet. There was no need; Peter had too many eyes on him to worry about him trying to run.

Peter had set his hearth at the center of a mossy clearing. The trees that stood around the open area were taller than any James'd ever seen, vines decorating their many branches like lace trimmings, and dawn turned the surrounding woods hazy with mist. At the heart of it all, there was a little pool. Its water was clear, moving like a lazy river, as if it were being filled by something unseen, though it never spilt over. *Peter's fountain.*

He would've called it a peaceful place, like a scene from a fairy tale, were it not for his former crew watching him with eyes that were cold or sorry – were it not for Peter, circling around him like a vulture every time he returned to the clearing.

His tormenter hadn't made a move yet, hadn't held the knife to his flesh, hadn't even *touched* him since the flight here. Peter liked him weak, he'd figured that much out by now. Give it a few days with no food, let the feeling of dread build with each passing minute. Wait until James was desperate, hungry, nearly mad with fear. *Then* he'd act.

When one of the sailors – a man known only as Green – brought him water on the first night, James tried to refuse it. The hope he'd scavenged, the thoughts of what his life could have become *after*, had faded the moment he watched Peter's broken flesh seal. The thought of survival was beyond him now; all he wanted was escape, even if the only escape was dying of thirst.

But he couldn't quite fight the men off when they forced his head back, pried his jaw open, and poured the water in. With that path taken from him, James started taunting the other sailors, calling them turncoats, *cowards*, anything that might goad one of them into an attack. It wasn't long before someone tore off his sleeve and gagged him with it.

For days, all he could do was lay miserably on the ground and watch the goings-on of the camp, the strength he'd worked so hard to recover sapping away. There only ever seemed to be a few men around at any given time, the others coming and going constantly. Peter himself was hardly seen at all.

With nothing else to do but wait, James spent much of his time thinking. He hoped against hope that Jeddy and the two others were still alive, *unharmed*. Perhaps even sailing away, back to familiar seas. Manning a ship so grand as the *Merry* would be a challenge with only three, but he was sure they could find a way. He'd made peace with his own death, but he found nothing but sorrow at the thought of theirs. Of Jeddy's.

All he had left to hope for was her safety, her happiness aboard the *Merry*. It was either that or drown in despair. After all, what could he do? Even if he were to escape now, Peter could no longer *die*. James could never rest, save for at the hour of his own demise, and he knew a swift ending was too much to ask of Peter.

As the hours passed, James found his thoughts straying from Jeddy to his captor, dreaming of ways to kill him. *Cut off his head, stab through the heart, slice open his belly and heave out the guts.* As morbid as it was, it did something to curb the fear that ate at him every waking moment.

If he were to cut Peter apart and scatter the pieces, could he still reform? James wished he could find out, but it was too late now.

He hoped Jeddy and Fiver and Scrap were safe, a small crew, but a crew nonetheless. He hoped Peter never left the island to inflict his games on anyone else.

***

In time, the hour arrived for James to die. The camp was nearly empty, with everyone off exploring or gathering food or whatever else it was they did during the day. Everyone except Peter. As he prowled closer, James knew this would not be just another taunt, another vulture's circle. This time, he would strike.

Peter had an easy time tying James down – the latter hardly had the strength to move, let alone *fight* – and the new position left him almost completely immobilized. James willed himself to breathe steadily.

This was inevitable. It would end, it was only a matter of when. It would hurt, but *it would end*. Still, he couldn't calm his racing heart, couldn't quell the rising fear.

Let it happen, he told himself. *Scream and weep if you must. It will end.*

Peter untied the gag, and the fabric was dry in James's mouth, pulling at his tongue. He couldn't hold back a whimper as Peter unsheathed the little knife, its golden teeth sharp and ready to tear away flesh.

Inevitable.

James tried to imagine breaking free, sinking the blade into its master's throat, but all he could picture was the way the flesh would bind itself back together, the way Peter would *smile*. He clenched his jaw as the other man sliced his shirt open, tracing the scars on his chest with the blade that had formed them.

"You thought it was all just a myth," he murmured. "But look where we are now. Did you ever dream it could be real?"

James didn't dignify that with an answer, but Peter didn't seem to care.

"X marks the spot," he said, knifepoint resting over James's heart. "Do you wish you could've joined me? I suppose it was never really a choice, but do you wish it were different?"

Did he? If Peter had entered the brig all those weeks ago with a proposition instead of a knife, would he have listened? To chase a fantasy and live forever beside a traitor didn't sound like him, and even the fear of what was to come wouldn't change that.

"No," he said, and winced as Peter applied just a bit of pressure to the knife, just enough to break skin.

"Even if I offered it now?" he asked.

Only for the chance to rip out your throat.

"Never," James spat. "I'd never follow someone so ... " *Cruel.* "Dull," he finished, and the word had the intended effect on Peter.

"Dull?" An incredulous expression quickly took the place of Peter's smile. "*Dull?*"

So it *was* possible to get the upper hand while bound, after all.

"You won't even finish our game," James continued. "And I hate to admit it, but I find myself getting rather bored – " Peter's hand closed around his throat, cutting off his words and his air.

"I'll finish our game when I *want* to finish our game," he hissed, leaning in close. James's head spun with the pressure, his mouth open, fruitlessly trying to draw in a breath. The terror at not being able to do so was instinctive, but with it came a sort of relief. *Would this be it?*

No. Peter released him just as his vision began to darken, and he lay there gasping.

"You want me to finish our game?" Peter was saying, his words dulled by the pounding in James's skull. "Fine." The little knife was in his hand. "But first, I have one more question." He seized his chin, forced him to look him in the eye.

James resolved not to plead for any mercies, though he knew he was only lying to himself. Only terrible things were to come when Peter was smiling like that.

"Can I cut out your heart?"

***

James didn't delude himself with the hope it would be anything but slow.

Sharp lines were drawn into his chest one-by-one, scarlet ribbons etched over each rib, the scarred map re-carved in red. He had hoped that at least the shock of the wounds would send him under, but he knew Peter was determined to make this last as long as he could.

A scream was torn from James's throat as the other man began to peel away the strips of skin, one at a time, like picking the petals off some grotesque flower. And when that was done, when the pain from the individual wounds had blurred into a continuous fire, the knifepoint dug into a rib, sending waves of agony through him as Peter began to saw through the bone.

James writhed against his bonds, his body shaking uncontrollably as he screamed and screamed and *screamed*. To hell with trying to beg, he couldn't even *think*, much less form words. He could no longer feel his limbs, couldn't see, couldn't hear – There was nothing left but the torturous white heat of the knife, steadily burrowing deeper and deeper into his chest.

But then ...

But then it stopped.

Did it?

Or was he just too far gone to tell what was happening?

He couldn't even tell if he was still screaming or not.

Maybe this was it.

Maybe it was finally over.

He hoped to *God* it was finally over.

Dying as nothing more than a sick source of amusement wasn't the end he'd wanted, not in a hundred years, but *it was an end*, and it was better than suffering under Peter any longer.

He only wished he could've dragged the son of a bitch down with him.

James was vaguely aware of a voice, of someone kneeling at his side ... *Jeddy*, her words soft and low.

Was he dead then? Were they *both* dead?

The despair that washed over him was almost enough to rival the pain, the *agony* that grew with every ragged breath. He'd thought – *hoped* it had at least been for something. That she'd be alright, back on the *Merry* where she belonged.

"James," she said, from somewhere far away.

"I'm sorry," he tried to reply, but his voice wasn't working. What good was it to be dead if everything still hurt so much?

Something bitterly cold splashed across his exposed ribcage, and he was almost certain he screamed again at the contact.

"James," Jeddy said again, and her voice was clearer this time. "James, *please* ... "

"We need to go." Another voice, somewhere further back, low and urgent. "He won't stay dead forever."

Stay dead?

Jeddy's face was coming more into focus, and behind her, near the edge of the clearing, stood Scrap and Fiver. And behind them ...

"What ... ?" he croaked out, and found he could breathe again, that the pain was steadily ebbing away. He knew what he would see before he looked down. The fibers of bone reforming, the ruined flesh repairing itself, everything settling back into place on his bloodied chest.

Jeddy cut him free, then tucked an arm under his back, easing him up. Even the dizziness and hunger pangs were fading. He stood with Jeddy's help, looking toward the others.

Behind them, Peter lay on the ground by the tree line, body spasming, hands fruitlessly clawing at the wooden spear that went right through his throat and into the earth, pinning him there.

"Can you walk?"

He tore his gaze away from his downed enemy. "I ... I think ... " His fingers grazed his stomach, the scars there still present, but fully healed. "What did you do?"

Jeddy's eyes went to the ground. "I – I took some water from the fountain. I tried askin', but you were too bad off to answer. I didn't know what else to do, I – " She looked up at him. "I'm sorry – "

"No. No, I'm not angry," James said quickly. "I just ... " He swallowed. "You came after me. I didn't think ... "

"You're the captain," she said, like it was the most obvious thing in the world. "Can't sail off without the captain."

"Jeddy ... " He wasn't sure which of them it was that initiated the embrace, but suddenly their arms were around each other, holding on like it was the only thing anchoring them to the earth.

"Y'promised you'd come back aboard and I'll hold you to it," she said, voice thick with emotion and muffled by his shoulder.

"That I did," he replied, unable to keep the waver out of his own voice. "But I couldn't have kept that promise without the best first mate I could ask for."

It felt as if a great deal of strength had been returned to him as they pulled back from each other and made for the tree line. He couldn't tell if it was an effect of the healing water or if it was something more.

"We'd best hurry," Fiver said, taking the lead. "Peter's boys could be back at any minute."

"Onwards then," James replied, his hand clasped in Jeddy's as they began to run. "The *Merry*'s waiting for us."

Epilogue: The Endless Game

"Am I ... like him now?"

They'd made it to *The Scarlet Merry* with little trouble, but hadn't yet set sail. Safely aboard, James's focus was currently on his makeshift hook. The water had healed him, closed his wounds like they'd never happened, but left him with the scars he'd had before. Peter's map. The whip marks. The missing left hand. As if the island didn't want him to forget.

Scars or no scars, he wouldn't.

"Dunno." Jeddy stood next to him, leaning on the ship's railing. "The legends say you must drink from the fountain, but it mended you all the same." She shrugged. "Might've touched me as well, seeing as I used this to fetch it." She tapped the flask at her hip. "Never runs out, so I dunno what water's what."

"What if it did?" He let his gaze drift to the waves below. "Do you want to live forever?" If the water had done more than just heal him, if it had changed him, changed *them*, was he happy with that? The concept of forever was a difficult one, a sprawling infinity that he couldn't grasp, but he imagined it would be easier if it were to be taken day by day.

"Forever at sea, forever aboard the *Merry* ... " Jeddy shrugged again. "I can imagine worse fates."

They didn't leave the cove that day or the next. James knew they'd be willing to leave at any moment if he just gave the order, but something held him back.

Unfinished business.

As much as he wished the spear to the throat was enough to keep Peter down, he knew it wasn't. It would take more than that to bury his enemy, and if it was true, if he was now undying as well, he had all the time in the world to find out what 'more than that' was.

Fiver, being the cook, was the first to discover that their food stores were as endless as Jeddy's waterskin. Nothing dwindled, nothing ran out. From the crate of hardtack, to the salt pork, to the little box of cane sugar.

It seemed Peter's neverland had no short supply of gifts to give.

Days passed without any trouble, the only sign of his old crew being a few men seen flying far overhead. Scouts, no doubt. James knew it was unlikely Peter would leave them alone. It was only a matter of time before the other man decided to stage another attack, and he knew he had a choice to make.

Sail or stay?

Peter didn't want to leave the island. If they set off, even with a crew as small as theirs, there was a chance they could make it far enough that he wouldn't follow.

But what would Peter do then? What would happen in a dozen years or more, when he at last grew bored of it all? True, the neverland was a great distance from any civilization James knew of, but Peter couldn't *die*, and he was certain if the other man set his mind to it, he'd make it somewhere. Unkillable, unconstrained. God help anyone who he decided to toy with.

James couldn't let that happen. Not when it was possible he'd been granted an opportunity to fight fire with fire. If he were immortal, who better than him to find a way to stop Peter? After all, they still had a game to finish.

But he wasn't the only one aboard the *Merry*. The others had the right to choose their paths forward.

***

"I find it's become my duty to put an end to Peter," James said one night as they had their dinner. "I can't in good conscience leave this island until I know for certain he's dead."

"And what if 'dead' is impossible?" Scrap said around a mouthful of food.

"There must be a way," James replied. "And if there is, I'll find it." He ran his fingers over his hook. "I won't try and order any of you to stay by me. If you wish, take the *Merry* and sail far away from here. I won't try and stop you, nor will I think less of you for it."

He waited, the room filled with an easy silence.

"I'll stay." Jeddy was the first to speak. There was a slight smile on her face, a warmth in her eyes. "What's a captain without a first mate?"

"And what's *either* of those without a cook?" Fiver added. "Can't very well let y'be cooking for yourselves."

"Suppose you'll need someone to tend the sails," Scrap cut in, then added in a softer voice, "Cotts taught me well. Hope I can do half as good a job."

A warmth grew within James, the seed of hope Jeddy had given him what seemed so long ago blooming. No matter the things they'd said before, it was only now that he truly felt like he was captain again, at last able to make his own choice and not have it be driven by survival or pure necessity. And beyond what he'd hoped for, he had people willing to stand by him in a task that may yet prove impossible.

"I couldn't ask for a better crew," he said, and meant it with all his heart.

The next day, they finally set sail. Not to flee or to seek safer harbors, but instead to circle the island in a sort of patrol. Even with land in sight, it felt freeing to be out on the water again, aboard his own ship. James found it easy to steer the *Merry* with the help of his hook, but even in fair weather, he knew looking after the ship was a struggle for only three.

So he sat down with Fiver and Scrap, coming up with a list of those who weren't fully loyal to Peter, who may yet be swayed to come back aboard *The Scarlet Merry*. James made another silent promise, right beside his vow to see his enemy to the grave: he'd find his former crew, however long it took, and make sure each sailor at least had a choice.

By day they sailed, singing the old shanties that somehow sounded just as full as they had when sung by dozens instead of four. By night they let the ship drift, sleeping or watching the stars. Jeddy was right. There were worse fates than living forever at sea.

And when Peter at last made his appearance, piercing the air overhead like a bird of prey, James was not afraid.

***

Years passed like days. Time was easily lost in the eternal summer of the neverland. James could sail the island's waters blind. By now he knew them like the back of his hand. Like the scars on his torso. The *Merry* thrived in these waters, never faltering, never wearing even when she should. In time, some of the sailors in Peter's band left him, returning to her. *Returning home.*

Peter came too. Came and went, fought James, fought Jeddy, fought any sailor who crossed his path. Sometimes Peter died. Sometimes James died.

But they always came back for the next battle. Even Peter's little knife couldn't put a stop to that.

It was a curse, a blessing. It was a game that never ended.

"What happens if you beat him?" Jeddy asked one evening. They'd tried to bargain with the merfolk earlier that day, seeking more knowledge of the fountain and finding very little.

"If I beat him?"

"For good," she added. The moon was full, casting a soft glow on her face and the tight coils of her hair, lighting up her eyes. He truly could not say how long it had been since they'd first come here, since those first pain-filled days at the skull-faced island. Be it one year or ten, Jeddy didn't seem to have aged a day. He supposed he'd make the same observation about himself, should he take his time in front of a mirror.

"If I should ... I suppose we could leave," James mused. "Pick a horizon and sail away. Leave the island's games behind forever." Even as he said it, he knew it would never be. The neverland was a part of them now, and they of it. Removing themselves would be no different from ...

From separating a man from his hand, James thought, the notion somehow as amusing as it was bitter. Not impossible to do, nor impossible to live with. Only strange, for a while.

"M'not sure I'd want to leave. Or even if I could," Jeddy said, voicing his thoughts.

"Whether we want to or not, the choice is a distant one. Peter is not an obstacle that will be easily buried."

"And if you can never find a way?"

"Suppose we'll be here forever then." *Forever playing Peter's game.*

Jeddy laid a hand over his. "It's not so bad a forever," she said, and he smiled.

"No. It's not."

Forever aboard his ship, his home. Forever with a good crew, with a first mate he trusted with all of his being. Forever hunting Peter, playing this endless game, and maybe, one day, he'd *win*.

It was his choice.

It was his forever.

And it was enough.

Acknowledgements

I owe a lot to the whump community for resparking my passion for writing. Without it, I don't think I'd be where I am today, and I am thankful for their support, inspiration, and friendship. I would also like to thank Nate for encouraging me to finish a project, and the Whumpy Printing Press for all the hard work they've put in to bring this collection to life!

About the Author

Callie has loved writing since elementary school, and devotes most of her freetime to crafting some kind of world, be it with words or with art. When not creating, she enjoys hiking, rock climbing, and playing ukulele.

Creatures From the Caldera

A.E. Pillow

Cover Design by Nicole Alessi

Cover Illustration by Hen Towers

To my mom and sisters

Contents

Content Warnings

This story contains the following content:

- Animal attacks
- Character death
- Whipping
- Broken bones
- Cave-ins

If this book isn't for you, no worries! But if it is, we hope you enjoy this story about some misfit guards and some very unfriendly cats ...

1

THE UNUSUAL

Ivy climbed to the top of the watchtower shortly after sunset, throwing her day pack on the floor of the small wooden structure with a grunt.

"Fucking tower duty," she mumbled. For the most part, Ivy liked being stationed as a guard on the Caldera. The population was sparse, the wilderness vast. She would much rather be out in the wilderness, though, not stuck in a tower watching for non-existent threats.

Ivy sat and looked out at the thick pine forest and the rim of the Caldera rising above it. The slope was gentle at first but turned into a sheer rock cliff for the last hundred feet or so. It was impossible to get over and into the Caldera. It did lend a bit of spookiness to the area, Ivy supposed.

"Nothing out there," she said. Nothing had come out of the Caldera ... ever. Children's tales. The three guard stations on the rim, the guard towers, the fort below, were all just there to get rid of subpar members of the guard, the weird ones that no one knew what else to do with. Again, Ivy quite liked that most of the time, but she had a realistic view of what duty on the Caldera was.

The trees below were bathed in shadows and the moon was just rising when Ivy decided she was going to sleep. She wasn't supposed to, of course, but who was going to catch her?

As she moved to the back of the wooden tower, the ground shook beneath her, sending her sprawling on the floor. Something snapped beneath her, and the hut pitched to the side.

"The fuck … " Ivy got up carefully, the lantern she had brought with her somehow still lit. She looked around, listened. As her pounding heart started to calm, her mind caught up to what had happened.

Earthquake.

A decently big one at that. Ivy was used to tremors, but it had been years since one so large had hit.

Well, at least she was going to be able to get off tower duty. She should get back to the station and report the damage. First she had to get out of the fucking tower before it collapsed and killed her. She moved slowly toward the door, which was now pitched toward the ground. She was surprised it hadn't been knocked open. Ivy took a deep breath and scooted on the floor to the door and got outside onto the little wraparound porch. She tried to ignore the way her arms were shaking. She looked down at the ladder, and it seemed to be intact to a point just above the ground, easy enough for her to jump off.

Ivy thought she heard something and glanced at the forest and the Caldera beyond. She squinted. Something felt a little off, but she couldn't figure out what it was.

She shimmied along to the ladder and started down. The gap between the bottom and the ground was a bit larger than she thought, but the base of the tower was mostly grass, so she took a chance. She tucked and rolled and got off with no more than a minor cut on her arm. Probably didn't even need stitches.

Ivy adjusted her pack and took off to East Station. It would only take a quarter hour or so if she walked quickly, and she would do so in the chilly autumn air.

She'd only been walking for a few minutes when thick fog rolled in through the trees. There was a strange smell to it, not a smell she would associate with any volcanic activity. It smelled like … sweet rot? Like apples that had fallen off a tree and had been on the ground quite some time. Ivy tried to ignore the smell and the fog, but it was odd. She'd been at the Caldera her whole adult life and had never seen fog that thick, and the smell was bothersome. She knew there were no apple trees around that part of the forest.

"Focus," she told herself. It was just fog. Normal fog. It was just an earthquake, just fog, there was nothing abnormal about anything going on, or at least not dangerously abnormal.

At last, she saw the lights of the station ahead.

Something darted across the path before her and Ivy blinked.

"What the fuck."

Ivy had been roaming around the Caldera for over twenty years and had never, ever seen anything like what just ran before her. It was perhaps the size of a bobcat but much too slender and, well, it might have been a trick of the light, but it looked green and somehow shiny in the moonlight. Something about it made Ivy want to run.

She walked as calmly as she could toward the station. If there was something predatory out there, it would chase her if she ran. She was almost at the station, and once she got in, she would be safe.

Someone screamed from inside the station. At nearly the same time, something growled behind her, a sound not unlike a house cat growling. Ivy drew her sword, or tried to, but something hit her from behind, landing on her pack, knocking her off balance, and sending her sprawling face-first into the grass.

Something was ripping and tearing, luckily just into her pack, giving Ivy a moment to regain her composure. She rolled over and drew her knife from her belt. The creature skittered away for a moment then jumped toward her chest. She managed to dodge, and the creature's claws tore into her arm.

Ivy grunted in pain and took a stab at the creature. She wasn't sure if it was a fatal hit, but the creature ran away. There were more screams from the station.

"Fuck!" Her arm was bleeding badly. She slipped off the path and into the forest for enough time to pull her med kit out of her backpack and quickly wrap the arm. She stood and immediately stumbled back against the tree.

There were more of them. A lot more. At least five creatures were staring at her, hissing and growling. Ivy knew she wasn't going to be able to deal with them all. There were more screams coming from the station.

One of the creatures jumped for her, and Ivy tried to hit it but slipped on the dewy grass and tumbled down the hill. She landed with a splash in the pond below. She looked out into the moonlit night and waited for the creatures to attack.

"Where are you, little fuckers."

They weren't coming. Did they not like water? Ivy started to shiver, but she thought maybe she should stay put for a little bit.

By the sound of the screams from the station, there was nothing she could do there.

***

Calla made her way up to the roof of the fort to look for the station lights. She paced back and forth while she waited. Most nights she was there at midnight on the dot, stood still, saw the lights, and went back to her room. It was, on a normal night, a ten-minute routine.

Tonight was different.

Earlier that evening, an earthquake shook the area, and Calla had a bad feeling that one of the stations wouldn't light. Everyone else had gone to bed as usual, sure that things were fine, but Calla knew something was wrong. Something bad happened hours ago, and she was going to be the one to see it. It was up to her to see it.

West Station lit up first, then, shortly after it, Mid Station. Calla looked to where she knew the light for East Station would be.

Nothing. No light. Calla looked at the other stations again and back to East Station. Still there was no light. Calla knew there was something wrong, but she waited a few more minutes just to be sure then went down and straight to Captain Marcus.

"Something wrong, Calla?"

Calla jumped. "Damn you, Zero." Zero laughed, standing up from where he had been crouching in the dark near the captain's quarters. He ran his hand through his light hair and, still smiling from scaring her, spoke.

"So, something wrong?"

"East Station didn't light," Calla said. "I need to inform Captain Marcus. I think we should lead a party tonight to see why."

"Always doom and gloom with you, Calla," Zero said.

"And you're never serious, are you? They didn't light for a reason, what if there was a collapse or something and people are hurt?"

"I know. Get your pack and meet me out front in five. Marcus authorized a quick foray in the dark," Zero said.

"Just the two of us?" Calla said.

"For now," Zero said. "Come on, better than nothing, isn't it?"

"Right," Calla said, leaving Zero and heading to her quarters for her pack. While she was worried about East Station, she didn't really fancy going on the journey with Zero and just Zero. The man annoyed her to no end. He annoyed most people and seemed to like doing so. But she didn't really have a choice in the matter, so with Zero she would go.

The night air was chilly but the moon was shining bright. Calla had been up to the stations many times in her years at the fort, but there was always something about going there at night that made it feel like one could get lost.

Zero took the lead, and Calla thought she could at least trust him to not get them lost. She'd rather be going through the dark forest with Ivy, though, an expert navigator, versus the joke of the whole Caldera.

As they wound through the forest and up to the stations, a thick fog set in. Oddly thick. Calla couldn't remember fog that thick before, especially when the weather had been so dry. It gave her an odd feeling. No light, thick fog, earthquake.

Calla had grown up on legends centered around the dangers of the Caldera. Most people discarded them as just stories, things that hadn't happened or were figurative and not to be taken literally. Tales of danger and monsters and brave deeds. There was truth there, Calla always thought, and all the stories were swirling in her head just as the fog was swirling around her and Zero.

Calla hoped it wouldn't take too long to get to the station.

"Bit like a scary story out here tonight, isn't it?" Zero asked.

"Indeed."

"Nervous, Calla?"

"A bit, you're not?"

"A bit, it is rather creepy out tonight. I wouldn't worry too much. We're guards after all, aren't we? We're supposed to be brave, right?"

"I know," Calla said, glad it was too dark for Zero to see her blush. She was being a bit cowardly, she supposed. They continued on through the fog with the moonshine almost making it worse.

Zero, on the other hand, almost seemed happy to be going to the station in the middle of the night.

Calla groaned.

"Yes?"

"You're going to the station because you want to sleep with someone there, aren't you?" Calla said.

"Well, that might be one of the reasons," Zero said with a smile. Calla scoffed, but they were at least going to the station, so she supposed she should be happy with that. She should have realized sooner what Zero was up to; he slept around with quite a few guards. It wasn't hard to see why; he was, by most standards, handsome. Calla could see it even though she never really cared to look at men that way.

Suddenly Zero stopped ahead of her. "Do you smell that?"

"What? No. I don't smell anything."

"It smells like blood," Zero said.

Calla scoffed, "Zero ... "

"No, really. You don't smell that?"

Calla took a deep breath. She couldn't smell anything, or, well, nothing unusual. She looked at Zero. He was standing still and looking around, his hand on the pommel of his sword. It looked like he was serious about it.

"Keep an eye out," he said.

"Yes, sir," Calla said. In all likelihood, the worst it could be was a coyote or some other animal killed nearby. There was danger there, but it was more likely they would scare off the creatures or see them long before they attacked. And Calla didn't even smell anything.

"Fuck," Zero mumbled ahead of her as he stopped. Calla approached and looked down at the ground.

Blood.

A rather large slick of blood in the grass on the path. Zero lifted his lantern and looked side to side. Calla did the same but didn't see anything. She didn't hear anything, didn't smell anything.

"We're almost at the station," Zero said. "Side by side." Calla walked with Zero, knowing that the station was dead ahead and wanting to run to it. They came upon the station, and for just a moment, Calla was relieved. Then she started noticing things.

The station was dark. There was no noise. She could smell the blood. Zero was right, the coppery smell of blood hung heavy in the air, and there were other scents with it that Calla didn't want to think about.

Beside her, Zero drew his sword and she followed suit. The door to the station was ajar and Zero pushed it open. The first body was right inside the door. They both froze. Calla looked around the courtyard, the dim light of the lantern revealing more bodies. Calla clapped a hand over her mouth to keep from screaming. She blinked away tears and tried to keep breathing.

There were a dozen people at each station. Calla counted the bodies she could see, the task the only thing keeping her sane. She looked at Zero and held up nine fingers then drew her finger across her throat; nine dead. So three were missing.

Zero pointed outside then up. Ah, there would be a guard out in the tower, but that left two missing in the station and no sign of what had caused the carnage. Zero moved forward and Calla followed. As they reached each body, it was clear there was no point in checking for life. Around the back they found the last two bodies.

Calla looked down at the closest body. So many of them were mauled beyond recognition, but the body nearest her was not. Lana. The guard's name was Lana and she had only been there a year. Calla had been the one to give her the orientation tour. Calla knelt and closed Lana's eyes. With her lantern closer to the body, she could see the wounds better. A few years back, a guard had been mauled nearly to death by a bear. Calla had seen the aftermath of the incident, and there was no doubt in her mind that the wounds that killed Lana were made by some sort of animal.

Zero shifted a little and Calla stood.

Eleven dead. No sign of what killed them. Zero led her back out of the station and down the path for a little bit before stopping.

"What the fuck did that?" he asked.

"I don't know. An animal of some sort."

Zero let out a shaky breath and ran a hand through his hair. He took a couple of deep breaths. Calla felt like the world around her couldn't be real.

"Right. We need backup, as quickly as possible. We need to warn the other stations and the fort, but if ... if we get taken down, no one will know. Thoughts?"

"This can't be real," Calla said.

A groan interrupted Zero, and both he and Calla jumped. There was something in the forest right off the path. It sounded human to Calla, and there was someone missing ... Calla stepped into the forest before Zero could say anything.

There was a body slumped against a pine tree just a few steps off the path. Calla lifted her lantern, expecting to see yet another corpse, but when the light hit the person's face, they looked up at Calla.

"Ivy! Zero, it's Ivy and she's alive."

Ivy's left arm was bleeding; she'd wrapped a bandage around it. Calla looked for any other wounds, sure that there must be something else keeping the woman on the ground. Ivy was soaking wet and shivering.

"Ivy?"

Ivy moaned and her hand twitched.

"What do we have, Calla?"

"Wounded arm and it looks like she fell into the pond, she's shivering," Calla said.

"We need to get her out of here," Zero said.

"Ivy, can you get up and walk?" Calla asked.

"Can try," Ivy replied.

"Good, we'll help you get back to the fort," Zero said.

"Station?"

"All lost," Zero said. Ivy grunted. They managed to get Ivy on her feet, and she could stand a little. It was going to be an awkward trip down to the fort; Ivy and Zero were both quite a bit taller than Calla.

It took a little bit to get a rhythm going, but once they did, they started making good time down the hill back toward the fort. As they went, Ivy regained some of her strength and was able to move better.

"Do you smell that?" Zero asked. "Smells like apples."

"Fuck, that's them," Ivy said. "Keep going."

"Did you see them?" Calla asked.

"Smaller than a bobcat, skinny. Green," Ivy said.

Calla could have done with a little more description, but that was good enough for the moment. Once they got Ivy back to the fort and they were all safe, they could talk more in detail.

Once they dipped out of the fog, the smell disappeared and Ivy could walk on her own.

Finally they made it to the fort, and Zero and Calla shut the fort door firmly behind them.

"Right, Calla, can you make sure Ivy gets to the infirmary, stay there with her, I'll get Captain Marcus and meet you two there," Zero said.

"Got it," Calla said.

"I can go there myself," Ivy muttered.

"Just to be sure," Calla said, "then Captain Marcus will know where to find us. I'm sure he'll have questions."

They walked into the infirmary where Ramona was sitting and reading something. She jumped a little as she saw Ivy and Calla.

"Oh goodness, what happened, Ivy?"

"Attacked. Sat in the freezing water too long."

"Well, I can see that, but what did this?"

"I don't know," Ivy said.

Ramona frowned and looked at Calla.

"It was some sort of unknown creature," Calla said, not knowing really what else she could say.

"Just sew me up," Ivy said.

"Working on it," Ramona said. "Let's get you out of these clothes first." Ivy nodded and Ramona led her behind a curtain to change.

Calla settled back and sighed. What a weird night, and it wasn't over yet. What the hell had just happened? What the hell had killed all those at the station? Eleven people were killed by a skinny green cat? How many had there been? Were the other stations in danger?

Calla tried not to worry, but images of the dead kept popping into her mind. The smell of blood. Calla had never seen such carnage. She knew every single one of the people there, and had known many of them for years. She tried not to cry and failed.

"Calla, you alright over there?"

"No, but I don't think there's anything you can do about it," Calla said, wiping away the tears.

"I'm assuming the captain is aware of whatever this is?"

“Yes, he should be here soon,” Calla said.

“Can you help me over here, Calla?” Ramona asked.

“Sure,” she said. She really didn’t want to see blood and injuries, but she wanted to help Ramona with Ivy. It mostly involved holding a light so Ramona could stitch Ivy up. Ivy groaned and cursed and twisted when Ramona would pull away.

“I could hold your hand,” Calla said.

“Fuck off, Calla,” Ivy said.

“Sorry,” Calla muttered. She didn’t like touching people without asking first. She didn’t like when people did that to her, but maybe Ivy had thought she was teasing or something. Or that was just Ivy. Calla didn’t know sometimes. She wished she did, especially with Ivy. Ivy was beautiful. Calla pushed the thought out of her mind. It wasn’t the time to think about such things. She really didn’t want to think of anything, actually.

Calla wished very much that nothing about the day had gone the way it had, and she couldn’t even be glad it was over because she had a feeling it was only the beginning.

2

Dawn

Ivy's arm was throbbing, and she really, really didn't want to have to talk to more than one person. She knew she was going to sound a bit crazy with what she had to report. She was also worried that strange, deadly creatures roaming the hillside would mean she would have to stay in the fort. Or worse, she would have to lead people through the forest in search of the creatures.

Ivy sighed. Ramona was busing herself with cleaning up, and Calla was staring off into space, looking rather dejected. Ivy felt a little bad about snapping at her earlier.

At last, Zero and Captain Marcus came in. Both looked tired and annoyed. Good. If Ivy had to be annoyed, everyone else should too.

"What Zero's just told me sounds like a bunch of madness," Captain Marcus said. "I'm in no mood for madness. I can see Ivy is hurt, so that's the truth. Calla, what did you find at the station?"

"The bodies of eleven guards," Calla said.

"Elaborate."

"The bodies were torn and bloody, the lights were out at the station, there was no sign of what had attacked."

"You're sure the bodies were dead?"

"Yes, sir."

"Have you ever seen a dead body before, Calla?"

"Yes, but not so brutally killed."

"Then how were you sure they were dead?"

"No movement, no breathing, the smell ... There's no mistaking it, they're dead."

"Hmm. Ivy, how were you injured?"

"I was attacked by some sort of creature, sir."

"You didn't get a good look?"

"It was smaller than a bobcat and looked feline a bit, but it was longer and slender. It was green."

"Why were you outside the station and why didn't you help those inside?"

"I was on tower duty. The earthquake damaged the tower so much it's unsafe. I was on my way to report it when I was attacked. I was able to get away from the first creature, but then five more showed up. I fell down the hill into a pond, and for some reason, they didn't attack me. I waited for them to leave, then I headed up the hill and ran into Zero and Calla."

"Ramona, do you know what caused the wounds you just sewed up?"

"Animal, but unlike any I've ever seen," Ramona said.

Marcus sighed and looked at the group. "I find this all very difficult to believe."

"So do we, sir," Ivy said. As fucking weird as it was, denying belief in the face of all the evidence was stupid, and she felt like saying just that to the captain.

"Sir, we just lost an entire station, we have to check in with the others," Zero cut in before Marcus could speak.

"Right. One last thing before we move on. If this is a prank or some sort of cover up, that's it for you three." Marcus indicated Ivy, Calla, and Zero. "Ivy and Calla, you'll be expelled from the guard, and you, Zero, you'll be tried and I will push for execution."

"Understood," Zero said.

"Right. I'm taking a squad to East Station; until then, you three need to stay here. Once I return and find out what's going on, I'll deal with you," Marcus said, leaving the room in a huff.

"That went well," Ivy said.

“Are ... are they really all dead?” Ramona asked.

“Yes,” Zero said. “I’m sorry.”

“Do you think the others really are in danger?” Ramona asked.

“I don’t know,” Zero said. “Who knows how many of those things there are. How much do they eat when they hunt, were they even hunting? We don’t know a damn thing.”

“Seems like there was a danger in the Caldera after all,” Ivy said.

Zero was pacing back and forth and frowning. It would almost be comical if things weren’t so dire.

Calla frowned. “What are you thinking?”

“That we really need to go warn the other stations. Marcus didn’t believe us, though I don’t fully blame him. This is insane, but we know better, and I don’t think we should risk lives for want of proof.”

“Marcus was very clear what the repercussions would be,” Calla said.

“If we were lying, which we’re not,” Zero said.

“I love it here, but I could survive expulsion from the guard. Zero, he threatened to have you killed,” Calla said.

“I know, but I think it’s worth the risk,” Zero said. “Will you come with me?”

“Not an order?”

“No. This is potentially dangerous and possibly seditious. I could use the help, but this is volunteer only.”

“I’m going,” Calla said.

“So am I.”

Calla and Zero turned to look at Ivy. She knew she looked like shit and that maybe it was safer to stay where she was, but she also knew she wasn’t fucking crazy and wanted proof of that.

“You’re up to it?” Zero asked.

“Yes, and it makes sense, I’m the only one that’s seen one of the things. And if we have to go off the path, I can get us safely home better than anyone here,” Ivy said. "Also it pisses me off that Marcus didn't believe us even though I almost had my fucking arm ripped off."

"That's good enough for me. Let's move out," Zero said. Ivy sighed and hoped she was making the right decision.

***

For the second time that night, Calla found herself leaving the fort in the dark. It still didn't quite feel real. If both stations were safe and well, they might be able to take a bit of a rest. If they weren't thrown in a cell when Marcus caught up with them.

"So, these things are small, green, cat-like creatures with claws. Did they make any sounds?" Zero asked.

"Hissing, it sounded like a pissed off house cat," Ivy said, "and there were a lot of them, but they were hard to see even with the moonlight."

"And they smell like rotting apples," Zero said. "That gives them away a bit."

"I just can't work out why they killed all those people in East Station but didn't eat them," Calla said.

"Maybe they like their meat a bit putrid," Ivy said.

"That's disturbing, but possibly true," Zero said.

"I'm glad we're not headed there," Calla said. "I don't want to see that again." She hoped that the other stations were alright. The images she saw earlier that night were starting to wind into her mind. She'd known all the guards who'd been killed.

The country was not at war and hadn't been for a few hundred years. Calla had grown up in a small town where there wasn't much violence. She'd lost family over the years, of course, but none of them violently. Prior to that night, the worst violence she had seen was a fellow guard who had taken a bad fall and broken several bones and had deep gashes. Now she'd seen eleven dead, torn into pieces. She didn't think she would ever forget the smell of blood and guts and excrement.

Calla took a deep breath.

"You're doing great, Calla," Zero said quietly. "Thank you for coming with me."

"Of course. I don't want anyone else to get hurt."

"Once we're sure everyone is warned, if you need to go off and cry or scream or break down in any way, let me know."

"I will," she said.

"Gonna let me cry too?" Ivy cut in.

"Of course, but I don't think you're shy about the whole thing," Zero said. "I'm guessing you'll take your anger and grief out by killing some of these beasts. Or hell, I could be wrong, and Calla will go for slaughter and you'll break down crying."

Ivy snorted. "Slaughter sounds about right for me."

"And what about you, Zero, crying or killing?" Calla asked.

"I'll start with making sure no one else is hurt, then we'll see," Zero said.

Calla hoped that she could shove the feelings aside to wait for a good time to break down. She knew emotion was one of the reasons she was stationed at the Caldera. It made sense that they would put her here where they didn't expect there to be any danger. She didn't blame them, and she desperately hoped she wouldn't embarrass herself.

Most of the people who were stationed at the Caldera were odd. Ivy certainly was. She was brash and kept to herself and didn't want to be around people for the most part. There was something about her, though, that made Calla wish she could spend more time with Ivy. Well, she was getting to spend a bit of time with her now, but the situation was less than ideal. As for why Zero was at the Caldera, Calla wasn't sure. There were a lot of nasty rumors about him. Calla supposed they really didn't matter as far as the present situation was concerned.

They made it to Middle Station in under an hour, and Calla felt nervous as they approached. It was quiet, but it was the wee hours of the morning. There was also light and no smell of blood or rotting apples.

As they approached the door, someone inside opened it, looking half asleep and confused.

"Lieutenant Zero?"

"Yes, I … "

"What are you doing here?" The door opened further to reveal Captain Marcus, arms folded across his chest.

"We really thought … "

"Silence. I don't actually want to hear whatever excuse you've got, not after what you've done."

"Sir?" Zero frowned and stiffened.

"What did you do at East Station and where are the bodies?" Marcus asked.

"What … I didn't … the creatures … " Zero looked back at Calla and Ivy.

"Get in here, you three," Marcus said, and they all three filed in. Zero looked at Calla again, and she gave a shrug. She had no idea what could be going on. What did Marcus mean, there were no bodies? How could that be?

"Sir … "

"Silence, Calla, you still have a chance to save your life. That goes for you as well, Ivy. Lieutenant Hana, please escort Zero here to a cell. Calla and Ivy, you go to the main hall and wait for me," Marcus said.

They made their way to the hall, and Calla sat down in a daze with Ivy across from her. She wondered if she was going crazy. How could the bodies be gone? She had seen them with her own eyes. Why did Marcus think Zero had anything to do with what was going on?

"Calla?"

"Sorry, what was that?"

"Things are fucked," Ivy said.

"Very."

Ivy sighed. "I'm leaving."

"What?"

"I'm going to West Station to warn them. Someone fucking has to and I think you'll do a better job than me of keeping Marcus from killing Zero."

"Fuck," Calla said.

Ivy snorted a laugh. "Fuck indeed, but are we on the same page here? Those fucking things are real. West Station needs to be warned and someone has to protect Zero."

"I didn't think you liked him."

"I didn't think you did either," Ivy said.

Calla shrugged. "He's annoying when nothing is going on, but tonight ... "

"An actual calm leader, who'd have thought?"

"I'll do the best I can to protect him. Be safe, Ivy," Calla said.

"I will," Ivy said. Calla sighed and put her head in her hands. This was all getting so wildly out of hand. She didn't understand why Marcus was being the way he was. People had died! They should be regrouping at the fort and figuring out what to do next! It was impossible to say how many of the creatures there were, but there were a limited number of guards to deal with them and they had already lost nearly a dozen.

"Calla." She jumped slightly as Captain Marcus entered. "Where is Ivy?"

"She went to the bathroom," Calla said. Marcus was going to be furious when he realized Ivy wasn't there, and Calla hoped she was far enough away by then. Of course, it was Ivy, and she knew the forest better than anyone and could easily evade anyone sent after her.

"Right. I want to talk to you alone, anyway. Calla, this is a serious offense."

"Sir, I'm sorry, I'm confused. What do you think happened? Zero was at the fort all evening until I saw East Station fail to light. Then he and I found the dead and rescued Ivy."

"No one saw Zero for several hours in the evening. He had time to go to the station and back," Marcus said.

"You really think he killed guards? What of Ivy?"

"I'm worried she helped. I wish I could have seen her wounds before they were sewn."

"I'm sorry, sir, that just doesn't make any sense."

"Doesn't it? I've seen guards go mad here. Ivy has never fit in, she dislikes most people. Zero has history," Marcus said. "They got bored, went to East Station, and slaughtered everyone there. Then Zero volunteered to go check things out with you, knowing you'd be easy to fool, especially with an injured Ivy lying in wait."

Calla couldn't help the blush that spread across her cheeks. Easy to fool. Was she? Ivy wasn't very social, but Calla really didn't think she would go off and kill people out of boredom. And Zero ...

"Zero's history?"

Marcus sighed. "Zero was stationed in the south for his first few years on the guard. He was on a training mission and his entire squad was killed. Poisoned. Zero claimed that they all drank from the same tainted water. He claimed to have almost died himself, but there was no proof. They couldn't charge him and moved him here."

Calla had to admit it was rather odd, but still, she couldn't see why Zero, or Ivy for that matter, would want to kill people. Ivy's wounds had looked like an animal had made them. The guards looked like they had been torn apart. How had Zero killed them all and gotten no wounds?

"The bodies were torn apart, quite different from poison."

"Unless he did the cutting once the guards were incapacitated."

"That doesn't seem likely. I'm sorry, sir, I don't think Zero or Ivy did this."

"Green cats did?"

"Yes," Calla said. "I know it seems crazy, but I believe it was creatures more than Zero and Ivy. That just doesn't make sense to me."

"Calla, you're risking expulsion or worse," Marcus said.

"I know."

Marcus sighed. Just as he was about to speak, one of his men walked in and whispered something in his ear.

"Ivy is gone," Marcus said.

"She is?" Calla frowned.

Marcus shook his head. "That's why they wanted you. Naive. A fool. Too stuck in stories to see what is really going on."

Calla knew she was right. She knew Zero hadn't killed anyone. She knew Ivy was telling the truth about the creatures. There were just too many signs that the creatures were there. Calla didn't know what she could say or how she could say it to get Marcus to believe her.

Calla started crying.

"You help me, side with me, and I can protect you, Calla. You don't have to worry about Zero or Ivy hurting you."

Calla shook her head. "I believe them. There are creatures out there, they are dangerous, and we should be doing something about them."

Marcus sighed and looked over his shoulder. "Lock her up too."

3

A Light in the Dark

Ivy made it out of the station easily. She just walked like she had purpose and no one stopped her. Marcus just thought she'd follow his order. She supposed she should have done it, it was how the chain of command worked after all, but Marcus was an ass and if Ivy stayed, she was going to blow up in his face and get in fucking trouble anyway. Better to let Calla deal with Marcus. Oh, the woman was a bit sensitive, but her heart was in the right place and she could help Zero more than Ivy could.

It was starting to get light as she left the station and headed to West Station. The fog was clearing as the light chased the night away. Ivy paused now and then to listen for any odd sounds and sniff the air for the smell of rotting apples. Nothing seemed off; the morning chorus of birds was starting to sing as usual.

"Fucking Marcus," she said. If the bastard didn't have such a problem with Zero, they could move forward with the fact that strange green cats were fucking killing people.

Ivy knew why Marcus was after Zero, or at least she knew the basics. Zero was the sole survivor of a training mission gone wrong. Everyone thought Zero had something to do with it. A lot of people didn't quite trust Zero, and it was clear that Marcus didn't trust him and more; he seemed to particularly have it out for Zero.

Stupid. The whole fucking thing was stupid.

Ivy picked up the pace as she neared the station. She was tired and would like to take a nap if she could before heading out.

At first all looked well; there were no bodies on display, no groans of pain, nothing on fire. It looked exactly as a station should look in the early morning. She knocked on the side door and waited for the night watch to open it.

Nothing.

She knocked again. Maybe it was guard switch time. Ivy sighed.

"Wake up, fuckers!" she yelled.

Still nothing. Ivy was just considering breaking in the door when the wind picked up a little and a horrible smell reached her. Blood. Shit. Death.

"Oh fuck no," Ivy groaned. She didn't want to see what was in the station, and it seemed likely everyone within was dead, but with fucking Marcus being a dick, she needed proof. Ivy stepped back, positioning herself so she could try to kick the door open. It took a couple of tries, but the door finally opened.The first body was just a few feet away from the door. Torn open, insides missing. Ivy took a deep breath and moved forward, trying to push it out of her mind that she knew who the body had been. The courtyard had blood and bits of bodies all around. She tried to ignore the fact that her legs were shaking and pushed forward.

"Fuck, fuck, fuck," Ivy muttered as she moved around. She went into the central building and made her way up into the tower to see if she could spot anything useful before she left the fucking place.

There was something odd about a patch of grass outside; it almost looked wet. It was blood. The sun rose above the Caldera and hit the blood, turning it almost golden. Ivy saw patches of blood here and there heading north and then east toward the Caldera, toward ...

"The caves. Fuck," Ivy said. She had to get back to Mid Station as fast as she could. Something crashed below her and Ivy jumped. Fuck, the things were still there. Ivy drew her sword as she descended from the tower. She saw movement.

"Ivy?"

Ivy looked at the bloody man before her and tried desperately to remember his name. "Asher?" Two more guards stood behind Asher, bloody as well.

"What ... what is going on?" Asher asked.

"The earthquake did something and released these things," Ivy said. "We're working on it. Are you three all that's left here?"

Asher nodded.

"We should get to Mid Station where the others are," Ivy said.

"Your arm," Asher noted, his unspoken question clear.

"East Station got attacked, all gone but me. Mid is alright and so is the fort."

"What the hell is going on," Asher sighed.

"An attack. I ... let's get reorganized as best we can and get out of here," Ivy said. She could tell that Asher and the others were fucked up, of course they were fucked up, but she didn't know how to get through to them through the shock. Fuck, this wasn't what she was good at.

"They're gone?"

"For now, I think. They seem to come out at night," she said and hoped that she wasn't wrong.

Asher nodded and got lost in looking around at the blood and carnage around the station. Fuck, they needed to get out of the damn station. Ivy kept her focus on Asher.

"How badly are you all hurt? Can you walk or do we need to figure that out?" Ivy asked.

"I ... I think we can go," Asher said.

"Good, just ... let's get you three cleaned up so we don't attract anything out there and maybe get some food ... "

"How can you think of food? What is wrong with you?" Asher asked.

"Look, we need to be practical about this. We've lost a lot of guards, and if we don't want to join the dead, we need to move forward," Ivy said.

Asher shook his head. "Fine, let's get out of here."

Ivy tried to ignore the looks Asher and the others were giving her as she raided the kitchen. She hadn't eaten in hours, and it was going to be a hike back to Mid Station, so she needed something to eat. It would do the others no good to pass out or be too weak to fight when the things came back again. It was the only thing she could do to keep sane. Do something normal, don't think about the blood and the guts and the people they once were. In the kitchen, doing something normal, she could almost pretend she was shaking because she was hungry.

"I don't think we should leave," Asher said.

"We have to. Marcus isn't believing what's going on, and we have to tell him he's full of shit, though maybe not exactly that way," Ivy said.

"They'll come for us," Asher said.

"Probably not in time. We need to be back at Mid by nightfall," Ivy said. Ivy knew that Asher was still in shock over the whole situation and that people reacted differently, but they really needed to be practical about the fucking thing if they didn't want to join the dead.

"I ... I don't ... "

"Asher. We need to leave this place, and if you don't want to fucking die, you should come with me. I'll give you a little time, I want to look around at something outside the station, but you really need to come with me if you want to live."

Asher nodded and Ivy hoped that he would come. She could give him a little longer. It was still early in the morning, and it didn't take that long to get to Mid Station.

Ivy had seen the trail of blood leading to the cave in the early morning light, and she felt the need to investigate. She had little hope of finding anyone alive, but then again, the creatures had left her and not come back, and Zero and Calla had found her.

Ivy followed the trail of blood toward a cave entrance she knew was too small for a person to enter, and she wasn't going to fucking die squeezing herself into a cave.

"You little fuckers," Ivy said. There were flies and bugs of all sorts flying around the mouth of the cave. There was a lot of blood and bits of flesh and bone. She lifted a hand to cover her nose.

"Disgusting. Fascinating," Ivy said. Well, there wouldn't be anyone left alive after being dismembered and dragged into a cave. Ivy looked around. There was an entrance to the cave nearby that she could go into, and it would get her close to where the creatures had entered. She started out that way, unsure if she was going to actually go in. It was probably stupid to go in alone with no one knowing where she was, but they were lacking information.

Ivy stood before the cave with a lantern in her hand. "Fuck it." Ivy had been in most of the caves in the area at least once. She liked to take shelter in them when the weather was shitty, and they were fun to explore. As long as they were unoccupied.

Ivy entered the cave and went toward where the creatures had taken bits of bodies into the cave. As she got closer, she could smell the blood and a faint odor of apples. She drew her sword and slowed down. The passage she was following was wide enough for two men to walk side-by-side and was two feet or so taller than she was; enough room to move around if she needed to.

"Oh fuck," Ivy closed her eyes and turned away. A mass of flesh, almost impossible to tell that it was ever human, filled the tunnel to the left. There was no sign of where the creatures were. Every instinct told Ivy to run and get the fuck out of there, but she pressed forward down the tunnel to the right, which she knew she could follow for quite a while.

Ivy heard something ahead of her and stopped to listen, but she couldn't hear anything else. Ivy concentrated on where her lantern light was ahead of her and was ready to turn and run at the first sign of danger.

She was concentrating so hard on the light ahead that her foot hit a patch of slick blood.

"Fuck!" Ivy tried to right herself but fell to the ground, hard. The lantern slipped from her fingers and hit the stone floor. The base cracked and the oil leaked out, briefly illuminating the cavern in a burst of flame before burning out and plunging Ivy into total darkness.

Ivy didn't notice at first, too focused on the pain shooting up her leg from her ankle and the throbbing cut on her cheek. She blinked a few times.

"Oh fuck, fuck. Okay, stay calm. Calm. Think." Ivy tried to get her breathing under control as her heart pounded in her chest. She pulled herself into a sitting position and tried to think in total darkness. She could get out. It wouldn't be that hard to find her way back, as long as she picked the right direction to begin with.

"Think, Ivy," she muttered. She had been heading into the cave, down into the cave. She luckily had a waterskin with her. She put her hand on the cave floor and poured water over her hand; the water trickled down to her left.

"Left is down, the exit is to my right." She poured water twice more with her hand in slightly different parts of the cave floor and found the same result. She stood and turned to her right but nearly collapsed again when she put her full weight on her left ankle.

"Fuck me," she said. No use worrying about it at the moment, though; she couldn't see shit and didn't really want to feel if she had a bone sticking out or something. She kept her left hand on the cave wall for support as she slowly moved forward in the dark. She knew she would come to the passage on the left to get out, and she'd run into the pile of bodies before she got lost that way.

Ivy fought against the sense of panic. She couldn't see. She had gone into a cave and not told anyone. There were bloodthirsty creatures somewhere in the cave with her. She wouldn't be able to fight them if they came upon her.

"Stop fucking thinking about them," Ivy said.

What was she supposed to concentrate on? How much her ankle hurt? She went forward slowly and carefully, determined to get herself out of the stupid mess she had gotten herself into. And for nothing. Well, maybe not nothing. They did seem to like rotting meat and they went into the caves during the day. Hopefully that was worth it.

Ivy stepped wrong on her ankle and tried not to scream. She tried taking deep breaths through the lightning shots of pain going up to her hip and back down.

Ivy heard something behind her, an echo in the cave. She couldn't tell what it was or how close it was. She took another deep breath and moved forward. She needed to get out and she needed to get the information to the others even if it turned out to be useless.

She ... wanted to see the others. She wanted to see Calla in particular.

"Don't go there now," she thought. "Stupid."

It was true, though. Of all the people she knew, most would probably not really care if she didn't come back. She didn't exactly endear herself to people. But there was something about how Calla looked at her. She always smiled. She was kind even when Ivy was being a bitch.

"We have to do this now, brain," Ivy huffed as she pushed herself forward. It was distracting, at least; it was getting her to keep going. She heard another noise behind her. She pushed forward.

Finally she came to the turn. She could smell the rotting bodies in front of her as she turned into the tunnel she knew would lead her out. Ivy couldn't go very fast. She wanted to run but couldn't. She still thought she heard something behind her.

When she first saw light, she thought she might be imagining it. She held her hand out in front of her and she could see it; she was getting closer to the exit. She could smell fresh air.

Almost out.

There was something behind her. There was no mistaking it for imagination. There was a skittering sound. Too big to be bugs or rats. Too small to be a bear or big cat. Ivy tried to keep calm. If she could get a little further, there would be enough light for her to put up a little bit of a fight even if she was hindered by the ankle.

She pushed past the pain to get to the light.

Something was behind her. Close.

She wasn't going to look behind her until she had enough light to see. It wouldn't make any sense to turn around to face what she couldn't see.

Ivy could smell them now, the rotting apple scent wafting close behind her. At last she could see well enough to turn around and see if there really was anything behind her.

Three creatures. Ivy walked backward into the light as best she could, which was very awkward with the fucking ankle.

"Why are you little shits not attacking?" she asked them. Maybe they were full; they had a lot of nice rotting meat not far away and didn't really have to risk anything to kill her.

"Fuck off!" Ivy yelled at them, and they did nothing. Well, sound didn't seem to scare them off. Ivy continued backing up and hoped she didn't fall; she was sure that if she fell, that was going to be it.

Ivy risked a look behind her and realized she was almost out of the cave, almost into the full light. So of course Ivy had to fall. Her ankle gave out and she fell on her ass. She scooted back as much as she could into the light.

The creatures started to hiss and lunge forward a little bit, but they wouldn't get into the light. Ivy watched them for a few moments. Were they just playing, or did they really dislike the light so much as to avoid it? Or was it again because they weren't quite hungry? If they were starving, would they come out into the light?

Ivy pulled herself up with a groan, and the creatures still lunged, not quite into the light.

"I guess that means we're safe for the moment and you hate light," she said. At least sunlight. She wasn't sure if the light of torches would be enough, and there were always shadows to hide in.

"See you fuckers later," Ivy said and started to walk away. The creatures hissed and skittered in the shadows. They did not come after her even though she was limping and crying out in pain. That would attract any other hunter.

The light. She could use that if she could get back down to the others.

It was a struggle, but she made it back to the station and then got Asher and the others ready to go. She wrapped her ankle as best she could. At least it wasn't broken. Then they headed out. She knew even then that they wouldn't quite make it before dark. Hopefully they would have enough light around them or somehow beat the creatures back.

4

The Second Night

Calla sat down on the wooden bench across from Zero with a sigh. She didn't know what to say to Zero or what was going on. She didn't believe that Zero could be the cause of such carnage, and even though Ivy was a bit odd, she didn't think that Ivy would do something like that either.

Marcus had called her naive and told her she was easily swayed and that's why Zero took her with him. She didn't know what was and wasn't true.

"Calla?"

"I ... I don't know what is going on," she said.

"What did Marcus say?"

Calla took a deep breath. She didn't know how Zero could be so calm, sitting in a cell with Marcus out to harm him.

"He's convinced the slaughter was you and Ivy and that you chose me to witness it because I'm gullible and an easy mark," Calla said.

"Fuck him, you know I didn't do that, right?"

"I ... think I do. I'm so confused. You're up here for a reason and there are rumors."

Zero nodded. "Parts of the rumors are true. I was part of a training exercise where all my squad died. I nearly died."

"Why did they think you'd done it?"

Zero sighed. "Two days before the exercise, I put ink in everyone's canteens as a prank. On the mission, it was something in the water that poisoned us. I tampered with the water before, so they thought I'd done it again. Then there was the fact that I chose to live my life and not let myself be destroyed by the fact that I lived."

Calla nodded. "I can see how people could think that was suspicious."

"I don't know what happened that night. We all filled our own canteens. Whatever was in the water didn't take long. My mouth burned then went numb. Everything started to turn numb. We all vomited." Zero sighed. "None of us were well enough to start a fire, we were all freezing. I could barely move, I was lying still but my heart was racing. People started dying. I could hear their labored breathing suddenly stop, and I was sure I'd be dying soon. I didn't kill my friends."

"I'm sorry, Zero. I believe you. I'm sorry I couldn't convince Marcus."

"Don't worry about it," he said.

"I do. He's going to try to kill you," Calla said. "Ivy was sure I could do it, that's why she left."

"He can't kill me without a tribunal," Zero said.

"I know the rules, but ... I think Marcus is willing to break them. And we still have the creatures to worry about."

Calla hoped that Ivy was having better luck than they were. She hoped that the creatures were nocturnal or at least had a small range or something else that would keep the other stations safe.

Calla tried to stay calm about the whole thing; Zero certainly was, but the day was passing by and she dreaded what night would bring.

It didn't look like anything was going to happen soon, though, and Calla tried to curl up in a comfortable position on the bench and get some rest. Maybe Marcus didn't believe there were monsters out there, but Calla knew better. Sleep would do her good.

Calla woke with a start, nearly falling off the bench as the door to the cell was opened.

"Have anything to say for yourself, Zero?" Marcus asked.

"No, sir, my statement remains the same," Zero said.

Marcus shook his head. "Have it your way." Marcus crossed the small cell in two steps and pulled Zero up off the bench by his collar. Calla was on her feet but couldn't do anything as Marcus punched Zero in the jaw, sending the man sprawling on the floor. Marcus took the opportunity to kick Zero in the stomach before backing up.

Zero groaned and coughed on the floor of the cell. Calla looked around. No one else was there.

"What do you say now, Zero?"

"Same thing, sir," Zero said quietly.

Marcus grabbed Zero off the floor and pulled his fist back again.

"Stop!" Calla cried out. "Sir, this is against the rules."

Marcus scoffed, dropping Zero on the bench. "You simple, idealistic, naive cunt. You think rules really work in the real world? This man is a murderer. He got out of punishment once before, and I will not let that happen again!"

"Sir ... "

"Do you want to join him? It would be easy for me to charge you with helping him."

"This is wrong," Calla said, voice shaking. She looked at Zero. She didn't know what to do. Marcus was twice her size and armed. She wasn't much of a fighter, truth be told. She wasn't much of anything.

"Calla, I'm going to make this very clear. I order you to leave this cell and wait in the mess hall."

"No, sir."

Calla was shaking, and she couldn't help the tears that ran down her cheeks. She wasn't going to leave Zero alone to be beaten to death.

Marcus looked between her and Zero. "You know, maybe you are right, Calla. This should be more of an example."

"Sir ... "

" ... and I'm well within my rights to have him flogged. And I don't need a tribunal for that."

"I ... " Calla couldn't stop it. She didn't know how to stop it without causing more trouble for herself and Zero. She looked down at Zero with his swollen jaw and didn't know what to do.

Marcus pulled Zero off the ground and pushed Calla aside. Everything was happening so fast that none of it made sense. She couldn't help but follow and watched as Marcus tied Zero to the pole. Calla didn't even know if anyone had ever been flogged in all her years there. Several people came out to see what was going on. No one seemed eager to stop it.

"Calla," Zero said.

"I don't ... I'm sorry ... I ... "

"It'll be night soon," Zero said.

"But ... "

"I can survive this, let's not ... "

"Shut up!" Marcus said, slapping Zero across the face. "And you'd better step back, Calla."

She did. She stepped back. She wanted to stop it, but Zero did have a point. If Marcus got any more riled up about the whole thing, he might lash out and kill Zero. This was horrible, but it was survivable.

The first hit of the lash made Calla jump almost as much as Zero. He grunted in pain, blood blooming across his back.

Another hit, more blood. Zero grunted again.

The third hit cut into one of the previous lashes, and Zero screamed in pain. He was shaking as blood ran down his back. Calla put a hand over her mouth; she was afraid she was going to be sick.

He screamed again as the fourth strike hit him, and it looked like he wanted to go to his knees, but with the way he was tied, he could not do so.

Marcus took his time between the fourth and fifth strike so when he finally brought the lash down, Zero screamed and writhed on the pole.

"There, all in accordance with the rules, and I can do this again in the morning," Marcus said. He rolled up the bloody whip then loosened the restraints, so Zero could fall to his knees. Then Marcus left without a word to anyone.

Zero was slumped against the pole, bloody and tired. They had maybe a half hour before dark. Calla approached Zero and knelt in front of him. He was still shaking and pale, and there were streams of blood running down his back, but his cuts weren't too deep, and it was unlikely they would prove difficult to heal.

Calla wiped tears from her face and took a deep breath.

"I'm going to get you some water," Calla said.

"Thank you," Zero said.

Calla felt shaky and sick as she entered the main room. Marcus was there, tucking into his dinner, and Calla couldn't believe he could just sit down and eat after torturing Zero all afternoon.

Calla wondered what had become of Ivy; had she run off or gotten killed? Everyone else looked a little stressed but probably because of the torture going on and not a sense of dread. Calla grabbed some supplies before heading back to Zero.

"I got you some water, a little soup if you can eat. I'll clean you up a bit," Calla said. "I'm sorry." She lifted the cup of water to his lips to help him drink. Then she cleaned some of the blood off Zero's back, as gently as she could.

"I have a feeling this will be over soon," Zero said. "At nightfall."

"You think the creatures will come?"

"Yes," Zero said.

"On the one hand, I hope not, but on the other, I don't want to see Marcus kill you. I ... don't know what else to do," Calla said.

"It's good to know that at least one person has my back," Zero said. A back that was currently torn open and bleeding.

"I think more would if they weren't so scared of Marcus," Calla said. She had brought bandages with her and a shirt and managed to get things wrapped up a little. Getting the shirt on over the manacles was harder, but at least Zero wouldn't be shivering in the night air. Calla sat with Zero, intending to keep her promise of not leaving his side. She was beginning to consider how far she was willing to go with it. She was near the point where she wanted to put herself between Marcus and Zero no matter the cost. Everyone else seemed scared and indifferent to the whole thing. Maybe if Calla was hurt, they would stand up to Marcus.

"Fuck," Zero said, looking around suddenly.

"Zero?"

"I smell them," he said.

"You're sure?"

"Yes." Zero pulled his hands and the chains rattled. "Marcus has the key?"

"Yes, I'll sound the alarm," Calla said. She couldn't smell the apple scent, but she believed that Zero could. The alarm bell was across the courtyard from where Zero was tied up. Calla rang it then started back to Zero.

"What is the meaning of this?" Marcus demanded.

"The creatures are coming," Calla said. "We're soon to be under attack."

Marcus stood stock-still and stared at Calla. She swallowed hard. She had to stand her ground; she knew that they were in danger, and everyone needed to know it.

"This is sedition. You and Zero are charged with sedition, and it is my right to take out a threat to the guard," Marcus said, drawing his sword. Calla's hand went to her own sword, but she stopped. If she drew against Marcus, there was no doubt about what she was doing.

"We are in danger from creatures that have killed an entire station before. We haven't had contact with West Station. One or two people could not have caused the slaughter I saw. I know it's hard to believe, but Zero and I are telling the truth. I'm not trying to betray the guard, I'm trying to save us!" Calla let out a frustrated sigh as tears started to slip down her cheeks. Of course she couldn't even stand up for things without crying. Stupid. She wiped the tears away.

Marcus took a swing at her with his sword, and Calla jumped back. She looked at all the gathered guards behind Marcus, hoping that at least one of them would intervene. She could see confusion and uncertainty on most people's faces, so that was something, at least. Calla continued to back up toward Zero.

She was only a few steps in front of Zero, and Marcus was still advancing with his sword drawn. Well, she wasn't going to give in. She couldn't let Marcus kill Zero.

"This is your last chance, Calla. Stand down now, and I'll only expel you from the guard. This is all Zero's doing. Stand aside, Calla."

"No."

"So be it," Marcus said. Up until the last second, Calla hoped that Marcus would stop or someone else would stop him. Marcus lunged forward, and Calla drew her sword and blocked him.

The station door burst open behind Marcus, and Ivy and three other guards came in.

"What the fuck ... "

"You! Someone get her before she escapes," Marcus ordered.

"Those things are right behind us," Ivy said.

"They killed all but three of us at West Station," Asher said. "What the hell is going on here? Why aren't you preparing for an attack?"

"You ... you're all in on this," Marcus said.

"You're in the wrong, Captain," Calla said. "You have more witnesses now. Let Zero go and let's get ready for ... "

Someone screamed in the crowd. Calla realized she could smell rotting apples. Ivy was wrong, they weren't coming. They were already there.

Calla saw another guard go down, swarmed by five of the creatures at once. They were real, she had been right. Zero was right. Ivy was right.

"Marcus ... "

More screams as another guard went down.

"Marcus, I need the key," Calla said. Marcus looked at her, at Zero, then turned around to face the onslaught of creatures.

"Shit!" Calla went to Zero and looked at the shackles. She knew good and well that there was no way she could get them off without a key, but she didn't know what else to do.

"Calla, get your sword!" Zero called out. She grabbed her sword and swung at the first creature to attack. Ivy was right, they looked quite feline. Longer claws, longer jaws, and an odd dark green, but very cat-like. Not solitary hunters like cats, though; they swarmed. That's how the others were slaughtered. Panicked and overwhelmed. And it was happening again.

Calla knocked another creature back as it jumped toward Zero. They were going to lose, going to be killed. There had to be something the creatures didn't like. Something fell near Calla, and she saw a torch from the wall knocked down and three of the creatures kicking dirt at it.

The light. They didn't like the light.

"Set things on fire, burn everything!" Calla yelled. She went for a torch and held it before her in her left hand and the sword in her right and tried to keep the creatures away from her and Zero.

She tried to spot where Marcus was in the fight; she still needed to get the shackle key off of him to free Zero.

A sudden burst of light erupted from the central tower. Good. Either someone heard her or figured it out themselves. The creatures screeched at the light and backed away from it. It didn't completely stop them, and Calla watched in horror as a guard was dragged into the shadows.

"Calla!"

"Ivy, did you set the blaze?"

"Yes. Where's the key?" Ivy nodded toward Zero.

"Marcus has them," Calla said.

"Fucker, I'll get it," Ivy said. The remaining guards, nine that Calla could see, were all heading for the light as the creatures backed away from it. Marcus was still alive, and several guards, including Ivy, were surrounding him and shouting.

Marcus came toward them, and for a second, Calla thought he might be coming in to try to kill them, but then he took the key out and released Zero. Zero fell slightly, and Calla dropped her torch to support him.

"We'll talk about this later," Marcus said. Calla nodded but kept her attention on Zero. There was a patch of darkness they needed to cross to get to the others and safety.

"We have to move fast, Zero, I'm sorry," she said.

"I can do it," he said, but he stumbled slightly as they started to move.

"We've got you!" Ivy called out, and Calla and Zero ran. Calla could hear the creatures leap forward — she thought she might have felt one try to grab at her ankle as she passed — but she made it into the light with Zero.

She turned to see if Marcus had made it, just in time to watch two of the creatures drag him down. Calla made sure Zero wasn't going to fall over and ran toward Marcus as he was being dragged away.

Calla cut down one of the creatures and managed to grab Marcus and started to drag him back into the light. Asher and Ivy came forward to help her, and they managed to get him back.

"Oh fuck," Ivy said, and Calla looked down.

Blood was pouring from Marcus' neck where the creatures had torn into him. Zero quickly clamped both hands on the bleeding wound, his hands instantly soaked in blood.

"He's losing too much blood," Zero said.

"Do we have a healer here?" Calla asked as she looked away.

The answer was no. Calla didn't think a healer could do anything as quickly as Marcus was losing blood.

"Med kit?" Zero asked.

"Across the way," someone said, pointing past a very dark patch with several creatures milling about in it.

Calla swallowed. "I'll get it." Marcus grabbed her with a shaking hand and shook his head no and frantically looked between Zero and Calla.

"Fuck," Zero said. "Don't go for it, Calla."

Calla nodded. Marcus was fading quickly, eyes dim and wandering as he took shallow gasps of air. Calla took his hand and held it in hers. It was only another minute or so until Marcus went still.

Zero stood, looking at the huddled guards. With Marcus and the station's lieutenant gone, Zero was the highest-ranking guard. Back wrapped in bloody bandages, covered in the captain's blood, Zero looked at them all and spoke.

"We keep the fire burning and stick to the light. The creatures have to go somewhere before dawn, then we'll figure out what comes next."

It seemed like such a simple order, but Calla thought this would likely be the longest night of her life.

The creatures tried again and again to pull people into the darkness, to kick dirt on the fire to put it out, to jump and catch them by surprise. They succeeded a few times.

Calla caught sight of one of the things about to jump on Zero and managed to pull him back and slice the creature enough to get it to run away.

"Thanks," he said.

"Hanging in there?"

"Trying," he said. More creatures, more fighting. The night seemed endless.

About an hour before dawn, the creatures started to leave, taking bits of bodies with them as they went. That was particularly hard to watch.

Dawn came at last. Calla was alive. Zero was alive, Ivy and Asher were still alive. There were eight of them left alive.

Just two days before, there were thirty-six guards spread out along the Caldera stations. Now there were eight, and most of them were wounded.

"Right. We need to take care of the wounded, then pack up and head to the fort and regroup," Zero said.

"We're just going to leave the dead?" Asher asked. "Again. I'm not surprised Ivy was like that, but I thought better of you."

"I would love to be able to bury the dead, but we need to leave," Zero said. "We need to get help for those of us who are still alive."

"I still don't like it."

"Neither do I," Zero said, "but it is what we have to do."

Calla took stock of her own wounds. Scratches and bruises, not much else. She was extremely lucky.

"Are you alright?" Ivy asked.

"Yeah, most of this isn't my blood. I noticed you limping."

"Twisted my fucking ankle trying to track the creatures into the cave," Ivy said. "They go into the caves during the day and don't like coming out in the light. We should be safe now."

"We know a little more, I guess. I ... don't know what we're going to do," Calla said.

"I don't know either. Zero's back looks bad."

"He claims it's not as bad as it looks," Calla said.

"We're going to have to stand up for him again."

"Probably," Calla said. She didn't want to have any other arguments about what was going on. She was really sick and tired of it. They needed to do something, not argue about what was happening.

It didn't take long for them to get ready to leave; even those who were hurt the worst wanted to get away from the station and get back to the fort. Calla wanted to get back to her room at the fort, and she wanted to take a nap. She wanted to sleep for several days, but that wasn't going to be possible. They had to act fast if they were going to stop the creatures from spreading further west.

Calla walked near the back of the group with Ivy, who was still limping even though they had wrapped her ankle. No one really felt like talking. It was quite the somber procession coming down from the station.

They were halfway down to the fort when Zero stopped. Calla made her way up to the front.

"I smell blood," he said, "fresh."

"I don't, but I trust that you do," Calla said. She drew her sword. There shouldn't be any creatures out and about, but just in case.

"Move on, eyes open," Zero called behind him.

They only had gone a little bit more when they heard someone calling out for help. Calla thought she recognized the voice. It was a human voice, that was certain. They pushed forward toward the voice.

"Help!"

Ramona. It was Ramona, but what was she doing out in the forest away from the fort?

"Ramona!" she called out.

"Calla? Help!"

Calla followed the sound of her voice and came to a thick patch of trees not far off the main path. The grass was slick with blood, and there were parts of bodies all around.

"Ramona!" Calla cried as she caught sight of the healer sitting up against a tree.

"Calla. I ... I ... We saw the fire, we tried to come see what was going on," Ramona said.

"How many from the fort came with you?" Zero asked.

"All but five," Ramona said. "What ... what ... "

"Calla? Can you look around for anyone else alive?"

"I will," Calla said. She didn't think she would find anyone else, but she set about it methodically to make sure she didn't miss anywhere. She tried to keep it out of her mind that Ramona said that there were only five people left at the fort. So they were down to fourteen people. And if the creatures got through them, they would spread out below the Caldera from village to village as far as the caves would allow them to, which was quite the distance. Once they spread, there would be no way to stop them. They needed to do something, but she didn't know what fourteen people, many of them wounded, could actually do.

Calla couldn't find any bodies, living or dead. She saw blood. Bits of bone.

"Calla!"

"Here!"

"Come back out, we need to move," Zero said.

"I didn't find anyone," Calla said. "Plenty of signs of where people fell but no one alive."

Zero nodded. "We'll figure it out once we get back to the fort. Let's get there and get people patched up and fed and see what we can do."

"Yes, sir," Calla said. Zero smiled at that. Calla usually didn't bother with honorifics. Most people at the Caldera didn't really worry about rank beyond the captain, but it felt like they needed a little more protocol with all that was going on.

The wounded, tired group made it back to the fort. It was clear once they got there that Zero was the highest-ranking officer left out of the group. Fourteen out of a hundred were alive.

Zero took charge the instant he got back. Calla had never seen him like that before. Calla helped Ramona with the wounded until they were taken care of, then went to the galley for some food, where Ivy was sitting alone.

"How's the ankle?"

"Still fucked, but a little better," Ivy said.

"Good."

"I'm glad you're alright, Calla," Ivy said. "I was worried when we saw the station under attack."

Calla smiled. "I was worried about you too."

"I shouldn't have gone into those caves alone. I broke my lantern about a mile in and had to backtrack through the dark and thought the creatures were gonna jump me at any second. I ... I was thinking about you, that I wanted to see you again."

Calla smiled. She hadn't thought that Ivy really liked her. It was a little overwhelming. "That's really sweet, Ivy."

"Don't tell anyone I fucking said that," Ivy said.

"Wouldn't dare," Calla replied.

5

New Leadership

Calla didn't think she would be able to get to sleep with all that had happened, but her exhausted body had other plans, and she more or less passed out. She knew she couldn't sleep long; a few hours, maybe. But there was going to be a lot to do before nightfall and a probable attack.

Calla wandered into the galley a little after noon to find Zero sitting with a cup of tea and staring at nothing. The fort was quiet; most were still sleeping or dealing with what had just happened.

"Morning, or afternoon, I suppose, sir," she said as she sat down. Zero looked ... well, he didn't look good, but he didn't look as bad as one might expect. Still, it looked like he could sleep for days.

"Thank you," Zero said.

"For?"

"Calling me sir. You've done it a few times now."

"Of course, you're our leader now," Calla said.

"For now." He sighed. "We have to get the word out, but I think it's too late in the day to send a messenger out; they won't make it down the hill before nightfall. So we'll have to survive tonight."

"We can set up enough fires, I think, we've got plenty of wood since we're stocked up for winter. I ... don't know what we'll do if we have to stay here all winter, but survival is our goal right now," Calla said.

"Agreed. We'll have to get going on it soon if fourteen wounded guards expect to get it done," Zero said.

"How are you feeling?"

"Better. Or at least not worse. Not looking forward to holding a meeting, but I need to," Zero said.

"I have your back and so does Ivy," Calla said. "We don't have time to fight each other."

"I know. We just have to convince everyone else," Zero said.

"The chain of command is a thing for a reason, and you're doing an excellent job so far," Calla said.

"Thanks, Calla."

An hour later, they were all gathered in a room that could hold a hundred people but now held less than a quarter of that. Zero stood up at the podium and looked at the gathered guards.

"First order of business is to get this fort ready for nightfall," Zero said.

"Shouldn't we go get help?" Ramona asked.

"I doubt anyone could make it down by nightfall, and I don't want to risk a messenger getting killed *en route*."

"Wait ... wait, isn't there something else we need to discuss? Is he really the one to lead us?" Asher asked.

"Captain Marcus is dead, so are the other lieutenants. The chain of command falls to me," Zero said. "We don't have time to bicker if we want to live. If, after this is all over, you wish to lodge a complaint, please do so, but for now, we need to focus on staying alive."

"I don't think a man who killed his entire platoon as a joke should lead," someone else said.

"My leadership is not up for discussion," Zero said.

"How do we know you didn't kill Marcus?"

"Because a creature ripped the captain's throat out, you fucking idiot," Ivy said. "I saw it happen and so did Calla."

“I still think someone should be able to get to town before dark,” Ramona said.

“I won’t risk it,” Zero said, “and we need everyone here to prepare for tonight. There aren’t many of us left, and I don’t want to lose anyone else if I can help it.”

“We should all just leave,” Asher said.

“We can’t make it down by nightfall, not with so many of us hurt,” Ivy said.

“We can’t do this,” Asher said.

“We must,” Zero said.

“We can’t lead those things down the hill,” Calla said.

“Do you really think we can stop them?”

“We have to try,” Zero said. “That is our duty as guards.”

“Our duty to die?” Asher scoffed.

“It is our duty as guards to protect people. Calla is right. We can’t lead those things to other people without trying to dispose of them first. We will send for help, but we need to hold this fort at the very least. We all swore an oath when we joined that we would lay down our lives to protect others. I will do everything in my power to prevent that from happening, but I will uphold my oath of protection to whatever end.”

“As will I,” Calla said.

“Well, fuck, how could I not after a speech like that,” Ivy said. There were murmurs of agreement in the crowd and then silence as Zero waited to see if anyone else would speak up.

“We need to get to work protecting the fort. We’re going to line the entire wall with fire so those bastards won’t want to try to attack us.”

“We should have lantern oil ready to relight as well. I saw some of the creatures trying to put out fires last night, they’re not stupid,” Calla said.

“Good point,” Zero said. “We’ll do that. Let’s get started, then. Calla, hang back a moment, I have something to ask you.”

Calla nodded and couldn’t help but feel a little nervous. She knew it was stupid, but that was just the way she was sometimes.

“Thank you for your support again,” Zero said.

"Of course," she said.

"I hope we can fend those things off tonight, but if I die, I need someone to lead, and I would like you to do it."

"Me?" She scoffed and shook her head.

"Yes, Calla, you have a good head on your shoulders. No one would argue with you leading, and I know Ivy would have your back. I need to make sure that someone is going to be able to lead if I die."

"I don't know if I'm qualified to do it," Calla said.

"You are. I would really like it to be you. I trust you to get the others to safety and keep a cool head," Zero said.

"Alright. I accept. But I really don't want to do it, so you'd better not die, Zero," she said.

Zero snorted. "I'll be sure to try."

Calla really hoped that she wouldn't have to take over. Even with a small group, she didn't think she could do it. It felt good to have Zero express confidence in her, but she didn't quite believe it herself.

She tried to ignore that particular anxiety and concentrate on getting the fort ready. They had a winter's worth of wood at the fort, which looked like it was going to be enough to have the fire burning all night.

They had a decent amount of lantern oil that could be used to quickly set things ablaze if they needed to. It all looked like it would work, but Calla thought they should still be very cautious about it since they didn't really know all that much about the creatures.

Or maybe she had just read too many stories and the creatures were simple in essence, but it was the amount of them that was the problem.

There were plenty of unknowns, though; how fast did they move, how much did they have to eat, how fast did they reproduce. It wasn't as if she'd had the chance to look closer and pick out any young while they were ripping her friends apart.

By supper time, they had the fort set for the night.

"Well, I think that's the best we can do," Zero said.

"I think it looks good," Calla said.

"I hope so. We just have to make it through the night with at least one person to get down and warn everyone else in the morning. Of course, I don't want to lose anyone," Zero said.

"I know that, Zero," Calla said.

"I'm going to assign Asher to the tower," Zero said. "So he can lock himself in there if worse comes to worse, and then he can go down to the village to warn people. I ... I can't be the only survivor again. I wish I could put you all in the tower, but I don't think Asher is up to the fight that might hit us, and you and Ivy are."

"I wouldn't want to be in the tower, anyway," Calla said. "And you're right about Asher. I would say put Ivy up there, but with her ankle being messed up, she might not get to the village in time to warn them."

"That's what I was thinking. Plus I really think she wants to kill those things, as many of them as she can," Zero said.

"Yes. I want to as well," Calla said.

"Me too," Zero said. "As many as it takes to protect people." They fell into silence for a little bit until Ivy came up and sat down with her tray.

"So, assuming we don't get ripped apart for food tonight, I have an idea," Ivy said.

"Alright, go on," Zero said.

"Since they spend the day in the cave, that's probably how they came out. That earthquake must have opened a passage in the caves from wherever they are. We need to find that place, where they sleep."

"Go into the caves," Zero said.

"I know it sounds insane," Ivy said.

"It is insane," Zero said.

"I know, but if we can block where they are coming from ... "

"If they go back to the same place," Calla said.

"That's what we need to know," Ivy said.

"I'm assuming you want to use fire powder to block them in."

"Of course," Ivy said.

"Do we have any experts in fire powder, or are we winging it?" Calla asked.

"I know enough," Zero said with a smile.

"That is disturbing," Ivy said.

"Disturbing but useful," Zero said.

"It might work," Calla said. "And destroying them before they have time to settle in, as it were, would be the best course of action. I hate the idea of just sitting around, waiting for another night of hell."

"Alright, we'll think on the idea. First things first, we have to survive tonight. I'm going to have everyone up on the wall and Asher in the tower. We have to keep the fires burning, and we need to have eyes on where the creatures are. I don't want to be caught by surprise. I want to know what those fuckers are doing. Calla and I will be walking the walls and checking in to see if we have any problem areas where we need more people. How's your ankle, Ivy?"

"Fucked but not bad, I'll be able to stand and fight," she said.

"Good."

"I'll push through this," Ivy said. "Tonight and when we go into the caves."

Zero nodded. "Good."

Calla wished there was more time to plan and time to rest; they only had a little bit of time to take a nap before they needed to be up and ready. Well, she supposed it was better than nothing.

Zero took the east and south walls, and Calla was on the west and north walls. Four people per wall seemed like it would be enough. It seemed a bit silly, actually; in all the training exercises, they had had two people per wall if there was nothing going on, and there was normally one person on the whole wall at night on a regular night.

They lit the fires just as the sun was sinking below the horizon. It was going to be hard to see the creatures until they were right on the fort, and Calla wondered if even Zero would have trouble smelling them with all the smoke in the air.

Now it was just a waiting game to see if the creatures would come. Calla had no doubt they would but really, really hoped that they wouldn't. One would think nearly a hundred people would be enough food for them, and they wouldn't need to hunt again.

Unless ... oh fuck, what if it was more a territorial thing? Had they thought of that before? Everything was starting to blur and go mad in her mind.

"Calla?"

"Sorry, what was that?"

"Nothing, you just stopped dead in your tracks and stared off into the distance," Ivy said.

"I did. I was just wondering if those things are being territorial and that's why they keep coming after us."

"Hmm, you would think they've had enough to eat," Ivy said.

"Exactly."

"Fuck, all the more reason to kill them off as quickly as possible," Ivy said.

"I wonder what kills them or keeps them in check in the Caldera?" Calla asked.

"I really don't want to think about that right now, Calla," Ivy said.

"Sorry, couldn't help it," she said. "I ... "

"Wait a second, I think we've got something out there," Ivy said. Calla peered with Ivy out past the light and the smoke and saw at least three pairs of eyes glowing in the dark tree line. Calla's heart started to pound.

"That's them," Calla said. "I'll go tell Zero and pass it on." Calla spread the word as quickly as she could and let Zero know.

"Surprised Asher didn't see them in the tower," he said.

"I think Ivy's part cat and can see in the dark," Calla said, and Zero snorted a laugh. Within the hour, the creatures were all around the fort in the forest. Calla walked the walls and waited. It didn't look like they were up to anything, but it wasn't like the guards knew how they hunted and acted. She found herself looking closer to the fire and even up in the air. She wondered if they could tunnel, or if they were smart enough to do things like that. She wondered how they communicated, and if there would be some sort of tell before they attacked.

There really wasn't; a group of ten of the creatures came out from the woods screeching and tried to kick dirt on the burning logs.

Calla was walking near Ivy when a few more tried it.

"Watch this," Ivy said and took a cup of lantern oil and tossed it at the creatures. The oil hit them and they burst into flames.

"Shit ... "

"Ha ha ha, you fuckers! Burn!" Ivy cackled. The creatures howled and dropped a few feet away from the burning logs. More creatures came out and tried to kick their fallen comrades into the fire as if that might put it out, which only made them burn more.

"They kind of smell like roasting apples," Calla said.

"They do." Ivy laughed.

Calla felt hopeful about the fires and their ability to keep the creatures out. But as the night wore on, the creatures got more riled up. They hissed and growled and made a strange howling noise.

"Ah fuck!"

Calla turned to see Ivy stepping back and using her sword to cut one of the creatures in half.

"They're jumping through the fire!" Ivy called out.

Three more creatures launched over the wall, and Calla looked over the edge to see how the hell they were doing it. They were standing on each other, and the creature on top was jumping over the flames and scaling the wall.

It was frightening and weird but fairly easy to see coming.

Calla met Zero to check in as the occasional creature came over the wall.

"I feel like we're not seeing something," he said.

"I know, but I can't figure out what it is," Calla said.

"I guess just keep your eye out," Zero said. More creatures came over, more creatures tried to put the fires out. Ivy and several others were pouring lantern oil to burn some of the creatures and keep the fires lit.

Calla saw a creature coming toward her and split it in half with her sword. Something hit her and she fell back and rolled off the wall and hit the ground below.

Calla's vision blurred and she couldn't breathe. The creature that hit her growled nearby; she couldn't really see where it was exactly and was having trouble moving at all. She patted the ground for her sword and couldn't find it. She drew her knife but knew she wouldn't have much reach with the damn thing. Her hand was shaking and her lungs just wouldn't draw in any air. She didn't know how badly hurt she was, if she had just knocked the wind out of herself or if she'd broken something. Perhaps many things.

The creature jumped up on Calla's chest, and she took a swing at it but didn't have the strength to land the strike.

Calla couldn't call out for help, but surely someone had seen her fall? The creature flexed its claws, and Calla felt her flesh tearing. The creature reared up to go for her throat, and Calla struck with her knife with as much force as she could.

The creature screeched as the knife pierced its belly. It stumbled away and died. Calla still couldn't quite move, but it didn't seem like there were any more creatures around.

"Calla!" Ivy was there with a lantern, looking at the blood on Calla while Calla tried to speak and tell her that most of the blood was the creature's and not hers.

"I ... "

"It's alright, I'll get Ramona," Ivy said.

"I'm okay," Calla managed.

"Are you?" Ivy asked. Calla nodded. Ivy didn't seem sure and examined the wounds the creature made and searched to make sure the blood wasn't Calla's blood.

"I'm okay," Calla repeated.

"Fuck. I think you are. Fuck, I thought that thing had got you," Ivy said.

"Help me up," Calla said.

"If you're sure."

Calla nodded. She still felt a little shaky but could breathe again. Ivy helped her back onto the wall, and the night continued.

6

Tracking

Ivy watched Calla go down and thought it was all over. She had to run quite a ways to get to the stairs and by the time she had, the creature was dead, but Calla was still very still and covered in blood. Ivy shook as she knelt next to Calla to survey the damage.

By some miracle, Calla was alive and only slightly injured. Ivy tried to keep an eye on her the rest of the night.

By dawn, they were all still alive. The creatures started to creep back into the shadows of the forest as the light started to penetrate it. When she was sure the creatures were headed back and the light was growing brighter, she went to Zero.

"I need to leave soon if I'm going to track them. I ... probably need help, just in case," she said.

"I'll come," Calla said.

"You're hurt," Ivy said.

"You are too, Ivy," Calla said.

"True. If you think you're up to it," Ivy said, "and Zero approves."

"I do, I can hold the fort," he said. "You two be careful. I need you both to come back."

"Yes, sir," Calla said.

"Might want to get the powder ready so we can get them before tonight, if we're lucky," Ivy said.

Zero nodded, then rubbed at the dark circles under his eyes. "Good luck."

Ivy gathered her things as quickly as she could and met Calla at the door of the fort, where Asher was also waiting to go out to warn the nearest village of what was going on.

"You two are fucking insane," Asher said.

"Probably," Ivy said. She didn't have time to deal with Asher, not again. The man didn't like her very much, anyway, and she was rather neutral towards him. She just hoped he would be able to get back to the village and warn people in time. Hopefully he wouldn't come upon an entire village of corpses. Ivy shivered at the thought.

"You alright?" Calla asked.

"Yeah, just had an unpleasant thought," she said.

Calla chuckled. "Imagine that."

"Fuck off," Ivy said and smiled when Calla smiled.

Ivy knew where the creatures were most likely headed and which route they would take: through the darkest parts of the forest to avoid the light. Ivy decided to take a path close to that but with a little more light. The last thing they needed was to walk right into an ambush. The creatures weren't stupid. They were fucking nuts but not stupid.

"I wish we could have brought Zero for his nose," Calla said. "I keep thinking I'm smelling them, but I'm not sure if it's real or not."

"Probably is," Ivy said. "We just need to be as careful as we can."

Calla grunted in response, and Ivy looked over at her to make sure that she was alright. She looked like she was holding up pretty well. Ivy was about the same. They were both exhausted, running on just enough food and rest to keep them alive. Ivy might have been able to stay up for a few days when she was in her twenties, but her forty-something body was protesting it hard.

"You know what? I don't think I'm ever going to be able to eat apples again after this," Ivy said.

Calla laughed. "Probably not."

"Fucking sucks too. I love apple pie."

"Now I'm hungry," Calla said.

"Maybe we'll catch one of those things and roast it on a spit," Ivy said. "Alive." Calla laughed again.

Ivy walked on with Calla by her side. Normally when someone was with her, she felt uncomfortable and annoyed. Not when it was Calla. Fuck, Ivy hoped that they would actually live through the whole thing, and maybe she and Calla could be more than just fellow guards.

Ivy caught a whiff of apples stronger than before and stopped to look around. The path ahead led through a dark copse of trees, but it was the best way to get where they were going.

"Swords out, I think," Ivy said. She wished there was another way to go, but if they were going to get to the cave in time to track the fuckers, they needed to go straight up. Ivy and Calla walked side by side with swords drawn, looking in every direction to try to spot movement. The coloration of the fucking things made sense; the dark green was perfect camouflage in the shadows of the forest.

A slight rustle was the only warning they got before two creatures lunged out of the bushes and another dropped down from one of the trees. Ivy managed to kill two and Calla the other before they moved forward slowly. They just needed to get to the top of the hill, and they would be in the open sunshine and be able to see the entrance to the cave Ivy was sure the creatures would be going into.

Another creature burst out of the bushes and missed Ivy's arm by inches.

At last, they were at the top of the hill in the sunshine; if there were any more creatures in the forest, they wouldn't dare come out in the bright morning light. Ivy walked to the edge of the depression. The rocky entrance to the cave was a good twenty feet below them and still bathed in shadow.

"Oh fuck," Ivy whispered as she looked at the creatures milling about the cave below. She felt frozen looking down at them. Calla touched her, and she nearly jumped out of her skin.

"At least two hundred," Calla whispered.

If the creatures caught sight of them, if they could stand the light, they would be dead and picked clean in a matter of minutes. And they were going to go into the caves with a few lanterns and torches to track the fucking things. It was madness.

"Are we really going to go in there?" Calla whispered.

"Fuck, I don't know. I might have another entrance point in mind," Ivy said. "I really don't want to go in there."

"If you have another idea, I'd like to try it," Calla said.

Ivy nodded. Waiting until all those things went in and then following them was starting to look like a really stupid idea. There was another entrance to the cave system and one closer to the area where the creatures probably came from. They attacked East Station first, so it made sense for them to have come from that area. Ivy hoped that she was right about it. She was used to tracking things and finding her way, and the wilderness had always made more sense than people.

Ivy hoped that the creatures made just enough sense that they could figure out how to kill them, where to kill them. The sun rose higher in the sky and the light came shining through the forest, and it felt much safer. Not safe enough to completely ignore the possibility of attack but enough that they could move faster.

They made it to the opening, a narrow split in the rocks that one could easily miss. Ivy had been in that particular cave several times. She often was out and about in the forest when storms would hit and knew good places to shelter.

"That's it?" Calla shifted and looked around.

"Yep, I know it doesn't look like much, but it'll do," Ivy said.

"If you say so," Calla said. They lit their lanterns, two torches, and grabbed some extra wood in case they were under for too long.

"Well, here we go," Ivy said.

"Please tell me we don't have to squeeze through narrow passages or swim under anywhere."

"Some areas are small, but I would say no squeezing. Shouldn't be much water this time of the year. I wouldn't want to try this one in spring."

The entrance narrowed a bit and sloped down into the cave system. Luckily there was only one way to go. There were other places in the system where one could easily get lost. Some people didn't have a good sense of direction underground, or at all, really, but Ivy was still as good underground as she was above it, maybe even better.

The air grew still and stale as they descended. Sound was strange underground. If their lights went out, it would go completely dark. Ivy had a little anxiety over the thought of it. She didn't want a repeat of the last time she was following the fucking things.

"The main passage is just around another bend. There's a little drop, so we'll approach slowly so we know if it's safe to drop down."

"Can the creatures get up if they can see us?"

"Maybe, it's a bit of a drop, but they'll try."

They heard the creatures, and smelled them, before they saw them. They were hissing and chittering as they moved through the tunnel. For the longest time, Ivy and Calla stayed just around the corner where the creatures hopefully wouldn't come after them. Hopefully the light was enough to deter them.

They waited a long time until the hissing stopped. Ivy took a deep breath, hand on her sword as they rounded the corner. Ivy couldn't see anything at the opening to the drop, and she couldn't see anything down in the main passage. She took several deep breaths and only vaguely smelled apple.

"That's quite a drop," Calla said.

"For a short person, maybe," Ivy said. "I'll help you down and back up."

Ivy dropped a torch down and waited just a little longer to make sure there were no creatures before she dropped down and helped Calla down.

"Alright, forward we go."

"How much longer is this passage?"

"There's a big opening maybe a mile ahead. That's where I think they are," Ivy said. "And I think we can trap them there because there is only one entrance."

"Hopefully," Calla said. They walked slowly, partly because they wanted to be cautious and partly because they were both hurting. But there was no one else who could be doing the job. Most of the people at the fort and stations never made it into more than one cave and probably went in to get out of the rain and only went in a little bit.

"Ivy?"

"Hmm?"

"You said this dead-ends, right? Like a big open room where all the things can fit?"

"Right."

"Then why is there light ahead?"

Ivy blinked and looked ahead. She blinked again. There looked to be sunlight, just a little bit, ahead of them. It wasn't light from the torches or lanterns.

"What the fuck," Ivy said.

"Maybe we found where they came through," Calla said. "Maybe the earthquake opened something, and now they can get through."

"Maybe."

They pressed on, and it was getting more and more obvious that it was sunlight coming into the cave. There were a few more twists until they got to the opening. Ivy paused and drew her sword, very uncertain as to what she was going to find.

There was so much light shining that there had to be an opening.

"Shit," Calla said. Ivy stared and waited for her mind to figure out what she was looking at. There was light shining in through a thick forest of trees, several of which didn't look like any trees that she knew. The trees around the Caldera were mostly pine, but these were deciduous and their leaves were just starting to turn. Any of the deciduous trees outside the Caldera were much further along.

"We're ... looking out into the Caldera," Ivy said.

In the distance, Ivy could see the other side of the Caldera rising above the trees, she could see the high walls all around it, but it was much, much bigger than she thought it would be. At the base of the nearest tree, there was an entrance to a burrow of some sort, perhaps a rabbit den. Birds were singing in the distance, familiar and yet a little off.

"That's amazing," Calla said. Ivy moved forward into the room, holding her torch high to try to figure out where the fucking creatures were hiding. The room was filled with light, so it was hard to believe that they were anywhere near.

"Where are you," Ivy muttered.

"Over here," Calla called out.

Right at the edge of the forest, there was a huge gash in the rock leading further downward. It was only maybe three feet wide but too long to fill in with anything. And it would still probably be easier to blow the tunnel just before it opened, but at least there were a few options.

"We should head back," Ivy said.

"Yes," Calla said.

Ivy looked beyond the cave into the Caldera and didn't want to go back. Every bone in her body told her to keep going forward, that this was a fantastic opportunity to explore somewhere no one had ever been.

"You know the old stories, Calla. Has anyone been out there?"

"No. And for good reason, probably. I bet the creatures crawl out of caves every night and attack whatever lives out there," Calla said.

"I want to go out there so bad," Ivy said.

"I know, I sort of do too. But we can't. If we just blow this entrance to their underground home, they can come out somewhere else and use the tunnel," Calla said. "We have to block it all."

Ivy sighed. She knew it was the right thing to do; they had to stop the creatures from coming out of the Caldera and killing people. Maybe someday they would be able to find a way in that didn't let the creatures out. Then they would be able to explore.

“Come on, Ivy, we really should be getting back,” Calla said softly.

Ivy nodded, and they left the bright new world and went back into the cave system. Her ankle was starting to throb again, but she pushed on; they had to get back to the fort as quickly as possible, and then they would have to set off again to make sure they could blow the cave by nightfall.

It had to end. There was no other way. Ivy could devote time to finding a way into the Caldera once everyone else was safe. There had to be some way to get back in, but first they needed to take care of business.

Ivy and Calla pushed on through the darkness. When they came to the offshoot again, they decided to head out the main entrance, as the creatures were all gone and underground again.

Coming back out of the cave seemed to take less time than going in, even with both of them moving slower because of their wounds. Ivy wondered if they were going to get some sort of award for the whole thing or if they would just be ignored. Zero would likely get a captaincy after it was all said and done. Maybe. Unless people started turning on him again. One thing was for certain, if anyone told Ivy she would have to move away from the Caldera, she was going to quit the guard.

“Still thinking about the Caldera?”

“Yep. Probably will for a long time. I’m going to find another way in there and figure out how to do it without the creatures being able to get out. I’ll work on it the rest of my life if I have to,” Ivy said.

“I’d like to help. I’m curious about it too.”

“Would you leave the guard to do it?”

“I don’t know.”

“We’ll have to replenish the guards we lost. We lost almost everybody,” Calla said.

“True. I don’t know, if they offer me a promotion, I think I’ll have to turn it down,” Ivy said.

“Even if you serve under Zero?”

"Ehh, maybe, fuck, I don't know. I guess we need to concentrate on surviving the current mission."

"We'll have to get back here pretty fast, and none of us are in good shape," Calla said.

"And we have to hope the powder goes off right and we don't just bury ourselves under the Caldera."

"We might be walking in our own tomb," Calla said.

Ivy laughed. "You have a morbid streak a mile wide, Calla. It's cute." Calla scoffed.

Finally they came out into the light, and Ivy felt a little better. It was a nice bright day, and there was no way the creatures were out. It was just a nice walk back to the fort.

***

Zero was pacing around the top of the fort as they approached and visibly relaxed when he saw them, meeting them at the door.

"Please tell me you found something."

"We found a lot," Ivy said.

"The earthquake broke a wall in the cave, exposing the Caldera. There's a whole forest in there, a whole habitat. But we're going to have to blow the entrance to that chamber to be sure to block the creatures," Calla said.

"Shame, but we really need to finish this as soon as possible," Zero said.

"Did something happen while we were gone?" Ivy asked.

"Yes. A whole argument about whether or not we should wait for back up to attempt anything. Asher and a few others still aren't happy that I'm in charge," Zero said.

"We need to do this. I don't know if the wood can last another night," Calla said.

"And I think we survived that by dumb fucking luck to begin with. My vote goes to leaving as quickly as we can and blowing the fucking thing. They can get mad at us later. We don't want new people sitting around talking and debating and wasting time," Ivy said.

"I agree, but it might be just us three going," Zero said.

"I think we can do it," Ivy said.

"Yes," Calla said, "the fewer people go, the faster we'll be."

"I don't know what's going to happen once more guardsmen get here," Zero said.

"I don't fucking care," Ivy said.

"I do care a little," Calla said. "But this is the right thing to do. We need to get this done. Last night we had good luck. Tonight we might not."

"Alright, you two go get something to eat and a quick nap. I'll take care of gathering all the supplies," Zero said.

"Yes, sir," Ivy and Calla said at the same time.

Ivy was starving and could use a few days' worth of naps but a little one would do. Ivy and Calla ate as quickly as they could to maximize nap time.

"Do you want me to come wake you up if I get up first?" Calla asked.

"Might be easier if we, uh, slept in the same bed? Just sleeping, I'm too tired," Ivy said.

"That would be nice." Calla smiled and Ivy smiled back. Nice indeed, a little comfort before going to certain death.

7

Blowing the Cave

Calla woke with Ivy's arms wrapped around her. She snuggled closer for a few moments. She knew that they both needed to get up and get ready for the upcoming mission. Calla hoped that all would go well and that there would be more time for her and Ivy. Calla smiled as Ivy slept beside her.

Calla had never really thought of being in a relationship before. She knew it was more important for a lot of people, but she'd always just thought if it happened, fine, and if not, fine. She suspected Ivy wasn't keen on relationships because she was not going to change herself to appeal to anyone and figured that no one would like her as she was.

Calla did. She very much liked Ivy just as she was.

"We should wake up," Calla said softly.

"No."

"I don't want to either, but we can't let Zero go by himself," Calla said.

"We can," Ivy said then sighed. "No, I guess we can't. He'd probably get lost in the caves."

"Probably," Calla said. She got up first and got dressed, trying to ignore her bandaged wounds and how it still ached to breathe too deeply. She watched Ivy get out of bed, stepping gingerly on her ankle and rubbing her arm.

Zero didn't look much better; there were dark circles under his eyes, his left eye was still swollen, and his lip was split.

Ivy snorted. "We're a fucked up bunch, aren't we."

"Indeed. Heroes in old stories aren't all bruised and beaten up, are they?" Zero asked.

"Not usually, but then it might just be the author leaving out those details. They are stories after all."

"Still, I hope we get our nice heroic ending, with everyone cheering for us," Zero said. "I'm at least hoping to not get kicked out of the guard for this."

"I bet there's going to be a meeting and discussions." Ivy sighed. "I fucking hate that."

"It'll be worth it to get rid of those things, though," Calla said.

"Indeed," Zero said. "Well, my lovely and brave crew, let's get going."

Calla didn't feel especially lovely or brave at the moment. She felt exhausted and wary of what was to come. Powder wasn't used all that often in the area; she knew further south they used it to blow into the mountains to mine for iron and other things, and during war it was used to blast into castles and such, but around here, there wasn't much use for it.

They only had it and briefly trained with it because all guards did. Now they were going to go underground and try to block a cavern by blowing part of it up. There was a not-so-small chance that they were going to end up burying themselves in the process. Calla could only hope in that instance that it was quick; she'd rather be crushed to death than be trapped in the darkness, waiting to die from lack of air or water.

"I know you're worried, Calla, and probably mostly for good reason, but remember, I do have a decent amount of experience with powder," Zero said with a smile.

"Do we even want to know?" Ivy asked.

"I grew up near a place that made powder. They'd pay good coin to young boys willing to test it," Zero said.

"Good that someone had experience with it," Calla said. "I don't remember how to use it. I'm not really good at anything."

"You are," Ivy said.

"I don't know about that," Calla said. She didn't really see herself as that, though she had done things in the past few days that she wouldn't have guessed she could possibly do. She was nervous the whole time, but she had done it and she was still there and still willing to push forward.

"I do," Zero said. "You are a phenomenal guard, Calla."

"Thank you," she said.

"Aww, you made her blush," Ivy said.

"Shut up, Ivy," Calla said. "I ... I believe you, Zero, I don't think I would have a few days ago, but now I do. And you are doing a fantastic job as well."

"Thank you."

"Ah yes, making each other feel good before we go to blow ourselves up in a cave," Ivy said.

Calla snorted a laugh and Zero chuckled.

"We're going to try to avoid dying as much as possible," he said.

"Of course," Ivy said.

"I'd rather not."

"But ... " Zero hesitated. "It might happen. I think we all know that."

"Yeah," Ivy said, and Calla nodded. She had no idea, really, what to expect. She wanted it to go like in a story where they would easily defeat their foes and come back victorious to a cheering crowd, but that wasn't really likely to happen, was it?

Three wounded, tired guards trying to do something nearly impossible. Surely something would go wrong. But she supposed things had been going wrong for a while now, and they just had to work with what they had and fight until they couldn't fight anymore.

The cave opening was clear of any creatures, and the cave itself was empty. Not a whiff of rotting apple or blood. If Calla didn't know better, she would say that the whole thing had been a dream, or a nightmare, really.

They walked through the cave as quickly as they could. Calla was surprised how much she remembered about the way even though she had only been there once.

“I see the light,” Zero said. “That’s insane.”

“We need to be careful,” Calla said. “With the sun behind us, there might be a shadow and enough darkness for the creatures to come out.”

“I hope they’re asleep, mostly because I want to surprise the fuck out of them,” Ivy said.

“So far, so good,” Zero said. “I can see why you don’t want to blow this, Ivy.”

“Has to be done, I’ll figure something out,” Ivy said. “Right now I just want it done, and I want to go back to the fort and nap for days.”

“Time to play with powder.” Zero smiled. “If you two would kindly keep a lookout.”

“Yes, sir,” Calla said. Ivy moved away from where Zero was setting up the powder bombs to look at the forest. Calla followed her over and looked at the strange landscape beyond.

“I want to know what’s out there, but then again, I don’t. I have a feeling I could find ten things that would kill a person just walking a few feet in.” Ivy paced back and forth a bit, looking at all the plants.

“Most likely,” Calla said. It was beautiful, though, and so different from anything she had ever seen, but she could imagine how many of those things would be crawling around the forest at night.

“I will find a way back out here,” Ivy said.

“I know you can do it,” Calla said. She turned around to look at Zero to see how he was doing and found that he was looking between the two of them. He gave her a thumbs-up and Calla blushed and turned away.

Two birds with odd-looking black and white feathers cried out and flew from a nearby tree.

“Fuck,” Ivy said, and Calla looked over and saw two of the creatures coming out of one of the holes in the ground. It was still a little light out, but they were clinging to the shadows. So far, it didn’t look like Ivy and Calla had been spotted, but it was only a matter of time.

Calla drew her sword as quietly as she could and Ivy did the same, and as they were doing so, three more creatures came out. Ivy took a few steps back toward Calla, and they both moved so they could be in between Zero and the creatures.

Calla turned to Zero, who was busy setting up the charges and seemed unaware of what was going on. Calla debated whether or not to try to get his attention; she could cause the creatures to notice them, but then again, if Zero started talking loudly without realizing it, they would attack anyway.

Luckily Zero looked up and saw Calla and Ivy then looked beyond them to the creatures. He stared at them for just a moment then went back to furiously setting up the charges.

Calla thought they were in a good position to ...

It only took an instant for the creatures to notice them and start an attack. They started hissing and stalking, and more creatures came out of the crack. But they didn't seem eager to attack as fast as they normally did.

"What are they doing?" Ivy asked.

"I don't know, maybe they get more defensive of their home?" Calla said. She started looking around in case there was somewhere else they were crawling out of or sneaking up on them from, but she couldn't see anything.

"Alright," Zero said not long after. "Ready to go."

Calla and Ivy moved back slowly. If they ran, the creatures would probably chase them, though every bone in Calla's body was telling her to run. A few of the creatures started to follow them as they retreated into the cave.

Calla hoped that none of the creatures would follow them back, but they could manage to take one or two of them out if they were left in the tunnel after the explosion.

"I'm going to light this, and then we'll run back a bit further. Once it goes, cover your heads. As messed up as it sounds, it's better to have a broken arm than a cracked skull," Zero said.

"Lovely thought," Ivy said.

"Ready?"

Zero lit the fuse, and they all ran back down the tunnel to where they thought would be a safe enough distance.

At least three of the creatures came after them, but something about the smell of the lit fuse made them stop, luckily just under where the explosion would be.

The powder went off, sending a near-deafening sound of rocks cascading down.

"That sounded about right," Zero said. "We should … "

The world dropped out from under them, and the sound of cascading rocks once again filled the air. The tunnel was collapsing, Calla realized. There must be something under them, another cavern that they were falling into.

They were doomed. There was no way they would survive. They would be crushed for certain. Calla tried to reach out for Ivy but couldn't find her. Her last thought before they hit the bottom was hope that at the very least, the creatures would be blocked, and they would not have died in vain.

8

In the Dark

Ivy could make out a little light; at least one of the torches or lanterns was still burning in the darkness of the cave. Everything was silent aside from her own breathing. Fuck. Was everyone else dead? Ivy knew she was very much alive because she was in pain, but she didn't really want to have to focus on how badly she was hurt. She didn't want to move, she really didn't, but it didn't sound like anyone else was alive, and she had to know.

"Fuck it," she said and moved her arms. Good there. She felt her head, and there was something sticky, blood, obviously, on the side of her forehead, but it wasn't enough to be concerned about. She felt her chest and stomach, and nothing felt too bad, sore, but not bad.

She moved her right leg. Fine. Left ...

"Oh fuck, fuck damn it fuck!" Well, at least it was the same leg as the twisted ankle. Something in her lower leg was broken.

"Calla! Zero!" she called out and listened. Nothing. She couldn't even hear anyone breathing nearby.

"Fuck! Please, I don't want to be alone ... "

Light. There was still light. She could find the still-burning torch and try to find Calla and Zero ... at least find their bodies. She had to try to get out for them. So someone would know what happened.

Ivy half-stumbled, half-crawled to the light of the torch. She stopped just before she got to it with a gasp.

Calla.

She was lying on her stomach, very still. Ivy took a deep breath before reaching for the torch. She moved some of Calla's dark hair aside and felt for a pulse at her neck, expecting to find nothing.

But there was something. A pulse, and a strong one at that.

"Calla?" Ivy moved around to the other side of Calla so she could see better. "Calla, honey, please wake up."

Calla groaned and Ivy looked over her body for any injuries. She had a nasty gash on her upper left arm, a cut across her cheek. Ivy carefully felt Calla's head and couldn't find any broken skin or bone.

"Ivy?"

"Calla! Oh thank the spirits, where are you hurt, honey?"

"Honey. I like it," Calla said. She moved slowly, and when she turned onto her back, she grunted.

"Calla?"

"Ribs," Calla said, holding her hand over her lower left ribs.

"Can I take a look?" Ivy asked, and Calla nodded. Calla's skin was bruised, swollen, and hot, and the ribs felt odd, probably broken. But the bruising didn't look too bad or so Ivy hoped.

"Where is Zero?" Calla asked.

"I haven't found him yet," Ivy said. "I'll try to, but my leg's fucked." Ivy saw a flash of light and blinked as Zero came into view.

"Zero?"

Zero let out a long sigh. "Thank goodness. Fuck, I couldn't do it again."

"Come here. How bad are you hurt?" Ivy asked.

"Broke a couple ribs for sure," Zero said. "Bloody and bruised. How are you two?"

"My leg is broken," Ivy said.

"Broken ribs," Calla said.

"We're still alive and still have light," Zero said. "We're going to try to get home as best we can. All of us."

"Yes, sir," Calla said softly.

"I'm not fucking done yet," Ivy said. She really didn't want to think about moving in her condition and trying to climb out and crawl through rocks with a broken fucking leg, but she really didn't want to die down in the cavern, and she didn't want Calla or Zero to either.

"Let's take stock of what we have and look around a bit. Gather our wits," Zero said.

One of the lanterns was still in working order, and once they found the wood from the other torches, they each had a light. Ivy closed her eyes and took some deep breaths. She was facing east. She could feel it, just as she had always felt it. There was no way out east; it was all blocked, which likely indicated that they had successfully closed the gap. Well, they would find out soon enough. If there were creatures and they could get through, they would undoubtedly come after wounded prey.

The tunnel they should have taken to get out ran west, and that direction looked passable. She told Zero and Calla as much.

Calla was searching nearby for their packs or anything useful. What they really needed was something to brace Ivy's leg with so it didn't break worse. She wondered if she was going to lose the leg. Fuck. *Don't think about it, not now.*

Ivy tried to focus on something else, and something made her focus in on Zero's breathing. She could hear his breaths hitch in pain, and it sounded like he couldn't take a deep breath. She lifted her torch slightly.

"Zero? How bad is it?"

He looked for a moment like he was about to deny anything being wrong, but he let out a shaky sigh. "Not good. I think a rib might have punctured my lung, it really hurts to breathe and it's hard to get a good breath."

"We should try to get going, then," Ivy said. "If you think you can."

"I can," Zero said.

"I found my pack," Calla said. "Most of what was in it was crushed, but I think we can use it and the straps to brace Ivy's leg a little."

"Sounds like fun," Ivy said.

Ivy cried out in pain as Calla worked on bracing her leg. Lightning bolts of pain ran down to her toes and then all the way up into her lower back. It felt like a million fire ants were in her leg, and she was half-tempted to take her sword and cut the fucking thing off.

By the time Calla was done, Ivy was shaking and tears were streaming down her face. Fuck, she didn't know how she was going to manage to get out of the damn cave.

"I'm sorry," Calla said.

"Had to do it," Ivy managed. "We should get moving." It was the last thing she wanted to do, but Zero was badly hurt and they needed to get him to Ramona at the fort so she could patch him up. They couldn't delay.

Ivy felt a little dizzy as she stood and tried to fight down the pain. The path before them was strewn with boulders and loose rocks, but it did lead in the right direction and in a vaguely upward trajectory.

It was a struggle. Every single step was a struggle. They were all moaning and groaning as they moved, trying to pick the best path through. They couldn't see where they were going. For all they knew, there would be nothing but a dead end at the top.

Ivy tried the best she could to move on her own. She had a feeling that Zero was going to need to be helped before long, and if Calla was helping her, it would be hard for her to leave Ivy to help Zero.

Zero was really starting to struggle. He was panting for air and groaning in pain. Every time Ivy glanced over at him, Zero looked like he was about to fall over. But he kept pushing forward.

Calla was doing well. She was being careful and holding her left side where her wounded ribs were, but she wasn't making as much of a fuss as Ivy and Zero were. She would make it out for certain. She was a lot tougher than she looked.

Ivy thought she would make it as well. She was very concerned about her leg, but she'd pull through.

Ivy wasn't sure about Zero.

Ivy tried to focus on the path ahead; they were finally nearing the top of what they could see. It felt right, like they could be just below where the usual path went, and they would pop up into the main tunnel and be able to stumble out into the light.

Calla made it to the top first and rested against a boulder and tried to catch her breath. She was quiet and didn't say anything, and it had Ivy worried. Then Calla lifted the torch and looked around.

"I think we're back up into the main tunnel," Calla said. Ivy pushed herself forward through the pain. She had to see it. She finally got to where Calla was and looked at the tunnel ahead.

It was the same tunnel. They made it. They would be able to walk out after all. Calla and Ivy stepped onto the main path. Zero came up behind them, stumbling forward and leaning heavily against the wall of the cave.

With a groan, Zero slid down the wall and started to cough.

"Zero? Fuck."

"I can't breathe ... " Zero groaned again.

"Just rest a minute, Zero. You said we're all getting out of here and we are," Calla said.

Zero nodded. Calla looked at Ivy, her brow furrowed and lips pursed. Ivy shrugged. It looked bad, but they were all pushing themselves hard.

"I'm going to scout ahead a little, make sure it's safe," Calla said. "You two rest."

Ivy was glad for a little break and even managed to find a position where she could rest more comfortably. Even Zero's breathing evened out a bit. It was still labored and rough, and Ivy really didn't like the sound of it.

"We'll get you out, Zero, we'll get you out into the light again. I know you can make it that far," Ivy said.

Zero nodded. "I think I can, but I don't ... I don't know ... "

"Just focus on the first part, getting out. Calla and I won't abandon you," Ivy said. She shifted slightly so their shoulders were touching, and she reached out and took Zero's hand. Calla came back and looked between the two, and Ivy could see fear in her eyes, not for the tunnel, she was sure, but for Zero.

"It looks good ahead," Calla said. Her gaze lingered on Zero, and she looked for a moment like she was going to say something but didn't.

"Good, let's get the fuck out of here," Ivy said. She managed to get up and managed to help Calla get Zero up. He groaned in pain, and as they moved on, he continued to cry out every so often from the pain. It was hard to support him; he had incurred so many wounds over the past few days.

They really didn't have far to go, but they had to move so slowly with how badly they were all hurt. There were times when Ivy thought that Zero was going to fall over. She didn't know, really didn't know, if they would be able to get him back to the fort.

She wondered how quickly Calla could run down to get Ramona and bring her back, if there would be enough time to do so before Zero succumbed to his injuries. One thing was certain, she was not going to leave Zero alone to ... die.

Ivy didn't want to think that way, but things didn't look good. All they could do was try their best, and at the very least, Zero wouldn't be alone. When she first woke up, she had been terrified of the thought of being alone. Zero wouldn't have to worry about that.

"I see light ahead," Calla exclaimed. Ivy saw it too, and hopefully Zero did as well. They were almost out.

"Almost there, Zero," Ivy said.

Once they got out into the light, they would have to rest. Ivy's leg was throbbing and she felt like she could fall over at any moment, and Zero needed to rest again. They needed to have a realistic conversation about what Zero wanted to do next.

All three of them managed to stumble out of the cave and into the early morning light. Ivy was just helping Zero sit down, and also trying to sit down herself, when she heard a noise.

"There they are," someone said. "Arrest them."

***

Calla glared at the man and looked back at Zero and Ivy, who were both absolutely worn out, and Zero really didn't look good.

"No!" Calla said. "There will be no arrests until we receive medical attention. That is the most pressing matter, sir."

"Who are you?"

"I am Calla. I have served at the Caldera for over twenty years. Due to the recent incident, Zero was temporary leader, and he made me his second in case of further emergency. There is a lot to be dealt with and handled, but first and foremost, we are all hurt, and Zero especially bad. Medical attention needs to be the priority, sir," Calla said.

The captain looked at her then over her shoulder at Zero and Ivy.

"You are quite right, forgive me. Medic!"

Calla breathed a sigh of relief. She was still shaking a little as she walked back to Ivy and Zero and as Ramona came from behind the captain and headed straight to Zero.

"Holding on, Ivy?" Ramona asked.

"I'll be fine, leg's just fucked," Ivy said. "Again."

Calla sat down opposite Zero and took his hand as Ramona began looking him over.

"That was awesome, Calla," Zero said. "I knew you had it in you."

"Thank you, Zero." Calla smiled. Now that they were out into the light, now that they were not fighting to survive, now that it was done, it was clear how badly hurt Zero was. He was breathing fast even though he was lying down. He was far too pale.

Ramona was listening to Zero's chest with a frown on her face. Calla still had a little hope that maybe, just maybe, they could help Zero pull out of this. Ramona lifted Zero's shirt, and Calla saw the bruising and her stomach twisted. Ramona put her hand on Zero's chest and then his stomach, and Zero let out a groan of pain.

"His lung's collapsed," Ramona said. "Broken ribs, internal bleeding."

"Dying?" Zero asked.

"Not just yet. I can put a tube in your chest to get rid of the air and blood. I don't know if I can stop the bleeding, but I can try. There is a chance you'll pull through."

Zero closed his eyes and let out a groan. Calla squeezed his hand.

"You can tell me to stop whenever you want, Zero, and I'll respect that," Ramona said. Ivy moved closer to them and put a hand on Zero's shoulder.

"We're with you no matter what," Ivy said.

Zero looked at them then focused on Ramona. "I'll try."

"Alright, Ivy and Calla, if you could each keep hold of one of his arms, be ready to hold him down a bit. We'll get the tube in and see if he stabilizes."

Ramona worked quickly; it seemed only a matter of moments between her rummaging in her bag and being ready for the procedure.

"Alright, Zero," Ramona said. "I'm sorry, this is going to hurt."

"Do it," Zero said. Zero cried out in pain and squeezed Calla's hand hard. There was a horrible gurgling, hissing noise as blood and air came out of the tube in Zero's chest. It looked horrible, and Calla looked at Ramona to see if it was as bad as it looked.

"That's it, Zero, just breathe," Ramona said. Zero did. His breathing hitched in pain and he still looked far too pale, but he was hanging on. Zero kept breathing, and after a few minutes, it even seemed like he was taking deeper breaths.

"Easier to breathe?" Ramona asked.

"Yes, still hurts," Zero said.

"I know, I'll get to that," Ramona said. The next few minutes were spent listening to Zero breathe and Ramona checking Zero's vitals. It didn't look like he was getting better, but it didn't look like he was getting worse either.

"Alright," Ramona said. "I think he's stable enough to move down to the fort. We'll take it slow and have to take breaks, probably, but I think we can move."

"I can do it," Zero said. His voice was shaky and weak, but there was a look of determination in his eyes that Calla thought was a good sign. They had to make two stretchers, one for Zero and one for Ivy, even though she told them to fuck off at first.

"Stay with Zero," Ivy said. "He needs it more right now."

"I'll see you at the fort," Calla said. Calla was a bit too short to carry Zero, but she held his hand the whole way down to the fort. He moaned in pain often, but he kept breathing and managed to stay awake.

"You're doing well, Zero, getting closer," Calla squeezed his hand and he squeezed back. Calla had never been happier to see the fort. She knew that there was still going to be a struggle to keep Zero alive, but it felt like it would be easier at the fort.

Calla followed Zero and Ivy to the healing room.

"Still holding on, Zero?" Ramona asked as she checked his pulse and listened to his chest.

"Still here," Zero said.

"Good. Calla, can you help me with Ivy?"

"Do we have to do this?" Ivy asked.

"You know we do. It's not going to take that much manipulation, it'll be quick," Ramona said. "It's a simple break, should heal cleanly."

"Fine," Ivy said and held tight to Calla's hand.

"You'll be alright," Calla said. Ramona got ready and Ivy groaned in anticipation.

"Ahhhh, fuck shit damn it all to hell motherfucking fuck!" Ivy yelled. Calla tried hard not to laugh at Ivy's profanity. Ramona wrapped the leg up quickly, and Ivy's breathing calmed down.

"That's it, Ivy, we're done, I'll get you something for the pain," Ramona said.

"Ugh, that sucked."

"I'm sorry," Calla said.

"How's Zero?" Ivy asked.

"Hanging in there," Ramona said. "His pulse is stable, and he's breathing well enough now. I don't think he's losing too much blood. It'll be touch and go for a few days, healing might take some time, but I'm hopeful. Right, Calla, let's take a look at your ribs."

The next few days were a blur for Calla. She spent most of her time in the infirmary looking after Ivy and Zero. Ivy was alright; she was mostly just bored and needed company.

Zero ... Ramona wasn't lying when she said it would be touch and go. He was unconscious most of the time, and his breathing sounded rough and painful. There were times when it was quiet in the night that it sounded like Zero might stop breathing.

When Ivy was asleep, Calla would spend some time holding Zero's hand and putting a cool cloth on his forehead to help with the fever.

It was rough for a few days.

The captain, Campion was his name, luckily was a patient man and wasn't insisting on talking to Ivy and Calla just yet. Maybe he was waiting to see if Zero pulled through before he decided what to do.

9

A New Normal

Calla and Ivy made their way to meet with Captain Campion. They had been back a couple of days, and so far everything was going well. There were no signs of the creatures, and Zero was recovering well.

Calla was a little nervous about why Campion wanted to talk just to her and Ivy, though. Surely he didn't think Zero was at fault for anything?

"We started off on the wrong foot, I apologize for that. There is a lot going on with this situation, and we are both partially in the dark. For one, the only reason I was in Hennan was because I was on my way to replace Captain Marcus."

"I didn't know that," Calla said.

Campion nodded. "I doubt he would have told anyone. Now, Lieutenant Zero had an incident in the past ... "

"I am aware of it," Calla said.

" ... Marcus was always of the opinion that Zero slipped out of any repercussions. Marcus may have been looking for a way to keep his position by bringing who he assumed was a criminal to justice."

"Ah, that would make sense," Calla said.

"It also seems like Asher didn't quite like Zero, or Ivy, for that matter."

"I'm well aware of that," Ivy said.

"I believe he was in shock as well. This was a situation none of us could have foreseen," Calla said.

"Tell me what happened here," Campion said.

Calla and Ivy told him in as much detail as they could the events of the few days when the creatures were attacking. It was hard to believe so much had happened in a few days when usually so little happened in a year.

Calla made sure to stick as close to the facts as she could. She didn't think anyone was really to blame, not even Marcus, and the man was not there to defend himself. Asher had been dealing with the shock of the situation. She did make sure that she mentioned all of what Zero had done. He had risked his life and almost died, and she wasn't going to let his name get dragged through the mud, and she was going to try to make sure he stayed in the guard.

Campion nodded when she was done, and for a while, they sat in silence. Then Campion spoke. "Now, there is a lot of cleanup and restructuring and rebuilding to do. You used quite a lot of wood in defending the fort, and winter is almost here. It's going to be a long hard winter here, and we can only keep a small squad. I would like you two to stay since you know the area well."

"I will stay, sir. I've been here all of my career and would like to help," Calla said. "As long as Lieutenant Zero remains here as well."

Campion smiled. "I thought you might say that. Yes, Zero is staying, if he wants to, that is. And I'll be training him to take over this fort. He'll need some help, of course, so

congratulations, lieutenants, I feel I'll be relying on you two a lot this winter."

"Thank you, sir," Calla said.

"Thank you, sir," Ivy echoed.

Campion smiled and left Calla in a daze. Lieutenant. She had been promoted. Less than a week ago, she was too scared to talk to Captain Marcus and now she had a promotion. Life was very weird sometimes.

"We're fucking lieutenants, what the hell," Ivy said, breaking Calla out of her mind.

"That's not really how I saw this going, to be honest," Calla said.

Calla and Ivy waited for Campion to get done talking to Zero before coming into his room to see what he had decided.

"I'm surprised you two waited until Campion was gone," Zero said.

"Barely," Ivy said. "So, are you staying? Future captain?"

"With you two as my lieutenants? Of course I'm staying. And I don't feel like having to move with these damn ribs," Zero said.

"So, what's the plan, captain?" Ivy asked.

"Survive winter, heal," Zero said.

"And ... plan to find a way into the Caldera?"

"As long as it doesn't involve me," Zero said. "It would be good to make sure we're safe, and if you can get in without those things getting out, that's fine by me."

"Yes!" Ivy said. Zero laughed a little bit then wrapped his hand around his ribs and winced.

"You alright, Calla?" Zero asked.

"Yes, better than that. Just I still can't believe all this happened," she said. "We almost lost you."

Zero smiled. "I'm still here."

"That was rough," Ivy said.

"I knew you cared." Zero smirked.

"Oh shut up," Ivy said, and they all laughed.

***

Ivy tried to be as quiet as she could, but it wasn't fucking easy on crutches. She didn't want to wake Calla just yet. Normally on such a cold winter day, she would want to stay in bed with Calla as much as possible, but she needed to look outside. She was absolutely sure it had snowed, and quite a bit, overnight.

The air just had a certain feeling to it. There was just something different about the first snow of the season. By the end of winter, Ivy knew she would be sick to shit of looking out at all the white, but the first snow? That was something to celebrate.

She opened their door slightly and saw at least six inches of snow. Well, fuck, it was going to be harder to hobble around with it, but it was still so pretty. The air was nippy, the fort in near silence as snow still fell.

It was beautiful.

"It snowed?"

Ivy jumped a little and turned to see Calla, who was almost doubled over laughing.

"Fuck off," Ivy said.

"Sorry, sorry," Calla said. "I'll get us some breakfast. You'll end up in the snow if you try to walk through this before we clear a path."

"Probably. Thanks, honey," Ivy said. Calla smiled and blushed, and it was so cute that Ivy had to pull Calla in for a kiss.

Ivy watched Calla pick her way through the snow and smiled. Winter was a hard season, but it was nice to have someone to go through it with for a change. It was nice to have someone around for everything for a change.

Ivy was standing and watching when suddenly a snowball hit her in the shoulder and she heard laughing. She saw Zero peeking out of his doorway.

"Oh, you are dead," Ivy said.

"No no no wait, mercy, I'm still healing!"

"So am I!" Ivy said and made sure to aim high enough to miss Zero's chest and hit him square in the face.

"Ugh, insubordination! Lashes for you!" Zero cried dramatically. Ivy was sure that if he were fully healed, he would flop down in the snow and pretend to be dead.

"Could you two stop trying to kill each other? Breakfast is ready," Calla said.

"Thank you, Calla," Zero said.

"Thanks, babe," Ivy said. "We're coming over to bug you, Captain."

The three sat down and dug into the oatmeal. It was oatmeal yesterday and it would be oatmeal for the rest of the winter. It was like that every winter, though. Looking around at her girlfriend and friend, Ivy wouldn't change anything.

ACKNOWLEDGEMENTS

Thank you to my family for always being supportive.

About the Author

A. E. has been writing since she was fourteen and has always had an interest in the whump genre.

Deepest Canyon: A Starslinger Tale

Kras Nebula

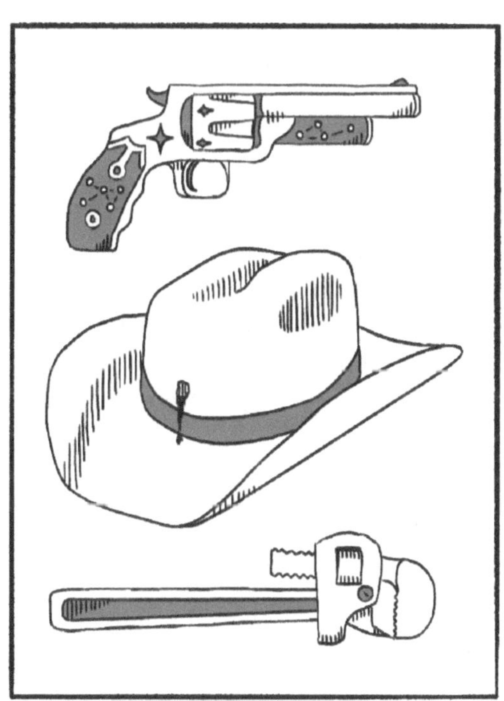

Cover Design by Nicole Alessi

Cover Illustration by Hen Towers

For my friends, who gave me all the feedback and support and encouragement a little guy needs to finish a book. We did it!

Also By Kras Nebula

The Starslinger Tales

The Well

Rattler's Moon

Contents

Content Warnings

This story contains the following content:

- Gun violence
- Offscreen animal death
- Broken bones
- References to terminal illness and loss of a loved one
- Character death

If this book isn't for you, no worries! But if it is, we hope you enjoy this story about the post-apocalyptic wild west and all the horrors therein...

1

There was a hole in Xal's head. A clean shot, too. In through the forehead, bursting through their thick skull, cleaving through the gray matter of their brains, and puncturing right back out the other side. If it were any other spot in the body, it might be a blessing. As it was, however, it was mighty hard to find a silver lining in a bullet to the brain.

The body of Xal, all of middling height and long legs, was a foreign thing. It was still in the worn leather duster they'd been shot in, their shock of white hair against brown skin going pink with blood. Nothing more than a dressed-up slab of meat and bone, lying silent where they fell. They couldn't move a finger, couldn't feel a finger to move. They felt cold. They weren't used to feeling cold, but it weren't unfamiliar neither. Not many things are cold these days, not out in the harsh sun of the Wastes. Someone, somewhere, had told them that they ran "hot as the sun," though they could no longer remember the person's face, nor the rest of the conversation. This grasping at fog for answers only to fill their lungs with smoke was familiar too.

They floated, adrift like a sunbeam, quietly tracing where their nerves began (their damaged brain) and where they ended (somewhere else). They probed gently around the shape of a body simultaneously familiar and forgotten – the scars from a knife through their lip and bullets clustered through their chest, whose context they'd lost a long time ago; the dust baked into the creases and wrinkles of their clothes and riding leathers; the strands of long white hair that had come loose from their mooring; the callouses on their gloved hands that spoke of a lifetime of gunslinging – and tried their damnedest to remember just what it was they'd been doing, or at least what it was they were supposed to be doing. It was something important; they knew that the same way they knew where they'd been shot. The thought sat uncomfortable and weighted like a physical thing in their body until it coagulated into unpleasant certainty:

They needed to breathe.

Xal took a single, horrible, drowned-man-wheezing-corpse breath, and just like that, the world exploded into chaos.

Someone was screaming. Scratch that, *multiple* someones were screaming, and Xal couldn't rightly make out where one began or the other ended or just who was saying *what* – it all was blending into technicolor mush, and they hadn't even opened their eyes yet.

Their second breath hitched on the inhale as their nerves began lighting up, one-by-one then all at once – their neck was craned up at a wrong angle against the rugged stone wall they'd slammed against upon impact, there was blood draining agonizingly slowly down their face and into their eyes and clotting in their hair, and their head –

If they thought about their head, they knew with full certainty they were going to pass out. Passing out seemed like a bad idea, given the commotion and that they still didn't know who shot them in the first place. Though they had to admit that it was tempting. Mighty tempting. Truly, undeniably tempting –

"Xal!"

Xal flinched, or at least they attempted to. Their body gave a weird shudder, like a dying fish not entirely sure what to do on land.

"Xal, can you hear me?" The stranger – someone who clearly knew them, though Xal wasn't about to pretend they could say the same – gently cradled their bloody face. Their hands were cold, small, and felt like coals against Xal's misfiring nerves. The best they could do was grunt and twitch. The stranger seemed to understand some of what plagued them, or at least assumed based off of the damage they'd already procured. Either way, the hands remained gentle, pulling the soaked strands of their hair away from their face. Someone further away snapped something, something that made the stranger tense. Like fog dissolving in the sun, Xal slowly became aware that the yelling had turned to stunned, anticipatory silence. Now it was just Xal, the stranger, and the ringing in their ears.

"Xal." The timbre of the stranger's voice had changed to something more serious. "I need you to open your eyes. Okay?" The stranger sounded young. Younger than Xal, at any rate. Scared.

It was the stranger's fear that prompted them to try more than anything else. The herculean task took just about all they had, redirecting all of their scattered focus to their eyelids and forcing the muscles to work the way they should.

The world was blurry. The light was dim. There was a face – pale, boyish, blonde hair sheared close to the stranger's head, bruise blossoming on the left cheek – hovering in front of them that lit up in sudden, hungry hope, only to immediately shift to terror as Xal's eyes rolled back into their head.

" – al!" Realistically they knew it was only a slap, and not even a particularly hard one, but the impact spider-webbed across their cheek nonetheless, and their pale eyes flew back open with a pained groan. "Xal, you can't pass out again, I'm sorry, but you can't." The stranger was babbling so quickly it would've been difficult to get a word in edgewise even if they could speak. As it was, it took all of their concentration to force the dead meat of their tongue and lips into the words "What happened?"

"Wha ... ?" was about as much as they could get out.

Silence fell, broken only by a few muffled swears and what Xal could now recognize as the other person who had spoken muttering in wonder, "Well, I'll be damned."

The stranger looked over their shoulder at the second voice only briefly before turning back to Xal. "You were shot. In the head."

Xal took another rattling breath. "Gath'r'd," they mumbled, resolving to stick to single-word answers. Maybe single-syllable, even.

The two stared for a moment, each waiting for the other to elaborate and, when it was clear an elaboration wasn't forthcoming, the stranger said with more emphasis, "Xal, you should be *dead*."

"Yup." This conversation was familiar too.

"Xal. How are you alive?!"

They shrugged, as though the answer weren't worth the effort that vocalization took. The stranger was growing increasingly horrified – personally, Xal thought they should have the opposite effect. After all, they were getting better, weren't they? But before the stranger could ask any further questions, someone else grabbed their upper arm and hauled them bodily away. They were tossed back almost nonchalantly to the others in the room, a group of blurry bandit-shaped forms Xal couldn't quite arrange into any coherent number. The person who'd tossed the stranger, a tall, thin man with slicked black hair, a thin mustache, and a suit *far* too nice and clean for the Wastes, loomed over Xal.

"Fascinating," the man said, looking Xal over like they were some kind of bug on the pavement. "No lattices, I didn't hear either of you sling a spell – not that there was time to do so. I've heard of mediums plying their trade and helping the departed move on, but I've never heard of any of them bringing someone *back*. I don't suppose you're one of those devils of the Wastes folks like to ruminate on, or perhaps one of the Wilder-Folks I'm told live among us? I've never met one before, so I can't say I know what to look for." He stopped examining Xal, his eyes roaming back up to the bullet hole in the center of their forehead. "Though, I suppose it doesn't matter. The real question is, does this happen every time you die? Or" – and he pulled out a gun, pointing it at Xal's head just a little to the left of the hole doing its best to close up – "is there a limit to how much brain matter you need to come back?"

"Alonzo, *stop*." The stranger had begun struggling against the bandits, blurry panic on their face.

The man, Alonzo, didn't take his sights off Xal and replied carelessly over his shoulder, "Sunny, darling, as curious as I am about how far this can be taken, I'm not about to waste ammunition performing this song and dance ad infinitum." He pulled the hammer back, the *click* echoing ominously in the small underground space. "I didn't have the chance to ask before, you understand."

"*Wait* – "

"Consider it a favor to your father's memory that I'm asking you now: why shouldn't I?"

"Because – " Sunny fished for words.

Xal swallowed, grumbling internally that they'd *just* been able to fully flex their hands, and now they were gonna have to start the whole process all over again.

"Because – "

They did feel bad about Sunny, though.

"Because they're an expert on 'Fore-Folk tech!"

Now, half of Xal's brains may have been splattered on the wall behind them, but they didn't think that sounded correct. Given the look of incredulity that crossed Alonzo's face, he didn't particularly believe it either.

"You're kidding me," he said. "They look more like a gunslinger than a researcher."

"Yeah, well, I wouldn't expect you to know what someone who does fieldwork would dress like." For their part, Sunny was dressed in a well-fitting pair of working boots and an ill-fitting pair of scrapper's coveralls, just a few sizes too big with both sets having seen their share of wear, tear, and repair. "That's why I hired them, we're down in this lab for the same reason you are. Though" – and their expression managed to reach even further scorn – "I'm surprised to see *you* down here. Tired of taking the credit for the work of others? Wanted to see what all the fuss was about?"

"*For your information*, I was scrapping *long* before you ever put on the coveralls," Alonzo sniffed. "Most scrappers would understand the honor of working with me."

The room was tense, but Alonzo's attention had drifted away from Xal and there was less intent behind his hand, so Xal let their attention slip. Sunny had called it a lab, but the location they were in looked more like a cave. Felt more underground, too, like there was a nontrivial stretch of dirt between them and the open sky. If they rolled their eyes to the right, they could see the way the cavern stretched onwards and upwards, into the darkness and out of sight. They must've come in that way. If they rolled their eyes back to the center, they could see the remnants of a campsite, disturbed and trampled. A long way underground, then. Sunny was still talking, something about the make of someone's guns. They didn't see Lacey anywhere, but they also didn't see any evidence that the large, white-feathered raptor had been in the cave to begin with; likely as not they'd hid her somewhere safe on the surface after they'd dismounted.

When they rolled their eyes over to the left, they were greeted with a solid, daunting blast door, half-buried in the earth and as incongruous with the landscape as a land mine in a flower field.

Ah. A lab.

A 'Fore-Folk lab, of course, as not many present-folks and sciencey types build their labs buried deep within miles of rock. Of course, neither had the 'Fore-Folks, but the hungry earth had devised other plans when the Shattering had cracked the firmament and sent everything tits-up. It still didn't rightly explain why Xal was in one with a hole in their head, but it did begin to slot things into place.

They'd been hired by Sunny for ... reasons. Reasons that involved the lab, likely as a bodyguard or something else requiring a gun. They'd decided to rest before braving the lab itself and had been cornered by Alonzo and his cronies – six of 'em, Xal could more confidently count. Potentially only good if Alonzo's money was good, but Xal weren't in a place to challenge that loyalty, especially seeing as one of them was likely a spellslinger. Four small lights floated around the group like leaves on the wind, providing the only illumination to the scene. Alonzo and Sunny knew each other. Alonzo and Sunny were down there for the exact same reasons, and Sunny was under the impression that Xal knew what those reasons were. Or Sunny was pretending Xal did. Or Sunny was lying to keep Xal from gaining another skull piercing.

"Fine," Alonzo snapped, interrupting Sunny's bargaining and pulling Xal's attention back to him. "They can come with us. But – if either of you try anything, I won't hesitate to see how far their little reanimation trick goes."

The two bandits that had been holding Sunny with bruising force released them, and they stumbled back to Xal, placing their little body between them and Alonzo, as though his gun only had one bullet.

"I hope you got some rest," Alonzo said, holstering his gun with an unimpressed air. "We don't stop until we reach the bottom. Pick them up."

He turned away, ordering his men to focus on the blast door. Immediately Sunny was on Xal, whispering hushed apology after hushed apology while trying to find the best way to get them to their feet.

"Don't worry about me, it's not your fault," was what they meant to say, but it came out closer to "*d'ntmesn'tult.*" Fortunately, Sunny either understood what they meant or hadn't heard them as they were largely ignored. Unfortunately, Sunny had gotten themself positioned with one of Xal's limp arms around their shoulders and was preparing to lift.

Their eyes widened. They forced their traitorous tongue to form "*Wait* – "

It was too late. Sunny hefted Xal up in one solid movement, and whether it was from the sudden change in altitude or the sudden movement of a body so recently un-necrotized, Xal saw white. Their hearing narrowed to a high-pitched ringing, their joints felt bathed in acid, they were too aware of every single tooth in their mouth –

" – al? Xal, *breathe.*"

They came back to themself in agonizing spits and spurts, with every muscle screaming in unison and their head fit to explode a second time that day. It took what felt like eons to blink away the spots in their eyes, to try and reclaim some semblance of self, and even longer to remember that breathing might help. The breath they took wasn't as dramatic as the one they'd taken earlier, but it ached on the inhale and caught on the exhale. Still, Sunny held them strong and steady through the coughing fit.

"S'rry," they apologized. Sunny scoffed. "Dunno ... how much help ... I'll be."

"Don't worry," Sunny whispered back. "I'm stronger than I look."

"Ain't ... what I meant. Um ... " They trailed off, unsure how to address Sunny.

Sunny seemed to pick up on it, quickly answering, "Oh, um, Miss is fine, anything, really, that ain't Mister – Xal" – concern colored her words – "we already talked about this." The concern was rapidly shifting to horror. "Xal ... how much do you remember about where we are?"

Xal didn't have the breath to explain nor the heart to do so, so they let their eyes fall away from her face and answered her question with a stilted shrug.

"I'll ... get us ... outta here," they promised. "Guessin' ... that's why you hired me." They paused to catch their breath. "Just ... gonna need ... a minute, first."

Sunny looked as though she had something more to say, but before she could, one of the bandits passed them – a taller man, black hair cut short, the lower half of his face covered with a purple half-mask – and plopped Xal's hat back on their head, effectively covering the now-almost-closed hole. "Quiet," he snapped as he passed, though he made no move to enforce this beyond the implied threat of his rifle.

At the door, Alonzo stepped back from a sparking control panel, the interior crystal lattice beginning to shine once more. The ground rumbled, and dust fell from the ceiling as the ancient doors began to open for the first time in centuries. Sunny, Alonzo, and the bandits all watched in awe as the ancient ruins took a fresh breath of their own. Xal, though, had eyes only for Alonzo and, more importantly, what hung on Alonzo's belt, glinting in the soft illumination of the spell-lights.

"Hell," they swore. "Fucker's got my guns."

2

After the Shattering rent the world asunder and started the horrid birthing process for the world we now call our own, folks for the most part stopped building things underground. Sure, there may have been benefits to diving down deep – protection from the sun, for one – but the fear of afterquakes crushing entire settlements to paste was reason enough to stay and build on the surface. With all this in mind, it stood to reason that the only folks who would go hunting for the buried relics and tech of the 'Fore-Folks – the ones who came before – were either those who had nothing to lose or everything to gain.

Alonzo, Xal decided as the group stepped cautiously into the wide-open entry room, was probably in the latter category. The man looked as though he'd never known want in his life, or if he had, he'd forgotten what it felt like – especially if the nice, clean-pressed outfit he had on were the clothes he wore around the *Wastes*. The bandits in his employ were likely the former. Most regular folks outside of settlements were like that. It weren't entirely uncommon to see folks with such diametrically opposed lifestyles working together. Or perhaps it would be more accurate to say it weren't entirely uncommon to see folks like Dr. Alonzo Morris hiring folks like the bandit pack for any number of things: protection, muscle, using them as a force to drive honest folks off their land while simultaneously keeping their precious little hands clean.

As for Sunny ... Xal supposed they would have known where she stood vis-à-vis gaining or losing had their memory of the proceeding events not been flushed through the hole in their head. She was focused, but then Xal supposed anyone in this sort of scenario would be. They were too closely watched to even attempt to speak, which meant that any context Sunny could have given them she kept locked tight in her mouth.

Though they couldn't bring up any evidence to back up their claim, the group of bandits in Alonzo's employ seemed smaller than a group of bandits should be. Mercenaries and hired guns like themself could work easily in small or smaller groups, but the six that Alonzo had hired on as muscle read *bandit* all the way down from the scars littering their bodies to the practicality of their clothing. Other than the bandit with the purple half-mask who'd been keeping an eye on them, none of the other five gave any real care towards Xal and Sunny, letting Xal observe them in peace.

Their leader was a big bruiser type named James, who sported a wastelander tan and had his brown hair cut short. He had a scar through the bridge of his nose that had clearly been broken in one hell of a tussle, and a mean-looking rifle slung around his shoulder. Next to him, near the front of the pack, was Sylvia: tall and wiry, hair tied back in a thick braid, head on a swivel as she picked up sounds Xal couldn't even begin to hear through the ringing in their ears. Jensen, an average-sized man who clearly spent more time on the long hair pulled back into a tail than the scruffy beard on his face, similarly had his head on a swivel, but in a way that read far more like nerves than the focused way Sylvia had. In the back were Levvy and Bernard, the spellslinger and another bruiser respectively. Levvy looked a sight like James – siblings, maybe. Same skin tone, same brown hair, though she sported a single blue ribbon braided into her locks. Bernard was the biggest one yet, but seemed to hang contentedly behind Levvy and watch the rear. The bandit with the purple mask was Shui, who put as many bodies between himself and James as possible. He hung back by the prisoners, but other than the harsh reminder to stay quiet, had yet to say another word.

While Xal had no memories to base the feeling off of, something about them felt as though they weren't moving like a bandit pack *should*. Desperate, maybe. Lot of folks out in the Wastes were desperate.

Their captors, for the most part, had fallen silent the moment they stepped beyond the blast doors, guns at the ready. Levvy's spell-lights floated as high as they dared, but there was no way to illuminate both the floor in front of them and come even close to touching the monstrously high ceiling.

"Air's good," Shui commented quietly. "Might mean vents."

"Or," Alonzo interrupted, though no less quietly, "there may still be power to the filtration system, which means there may be power to other systems as well." There was a hunger to his voice that had Xal's arm hair raising and Sunny clutching them that much more tightly.

The ghost of what the entryway to the lab had once been haunted the room – the broken furniture, the decayed crystal lattices, the dead lights all hinting at a past long since left to rot. It felt unbearably empty, both achingly lonely and actively rejecting its new intruders. The small group couldn't help but feel that they shouldn't be there, that the building wanted someone *else*. But places can't think, or feel, or want the way we do, they can only groan and creak.

Perhaps that was what set everyone's spine on edge. The silence. This far underground one would expect the building to shudder with all that weight, but she held firm. Which meant any noise beyond the echoing footsteps of the group belonged to something else –

At the head of the group, just before Alonzo, James gestured sharply for the rest to halt. In the sudden silence every tiny sound was deafening: the gentle trickle of dust, the wind from further up the tunnel, the quiet scuttling of feet –

Quick as a viper, Jensen twisted and shot, his muzzle-flare bright in the darkness, and a horrible screech echoed in reply. Suddenly the room was alive with the sound of scurrying once more, but further out now and further still, squeaking in fear as they retreated. The critter that had been hit continued to make its horrible, screeching, wounded animal cries all the way up until James stalked over and shot it again.

"Burrowers," he said, curling his lip.

Given the raptors and tri-horns and spikebacks of the surface world, burrowers could hardly be considered large. At a little under hip-height, though, they weren't exactly small, closer to a good-sized dog than anything. Between the feathers, the two legs, and the two short arms hosting their digging claws, they weren't unlike raptors. Save, of course, for the lack of meat in their diet and their propensity to scurry around and dig tunnels into the earth instead of run out under the sun. Most of the time they kept to their tunnels and to themselves, and were generally considered not much beyond a nuisance.

"Ah, yes, a worthy adversary and one well worth waking up anything else still around," Alonzo snapped scathingly. Jensen had the good sense to look sheepish, though no less nervous.

"Come on, Doc, no need for that," James drawled before looking over at one of his own. "Sylvia?"

Sylvia had taken her station crouched by one of the disintegrated chairs. "Just more burrowers, Boss," she called. "Don't seem like they're nesting here, but based off the droppings and tracks, I'd wager there's a host of burrower's tunnels in these walls. This place is just a juncture, a, uh, train station, if you will," she elaborated, seemingly for Alonzo's benefit. The doctor did not look particularly appreciative of this gesture.

"What she's saying," James stepped in once more, "is that if they feel safe enough to move about in the open like this, then ain't nothin' eating them down here. Nothin' else has been living here since the 'Fore-Folks were. Ease up a little."

Doctor Alonzo Morris did not, in fact, ease up, and instead only prickled further at the insinuation that he should.

"Just because these ruins are derelict," he bit out, "does not mean they are dead."

Underneath Xal's arm, Sunny flinched – an almost mechanical movement and one she clearly had tried to stop. At Alonzo's words the rest of the bandits shifted uneasily; Jensen had his head on a swivel, twitching at any sudden movement or noise; Sylvia had made herself smaller, looking quizzically around and focusing on the layout of the room and the patches of particularly deep darkness; Levvy had stepped closer to Bernard, who'd made himself a larger target; James kept his head high and the grip on his gun tight; Shui inched ever closer to his prisoners, just within grabbing range. Whether that was to pull them into or out of danger, Xal couldn't rightly tell.

"Well," Alonzo spoke, causing the entire group to jump, "if something were to attack us, I assume it either would have done so, or it already has us in its sights. Let us move forwards, hopefully having learned something from this."

Their steps echoed in the empty room, maybe not as deafening as the gunshots had been but loud enough to set the group on edge. Every now and then Jensen would startle-flinch and point his gun at shadows or more burrowers, sending them skittering away to safety.

"Weak link," Xal murmured out of the corner of their mouth. Sunny hummed a question back at them. "Jumpy one," Xal elaborated. "Could be easy to distract."

"Maybe," Sunny muttered back just as quietly. "But what 'bout the others? 'Sides, you can hardly move."

"I'm" – Xal paused to tamp down on a groan as Sunny maneuvered them around a pile of debris – "workin' on it."

Problem was, Sunny wasn't wrong. The forces piecing Xal's brain back together had apparently decided that sensory input was more important than motor control, leaving them uncomfortably awake and alert as their limp body was dragged across the room. They felt every single nauseating bump and sway but could do absolutely nothing about it but brace and pray. Talk of escape aside, a nontrivial part of Xal was already wishing for a break. "Listen – " they started.

"Quiet," Shui interrupted sharply. Xal half-expected a shove to accompany his words, but Shui kept his hands carefully on his rifle. He clearly knew where his priorities lay, and they were not in shoving around prisoners who could barely walk. That alone had Xal on edge. Jensen may have been the weak link, but they would be hard-pressed to find an opening with Shui watching them like a hawk.

At the other side of the room, past the decayed remains of some kind of front desk, there were two sets of doors. The first set were the same sort of imposing, solid blast doors that had led into the ruins. The second were smaller, set into the wall a story above and connected to the ground by a set of questionable stairs. With neither discussion nor hesitation Alonzo led the group up the stairs, wincing with every creak and groan of the ancient metal.

Xal clung tightly to Sunny as best they could as they ascended, step by step, each one an effort. Sunny bore them wordlessly, save for a few quiet apologies when their brown face turned white and their sweat glistened in the spell-lights.

"Sunny, be a dear and hurry it up, would you? I need your hands in here," Alonzo called from somewhere beyond the doors.

"Might've been faster," Sunny grunted, heaving Xal's body up another step, "if you hadn't shot one of us in the *head.*"

Despite the nauseating agony still beating from their brain, Xal huffed a breathless laugh. "Think ... if we take too long ... " they said between breaths, "he'll shoot me again?"

"Don't tempt me."

Xal began a retort, but before they could fire it off, Sunny's grip on them tightened like a vise. Not something to joke about, then.

They had barely a moment to catch their breath at the top of the stairs before James grabbed Sunny by the arm and hauled her into the room, leaving Xal to tumble bonelessly to the floor.

"Hey – !" She attempted to lunge towards Xal, but James's grip was locked tight around her arm.

Alonzo rolled his eyes. "They survived a bullet to the head, I'm sure they're fine." Xal, for their part, gave a wheezing groan from the floor but otherwise made no move to get up. "You, however, I need over here." He gestured to the larger part of what could now be recognized as, likely, some kind of security room. A jumble of identical screens sat bolted to the wall, an input terminal underneath; the entire thing was dark and dead as could be, not even leaving an errant spark of life. “I would like to have an idea of the layout of this place before we go any deeper. Get it working.”

There was a danger to Sunny’s glare, but it just as quickly fizzled out into something more resentful but resigned as Shui took his place once more over Xal. “Fine,” she spat, yanking her arm out of James’s hold and disappearing into the workings of the machine, “but I’ll need your spellslinger.”

There are very few folks these days who can work the tech of the old world, who can even begin to wrap their mind around the complicated crystal lattices and magical frequencies the ‘Fore-Folks used before they blew themselves into the firmament, but of that small group of folks, Scrappers make up a solid percent. Sunny quickly grew silent as her deft hands wove their way into the wires and lattices, muttering to herself as she puzzled her way around the ancient technology and occasionally asking Levvy for a whistled note.

Xal lost time. They didn’t have the mobility to maneuver themself out of the heap they’d landed in, and it didn’t seem like anyone else was about to help them out of it, so they drifted. They let sound filter in and out of their ears and the now mostly-closed hole in their head; Sunny’s tinkering, Alonzo’s cruel remarks, dust falling from the ceiling, the skittering of burrower claws, and, further, something else.

They must’ve lost more time than they thought, as when next they opened their eyes – eyes they didn’t remember closing, granted – Shui had just finished propping them upright against the wall of the security room. “Y’all hear that...?” they rasped. The room immediately fell still.

“Hear what?” Alonzo asked after a beat. The bandits shifted, Jensen in particular gripping his gun a little more tightly.

Xal took a breath, then another. “There’s somethin’ out there.”

Every occupant strained their senses to try and hear what it was Xal had picked up on. Dust. The scrabbling of tiny claws. The tapping of something metallic against the stone cavern –

Just as quickly as it had sounded, the noise stopped as though someone, or something, had silenced it.

"I – I don't like this," Jensen stammered.

James grunted before turning back to where Sunny was still half-inside the terminal. "How much longer?"

"Almost got it – " came the strained reply.

"Alright. Jensen, take the door. 'S probably nothin', but I ain't taking chances."

Jensen didn't look happy at the posting, but he did seem to prefer it over waiting to be ambushed. The silence that fell afterwards was tense, each person straining their senses just in case, none of them daring to make small talk on the off chance something else was listening.

"Got it!" The entire room started – or, in Xal's case, made an involuntary twitch – as the monitors lit up and Sunny pushed herself back out from the terminal. As the monitors lit up one by one, the emergency lights gave their best flicker, casting a dim light around the room.

"Well, I'll be," James muttered in wonder. "Shit down here's usually dead for good."

"No, most folks just don't know how to turn it back on." There was a hint of pride in Sunny's voice, even as she shook her hands out. "'Fore-Folks had a greater handle on their tech than the rest of y'all, these babies can hold a charge indefinitely so long as the lattice ain't broke and you can get a spark – hey!"

At a look from Alonzo, Sylvia had grabbed Sunny and shoved her next to Xal. "Yes, yes, very interesting, I'm sure," Alonzo said without looking back and began flicking through the readouts on the monitors. Images and words too far away to read flashed by, though Xal was certain some of that had to do with how their vision hadn't fully cleared.

"How're you doing?" Sunny asked quietly, taking advantage of Alonzo's focus on the machine.

"Been better," they grunted.

"Xal."

"Right, right." As best they could, Xal widened their hands, stretching out their fingers before curling them into weak fists. It wasn't much, but it was progress. They moved their arms slowly – not for any kind of notion of stealth, but because that was the one speed they had at the moment – and placed their palms flat on the concrete floor and *pushed*. They made it barely an inch before their arms gave out, and they collapsed back against the wall with an exhausted breath.

"Might be a bit yet," they grumbled after taking a moment to catch their breath.

"That's not what I'm asking," Sunny admonished quietly.

"Head hurts. Can't shoot. Not sure what else you want." Their words were short, curt, but they got the point across, and Sunny sat back with a huff.

"*Xal.*" At this Xal finally looked up and met Sunny's eyes. They might not've remembered her or how circumstance had thrown them together, but they could recognize the kind of emotional cocktail of someone worried out of their wits for someone who couldn't quite understand *why* in her face. "You *died.*"

"Didn't stick ... " They trailed off into silence as Sunny's frown deepened.

"How much do you remember?" Sunny asked, lowering her voice further.

"My name. Lacey. How to ride." The words felt familiar, like they'd answered the question a million times before. Their eyes moved away from Sunny to the two elegant pistols, mother-of-pearl, golden inlay, that had been shoved into Alonzo's belt. *Xal's* pistols. "How to shoot." They turned back to Sunny. "But ... as for why we're here, ain't got much to say. Mind filling me in?"

Sunny sat back and dragged a tiny, exhausted hand across her face. When she opened her eyes, they'd hardened. "Right," she whispered. "Keep that to yourself." So much for context.

Xal frowned. "Sunny?" they said, with all the gravity they could muster. "I'm gonna get you out of this." That was likely their job, far as they could guess.

Sunny, however, didn't seem to agree. Her expression shifted into something darker still, her hands clenching into solid fists.

"Sunny!" Alonzo barked from the monitors. "Get over here."

Sunny bit down on whatever she'd been about to say and moved out of Xal's reach.

"Most of the cameras are either non-functional or in rooms too dark to get a look at, but we've found a map." Alonzo carelessly tossed a miniature lattice to her. It was formed of a single circle, with pink crystals inlaid equidistant from one another and all pointing towards the center, which held another crystal that had been cut into a perfect cube. The entire thing buzzed in her hand with untapped energy. Sunny's eyes widened, turning the delicate lattice in the dim light.

"Where did you ... ?" she wondered.

"Transfer the map to the lattice," Alonzo interrupted. "I have no doubt certain sections have been affected by time, and I would rather not stumble around such sections blindly." When Sunny hesitated, he quirked an eyebrow. "I know you know how to do this. Your father used to rave about your skill with 'Fore-Folk lattices."

Xal hadn't thought Sunny's glare could reach new depths, but there was a shift in her stance. A stiffness, a danger.

Alonzo sighed, pulled out one of Xal's guns, and aimed it at them. They tensed, grasping for any possible way they could avoid the shot and coming up empty. "*Now*, Miss Quill."

The panic left Sunny's eyes only to be replaced with cold resignation, and she stepped back to the console.

"Pity," Alonzo purred, admiring Xal's gun. "I would have loved to see what these do. Plasmashot, it looks like, but not a make or model I recognize. Where did you get these?"

"They're *mine*," Xal growled.

Alonzo frowned. "Not anymore, and not what I asked. Were they custom? They must be, from the seal on the handle. Who is your gunsmith? Unless you found them somewhere, which, if you're half the 'expert' Sunny says, I could almost believe."

"*Bite me.*" Xal was growing increasingly tired of their captor. Unfortunately it seemed the opinion went both ways as, with a sharp look from Alonzo, James's boot collided with Xal's face, snapping their head to the side and making them see nothing but stars. When they pulled themself back, blood sharp against their numb tongue, Sunny was shouting again.

" – re harmless! You don't have to do this, I'm doing what you asked!"

"They bounced back from a bullet to the head, I can't imagine a boot to the face will do much worse." Alonzo wasn't wrong, but Xal couldn't help but feel apprehensive of the fact that he was beginning to collect data on the subject. The shouting continued as Xal did their damnedest to pull their eyelids back open, interrupted only by Shui's occasional interjection, and amongst it all they could hear the echoing metallic tapping growing closer –

Xal pried their eyes open just as the building lights plunged into darkness, only to be replaced a moment later with flashing red lights. Garbled messages that may have once been words echoed from speakers long since decayed, the voice who had recorded them long since dead.

"What did you do?!" screamed Jensen from his place at the door, aiming his rifle wildly into the room. "*What did you do*?!"

"Me?! I didn't do anything!" Sunny protested, the miniature lattice held tightly in her hands.

"Then – "

Whatever Jensen had been about to say was lost. From beyond and above the doorway, two metallic, reticulated arms stretched forward, ending in wicked, articulated claw-tipped hands. The most Jensen ever saw of his death were the red lights reflecting off of black metal in his periphery before the claws dug into his neck and shoulder and *pulled*, yanking his flailing body out and upwards towards the ceiling, screaming all the way.

For a moment no one moved, stunned to silence in the cacophony of Jensen's final gargled cries and the garbled message over the ancient intercoms.

James moved first, swearing loudly and bolting for the doorway, finger already on the trigger –

"*Stop*!" Alonzo yelled. "He's already dead. I hired you to protect *me*."

James turned on him, looming with his full impressive height. "*You don't know that*!"

Shui shook his head. "It's carrying him upwards, even if we shot it down, he wouldn't be able to survive a fall like that – " Right on cue, Jensen's cries were cut off horribly quick, and seconds later there was the unmistakable wet *thump* of a body hitting the floor somewhere in the greater chamber.

"We can't stay here!" Sylvia hissed.

"And I suppose going outside where *it* is waiting is the more intelligent option, rather than where it only has one avenue to attack us?" Alonzo sneered. "What am I saying, I don't pay you dogs to *think*."

At the corner of the room, much forgotten, Sunny had quietly moved back to Xal and slipped their arm over her bony shoulder. "When I say 'go,' jump with whatever you got."

Xal didn't think they had much to give, but they curled their fingers in her coveralls with one hand, braced against the ground with their other, and bent and tensed their legs as best they could.

"Be *very* careful about the next thing you say," James growled.

"Or you'll what? Shoot me? Lose out on your payment?" There was a dangerous glint in Alonzo's eye. "Already down a pack member with nothing to show for it. If you back out now, you'll wind up worse than you started with – "

"*Go.*"

Xal did their absolute best to help, but they didn't need to hold as much of their weight as they thought they'd have to as Sunny sprang to the door with shocking speed.

"Stop her!" Alonzo screeched.

She descended the steps two at a time, jarring Xal with every step. Bernard sprang first out of the doorway and fired a shot that cracked the stairs under Sunny's feet, sending them both tumbling to the ground in a heap.

"Not another step!" he called. "Not if you want another hole in the – " His voice broke off into a scream as the shadow that had been advancing down the wall above him snapped out, horrible arms reaching down to grab him by the face and shoulders and bodily fling him from the landing, tearing bloody chunks from his body as he went ragdolling through the air to *slam* through one of the ancient desks.

"*Bernard*!" Levvy screamed from inside.

"*Up up up* – " Sunny mumbled frantically, getting her feet under her and hauling Xal upright.

"Sunny – " Xal sucked in a breath as the room tilted alarmingly. "Sunny, I'm dead weight, you gotta *go*."

"No." Sunny slung Xal's arm back over her shoulder.

"*Sunny* – " But as she took a step, Xal's busted brain realized something. "Sunny, the exit ain't that way."

"*I know*," Sunny growled as she dragged them to the heavy blast door that led deeper into the laboratory.

With a furious yell, James flung himself onto the landing and began unloading bullet after bullet into the creature clinging to the wall – only for the bullets to ricochet harmlessly off the metal carapace. In the light of the gunfire, pieces of the creature could be made out: the heavy black metal plating, the humanoid body structure tilted sideways with heavy claws and flexible joints, the unflinching faceplate staring down the barrel of James's gun.

"*Move*," Alonzo ordered before raising Xal's pilfered pistol. With a single shot, the cavern was bathed in blinding light, the plasma breaking across the faceplate like a wave. The creature reared back, sparks flying and illuminating the metal joints, hissing and clawing its way back up into the darkness.

"Grab her, you idiots! *She's got the map*!" Alonzo shouted as he shot wildly with Xal's gun. The cavernous space lit up with each shot like a crack of lightning, blindingly bright then plunged back into darkness. Each shot illuminated a different scene – Sunny dropping Xal to the ground to fiddle with the door; James and Sylvia sprinting after them; Levvy searching frantically around the cavern with her spell-lights while Shui kept his rifle at the ready; the mechanical creature clinging to the side of the cavern, watching.

In a flash, James had reached Sunny, cracking the back of his hand across her face and sending her sprawling to the floor. The control panel she'd been tinkering with sparked and fizzed, and the blast door began opening and closing, opening and closing.

"Just come with us, nice and – " Sylvia ended her sentence with a *whoop* as Xal snagged her ankle from the floor and gave a mighty *tug*, sending her toppling to the ground. Before they could make good on their move, however, Sylvia scrambled out of reach, drawing her gun and aiming it directly at Xal.

"Not another move, neither of you," she snapped, "or it's bullet number two."

"Alright," James said, hauling Sunny upright by the arm. "Let's get a move on while we still can." He took a breath then, in the brief second that the door was open, leapt through to the other side, pulling Sunny along with him. "You next, Doc."

Alonzo stumbled over Xal's body, eyes wide and limbs jittery, before returning to the door and jumping through as quick as he could.

In the dark, something moved.

"Shui."

Shui backed in slowly, eyes scanning the darkness, before ducking through.

"Levvy."

Levvy's hand was glued to her mouth, and with a sharp whistle, her four lights followed her through the door, leaving the room solely lit by the emergency lights.

"Sylvia."

Sylvia kept her gun trained on Xal until the last possible second as she followed suit.

"Wait, what about Xal?" Sunny protested, struggling against the iron grip on her arm. Xal, for their part, looked at the rapidly opening and closing metal of the blast door, then down at their tangle of legs. There was no way they would be able to get themself through on their own.

With one person left outside the safety of the blast doors, the metal creature dropped to the floor, running on all fours at a gallop.

"Aw hell – " Xal summoned what strength they had and *dragged* themself as best as they could backwards – but nowhere near fast enough. Their legs refused to push under them, to carry them to safety, but they crawled with all they had in their arms until their back hit the chomping maw of the blast door.

"It's coming – "

"So shoot it!"

Alonzo fired Xal's gun once more, the heat and light of the solar pulse burning the ends of their hair as it blew past, only to miss wildly. Again the gun fired and *again* the bolt missed, and despite the situation Xal couldn't stop the bloom of rage in their stomach at the waste.

"*Levvy, take it down*!"

"But my lights – "

"Do it!"

Levvy released four sharp notes, and as the spell-lights winked out of existence, the air around the creature pulsed violently, vibrating its joints and causing it to shudder and shake and grind against itself – but the creature kept coming, no matter how the ancient machinery around them vibrated with Levvy's frequencies.

"For fuck's sake – " Shui's muttered swearing was the only warning Xal got before they were grabbed by the scruff of their duster and *hauled* through the door. They blinked the spots from their eyes just in time to witness Shui snatch the gun from Alonzo with his free hand and blast the creature right in the face.

A metallic screech echoed through the halls from the creature, causing Sunny to slap her hands over her ears.

As the door slammed shut once more, Shui grabbed the ends and held them closed on his own steam. "James! Give me a hand!"

With Shui on one side and James on the other, Sylvia grabbed Xal's gun from Shui and melted the door shut.

Not a moment too soon. The blast door *buckled* as the creature flung itself at it, the metal bending and warping under its onslaught. Metal upon metal shrieked as it shifted to using its horrible claws.

BOM

BOM

BOM

... And then silence, save for the distorted alarm echoing throughout the facility.

3

For a moment no one moved – they all stood still in the hall, staring at the welded blast door and breathing heavily in the dim, red light.

"What in every hell – " James murmured before he was cut off by Sylvia delivering a thunderous kick to Xal's torso.

"Snag me by the ankle, huh?" she snarled, kicking them again. "Thought you could scrabble off and get the best of me, huh?" Another kick. "Should've just left you out there to get torn apart by that metal devil!" Kick, kick, kick. Had they the chance to catch their breath, Xal would've snagged her and toppled her a second time. As it were, they were finding it mighty hard to do much of anything beyond cough and wheeze on the dusty floor.

"*Stop it!*" Sunny rushed forward. "They're – "

She pulled up short, staring down the barrel of James's rifle. "We know how they're doing. We made 'em like that," James drawled, low and dangerous. "And the next time you two get it in your heads to run, I'm shooting both of you, 'expert knowledge' be damned. Are we clear?"

Sunny watched as Sylvia delivered one final blow, leaving Xal wheezing on their back, before leveling her gaze back at James. "Crystal," she said, not quite hiding the tremble in her voice.

James held her gaze for a moment longer before nodding at Shui to stand over Xal. "Good. Levvy, lights." A short set of whistles and Levvy's spell-lights had returned. Folks breathed slightly more easily, even if they didn't notice. "Now, seems to me you two have lost close quarters privileges. Shui, keep the gunslinger with you in the back; Sunny here gets to go with us in the front." He paused, waiting to be interrupted or reprimanded for taking charge, but no words ever came. He turned back to Alonzo, who was still standing stock-still, staring at the door. " ... Doc?"

"Did you see how it moved?" he murmured, the glow from the gun in his hand casting flickering shadows on the wall as his hand trembled. "The articulation, the construction – it hardly *flinched* at the bullets ... What a marvel."

"*Doc*!" James repeated himself, sharper this time. At this Alonzo started, almost dropping Xal's gun before remembering where exactly he was and, more importantly, who he was with. He straightened himself out, holstered Xal's gun, and coughed awkwardly.

"Yes, yes, what is it?" he snapped.

"What the hell was that thing?" Levvy asked quietly.

"A construct, of course," Alonzo said, as though it were the most obvious thing in the universe, which, within certain contexts and preconceived notions, it was. Most folks out in the Wastes and beyond had at least heard about constructs: the fallen corpses of the old world, rusted shut with their lattices crumbled to dust. Rare up on the surface, but common enough for scrappers and the like. No one was quite sure what they were made of, or how the 'Fore-Folks had gotten them to move as they supposed they must have, but they were built for a variety of purposes from the smallest, most delicate tasks to the largest hauling ventures. Farming, guarding, medical ... well, most of that was all speculation from where they were found and what they looked like, and most of them had been found in pieces, anyways.

"No, no, that can't be right," Sylvia said, shaking her head.

"And why not?"

"Because it *moved*." Sylvia threw an arm out towards the crumpled blast door. "No one's ever seen one *move* before, they're all supposed to be *dead*, how the *hell* is it moving?!"

"I … I'm not sure," Alonzo admitted. "According to most records, what the 'Fore-Folks had built was destroyed in the Shattering; by all rights it *shouldn't* be, but if I could get my hands on it … "

Sunny shifted nervously.

"Alright," James sighed. "Do you at least know what kind it is?"

"Silencer Mk. 5." Everyone's heads snapped to the floor where Xal had spoken. "Or somethin' similar. I don't think the Mk. 5's were quite that big, they were supposed to be small enough to get into places, take folks out all quiet-like. Didn't think they ever made it to Mk. 6, though."

" … How the *hell* do you know this?" Alonzo asked, clearly more befuddled than sore that someone knew more than him.

Xal had no right clue any more than he did, but they weren't about to tell him that. "Didn't Sunny say I was an expert?"

Sunny very quickly tooled her expression away from surprise, as though she'd known the whole time. "Told you."

"Great. We've got an ancient assassin construct after us," James sighed. "Frankly that don't change too much. What's our next move, Doc?"

With the conversation shifting away from the marvel hunting them through the building, all wonder left Alonzo. He snagged Sunny by the arm and wrenched the map away from her. Once again the delicate crystal lattice sparked to life, displaying a series of flickering maps and floor layouts. Alonzo flicked through them in silence before pointing a finger.

"We are here," he said, causing the others to peer over his shoulder – all, save for Xal and Sunny. The two made eye contact. Sunny made a concerned face. "This building goes down several floors, and I find it doubtful we'll get too much up here beyond office space and administrative areas."

"I take it you've done something like this before?" Shui asked carefully. From the ground, quite unnoticed, Xal gave a shaky thumbs-up.

"Of course," Alonzo sniffed. Sunny's face shifted from concern to suspicion. "What do you take me for, an amateur?"

Shui didn't respond immediately to that, but though his expression was difficult to read under the half-mask, he set his shoulders a bit more defensively. Under him Xal paused, thought, then delivered a second thumbs-up. Sunny relaxed slightly.

"We won't be getting out the same way," Shui tried again. "Should probably keep on the lookout for another exit." Xal's eyes flicked up towards Shui, then Sylvia, James, Levvy, and finally Alonzo before silently holding up a hand with all five fingers splayed.

"Of course," Alonzo snapped, flicking through with increasing speed. Sunny gave a hint of a nod before frowning and mimicking a gun with her hand. Her frown turned into a look of incredulity as Xal waved dismissively. She shifted her hand to her mouth, mimicking a whistle. When Xal was equally as dismissive, she rolled her eyes in disbelief. She looked as though she were about to mime something else when Alonzo turned back towards Sunny.

"You," he snapped. "This lab is the sister lab to the one Dr. Quill excavated, yes?"

Sunny stared. "How do ... how do you know that? How did you even know where to find this place?"

To his credit, Alonzo's expression slipped. "Dr. Quill sent me a letter detailing how to get here," he said quietly. "I was supposed to do this with him."

Sunny's mouth hung open. "He – he would *never*. You two hated each other."

"He didn't run it by you first?" Alonzo tutted. "A pity. Of course, I'd originally refused but then, well." There was a beat before he asked, "How did it happen?"

It took Sunny a few tries to get the words out. They were still too heavy for her small mouth, even in a place like this. "A heart attack," she said, finally. "Three weeks ago."

To his credit, a hint of confused grief made its way into Alonzo's expression. "I ... can't say I'm overjoyed to hear that. I had lunch with him just before. A heart attack of all things ... " He trailed off before returning to the topic at hand. "Still, he must have told you about the other lab, yes?"

"That ... that was before my time." Sunny couldn't meet his eyes, even as he pressed further into her space.

"But not by much, not by much at all." He towered over her, and she shrank back. "Don't lie to me, Sunny Quill."

She swallowed, took a breath. "Experimental 'Fore-Folk constructs," she said finally. "They were very early, hardly anything completed. It was likely they'd gotten to work just before the Shattering, so they'd never managed to get particularly far with any of them – not like the one outside. Weren't nothing of use beyond the historical, most were broken beyond repair."

"But there *were* some things of value, yes?"

Sunny seemed to glean what the Doctor was getting at, and for a moment that steel slipped back into her spine. Her eyes flicked back to Xal, however, and when she turned back to Alonzo it was with less resolve. " ... The basement levels," she said, looking away. "That's where they'll be keeping the bigger projects."

"Good girl." Alonzo ruffled her short hair and Sunny bristled.

"There's no guarantee the lower levels even survived the Shattering," she said, raising her voice. "Or if there's even still a way down!"

"We also don't know what else is awake down here." The attention in the room shifted as Shui spoke up. "It's a safe bet this is also some kinda construct lab, if that thing that attacked us is any indication." He shook his head. "We need to find a new way out and take it. We're already down two and – "

In two strides James had crossed the distance and grabbed a strangling hold on the back of Shui's neck, forcing his head down. "Tryin' to give orders again, Shui? Thinkin' of turning your back again?" The pressure increased. "Because that worked out so well for you last time, didn't it?" Shui stayed silent, his eyes trained on the floor. "If you weren't so good a shot, I would've tossed you to the Wastes after the last stunt you pulled." Levvy looked away, clearly uncomfortable with the confrontation; in stark contrast, Sylvia looked on in glee. When it was clear Shui had no intention of speaking up, James pulled back, clapping him on the shoulder. "Just think of the payout when this is over."

Xal and Sunny shared a look, and for once there was no need for exaggerated pantomiming. They both could tell what the other was thinking: this was something they could use.

"James, he's got a point," Levvy spoke up quietly. "We don't know what else is down here."

In sharp contrast to how he'd spoken to Shui, the way James looked at Levvy was downright saccharine. "It'll be fine, Levs. We'll take it slow, keep an eye out. Like I said, think of the payout." Levvy clearly was still worried, but she nodded along anyway.

Alonzo sniffed. "If you're quite done, I suggest we get moving ... "

BOM

He trailed off into startled silence as noises echoed through the halls. It was hard to tell which direction they came from, but everyone's eyes snapped to a different angle, the arguments largely forgotten. The seconds ticked by agonizingly slowly before the rumbling stopped, somewhere off in the larger labyrinth of the dilapidated building.

The coast was clear, at least for that moment. James nodded to Alonzo. "Right. Let's get a move on."

Now, a scrapper's life ain't an easy one, and that is namely due to the location in which a scrapper scraps. Sure, folks might argue of the dangers those that travel the Wastes from settlement to settlement have to deal with, but frankly all the ways those folks die – bandits, heat exhaustion, falling into a canyon when they weren't lookin' – are right natural. No one knew precisely what killed the 'Fore-Folks, but from the environments they left behind, "natural" didn't come even close to describing their fate. The ruins in which scrappers scrapped were, more often than not, museums of the unnatural: spellwork common folks couldn't even begin to comprehend, constructs and machines and lattices that made the soul ache just to look at, experiments left behind where the only understanding of what they'd been trying to accomplish was from horrific implications. Every scrapper worth their salt knew the dangers of touching something unknown in a 'Fore-Folk ruin, and every scrapper had at least one story about a friend who was never quite the same after they'd done just that. It's common knowledge, after all, that the 'Fore-Folks had caused the Shattering, and thus had been the ones to blow themselves to smithereens alongside half the world.

And if they could do that, who knew what else they had gotten up to?

It was with this thought in mind that the group moved slowly down the hall, everyone on high alert despite the seemingly benign office spaces they passed. Some doors remained open, others barred shut, and still others had cracked and fallen when the world had ended. In this day and age there generally weren't skeletons to find – bones crushed or eaten or absorbed or in some other way succumbed to entropy – but the resulting emptiness of the labs, decaying desks and chairs and other such things, created the illusion that those who'd once spent their lives working there just ... got up and left one day.

"Shouldn't we be checking these rooms?" Sylvia asked from her spot in the middle of the group.

"If you want to lug equipment around for the rest of the excavation, be my guest," Alonzo sneered, "but I doubt you'll find anything of use up here. Why bother with the small things when a treasure trove awaits us?"

If Sylvia had anything more to say, she was distracted by the hall ending in a T, the doors of the building elevator sitting rusted shut. James sighed. "Shui, help me get this open."

"Are you sure the elevator is the smartest option?" Sunny asked as the two men began struggling with the door.

"According to the map, there are thirty floors. I don't know about you, but I, for one, have no interest in climbing that many steps if I do not absolutely have to." Alonzo pulled the map back up, studying the various floors as though to confirm his own statement.

With a grunt and the screech of rusted metal, the elevator doors were opened, revealing a pitch-black shaft, the echoes traveling for much longer than anyone felt comfortable with.

"Sunny, if you will," Alonzo ordered.

"Yeah, yeah," Sunny grumbled as she elbowed her way to the ancient control panel and pried it open with some effort. Immediately the dim red emergency lights were overpowered by a sharp flash of fuchsia as the crystal lattice sparked violently before crumbling to dust with a horrid purple fizzle. Sunny coughed, waving the smoke away.

"Don't suppose you can lower us down easy-like?" James asked, turning to Levvy.

Levvy chewed on her lip, looking down into the abyss before shaking her head. "Not that far. That spell only lasts as long as I can hold the note, but I can't do that for thirty floors, not on your life."

Alonzo huffed, closing the map and shoving it in his pocket. "I guess we shall have to settle for the stairs after all. This – "

BOM

Alonzo started, then coughed awkwardly. " – Um, this way."

It was with a slightly quicker pace that the group pressed onwards, everyone keeping a watchful eye out. Every darkened room was a space to be hidden in, every shadow a creature waiting to strike. Occasionally more noises would echo through the building, but it was difficult to say just where they were echoing *from*, and how whatever made them seemed to be getting there. There was no question that the construct knew the building better; it was just a matter of time before it caught up with them. Without speaking, the various members of the group came to the same conclusion on their own, and all clumped a little closer together.

"The stairs should be right around this – " Alonzo's words left him in a gasp as he turned the corner and stepped nearly over the edge of a massive pit that swallowed the hallway. Had it not been for James's hand snagging the back of his well-pressed shirt and dragging him back, that would have been the end of Doctor Alonzo Morris. On the other side of the pit where the stairwell should have been was nothing more than rubble and debris and further cracks in the masonry. Alonzo huffed a sigh, attempting to cover his panic at nearly falling to his death, and scrubbed a hand through his hair that was no longer quite so in place as it had been only moments before. "Well, I suppose we'll just have to find a new route." He pulled up the map and began frantically scanning through it, muttering to himself.

James peered over the side of the pit. "Lights," he ordered, and with a sharp whistle, the spell-lights moved from where they'd encircled the group and floated down the pit like a strand of glowing pearls. The light only reached so far, but the pit reached fairly deep. James clicked his tongue against his teeth. "That's what, fifteen? Twenty stories?" He looked back at Levvy, who immediately began shaking her head.

"No, that's still too far, there's no way I can hold a note that long," she protested.

James slung an arm around her shoulder. "You won't have to, just long enough to get down a few stories so you can catch your breath, y'know. Do it in spurts instead of all at once. What do you think, Doc? A sight faster than trying to find a new route that might not exist."

"And how exactly are we supposed to get back up?" Sunny muttered under her breath. She was ignored by everyone save Shui, who sent a sympathetic glance back.

"Surely you don't expect me to just *jump* that, do you?" Alonzo asked, peering down into the darkness.

"Naw, we can make it." James slung his rifle across his back and gave Levvy a wink. "You won't let me fall, right?" Levvy looked unsure but shook her head nonetheless. Without further comment, James took a running start and leaped into the pit. There was a fraction of a second before Levvy got her hand to her mouth and whistled out a sustained note that vibrated out from her spine and through her hand and caused the long-broken lattices still scattered in the various offices to hum with confused echoes. James's downward descent slowed like he'd fallen into water, still moving forward with his momentum, but when he reached the other side about three floors down, he hit the ground as though he'd only leaped off a six foot wall.

"What did I say?" He pulled himself to his feet and gave a mock salute. "Ain't nothin' to it, and a sight faster than going the long way." Levvy shook her hand out and caught her breath. "I figure if we station folks every few floors, we can catch them as they come down, ferry 'em easy-like." When Alonzo still looked unsure, he continued, "It's this or the elevator shaft, Doc. I dunno about you, but I'd rather do this than try to rappel down for thirty stories."

"Fine," Alonzo sniffed, "but I'm not going next."

Sylvia went next, followed by Shui, the two of them situating themselves on either side of the pit with roughly three floors between them. Those left on the top floor waited anxiously, knowing that the longer they took, the closer the construct got. As such, when it came his time to jump, for all his loud hesitation earlier, Alonzo jumped with perhaps a bit *too* much eagerness, spindly limbs windmilling as he crossed the gap one, two, three times over. Once he'd landed safely next to Shui, Levvy called for a break, breathing deep to try and get her wind back.

"Think you can do it?" Sunny asked Xal quietly. They'd been shoved at her when the others had gone down; apparently the bandits were confident in their lack of places to escape to, or confident in Levvy's ability to stop them. Xal's own confidence in their ability to make it to the bottom wasn't quite so firm, but they weren't about to say that out loud.

"Don't think I got much choice – " They paused, mid-sentence, listening. Sunny froze, listening as well –

BOM

Closer, now, uncomfortably close. Alonzo's voice echoed up from below, "Alright, that's enough of a break. Move along, now."

Levvy took another deep breath and let it out slowly before looking between Sunny and Xal. "Which one's next?"

"Xal," Sunny said quickly, hauling them over to the edge. Levvy took another breath –

BOM

– only for it to shudder out uncertainly. "Okay. On three, push them over the side with as much force as you've got. One, two, *three* – "

Sunny shoved Xal over the side with all her might, and for a second they were falling – before Levvy's whistle filled the air and caught them, making them light and buoyant like a stick sinking gently in a pond. For the first time in about an hour, Xal felt relatively painless with the spell lifting all their weight off their bruised and battered nervous system. They drifted slower than the others, though; not as much momentum. Levvy was forced to hold the note longer than she had for the others.

BOM

It was getting closer.

BOM

Closer. Xal was almost halfway across the gap. James reached out impatiently towards them.

CLANG

One of the vent covers went flying across the hallway, bouncing off the far wall and clattering to the ground. From the vent emerged the sleek black shape of the Silencer Mk. 6, its claws finding purchase along the tiled floor as it turned and faced down the hall. Levvy and Sunny turned in horror to the thing sprinting towards them, Sunny calling out a warning.

Levvy gasped.

All of a sudden, gravity returned to Xal as though some giant hand had closed around their body and given a mighty *yank*. They plummeted past James, past Sylvia, all the way down, and had Shui not thrown himself desperately at the gap to snag Xal's wrists as they fell by, they might've hit the bottom. Shui's ribs *crunched* as he was dragged flat against the floor by Xal's weight, and Xal's vision flickered in and out as they came to a very sudden stop. They couldn't see. They couldn't *breathe*. It was as though every bone in their body, every bruised muscle, hell, even their busted brain had been cracked like a whip, and the tendons in their shoulders were threatening to give.

Above them, Levvy had turned away from the Silencer and leaped the gap, aiming with all her desperation towards the outstretched arms of James, hand in her mouth, spell in her mind –

But she was out of breath. With nothing left to give the spell, Levvy fell like a stone, her outstretched hand slipping through James's, body falling past Sylvia, past Shui and Xal, with no wind in her left for a final scream. James's mouth hung open, his eyes wide and staring all the way until Levvy plummeted out of sight. All four spell-lights were snuffed out of existence, plunging everyone into darkness.

" – al! *Xal*!" The words slipped back into Xal's battered mind. Shui's hold around their wrists was shaking. "*Don't pass out!* Doc, help me!" They felt more hands reach down to grip their arms but with less surety than the two already holding them.

Sunny dove over the side right as the Silencer pounced, but instead of attempting the same leap Levvy had failed, she clung to the edge and swung below to the floor just beneath her. The Silencer paid her no mind and continued on with its target – James. It struck him clean in the chest, claws puncturing leather and flesh indiscriminately as it bowled him over. He cracked his head against the floor, holding the creature back solely by his legs bowed up against his chest and a hand pressed against its sternum, while his other arm shielded his head in a desperate attempt at cover. "Doc! Shoot it!"

"I'm – ! A little busy here!" Alonzo snapped back. Xal was just about over the lip of the hole. With one last mighty pull, they cleared it, left flat on the floor like a discarded toy. Shui immediately curled in around his ribs, breathing through the agony.

Sunny's grip on the lip of the hole slipped out of her fingers, and she screamed as she fell a story before landing hard on the next floor down, directly onto her wrist. The Silencer's head snapped up at the scream, twisting unnaturally around to look backwards at her. It was the opening James needed. He pushed with all his might, shoving the construct off him and into the pit. It snagged a hold of his leg, however, dragging him over with it even as he clung desperately to rubble and debris and finally the edge. "*Alonzo*!" he screamed again.

Alonzo scrambled to his feet, moving around the hole to get a better aim – and paused, eyes wide and glassy and full of wonder at the construct.

"It's hardly even scratched," he wondered aloud. "How has it stayed in such good condition?"

"You can figure it out when it's dead!" James yelled, holding on with all his might.

The mortal danger of his hired muscle snapped Alonzo out of his daze, and he fired three shots with Xal's gun – the first seared in front of the construct's visor to blast the ceiling beyond it. The second struck it in what could generously be called its thigh. The third caught it full in the face as it turned and leaped towards Alonzo, shorting out its trajectory and causing it to miss its mark, *thunk* against the edge, and fall into the darkness below. The echoing fall seemed to last for years, and while it weren't even close to that in actuality, it lasted for longer than echoes had any right to. The lab was *long*, and *deep*, and for the first time that realization seemed to cement itself in everyone's mind. When the quiet horror had released its hold on the small group, they moved with a silent efficiency down towards the floor with Xal, Shui, and Alonzo, and through the nearest set of doors. The moment everyone was through, James toppled an ancient filing cabinet in front of the door, then began piling whatever else he could find, desperation bleeding through every movement and every extra layer to the barricade.

"Lights!" he yelled. "Lights, damnit – !" James's voice broke with the realization that the only lights they had were the dim, red emergency lights that flickered in the hallway. His eyes widened in horror, then sunk closed. He pinched the bridge of his nose, and slumped against the barricade.

"I don't suppose either of y'all are spellslingers?" Sylvia asked, looking away.

"Can remember a few tunes, can't whistle for shit," Xal said from where they'd been dumped against the wall. Sunny shook her head.

For a moment no one spoke, each in their own state of revelation that they were all now, truly, in the darkness of the lab without Levvy. Sylvia returned to the barricade efforts, quietly encouraging James to do the same. Shui made no effort to join in whatsoever.

"Don't look at me like that," James snapped, bristling. "She slipped! There was nothing I could've – !" He cut himself off, turning away and focusing on the barricade. Shui said nothing, but his glare never wavered.

Sunny crouched down next to Xal. "How are you holding up?" she asked quietly.

Xal sucked in a breath between their teeth, but the gaze they leveled at Sunny was the most alert she'd seen in an hour. "Can't say I wanna do that again anytime soon," they said, giving an exhausted, breathy chuckle. They nodded towards Sunny. "How's your wrist?"

Sunny straightened back to standing, pulling her wrist farther out of eyesight. "It's fine," she said, too quickly.

Xal frowned. "I heard when you landed. Didn't sound pretty."

"Xal, drop it," Sunny snapped.

Xal's frown deepened, but before they could say anything, Alonzo strode over to snatch Sunny's wrist. "What are you hiding, you little – "

Alonzo's eyes widened, and he dropped her wrist like a hot plate. Sunny snatched her arm back, covering it once again with her other hand, her eyes just as wide and startled as Alonzo's.

"It's not what you think," she whispered desperately.

"No?" Alonzo's expression had shifted from shock to pure hunger. "And what should I be thinking, Miss Quill?"

Sunny shook her head. She took a step back. Alonzo took a step forward, putting him in front of Xal.

Xal's eyes were on their guns.

"Sunny, that's an interesting designation, isn't it? I never took Dr. Quill as a sentimental man."

"*It's my name.*"

James and Sylvia were occupied with the door. Shui was injured. Alonzo was focused on Sunny. If they were going to get their guns, it had to be *now*.

"I always wondered where Dr. Quill found you, why he suddenly showed interest in becoming a family man instead of just hiring you on as an assistant."

They just had to get there first. Xal summoned whatever strength they had left, sliding their knees towards their chest. They were sweating, face pale, limbs shaking, but they pushed through with all they had. This was their shot –

"Doc!" The opportunity slipped through their hands just as Levvy had slipped through James's, as James and Sylvia finished with the barricade, both still clearly wound with restless energy. "I don't know how well that'll hold, we gotta get going ... " James paused, glancing between Alonzo and Sunny, who shrank even further from view. "Am I interrupting something?"

Alonzo leveled one last, long glance at Sunny. Sunny pulled the sleeve of her coveralls so far down it nearly covered her fingertips.

"Not a thing," he said, his eyes still sparkling with hunger. "Not a single thing."

4

Now, Xal's brain wasn't one for numbers even before the bullet, but they could feel their body making the calculations their brain didn't care to. Though they kept their weight on Sylvia, they could feel control over their legs finally turning into something useful. Maybe not consistent, but a bullet only needs to strike true once.

Shui was injured; it was clear from the way he walked he'd busted his ribs something fierce. His standing within the group seemed equally rocky; the argument he'd had with James seemed as though it weren't the first by far, and the tension had only gotten worse with the loss of Levvy. He seemed intent to burn a hole in James's skull with his glare alone, hands gripping his rifle with a force they did not need. With the numbers they'd first come down with, Xal wouldn't have had a chance. But then, they didn't have the numbers anymore, now did they? And while it was difficult to quantify a human life as being more or less obtrusive to their survival, with the bandits' spellslinger out of the way, their chances had gone up significantly. The original pack of six had dwindled down to three, not counting Alonzo. Truly, Alonzo hardly registered on Xal's radar; the man couldn't shoot for shit and was clearly unliked by his hirelings, and money would only stave off starving dogs for so long. If they could somehow force the issue, they could get a chance to skedaddle while the rest tore each other apart.

'Course, much of that plan relied on Xal getting their guns back and Sunny working with them, not against them. The first part was doable. Alonzo had them and couldn't hit nothing with them. Were it a fair fight, they would trounce him no problem. Of course, with the bullet to the brain, it was going to be an unfair fight no matter what, so they were gonna have to keep an eye out for some way to tip the scales in their favor.

Sunny ... Sunny was a problem. They could feel their plans and calculations stutter to a halt every time Sunny was thrown into the picture. She'd hired them, but beyond that, there was nothing. No reason they were down in the lab, no reason she was so insistent on reaching the bottom, nothing to explain whatever history or tension there was between herself and Alonzo beyond whatever history Alonzo had with Dr. Quill, and Xal hadn't caught a glimpse of whatever it was that Alonzo saw. She was hiding something, and Xal wasn't sure if she was hiding it from just Alonzo and his dogs or from Xal as well.

Xal didn't like not knowing, but then, at the same time, not knowing felt about as familiar as anything else, so they supposed they may as well make peace with this as well.

Alonzo had eyes only for Sunny. Even with their suspicions, it still set a knot tightening in Xal's stomach the way Alonzo looked at her as though she were a thing. Their brain may have been full of quite literal holes, but they knew nothing good ever came from looks like that. Sunny, for her part, dutifully ignored him or, at the very least, made her best attempt.

As such, despite Sunny and Alonzo being in the front of the group, with Sunny's eyes on the floor and Alonzo's eyes on Sunny, and Xal's eyes on Alonzo and Shui's eyes on James, it was James who spotted it first.

"Doc, hold up," he said, pausing mid-stride and peering through the cracked glass of one of the larger windows along the hall. Parts of the building had been shaken to pieces this far down, either by the Shattering or the afterquakes or the regular, non-apocalyptic earthquakes, or just from a burrower digging through a load-bearing wall. The red lights flickered and spat, casting most of the floor into shadow that left folks blind in a way they'd never been with Levvy's lights. Most of the rooms they had passed so far were the same as those higher up, offices filled with monitors and pieces of equipment.

"What?" Alonzo snapped.

"You're gonna want to take a look at this."

"If this is more long-broken tech, then I have already made myself clear – " Alonzo stopped mid-sentence as he caught a glimpse of what James had spotted: another construct, though bulkier than the one that had attacked them. Unlike the Silencer, this one was motionless, still strapped into some kind of dock as though merely asleep.

"Do you think it's alive, like the other one?" Sylvia asked, her voice barely above a whisper.

"They're not *alive*," Alonzo corrected, staring intently at the new construct. "They're merely pretending to be. A facsimile, that's all. Isn't that right, Sunny?"

Sunny refused to meet his eyes. Alonzo eyed her for a long moment before moving towards the doors to the chamber. "Well, in that case, if our resident construct expert has nothing to add, we should go investigate, hm?"

" ... I thought Xal was the expert?" Shui said.

All eyes turned towards Xal, still slung over Sylvia's shoulder. For their part, they were staring through the fogged glass, squinting and trying to get a better view of the thing before speaking up. "Don't think this one ever made it to market," they commented.

"All the more reason to investigate," Alonzo said cheerfully.

"Wait – we shouldn't – " Sunny seemed to war with herself before she ran after Alonzo. "Leave it alone!"

"Don't worry, as long as no one touches anything, I'm sure nothing will happen." The doors had been covered in debris, but there was a small enough gap for Alonzo to squeeze into the room. Dread began to pool in Xal's stomach.

"He's lost it," Shui muttered, only to get cuffed on the head as James passed by. For a moment Shui stood still, a dangerous set to his shoulders, glaring at James's back, and only once Sylvia and Xal had squeezed in did he enter the room.

It was difficult to see in the dim light, but the chamber they entered was larger than the ones they'd seen thus far. Desks and broken-down monitors surrounded the looming figure of the construct docked in the center of the room. Thick wires and tubing shot off away from the dock back to the monitors and beyond, like the roots of some twisted tree. The slumbering beast was easily several feet taller than any of them, and twice as wide as even James. The rest of the group kept their distance, but Alonzo strode purposefully up to the construct with Sunny hot on his heels.

"Alonzo, *stop*!" Sunny yelled, only to flinch back as he turned on her.

"Why, feeling some kind of kinship with it, are we?" he asked, stepping forward. "You know, Sunny, your father never did say what he found at the first lab."

"I-I told you earlier." Sunny took a stumbling step back. "Just some broken experimental constructs and references to this lab. That's all."

Shui shook his head and turned away, but James and Sylvia watched the argument with rapt attention. "And – remind me, Sunny, dear." Alonzo took another step forward. "What exactly brought you down here?"

"I'm a scrapper. It's my *job*." But she no longer sounded as sure of herself as she once had. "I – "

Whatever Sunny had been about to say was lost as she tripped backwards over one of the thick wires. She crashed to the ground, hard – and from one of her pockets skittered a single, complex crystal lattice glowing a pale blue against the darkness of the floor. Alonzo stopped, staring. Sunny froze as well, eyes wide. The lattice was clearly modern – clunky and unwieldy in comparison to the ancient lattices they'd already seen that day – but for a modern lattice it was shockingly intricate. The frame was two concentric overlapping triangles all hooked into one another, the blue crystals shimmering and pointing in a spiral as they wrapped around the frame, the shape of the entire thing wholly unfamiliar to everyone in the room but Sunny.

"What ... is that?" Alonzo asked, low and dangerous.

Sunny's eyes were wide and terrified. All the eyes in the room were on her. And as she opened her mouth to say something, *anything* – Xal made their move.

Xal stomped with all the weight and force they could muster down onto Sylvia's foot and felt bones give way under the heel of their boot. There was no time to revel in the strike; the moment Sylvia began to howl and curl in pain, they followed the motion and shoved her over their leg – and as she went sprawling, they snagged her gun.

They shot once – twice – the first bullet cracking against the control panel by James's arm, the second missing Alonzo's head by a hair. Sunny shoved Alonzo back into the construct and dove along the floor to snatch the crystal and shove it back in her pocket. James pointed his gun towards Xal, and Xal pointed Sylvia's gun right back and fired – only for the gun to click empty. They swore, ducked under James's shots, and flung the empty gun at him.

Sylvia's gun flew through the air in what could have been considered a perfect arc, dead-shot aim, eagle-eyed and one in a million, were it not for the fact that Xal's vision still had yet to fully clear and they'd been aiming for James, who hadn't hardly needed to dodge the gun as it sailed by and perfectly struck the control panel.

Brilliant blue sparks crackled along the ancient control systems, drowning out the red emergency lights and blinding the room's occupants. Xal dove behind one of the control panels, and Sunny rolled under another; James flinched back, and Sylvia curled up into a protective ball; Alonzo took a startled step away from the construct, and the construct *screamed*.

It was a horrible noise, one that was so irrefutably human but forced out of parts no human had, like a construction site trying to speak. The construct screamed and strained and Alonzo had barely enough time to draw Xal's gun before the construct had pulled its bonds up by the root and *slammed* a flailing arm the size of a tree trunk into his side. Doctor Alonzo Morris went flying, and Xal's gun went clattering to the ground.

Xal and Sylvia shared a single look before they both scrambled for the weapon. They reached the gun at the same time, wrestling for it as best they could while, in the center of the room, the construct freed another of its gargantuan limbs, screaming that same horrible, mechanical scream.

"Shut it down, *shut it down*!" James was yelling, trying to distract it from Shui who was desperately pressing random controls in the hopes that *something* would change. "Where the *fuck* is the scrapper?!"

On the ground, Sylvia held on with all her wiry might, even if she was half the size of Xal. "Give me the gun," she spat, "so I can shoot the damn thing!"

"Sorry," Xal grunted, "but I think I'd rather take my chances with *it*." Before they could stop to consider the consequences, Xal *slammed* their head into Sylvia's, knocking her skull against the concrete floor. Both of them lost dizzy seconds, but Xal swam back to the surface first, slotted their gun back perfectly into their hand, and fired.

No one could be quite sure where exactly they were aiming, but sunlight spat from the mouth of their gun to sheer past the construct and clip James through the thigh, filling the ancient air with the pungent smell of burning meat. James howled in pain at the same moment the construct screamed that same metal scream, hauling its legs out and away from where the bolt had burned its way across its armored shell. It reeled back, flailing its horrific arms along with the wires still stuck deep in it like IV lines, smashing controls and lattices and nearly Shui if he hadn't ducked and rolled and –

"XAL!" Sunny screamed.

Xal moved, but not fast enough. The flailing arm struck them like a meteor hits the atmosphere: brutal, merciless, and entirely unaware. They felt their bones move in a way bones should not move and their skeleton rattle through all the aftershocks, and they squeezed their eyes shut and braced for the impact they knew was coming.

"*XAL*!" Sunny screamed again as their body *smashed* into the far wall and crumpled boneless to the floor. Xal didn't respond, but the construct had turned to where they'd been flung and was advancing. There was enough intelligence in it to recognize the threat in the hand that wielded such a gun. There was no time to think. Sunny sprinted out from her hiding place, ducked around James and Shui, and snagged the gun from Xal's limp grip.

"*Stop*!" The gun shook in Sunny's small hands as she placed her tiny body between Xal's prone form and the looming figure of the construct.

The construct stopped.

Sunny's breath caught in her chest, eyes wide. The construct leaned forward but not as a threat – it was almost as though it were confused. Another horrible, garbled, twist-of-metal noise groaned from it, but instead of a scream, it was a question.

The gun rattled in Sunny's hands. "I said – "

Sunlight burst through the air and exploded across the back of the construct. It reeled back, screeching and screaming and turned on the shooter – Alonzo, who'd just barely picked himself up off the ground.

"Xal, *wake up.*" Sunny shook them by the shoulders. "*Xal.*" Their head flopped over, fresh blood once again dripping slowly from their forehead.

"Get them up." Sunny started as Shui spoke; she hadn't even heard him move. On the other side of the room the construct was still fighting with Alonzo, James, and Sylvia. "This is your chance, but we need to move *now.*" When Sunny didn't immediately move, Shui knelt down and hauled Xal up before shoving their dead weight back to her. "In the storage room there's a vent. Drag them if you have to, but this is the best chance you'll get."

Still, Sunny hesitated. "Why are you – ?"

"It don't matter none, now *go.*" Shui shoved them along, watching the fight in the room. James had begun yelling for him, a yell Shui was blatantly ignoring. Sunny spent only a second more before stowing Xal's gun in her coveralls and getting a move on. The storage room was filled top to bottom with pieces and parts of lattices and crystals and tools for activities Sunny couldn't even begin to imagine, all long since rusted or shattered or claimed by entropy in one way or another.

True to Shui's word, there was a vent near the floor, just large enough for the two of them. Sunny popped the cover, then looked back.

"I'll make sure they don't follow." Shui pulled a wicked-looking knife from his belt and began prying open the door controls. "Don't worry about me."

"Thank you," Sunny said, and from the look in his eyes, she didn't think anyone had told him that in a very long time.

"Stop wasting time," he snapped instead, already prying off the casing to the control panel. "Get going already."

Sunny steeled herself, took a breath, and hauled Xal into the darkness.

5

There was no light in the vents. After a few twists and turns while dragging Xal backwards into the unknown, the red emergency lights and the odd flash of gunfire no longer reached Sunny. Not that it mattered. There was no real way for her to both see where she was headed and take Xal along easily. Time stretched and distorted with nothing to see; all sounds were garbled and echoed and blended into the natural groans of the ancient structure. There were times where her eyes would play tricks on her in the darkness, where out of the corner of her eye she would catch sight of some soft glowing emanating from the bloodied plane of Xal's forehead – but when she would turn to look, there would be nothing, only darkness.

"Xal," she said, not for the first time. "Xal, you need to wake up."

Xal didn't so much as twitch. Sunny was tempted to search for a pulse, but then she'd seen them get back up from a bullet to the brain, so she dutifully ignored the way their bones seemed to shift and move in ways they shouldn't. They were alive. They had to be alive. If they weren't alive, if Sunny had just been dragging a corpse down who knew how many vents –

"*Xal,*" she called again, desperately trying to pull herself out of her spiraling thoughts. "Xal, *please.*"

Sunny had never liked the darkness. She hated being alone, and loathed feeling helpless most of all. She'd fallen into a routine by this point, a muscle memory loop of dragging Xal deeper and deeper down, and as the loop became rote it freed her mind up to think and dwell.

"If I ever see Alonzo again," she growled, dragging Xal another length backwards, "I'm going to kill him. I don't give a shit if he was my dad's colleague, I don't *care*. I'm going to shoot him, but I'm a bad shot, so I need you awake to finish him off."

Silence.

"He's still got your other gun, yeah?" she said, switching tactics. "You're real possessive about those, aint'cha? I ain't seen guns like that since – since – " Even with her charge unconscious and unhearing, Sunny couldn't bring herself to say it aloud. "They're unique, you ain't findin' shit like that in the Wastes, not in such good quality either. They're important to you." She dragged them back another length. "You wanna get it back, right? Can't do it like this."

Silence. Sunny's grip trembled, thoughts of pulses and brains splattering a cave wall swirling through her mind.

"Xal." Her voice was small. Almost inaudible. "Xal, you have to wake up." She tried to put more strength into the words, but her resolve cracked at the end. "Xal, *please* – "

Her voice broke at the same time the vent behind her dropped suddenly and dramatically, sending them both sliding down at a sharp angle. Sunny didn't have the breath for any more than a surprised gasp as they tumbled backwards for what felt like an eternity. Metal hit Sunny's back and nearly dislodged the sob she'd been desperately burying. She bit down, tried to hold it in with the force of her jaw strength. When that failed, she clamped both hands down across her mouth. She screwed her eyes shut and held on, scarcely bothering to breathe.

She could not break here.

She would not break here.

There was still so much else she needed to get done.

She held herself there, submerged in that breathless state until her systems alerted her to the need to breathe. She held a second or two longer, just to remember what it felt like to hold her breath, and opened her eyes.

Xal still had not moved from where they lay, sprawled on her lap. She held the disappointment and let it wash away. She took the advantage laying on the ground had granted her and looked ahead.

Ahead of her, there was faint red light slipping in through the slats on the bottom of the vent. To the right of her, sitting in an offshoot of the vents that went deeper into the building, the Silencer Mk. 6 stared back.

Sunny's eyes went wide. She froze like a mouse in sight of a hawk and pulled Xal's body protectively closer. The Silencer was crouched on what could generously be called the tips of its fingers and toes, almost invisible in the darkness save for the faint red light reflecting off its black chassis. Sunny didn't move, couldn't move, Xal's gun in her coveralls too buried to be of any use. The construct moved too fast; there would be no way for her to get it in time.

The two stared each other down for what felt like an eternity, every fiber of Sunny tensed to move the moment *it* did –

The construct slipped further into the darkness and crawled silently away deeper into the vents.

Sunny's breath left her in a *woosh*, and she let her head fall back to the vent in horrid, confused relief. It should have ended her. It should have killed her the way it had already killed three people. She should be –

She closed her eyes and counted down. Thought of all the ways one could dismantle an ancient lattice. Mentally organized all of the tools waiting for her at her workbench back home. Looked back down at the body in her arms. It didn't matter why they hadn't been torn apart, she would have to take her gifts where they were.

"I'll be right back, okay?" she said, patting Xal on the shoulder as she disentangled herself from them and peered through the vent cover. It was hard to tell how far down the floor was, and it would be nearly impossible to close the hatch back up to hide their tracks, but Sunny was tired of dragging Xal through the darkness. It was worth the risk.

Sunny got to work prying open the vent cover. After everything else she had dealt with so far, the action was refreshingly mundane. It was held closed only by a few screws, which came loose easily under her deft hands.

When she looked down to the room below, it was difficult to say just how far the drop would be. She would be fine, she'd dealt with harder falls than this, but Xal had yet to wake up. She looked at their prone body guiltily a moment longer before pulling herself together. They didn't have a choice.

"I'm sorry," Sunny said, hooking her arms back under Xal's and dragging them into position. "I wish I didn't have to, but – but you'll be okay, alright? You survived being shot in the head, you survived that construct rearranging your skeleton, you'll survive a fall like this." She breathed in, steeling herself in their stead. "Okay. Okay. Let's go." She pulled their leather duster off their limp frame and dropped it to the ground below, figuring that any cushion she could provide would be better than no cushion at all.

Xal dropped like a doll, all floppy limbs and ligaments, but by some miracle they didn't seem to hurt themself any worse than they already had.

After a second of steeling herself, Sunny followed suit, dropping and rolling and hearing something clatter and skitter away while she caught her breath. Then her brain caught up with her ears and she patted down the many pockets of her coveralls before her gray eyes flew wide and scanned the floor – there! The crystal lattice she'd so jealously guarded had escaped again, rolling to a halt at the center of the room.

Sunny scrambled to pick it up, turning it over to search for cracks or blemishes or any possible sign of damage. The crystal lattice remained intact. She clutched it to her chest and screwed her eyes shut.

When she opened them, she got her first real look at the room. It was similar to the room they had just left, control panels and office chairs and fractured lattices and wires thick enough to be vines all in similar places – and in the center of it all was a chair. A padded chair, raised slightly from the ground, with leather straps at the arm rests. Every single part of the chair was adjustable, from the footrest to the headrest, all able to move to fit a wide range of bodies. Able to fit perfectly around a girl, just barely an adult, thin and sick.

There are as many ways a brain can react to something awful as there are brains. Some burrow deep in the pain, make a nest of it and then turn that nest into a fortress, letting no one in or out. Others turn it into a weapon, sharpen it over years so that they could hurt others before hurt could be done to them once more. Some carry that pain, learn to live with it, learn to love with it. Others just drown.

Sunny had done what a nontrivial amount of folks do and buried her pain so deep she couldn't even begin to think about it with any kind of clarity, only able to conceive of it in the abstract as though it had happened to someone else. See, the problem with this method is that pain don't forget – and all it took to bring the abstract into sharp relief was to get a glimpse, a reminder of the real thing.

The straps around her wrists were strong, well-made, and didn't allow her to move an inch. She couldn't try if she wanted to – weak, sick, in so much pain she almost couldn't wait for it to be over. The overhead lights burned her sensitive eyes, but she couldn't flinch away. Her breath caught in her throat and held there, even as they turned the horrid machine on – and the tugging, the extraction, the taffy-pull of something untouchable being wrenched piece by piece away from her physical form, torn away from tendons and sinew and nerve endings all the same – she screamed, she knew she screamed, but no one could hear her, or no one *cared* to hear her –

And then she was spun like thread into wires and cables and something cold and unforgiving with only a fractal understanding of what her life had been, and what it was now.

Sunny was pulled back into the present with a gasp as noise echoed down the vents. Her breathing sped to a breakneck pace and did not slow, and the hands that pulled Xal's gun from her coveralls shook like the Shattering itself.

"Sunny? Are you – "

Sunny fired, her shot going wild and blasting into the metal of the vents. Shui lost his grip and dropped to the floor in surprise, landing gracelessly among the debris. "*Sunny*! Don't – Fuck, don't shoot, I'm not here to hurt you!"

"No, you're just here to take me back to people who will!" Sunny yelled back, not moving her shaky aim from where Shui had landed.

"I left them back there," Shui said, calmly and slowly. His hands were in the air; he hadn't moved from where he'd fallen. "If they're still alive, they'll have to find a different way down."

"Why should I believe you?" Sunny's grip on the gun wasn't quite as strong as it had been.

"Because they're a bunch of idiots who are going to get themselves killed, and I'm done pretending they won't." Slowly, Shui moved from the ground to his knees. When he wasn't blasted to pieces, he began moving slowly closer. "I wanna live. And I'm guessing you do too."

"You know *nothing* about me."

Shui stilled, certain he'd crossed a line. The seconds ticked by, and he remained un-shot. "You're right, I don't." He was close enough now that he could reach out and grab the gun itself if he wanted. "But I do know that out here, rates of survival tend to be higher the larger the group. And, not for nothin', but with your gunslinger the way they are, I don't know how much help you're getting."

"Their name's Xal," Sunny corrected miserably. Shui's hands rested on her own, not forcing, just asking.

"Put the gun down, Sunny," Shui said. "Please."

He covered her vision, obscuring the hateful chair and the rest of the lab. For a moment, Sunny could almost pretend that they were in any other room in the ruins, lit only by the dim emergency lights. She squeezed her eyes shut, pulling herself back piece by piece. Not here. Not now. She lowered the gun. Shui's relief bled through his fingertips as he pulled away – and froze.

Sunny opened her eyes and followed his gaze. The sleeve of her coveralls had slid down, exposing her wrist. On the back of her forearm, where she'd landed hard, the dermal layer covering her body had split open. There was no blood, no open wound to risk infection, merely synthetic skin peeling back to reveal the metal of her body.

Sunny flinched back, finding her escape blocked by one of the consoles. Shui's eyes were wide, but, unlike Alonzo, Shui looked rightly horrified. Sunny rolled her sleeve back down as best she could without letting go of the gun.

Shui merely stared as his brain tried to figure out what exactly was the appropriate response. " ... Does Xal know?" he asked, finally.

"No one knows," Sunny whispered. "Are you serious about this? About helping get us out of here?"

If Shui was surprised by the sudden resolve, he didn't say anything about it. "Yes."

Sunny nodded and finally put away the gun. "Then help me get them out."

Xal, still sprawled out cold where they landed, said nothing.

Sunny kept her eyes anywhere but the center of the room as the two of them struggled through hoisting Xal's duster back on them, and then hoisting Xal onto their shoulders. Shui had originally attempted to muscle through the act himself, but his ribs had all too quickly decided they were not up to task. She had a fleeting thought of how none of them had gotten through this unscathed, followed by an unfortunate thought of just how far they had yet to go. Down in the depths of the lab, the emergency lights held even less power, barely illuminating a foot around where they were embedded in the ceiling, some dead completely. It was such that when Sunny produced the map from her pocket, the pink light nearly blinded the both of them.

"I thought Dr. Morris had that?" Shui commented.

"He did before I snagged it." Sunny paused a moment, analyzing the projected light. "Alright, I think we're about ... here." She chewed at her lip, thinking. "I doubt we'll have any luck with the stairs, and without a spellslinger, there's no way we can pull that stunt that took us down again, but maybe we could scale the elevator shaft? See if we can't haul Xal up after us?"

"What about the Silencer?" Shui asked.

Sunny turned her encounter with the construct over in her mind. "We ain't seen it since," she said finally. "It might be safe to say it's more interested in Alonzo and the others. Elevator's still our best bet."

Shui had half a mind to point out to her that the Silencer was able to climb walls and had hunted them through the vents and they were likely to be easy pickin's no matter *which* vertical shaft they attempted to climb, should the construct chance upon them again. Sunny, however, had begun moving them down the hall as though the argument had been solved one way or the other.

According to the map they were roughly two-thirds of the way to the bottom. Despite knowing it was theoretically possible to go even deeper, the bowels of the earth made themselves known in the darkened underground halls. The walls seemed to press in on them, the air heavy and forceful like water at the depths of the ocean. Despite this, despite the almost humid feeling of the earth, it had become increasingly frigid the further down they'd gone. Where once there might have been climate-spells woven into the rest of the building, now it was bereft and subjugated to the whims of the rocks so far away from the sun.

Shui shivered, not wanting to dwell too much on just how deep they were.

"Not too far now," Sunny said. "Then we can get you two back to the surface."

Shui frowned, something in her phrasing tickling the back of his mind but nothing more. On his shoulders, Xal twitched. Just a hand at first, but the movement traveled up their arm into their shoulder.

"Xal?" Shui called. Xal didn't respond, but they did twitch again. "Sunny, I think they're waking up."

Sunny paused, but her eyes were on the end of the hallway that was lost in darkness. They lowered Xal as gently as they could against the wall. The twitching was stronger now – not quite spasms but something more intentional. Their eyes went from peacefully closed to screwed shut in concentration as their chest bowed forward, then side to side. There was a series of horrifying cracks and pops as their skeleton forced its way back into place. Xal let out a groan that was half agony, half relief, before opening a bleary pale eye.

"'D'ja see the ship that hit me?" they slurred.

"*What*?" Shui asked.

"What?" Xal responded, equally confused. Shui shook his head, setting aside the millions of questions he had for the task of checking the rest of Xal over. Xal frowned as Shui checked the bullet hole; it had scabbed over, but if he squinted, there was almost an afterglow to the dried blood on their forehead. "Ain't you one of them folks that kidnapped us?" they slurred.

"Not anymore," Shui said, checking their neck.

"That's good." Their speech was getting better by the second, which meant whatever blow they'd taken hadn't been *too* bad. Or, at least, it wasn't any longer. They groaned again, their hands moving to their empty holsters by their sides. " ... Thought I'd grabbed one of my guns." They swore under their breath and knocked their head back against the wall in frustration.

"Sunny has it. Sunny – " Shui turned down the hall to call her over, but when he looked, she was already running headlong into the darkness. "Sunny, what the hell – ?!"

The light from the map illuminated her path as she sprinted, all the way up to the partially crumbled door to the elevator with a hole just wide enough for her to slip through.

"Damnit, Sunny!" Xal was up and moving with shocking speed for someone who had just reset their spine. They ran with the most sure footing they'd had in the last few hours, which wasn't saying much, but did mean they weren't too far behind her.

"Go back to the surface!" she yelled from the elevator shaft. Something else groaned underneath her, ancient and metallic. "This ain't your problem!"

"Like hell it ain't – " Xal stopped against the crack in the door, heaving for breath even after the short run. "I may not know why you hired me, but I *know* you hired me and I ain't leaving you down here in the dark – !" With a last burst of effort, Xal squeezed their way through and tumbled down through the darkness to land on the ancient elevator car next to her. The car groaned again, louder this time but just as ignored by the folks sitting on top of it.

"I'm serious, Xal," Sunny warned. "I hired you and now I'm telling you to *go back to the surface*. End of contract, go back to your raptor and *leave me alone*."

"*You still have my gun* – !" Xal spluttered as Sunny threw it at them. "Fine, *Alonzo* has my other gun."

"Who cares about your guns?!"

"I care about my guns!"

"Xal, they already shot you in the head!"

The indignant squeak Sunny made when Xal rolled their eyes damn near reached dog pitches.

"*One time*, and if anything, that should be reason enough to keep me along."

"*Folks*," Shui called from above, hanging off the entrance. "This ain't the time or place, simmer down and let's talk this – *oop* – "

Shui slipped, and fell, and thudded onto the ancient elevator car, which had weathered all the quakes and aftershakes of the Shattering and all the centuries after but was drawing the line at three adult bodies. The trio had just enough time to hold on before the elevator car began moving – slowly at first with a bone-breaking groan, then fast as lightning plummeting to the depths below, sending them all crashing into absolute darkness.

6

It was dark at the bottom. At least, Xal hoped they were at the bottom. The idea that at any moment they could plummet down who knew how many more floors was an unpleasant one. The alarms had stopped working altogether this far down. In the distance above them Xal could faintly see red light flickering in through the elevator doorways. The only sound was the echoing groans of the ruins. When it was clear they were in no immediate danger of plummeting further, Xal shifted and groaned.

"Shui?" they called. "You alive?"

"Close enough," Shui grumbled, shifting as well. The sounds of fabric and leather and the metal of his rifle clanging against the metal of the elevator car was somewhere off behind and to Xal's left.

"Sunny?" There was no immediate answer. "Sunny, you there?"

A choked-back sob broke through the quiet before it was wrangled back to something more manageable. Xal felt their heart break a little. They followed the sound to its source, where Sunny lay curled up on her side, crying silently with all she was worth.

"I'm sorry," she managed between sobs. "I didn't mean to."

"Aw, Sunny." Xal sat down next to her and placed a hand on her shoulder. "Sorry I yelled."

"I'm just so *tired* of all of it," she sniffed. "I'm tired of Alonzo, I'm tired of you dying, I'm tired of these *stupid fucking labs*. It's been hundreds of years, it shouldn't matter anymore."

Now, Xal wasn't particularly versed in conversation – their attention span was shit and they were adept at saying not necessarily the *wrong* thing, but somethin' that certainly weren't the right – but even they knew sometimes you just had to let a fella talk. So they waited as Sunny cried herself back to a somewhat more even keel, then waited some more in the darkness and silence, listening to Shui shift nervously.

"I'm not a real person," Sunny said finally. It took every inch of willpower Xal had not to argue. The only thing that stopped them was the knowledge that if they stopped her now, Sunny might never start back up. "I'm ... " She pulled a hand down her face, wiping away tears and snot that simply didn't exist. "The 'Fore-Folks were developing things they shouldn't've, right up until it killed them. We know this. You've all seen it. But a decade before the Shattering, the big, new, shiny thing was constructs. The 'Fore-Folks made them more and more complicated for increasingly specialized jobs, but that took time and effort and so much intricate spellweaving that they started looking into easier ways to ... get results." Sunny paused, taking a breath. "So they started putting folks in them."

For a moment the elevator shaft was silent, before Shui shook his head. "No, no, that ain't possible – "

"Folks ain't even *begun* to unravel everything the 'Fore-Folks could do," Sunny said gravely. "But they made something that could pull" – her voice cracked, but she continued on nonetheless – "the soul out of – out of someone and attach it to something else. It was supposed to allow for more complicated constructs, but it just ... "

"So then, that room back there ... " Shui trailed off in horrified silence. Sunny nodded, even though no one could see. "And – and the constructs we've seen so far ... "

"They weren't supposed to go that far," Sunny said miserably. "It wasn't – I didn't think they would. I didn't think *he'd* sign off on it."

Xal and Shui exchanged a glance. "Didn't think *who* would sign off on it?" Xal asked.

"It doesn't matter," Sunny said, too quickly. It was a longer pause this time before the words could be pulled out of her. "It was the lead researcher's daughter. They – " Sunny swallowed the words in her throat and thought more on them before continuing. "She was sick. Dying. So they made her the prototype, made a whole replacement body to put her in just to see if it would work, but the process – it scrambles you. It wasn't perfect." The bitterness that had crept into her voice was nearly all-encompassing now. "But I guess that didn't matter much, considering the kind of bodies they were making down here. Didn't matter much whether the person was whole or fractured if they're just making a weapon that can *think.*" Her hands came up and slowly covered her face, gripping her short hair. "I'm so *stupid.* I should've known that they wouldn't stop with ... " Even now, even after saying everything else out loud, she still couldn't say it. The truth held itself in her mouth like a rock someone else had placed there, weighty and unmoving and waiting for her to choke.

"Aw, Sunny," Xal said quietly. She closed her eyes, held them shut.

"You're a 'Fore-Folk," Shui said – just as quietly as Xal had, but it was as though he'd shouted the words in her ear. Sunny's eyes snapped open and she sat up, glaring at him.

"A *real* 'Fore-Folk wouldn't have a fake body!" she yelled. "I ain't her, I can't *be* her, I'm just – I'm just a scrambled up *ghost* in a body someone else put me in!"

"Sorry, sorry." Shui backed down.

"You *don't* know what it's *like,*" Sunny continued. "I was scrambled up *before* they shoved me in stasis. I could hardly remember who I was half the time or how I was supposed to act, only that my body was *wrong*, that *I* was wrong, that I'd been given this beautiful second chance at life and I'd *fucked it all up*. And now – " She slammed her fist down against the roof of the elevator car, the dull *thud* echoing around the elevator shaft. "And now I find out hundreds of years later that they didn't stop with me, they took all of that and kept *hurting* people the same way they hurt me, and it doesn't even *matter* anymore because they all blew themselves up anyways but I still have to live with the fact that my father – that my father – " She covered her face in her hands and *breathed*.

Xal sighed and snapped their fingers in frustration. "Shoot, that means you were asleep during it."

For a moment Sunny was lost in the tonal whiplash. " ... What?"

"The Shattering. No front-row primary source to the end of the world. Shame." Xal said it so casually, like they were disappointed in something trivial like losing at cards or missing a train, that Sunny couldn't help herself. A giggle snorted its way out of her.

"Sorry," she said, "'fraid I slept right through it."

"That's all – well, shit, this is a *lot* to absorb," Shui said, apparently the only one of the three to truly appreciate the enormity of what Sunny had just confessed. "But that don't explain why you'd want to come here."

"Or why you're so insistent on *not* going back to the surface," Xal grumbled.

"We weren't hunting you. Dr. Morris was shocked to find you here. I can't imagine why you'd want to go back to somewhere like this so badly."

"Does it have something to do with that lattice?" Xal prompted after a bit.

When Sunny spoke, weariness bled into her words. "When Dr. Quill uncovered the original lab and what was inside it, he became fixated on immortality. Started trying to figure out if he could do to himself what they'd done to – what they'd done. Started trying to recreate the tech, but he didn't have much to go on, didn't have any idea what he was doing. Eventually, though, he got *somewhere* ... " She reached into her coveralls, pulled out the lattice, and held it in the air. A gentle glow emanated from it, illuminating the darkness with a soft blue light. "He copied himself into this, and said that if something were to happen to him, he wanted to be – to be put in a construct, if there were any left whole that could be found. He wanted *me* to plug him in. Made me promise." Her fingers tightened around the crystal and she held it to her chest. "Two weeks later, he died."

The elevator shaft was quiet for some time, each person absorbing the information as best they could.

"Hell of a last request," Shui said, breaking the silence.

"He took care of me. He gave me a home when mine was ... gone. He woke me up, he could have been so much worse to me. Could've done whatever Alonzo will do if he gets his hands on me. How can I say no to that?" Her voice was small at the end, the last question not entirely rhetorical. Shui wanted to answer her in some way, but he held his tongue. He understood the way loyalty chained folks to one another and left them unable to stray from the path set out by someone else, no matter how dangerous.

Xal gave a big sigh and sat up. "Welp, you've still got my help," they said easily, as though none of this were particularly out of the ordinary. "I'm still missing a gun, and I've been itching for payback for the hole in my skull."

"Listen – " Shui started haltingly, unsure of how exactly to ask. "How *did* you survive that?"

"Survive what?"

"The bullet to the brain?"

"That was hours ago." Xal waved their hand dismissively.

"Xal, you *should* be dead," Sunny said patiently.

"I don't want to hear that from a *ghost*."

Realization hit Shui like a train. "You don't know," he said.

"Know what?"

"You have *no* idea why you aren't dead," Shui said again.

Xal shifted uncomfortably. "Listen, it just ain't that important." Sunny spluttered in the background. "I know my name. I know how to shoot." Xal took out their pistol, the inner fission radiating light dizzyingly on the walls as they spun it and re-holstered it. "And I know that Alonzo fella's a bastard who won't know what hit 'im. That good enough for y'all, or am I gonna have to sit through another hour of 'I don't know's?"

Sunny and Shui looked at each other, then back at Xal. "Yeah, I can work with that," Sunny said. "Shui?"

Shui breathed out a long sigh. "Well, I ain't climbing all the way out of here by myself. 'Sides, might as well make sure James doesn't follow me out to try and make it even between us. Not his kind of even, anyways."

"Naw, if I gotta try and explain whatever's up with me, *you* can elaborate on what's going on between you and James," Xal said.

"Frankly, after 'literal ghost' and 'mystery immortality,' I think my story's a bit bland." When it was clear the other two were waiting for him to continue, Shui sighed and scrubbed a hand through his dark hair. "Ain't nothin' no one's ever heard before. Joined up with this pack years ago, when it was under different leadership. Different leadership had planned to make me something more, James took offense with both that and said different leadership. Different leadership had an unfortunate accident, James and I had a scuffle, James won."

"That's it?" Sunny asked.

"Up until about five minutes ago it felt like reason enough to be mad at someone." He paused, thinking. "And, frankly, I think it still is. James's already gotten the majority of them killed, might as well finish the job."

When Sunny smiled, it was with a stronger smile than she'd had in hours. "Thank you both." Shui looked away, embarrassed. Xal beamed back. "Alright, let's hope this works." She rummaged around in her coveralls and pulled out the map, blinding everyone once again in the process. Once she'd blinked the spots away from her vision, Sunny scanned through the projected light. "Let's hope we're at the bottom. Everything I learned about this site said that this was where they were building the constructs." Her hands trembled, and though she did not need to, she swallowed nonetheless. "If we're going to find an empty construct, this is our best bet."

The three nodded to one another, then got to work. The elevator car that had buckled under their weight was so crusted over in grime they almost missed the hatch and, in fact, felt right by it several times, before Sunny's clever fingers finally found the lip. The hard part over, it was mere moments before she had it open, sending rust and debris falling into the pitch-black car. Sunny went first, dropping to the ground experimentally and feeling about with her hands and feet before declaring it safe enough. Xal went second, Shui lowering them down by their wrists for Sunny to catch around the waist. Shui went last, landing solidly and efficiently.

The doors were crumpled beyond repair, and it took all three of them to wedge it open – and when it was barely an inch apart, some small bit of leftover power that had survived the end of the world must've sparked, because the doors slid the rest of the way open on their own, overbalancing the trio and sending them sprawling to the floor.

"Now, isn't this a wonderful gift."

Three heads snapped up. Three pairs of eyes met the muzzles of three guns aimed directly at them. Doctor Alonzo Morris, with one eye swollen horrifically and crusted blood smeared along the side of his jaw, sneered down at them. "I do just love when things go my way."

7

The miracle that occurred deep in the depths of the abandoned lab that day was not Shui switching sides. It was not Sunny telling her story to people who were uninterested in dismantling her to see how she worked. It wasn't even Xal surviving a bullet to the brain. No, the real miracle was that James, Alonzo, and Sylvia had survived long enough to point guns at the other three.

Any good wastelander knows the rule of "loyalty is king." Humans are social critters and do best by working together in whatever manner that is. The second part of that rule is that there is nothing more dangerous than a pissed-off coworker, no matter how close you were, and it was clear to anyone with eyes that the loyalty between those three was hanging on by a thread. Doctor Alonzo Morris would never know just how far the sunk cost fallacy had gone in preserving his life a little longer.

Of course, the third part of that rule is that there ain't nothing better for morale than a common enemy.

James didn't wait for the order to be given before he hauled Shui up by his shirt, twisted his arm behind him and *slammed* him against the wall. "Thought you were real clever locking us in with that construct, didn't you? Thought it would take care of your problems for you instead of dealing with us yourself?" There were fresh tears in James's clothes and leathers, the leg Xal had shot wrapped in a field bandage. "The problem with running from your fights is sometimes your fights've got legs."

"Frankly," Shui said gruffly, "I was expecting this particular fight to trip down a garbage chute – " He cut off with a grunt of pain as James twisted his arm up higher.

"I'm going to enjoy this," he growled in Shui's ear.

Sylvia didn't bother hauling Xal to their feet. She kicked their hat aside then placed her boot on top of their head. "One false move, cowboy, and we find out just how much damage that skull of yours can take," she warned.

"Couldn't move if I tried," Xal said. "Take it your foot's doing better – " They cut off as Sylvia began applying pressure.

"As for you, Miss Quill, I do hope you're done running." Alonzo smirked. "It would be a shame to damage your chassis." He gestured with the gun. Sunny rose to her feet slowly, eyes locked onto Alonzo.

"How'd you get past the construct?" she asked warily.

"There are very few things that survive a blast from something like this " –he gave Xal's gun an incredibly clumsy twirl– "directly to the crystal lattice."

Sunny's hands flew to her mouth in horror.

"Boy, you must tell me where you got these guns," Alonzo said, oblivious.

"I ain't a boy," Xal ground out, "and even if I remembered, can't say I'd be right interested in turning you loose on some poor gunsmith." At Alonzo's frown, Sylvia dug her heel into their head further.

"A conversation for later, then," Alonzo said.

"You have no idea what you've done," Sunny hissed.

"Worried about your fellow constructs?" Alonzo sniffed. At that, both Sylvia and James looked over at Sunny. "It had gone mad with decay. Putting it down was a mercy. Besides, there's still so much we can learn from its corpse."

"*You have no idea what you've done*," Sunny repeated, louder this time. "You're just flailing around with tech you don't understand and consequences you can't even imagine! At any time, you could trigger the wrong lattice, the wrong ancient doomsday device, and melt someone, but as long as it ain't you, you couldn't give less of a shit!" Sunny's voice grew in pitch and volume, echoing off the dark walls.

"No wonder you ain't had any reasonable contributions in the last ten years that weren't riding on my dad's coattails, you absolute dust-brained *idiot*! What could you have possibly imagined you'd find down here to make this all worth it?"

"That's the beauty of these jobs." Alonzo's voice shifted into a lower, more dangerous register. "I don't need to imagine, I just need to know what investors would purchase because they didn't know any better."

"That's it? That's all you have to say for yourself? Four people are *dead* because of you," Sunny whispered.

"And I'm not afraid to raise that number. Now." He held out a hand. "The map."

Now, folks are often surprised just how much you can see while on the floor, even if your head is under another person's boot. Debris that would be otherwise hidden, for example. Holes the little burrowers had left, even this far down. And, what folks least expect, the ceiling. And holes in the ceiling, left by eons of decay among other things.

"Y'all might consider moving," they said, largely to the ground. One pale eye looked skyward past Sylvia, even as she ground her boot into the flesh of their cheek.

"Quiet!" she snapped. "I will squash that head of yours, don't tempt me."

"Naw, alright then, don't mind me – " They broke off in a quiet, pained gasp as Sylvia pressed harder.

"You genuinely do not know how to shut up, do you?" she snarled. Xal continued to watch something behind her. "I'll bet every person who killed you did so to finally get some peace and quiet – "

The Silencer Mk. 6 struck much like it had the first time, clawed hands snapping down to snag the bandolier strung across Sylvia's body, only to miss and tear into the meat of her shoulders and haul her into the air screaming.

Alonzo turned and aimed and was close enough that he may have actually been able to hit the thing, but the moment his eyes were off her, Sunny ducked her head and shoved him off-balance to the ground. Sunny sprinted past him down the hall, the pink light of the map illuminating her path as she ran.

"Get back here!" Alonzo screeched and scrambled after her.

"Hey – !" Sylvia choked around her bandolier, legs flailing. "Don't just leave – !" Before she could finish her sentence, the Silencer had hauled her up and slammed her against the walls with a sickening *crunch*, again and again and again and again –

In one fluid motion Xal rolled onto their back and drew their pistol, and in the darkness of the hall the bolt from its mouth shone like the sun before it was extinguished in the bloody forehead of Sylvia.

"Sylvia?!" James turned to look, and his hold on Shui loosened, letting Shui break free and wrap his arm around James's throat.

"Shouldn't've turned your back on me," he muttered before sinking his knife into the meat of James's back over and over until the larger man finally stopped twitching. Shui let the body slump to the floor.

The two still alive looked back to the ceiling. The Silencer stared back. It dropped Sylvia's corpse with a wet *thud*. The two flinched back as it leaped from its hiding place, only for it to ignore them and speed down the hall instead on all fours, chasing the trail left by Sunny and Alonzo.

Sunny didn't have a plan. She'd never had a plan, were she being completely honest with herself, no plan beyond hiring some help and fulfilling Dr. Quill's final wishes along the way. Now, sprinting as fast as she could down the hallway, she kept one hand on the map and the other pulling debris and ancient filing cabinets down behind her to slow Alonzo down.

If she could just get to the manufacturing ward, it would all be over. It was an irrational thought, but one she clung to nonetheless. Just another step. Just another step.

She slowed down as she came to the large double doors separating her from her goal and wasted no time prying open the lattice. Alonzo's voice, yelling and swearing and gasping for breath, was becoming too close for comfort, and the moment the doors rumbled open wide enough for her to slip between, she was through.

Sunny stumbled out onto a catwalk suspended over even deeper darkness than she'd thought possible, her footsteps echoing around the cavernous room. Around her all manner of machines lay inert, armatures and tools and pieces of other constructs held suspended where they'd died. In the center, suspended at the end of the walkway, was the largest construct that had ever been created. Easily the size of a house or larger, the construct was humanoid in the same way the last two constructs had been humanoid: enough that a soul could inhabit it without too much confusion, but no closer. It was mostly completed, armored like a tank and kitted out with weaponry built into its limbs and back.

Sunny swallowed around her frantic heartbeat, an echo of the biological impulses she no longer had. She stumbled forward, forcing herself to analyze it, to make sure it was unfinished. If it was unfinished, then it was uninhabited. If it was uninhabited, then ...

Sunny hesitated, halfway across the catwalk, staring up at the partially built monstrosity before her. It chilled her to think that however it was the 'Fore-Folks had destroyed themselves, they hadn't even gotten to the point of deploying such a thing. She could no longer sweat, but the hand clenched around the crystal lattice was cold and clammy all the same.

A bolt of sunlight cast horrific shadows on the walls of the room as it fizzed past Sunny and struck the railing, leaving it red-hot and smoldering.

"Nowhere to run, *construct*," Alonzo wheezed, aiming Xal's gun down the walkway. "It doesn't have to end this way. We could work together, you and I. You'll need someone on the surface to keep other scrappers and investors off your tail. I can be very ... persuasive." He caught his breath then straightened up, a pained look on his face that Sunny didn't trust for a *second*. "I don't want to do this. Dr. Quill was my friend, and I know he cared for you."

Sunny screwed up her face in rage. "You don't even think we're people!" she yelled. "We're just a meal ticket to you, you said it yourself!"

"Do you think Dr. Quill was any better?' Alonzo asked. "I respected that man, may his soul be at peace, but he was just as opportunistic as the rest of us. That's the only way anyone gets ahead out here. I'm sure whatever reason he sent you down here was *still* for his own gain, even now." Alonzo took a step forward, and Sunny backed away.

"Stop talking about him that way!" Sunny clenched the lattice tighter.

"He's not your father, and he's dead. Look around you! Look at what we could learn from this place, and from you! No one would ever have to go through the pain of losing a loved one ever again!" Alonzo threw his arms wide. "We could conquer death!"

"No one conquers death," Sunny whispered.

Alonzo smirked and looked as though he had more to say, but before he could, a sound echoed into the room through the doors and down the hall, the sound of metal slamming against concrete. Alonzo whirled behind him as the Silencer burst into the room and onto the walkway. He fired once – twice – three times. The first two were wide, the third sparking off the construct's shoulder. It didn't slow down.

The Silencer Mk. 6 sliced through Alonzo's chest with its claws, then snagged him by the arms and flung him like a ragdoll against the railing. Xal's gun went flying from Alonzo's grasp, and Sunny dove to keep it from clattering off the walkway.

"Stop – ! Please – !" Alonzo's pleas went unheeded as the Silencer rounded on him. He scrambled to his feet, running towards Sunny. "Sunny – !"

His words died in his mouth, his face frozen in shock as Sunny burned a hole through his gut from where she lay on the ground, hands steady around Xal's gun. Blood dribbled from his mouth as he tried to speak – only for the Silencer to snag him by the head and *slam* him against the ground. There was nothing left in him to resist as it smashed him against the ground again and again until he was hardly recognizable. He was hefted up over the Silencer's head with finality, and then the bloody pulp that had once been Doctor Alonzo Morris was thrown to the darkness below.

Shui arrived first and promptly skidded to a halt, staring down the construct which twisted its form to look at him. Xal was next, a sight slower but still miraculously on their feet. "What's the holdup – *woah*!" Xal peered around Shui and looked past the construct to look at Sunny. "Sunny?" they called nervously.

Sunny said nothing, staring down over the edge where Alonzo had been thrown. Her heart pounded in her chest, but her hands did not shake. It almost felt like a dream.

"Sunny?" Shui called, louder this time, and she blinked and looked up to find the Silencer still standing protectively between her and her companions.

"It's alright," she said. She pulled herself to her feet. "It's alright," she said, more softly this time, directly to the Silencer. "You know, don't you?"

The Silencer eyed her with its blank faceplate. It straightened up, towering over everyone by at least a head, and shifted into a different stance. Not a relaxed stance, but no longer quite such an aggressive one.

"Sunny, I hate to ask, but ... " Xal had already forgotten the first construct, their gaze drawn to the monster in the center of the room. "You're not ... you're not about to plug your dad into that, are you?"

Sunny looked back at the behemoth. "Yes," no longer seemed like the right answer. "I was going to," didn't ring quite true either.

"It's what he wanted," Sunny said, but even those words rang hollow in her ears.

"Sunny ... " Shui winced. "I know I said we'd help, but this ... " It was hard to explain the enormity of it, the canyon between the idea and the horrific reality.

"I know." Her voice trembled, and her hand shook. "I know," she said again, stronger this time. She shook her head. "I don't think I can do it." She held up the lattice, turning it this way and that. "It ain't him. We don't have the technology to pull ghosts outta folks anymore, this is ... it ain't him. He's already moved on to whatever's next, like we were supposed to."

The construct dipped its head, as though it were agreeing.

"And – and even if we did have the tech, and it was his ghost in here," Sunny barreled on, "it still wouldn't be him, not like how he was." The same way she wasn't who she'd been. "And even if it was perfect – " Her voice got real quiet. "This ain't living. It's just prolonged death."

Silence fell heavy in the room.

"Not for nothin'," Xal drawled after a bit, "but maybe we shouldn't be putting nothin' in that thing regardless." Followed by a soft "*oof!*" as Shui elbowed them in the ribs.

Sunny held the lattice heavy in her hand. It was small, had been small this entire time, but now it suddenly felt enormous. This was it, she realized with a sudden jolt of panic. This was the last piece she had of Dr. Quill.

All the bitterness in her, the anger over the enormity of his ask and his disregard for everything she was, warred with a sudden and profound emptiness yawning in her. She hadn't thought about it all. It was too soon, too fresh, and it hadn't mattered anyway because he said he'd be with her again.

Except, now, he never would.

The wound in her split apart, ragged and sore and bloody. She held the lattice to her chest. Would it be so bad to keep the copy? They'd never tested it; maybe it would be so like the original that she wouldn't notice. That she could pretend. It would be like he never died.

With a sudden start, the pit in her widened into a gulf. Those were probably the same thoughts running through her father's mind before he put her in the machine.

"Sunny ... " Shui started to approach, but stopped at the look the Silencer gave him.

"I know," Sunny whispered. She breathed, felt her chassis expand and contract, felt the false nerves relaying the information to her brain. Breathed again, one last time. Lifted her arm, and flung the crystal lattice into the depths to join Alonzo's body.

She didn't cry. She couldn't cry. She'd done enough crying.

Sunny wiped her cheeks anyway, even though there weren't any tears, and turned to the other construct. "Can you speak?" she asked.

The answer was a horrible garbled "Yes," and nothing more. Sunny nodded sympathetically.

"Were you awake during the Shattering? The, um, the big earthquake," Sunny elaborated. The construct paused, then shook its head. Whatever question Sunny had planned to ask flew out the window to make room for a more important one: "Do you want to see the surface?"

"Sunny, I don't think this is a good idea," Shui said quickly.

"Why not?" Sunny protested, though she already knew. "Why do I get to go around while they – " The construct held up a hand and shook its head. Sunny vibrated with the unfairness of it all before an idea came to her. "What if I added your lattice to my own?" she asked. "Then I – I could smuggle your ghost out next to mine. Find a medium, someone who can help us both move on."

Xal whistled low. "Is that really somethin' you can do?"

Sunny gave a wry smile. "I'm a scrapper. I'm good at this kind of thing." She looked back to the construct. "Would you – ?"

The construct folded in a perfect bow, and it emanated a single, garbled, "Please."

8

All in all, the process took what felt simultaneously like an eternity and a second, but in reality was close to an hour. Xal and Shui left the constructs to their work, occasionally looking up whenever Sunny said something particularly interesting or the magi-mechanical frequencies caught their ears. Mostly, they focused on the map.

"It'd be rough, but I might be able to climb out," Xal said, rolling a shoulder. "I feel a sight better than before."

"I couldn't," Shui said, sighing exhaustedly. The longer Sunny worked, the more his adrenaline had faded, and the more his bodily aches came to the forefront. He had his water on him, like any good wastelander, but water could only go so far. His ribs ached, and he felt as though he were more bruise than body. He chewed thoughtfully on a strip of jerky before offering Xal some. Xal took the offering with gusto. "Shame about the elevator, would've been nice to take it back up."

"The what?" No matter how long Shui squinted at Xal's expression, it never shifted from blank confusion.

" ... Nevermind," he said, deciding he was too tired to deal with it. "Don't worry about it."

"Can't wait to get back to Lacey," Xal said, taking Shui's words to heart.

"Lacey?"

"My raptor, sweetest li'l thing. Gorgeous white plumage, fastest ride in the Wastes," Xal bragged, puffing their chest out.

"Did y'all hide her? I don't think we saw her on the way in."

"Prob'ly." Xal folded their hands behind their head and leaned against the wall. "Don't 'xactly remember, but I wouldn't be without her if she weren't safe."

"What do you mean you don't remember?" Shui's attention had completely left the map by this point, fully focused on Xal.

Xal shrugged, then looked at him pointedly and tapped their forehead. "Ain't easy thinkin' with holes in your brain."

Shui's mouth hung open. "You're saying this entire time you had ... *no* idea what was going on?!" Xal grinned. "You seem *very* calm about this."

Xal shrugged. "Bigger things to worry about."

"And now?"

Xal shrugged again. "Don't seem to matter none now either."

"Is – is this normal? How do you live like this?"

"Being hard to kill probably helps."

Shui was saved from having to figure out how to respond by Sunny approaching. "All done," she said, causing the other two to sit up with their full attention.

"What's it like?" Xal asked.

"Strange." Sunny gave a lopsided grin. "I'm the only one with access to my body, but it's like he's riding side-saddle."

"He?" Shui asked.

"His name is Randal Watch." Sunny's eyes grew distant, and Shui and Xal watched as she flipped through memories that did not belong to her. "He was a soldier – well, emphasis on *was*, he was a military convict. They figured using someone who was already combat trained for something like this" – she gestured blankly back towards the empty killing machine behind her – "would make things easier." She paused, cocked her head to the side as though she were listening to something. "He says he knows a way out, but first he has a favor to ask."

"Another favor?" Shui asked.

Sunny ignored him. "He wants us to destroy this place, and I agree." She shook her head. "This place should be left in the past. We can't risk anyone like Alonzo finding it and attempting to pick up where the 'Fore-Folks left off."

"That would require a pretty big explosion," Xal pointed out. "'Fraid I left my dynamite in my other chaps."

"All of the chassis were built with a self-destruct sequence in case they ever fell into the wrong hands." Sunny didn't elaborate on who the "wrong hands" might belong to, nor that the 'Fore-Folks' hands maybe hadn't been entirely "right." "We set the big one to blow and call it a day."

"Alright, but how do we keep from getting caught in that?" Shui asked.

"Burrower tunnels," Sunny answered simply. "Watch has been keeping an eye on them, he says he knows where the tunnels are. We can take them to the surface."

Shui closed his eyes, mentally preparing himself for more effort.

"Shame about any of them getting caught in the blast," Xal lamented. "They're cute li'l rascals."

"If we blow up Watch's chassis first, it might startle them enough to get moving. They've mostly cleared out with all the commotion, anyway. We'll just have to take the risk."

"Well I, for one, cannot *wait* to get out of here," Xal said, getting to their feet. Shui followed suit, albeit more slowly and with more grumbling. Sunny waited, staring at him until he responded.

Shui sighed. "No time like the present."

Sunny's smile was exhausted and small and filled with the giddy joy of anticipated relief.

"Get ready to run," she said, then jogged back across the catwalk. She stopped at Watch's chassis, then climbed the metal stairs to lean precariously over to the monstrous construct. Then she was done and racing back towards them at a dead sprint. She said nothing, didn't hardly slow, just blew past them knowing they would follow.

Xal and Shui were hard-pressed to keep Sunny in sight, but they didn't dare ask her to slow down. She twisted through the halls without even needing to glance at the map, directed by a voice only she could hear. She skidded to a halt at the end of a hall that had been mostly destroyed, covered in rubble and debris, and at the end where the wall had been pulverized the most, a hole had been burrowed through.

"Up here," Sunny said, not bothering to gasp. "They head out to the surface." Without waiting for a response, she dove in. Xal followed without hesitation. Shui followed with as much hesitation as he dared, which wasn't very much at all. The tunnels were lightless, cramped and suffocating, barely large enough for Sunny to scramble through, much less Shui. Their heads scraped along the soil, their hands growing dirtier and dirtier as they dug their way through. All around them were the sounds of small, scurrying feet.

The first explosion was small, relatively speaking, just enough for sound and noise, but it did what it was supposed to. Between the intruders and the loud noise and the commotion that had been raging all day, the little colony of burrowers decided enough was enough and took to the proverbial hills. The skittering of little feet quickly became a torrent, buoying them and carrying them along with the tide.

"Faster – !" Sunny hissed. Neither Shui nor Xal had the breath to tell her they were moving as fast as they could.

They felt the rumbling before the roar of the explosion echoed its way through the tunnels. The squeaks and squawks of the burrowers grew louder and more panicked as the ground shook and danced and all three of them discovered that maybe they could, in fact, go faster. The second explosion shook the earth like the Shattering itself, causing a chain reaction in the ancient and fractured laboratory. Eons of suffering broke and exploded, and the heat hunted its way through the tunnels after them like a hungry predator. They scrambled as best as they could, even when their best seemed like it couldn't possibly be good enough to escape the hungry earth. They dug and dug and dug until –

Sunny gasped like a diver coming up for air as she breached the surface. Xal and Shui crawled out after her, hacking up dust and dirt as, around them, panicked burrowers fled into the night.

The trio fell to the ground as the aftershocks shuddered and shook and finally fell silent. For a moment no one spoke. The dust and sand beneath them was coarse and grainy; a cool wind nearly took Xal's hat with it, blowing off to some of the distant plateaus and mesas rising up from the earth; not too far away from the three of them was the entrance to the deep, deep canyon they'd all ventured into to start the whole mess; above them stars littered the darkness, slowly dimming as the sky quietly began to lighten.

Xal broke the silence with a sudden, whooping laugh. "How's that for an exit?" they crowed, giddy with elation.

Despite herself, Sunny found herself giggling along. Shui focused on catching his breath but did crack a smile under his half-mask.

"Hey, Sunny?" he asked when his breathing had evened out.

"Yeah?" she said, still a little breathless herself.

"When you leave to find that medium, I could, y'know, go with," Shui offered. "Make sure no one gets your body when it's empty. If, y'know, you're interested."

Sunny was quiet with thought for a moment. "Honestly," she said, "I just want to make it to the next town over. We can figure things out there. And, well" – she rolled her head over to look at him – "if you wanted to come with, I can't rightly say I'd mind having someone extra to talk it over with." She looked back to the third member of their little trio. "Xal?"

Xal had sat up and was looking off to the distance, as though they were listening to a sound only they were privy to. Sunny couldn't hear a thing.

"Xal?" she tried again, and this time they looked back to her as though they'd forgotten there were other folks they were sitting in the Wastes with. "What about you? Are you gonna join us?"

Xal turned back to look off into the distance. "Not sure I can," they admitted.

"What about – just – just until the next town, then?" There was a sudden, familiar desperation building in her, the vertigo of sudden ends, the abrupt understanding that she would never see her strange friend again. But, then, Xal smiled back at her as dawn's rosy fingers began slipping over the horizon.

"Don't worry 'bout me, I'll be alright," they said. "But ... I reckon I could make it that far."

Across the dunes, a lone raptor crooned into the dawn. Xal's attention snapped to it, and they whooped as though the melancholy had already been forgotten. They put their hand to their mouth and whistled four sharp notes in response, and Lacey crooned the four notes right back as dawn fully broke.

Glossary

Burrower. The common name for *Oryctodromeus*! They were a small, fast-running dinosaur that dug tunnels and burrows. Despite being non-avian, they were still feathered like their raptor cousins!

Construct. An artificial creature created by the 'Fore-Folks out of metal and magic for various tasks.

Crystal Lattice. A device made of interlocking rings inlaid with crystals for the purpose of storing and releasing magic and spellwork. Size can range from small enough to fit in your hand, to ancient ones that encircled the planet. Most tech these days runs on them, though they are significantly less impressive than they were before the Shattering.

'Fore-Folks. The colloquial name for the civilization that existed before the Shattering – as well as the civilization that caused it. Any knowledge about them is merely speculation based on what they left behind.

Medium. Someone who speaks to and deals with ghosts.

Plasmashot. A type of gun that fires concentrated magic rather than bullets. It's very difficult to make; anyone seen with one in the modern era either scrapped it from some ruins, or they paid very handsomely for someone else to find or make one for them.

Raptor. A catch-all term for dinosaurs in the Dromaeosaur family! They aren't very useful for hauling, but they are quite popular for solo-riders and bandits. The most common breed of raptor is based off of the *Utahraptor* –

the largest known Dromaeosaur! Lacey, meanwhile, is a *Dakotaraptor*, which are slightly smaller but faster and more agile.

Scrapper. The job title of those who undertake the lucrative and deadly job of taking things the 'Fore-Folks left behind and turning them into something useful.

Spellslinger. A person with the capacity and talent to bend magic to their will by whistling specific frequencies. Most tunes are taught and passed down from person to person, but that's not stopping folks from experimenting – leading to wondrous and disastrous results.

Spikeback. A catch-all term for Thyreophora dinosaurs, such as the *Stegosaurus* or the *Ankylosaurus*! They're popular with caravans for their natural protections and overall sturdiness.

The Shattering. An apocalyptic event brought on by the 'Fore-Folks that rendered most of their tech destroyed or inert and killed most of the population. There are no firsthand accounts of the event, so there is no way to know just what happened. Most folks have surmised, however, that whatever happened, it ended with planet-cracking earthquakes and pockets of magic erupting that were so concentrated and wild that hardly anything can live there anymore.

Tri-horn. A catch-all term for Chamosaurine dinosaurs, the most common being the *Triceratops*! They're generally used for hauling heavy loads.

The Wastes. Colloquial term for the stretch of battered, dusty, deadly wasteland that stretches from settlement to settlement.

Wilder-Folks. A catch-all term for intelligent, non-human creatures that live out in the Wastes and sometimes co-mingle with humans, often as tricksters or dealers.

ABOUT THE AUTHOR

Kras Nebula is a little guy who's been writing things since they were even littler. They are a lover of everything sci-fi and fantasy. When not writing, they're probably playing with fiber, and have just recently gotten into drop-spinning their own yarn! Wow!

Also by The Whumpy Printing Press

Anthologies

Hurt and Comfort

Once Upon a Blade

The Whumpboratory

High Stakes and Bloody Business

Zines

ABCs of Whump

Novels

Cry of Fangs

Magnanimous Moonrise & Savage Sunset

Novellas

Bloodbag

Lux in Tenebris: Poena et Salus

Hunting Static

The Windows to a Shapeshifter's Soul

Never, Never

Creatures From the Caldera

Deepest Canyon

Showstopper

The Kill Touch

Chipped

Silence

Bonnie and Guy

The Dark Side of the Sun